Praise for *Grace* and the previous novels of T. Greenwood

"*Grace* is a poetic, compelling story that glows in its subtle, yet searing examination of how we attempt to fill the potentially devastating fissures in our lives. Each character is masterfully drawn; each struggles in their own way to find peace amid tumultuous circumstance. With her always crisp imagery and fearless language, Greenwood doesn't back down from the hard issues or the darker sides of the human psyche, managing to create astounding empathy and a balanced view of each player along the way. The story expertly builds to a breathtaking climax, leaving the reader with a clear understanding of how sometimes, only a moment of grace can save us."
—Amy Hatvany, author of *Best Kept Secret*

"*Grace* is at once heartbreaking, thrilling and painfully beautiful. From the opening page to the breathless conclusion, T. Greenwood again shows why she is one of our most gifted and lyrical storytellers." —Jim Kokoris, author of *The Pursuit of Other Interests*

"Greenwood has given us a family we are all fearful of becoming—creeping toward scandal, flirting with financial disaster, and hovering on the verge of dissolution. *Grace* is a masterpiece of small-town realism that is as harrowing as it is heartfelt."
—Jim Ruland, author of *Big Lonesome*

"*Grace* amazes. Harrowing, heartfelt, and ultimately so realistically human in its terror and beauty that it may haunt you for days after you finish it. T. Greenwood has another gem here. Greenwood's mastery of character and her deep empathy for the human condition make you care what happens, especially in the book's furious final hundred pages."
—*The San Diego Union-Tribune*

"Exceptionally well-observed. Readers who enjoy insightful and sensitive family drama (Lionel Shriver's *We Need to Talk About Kevin*; Rosellen Brown's *Before and After*) will appreciate discovering Greenwood." —*Library Journal*

Praise for *Keeping Lucy*

"A baby born less than perfect in the world's eyes, a mother persuaded that giving up her child is for the best, a lingering bond that pulls and tugs yet will not break. *Keeping Lucy* follows a mother willing to give up everything to save the child she's been told she must forget. **This story will have readers not only rooting for Ginny and Lucy, but thinking about them long after the last page is turned.**" —Lisa Wingate, *New York Times* bestselling author of *Before We Were Yours*

"In T. Greenwood's latest page-turner, a betrayed mother discovers just how much she is willing to sacrifice for the safety of her child, deemed unwanted by even those most trusted. *Keeping Lucy* is a wholly absorbing tale in which the bonds of marriage, friendship, and family are pushed to the ultimate limit. **A heartrending yet inspiring novel that kept me reading late into the night.**" —Kristina McMorris, *New York Times* bestselling author of *Sold on a Monday* and *The Edge of Lost*

"With *Keeping Lucy*, Greenwood once again **mines emotional depths that have become the hallmark of her writing**. In fighting for the right to raise her daughter with Down syndrome, a mother in the late 1960s harnesses the courage and confidence she didn't know she'd possessed. Readers can't help but be drawn into her **heartbreaking and uplifting journey**." —Mandy Mikulencak, author of *Forgiveness Road* and *The Last Suppers*

"How much would you be willing to sacrifice for a child you didn't know? This is the question posed in T. Greenwood's *Keeping Lucy,* the story of a young mother betrayed by those who claim to know best, including her husband, and the harrowing journey she must take to find her voice and take a stand even if taking a stand means losing everything. **Compas-**

sionate, clear-eyed, and often wrenching, *Keeping Lucy* is the kind of story that's meant to be read with the heart, and one that will resonate long after the reading is done."
—Barbara Davis, bestselling author of *When Never Comes*

"Greenwood's (*Rust & Stardust*, 2018) heart-wrenching, emotional roller coaster of a read also seamlessly captures the transformation of women's roles in the early 1970s. A heartfelt tale of true friendship, a mother's unstoppable love, and the immeasurable fortitude of women."
—*Booklist*

"An unabashed heart-tugger . . . a moving depiction of the primal power of a mother's love." —*Publishers Weekly*

Praise for *Bodies of Water*

"A complex and compelling portrait of the painful intricacies of love and loyalty. Book clubs will find much to discuss in T. Greenwood's insightful story of two women caught between their hearts and their families." —Eleanor Brown, *New York Times* bestselling author of *The Weird Sisters*

"*Bodies of Water* is no ordinary love story, but a book of astonishing precision, lyrically told, raw in its honesty and gentle in its unfolding. What I find myself reveling in, pondering, savoring, really, is more than this book's uncommon beauty, though there is much beauty to be found within these pages . . . A luminous, fearless, heart-wrenching story about the power of true love." —Ilie Ruby, author of *The Salt God's Daughter*

"T. Greenwood's *Bodies of Water* is a lyrical novel about the inexplicable nature of love, and the power a forbidden affair has to transform one woman's entire life. By turns beautiful and tragic, haunting and healing, I was captivated from the very first line. And Greenwood's moving story of love and loss, hope and redemption has stayed with me, long after I turned the last page." —Jillian Cantor, author of *Margot*

Praise for *Breathing Water*

"A poignant, clear-eyed first novel . . . filled with careful poetic description . . . the story is woven skillfully."
—*The New York Times Book Review*

"A poignant debut . . . Greenwood sensitively and painstakingly unravels her protagonist's self-loathing and replaces it with a graceful dignity." —*Publishers Weekly*

"A vivid, somberly engaging first book." —Larry McMurtry

"With its strong characters, dramatic storytelling, and heartfelt narration, *Breathing Water* should establish T. Greenwood as an important young novelist who has the great gift of telling a serious and sometimes tragic story in an entertaining and pleasing way." —Howard Frank Mosher, author of *Walking to Gatlinburg*

"An impressive first novel." —*Booklist*

"*Breathing Water* is startling and fresh . . . Greenwood's novel is ripe with originality." —*The San Diego Union-Tribune*

Praise for *Undressing the Moon*

"This beautiful story, eloquently told, demands attention."
—*Library Journal* (starred review)

Books by T. Greenwood

Two Rivers

The Hungry Season

Undressing the Moon

This Glittering World

Nearer Than the Sky

Grace

Breathing Water

Bodies of Water

The Forever Bridge

Where I Lost Her

The Golden Hour

Grace

T. Greenwood

KENSINGTON
PUBLISHING CORP.
www.kensingtonbooks.com

KENSINGTON BOOKS are published by

Kensington Publishing Corp.
119 West 40th Street
New York, NY 10018

All Kensington titles, imprints, and distributed lines are available at special quantity discounts for bulk purchases for sales promotion, premiums, fundraising, educational, or institutional use.

Special book excerpts or customized printings can also be created to fit specific needs. For details, write or phone the office of the Kensington Sales Manager: Attn.: Sales Department. Kensington Publishing Corp., 119 West 40th Street, New York, NY 10018. Phone: 1-800-221-2647.

The K logo is a trademark of Kensington Publishing Corp.

ISBN: 978-1-4967-3028-2

ISBN: 978-0-7582-7815-9 (ebook)

First Kensington Trade Paperback Edition: April 2012

10 9 8 7 6 5 4

Printed in the United States of America

In memory of:

Justin Aaberg
Cody J. Barker
Brandon Bitner
Asher Brown
Harrison Chase Brown
Raymond Chase
Tyler Clementi
Alec Henrikson
Jaheem Herrera
Nicholas Kelo, Jr.
Lawrence King
Billy Lucas
Lance Lundsten
Eric Mohat
Caleb Nolt
Felix Sacco
Carl Walker-Hoover
Seth Walsh

and all the other tragic casualties
of hatred and intolerance.

We don't see things as they are,
we see them as we are.

—Anaïs Nin

I found that snowflakes were miracles of beauty; and it
seemed a shame that this beauty should not be seen
and appreciated by others. Every crystal was a master-
piece of design . . . When a snowflake melted, that
design was forever lost. Just that much beauty was
gone, without leaving any record behind.

—photographer Wilson "Snowflake" Bentley, 1925

WINTER

Kurt is suddenly aware of the way the snow looks like something living, like something with a purpose. He has always thought of snow as simply *falling* from the sky, at mercy to gravity. But now, as he marches out across the snow-covered field behind the house, his rifle drawn and aimed at the back of his only son's head, he sees that it is intent in its falling. Resolute, determined, even calculated in its descent.

Trevor is three feet ahead of him, trudging through the snow, bare hands shoved into his pockets, head bowed in deference to the blistering assault. It is midnight, but the sky is opaque and bright. It is only December, but it has been snowing for two days straight; they are up to their shins in it. Trevor is not wearing a coat, hat, or gloves. He is in jeans and the navy chamois shirt he had on when Kurt dragged him from his room into the mudroom, where he had allowed him to put on his boots before pushing him through the door into this cold, white night.

As they pass the unmarked boundary between their property and their neighbors', Trevor hits a deep patch of snow and sinks in up to his knees. If you didn't know better, you might think he was praying, only genuflecting to the falling snow.

As Trevor struggles to move forward, he glances over his shoulder at his father. For years, the arch of his brow, the thick dimple in his chin, the boyish smirk have been like reflections in a mirror held up to Kurt's own boyhood. This used to make him swell a bit with proprietary pride. But now these similarities seem to mock him, accuse him. *You made this,* they say. *You are this.*

"Dad," Trevor says, but Kurt can't hear. It's as though his head is full of snow—cold, thick, numb. "Daddy." Snot has frozen in two slow paths from nose to lip. His eyes are swollen.

Trevor is thirteen, and he looks exactly like Kurt did at thirteen. He is the same height, the same weight. He has identical ears, the same bent pinkie finger, Kurt's slight overbite and white-blond hair.

When they finally get to the top of the hill where Kurt used to take Trevor sledding when he was a little boy, to the place where the entire world shimmers then disappears in the valley below, Kurt says, "Stop."

The sound of his voice is like ice breaking. Like springtime at Joe's Pond when the ice goes out. The crack, the shift, the signal that the thaw has begun. But Kurt knows that this is a weakness he cannot afford. He must stay solid, frozen, numb. There cannot be any cracks, any fissures in this ice.

They are far enough away now from the house where, on any other night, they would be sleeping. But the house is empty. There is no one to hear the gunshots.

"Turn around," Kurt says.

Trevor turns to face him again. But this time, it's not the face of a child he sees. Nor is it the face of the monster he has turned into. Instead, his hair is covered in a thin layer of white, and Kurt can see the old man each of them might one day become.

Trevor puts his hands up, as if his palms might be enough to protect him. "Don't, Daddy," he pleads.

At this, Kurt lowers his rifle, turning his gaze from his son to the sky. He watches the shards of ice, the intricate, gorgeous filaments, as they continue to fall. And he thinks of the news footage he saw right after the attacks on the World Trade Center, before the media realized what they were showing—the men who broke windows, climbed ledges, and leapt to their deaths. The *falling* men, the men forced to choose one kind of death over another.

Kurt looks back at Trevor, who is crying now, tears and snot freezing upon impact with the air. He lifts his gun to his shoulder again, and the snow makes a lens of ice as he peers down the sight.

LAST SPRING

It started with a gift.

The box was blue, the same color blue as the eggs Trevor found up in the eaves of the shed earlier that morning, the color of crushed-up sky. Mrs. D. gave it to him after the bell rang and almost everybody else had already packed up their stuff and headed out the door. He was messing around in his backpack, worrying about where he was going to sit at lunch, and didn't know that she was trying to get his attention. But then she touched his arm, real soft, with her talcum-powder hands and said, "Trevor dear, can you wait just a minute, please? I have something for you."

Mrs. D. was the art teacher at Trevor's school. A lot of kids were creeped out by her; some of the younger ones even thought that she was a witch or something. She did look a little bit like a witch, with the small hump underneath her moth-hole-riddled green sweater, with the threadbare black wig she wore. She smelled dusty and old too, like wet books. Some kids cackled whenever she turned her back, called her Nanny McPhee, but Trevor liked Mrs. D. So what if she was old and strange? She was a good artist, a good teacher. The fruit she drew always looked like fruit: bananas and apples and a pomegranate, its seeds spilling out all over the table like the insides of the buck that Trevor's dad shot last year. Plus, Mrs. D. was always giving him things to bring home— a box of waxy oil pastels, some tubes of acrylic paint that she was about to throw away. One time she gave him a set of colored pencils that weren't even opened yet. Besides, Trevor liked being in the art room. He loved the smell of paint and paste, the dusty, musty scent of it all. He liked the way the canvases looked like boys leaning against the brick walls. He liked the paint-splattered floors, the rough wooden worktables, the high ceilings, and the quiet. It was almost like being in a library here; and when the doors closed behind him, he felt suddenly secure, sheltered, at peace.

He opened the box and pulled out a camera. A *real* camera, heavy and black with a glass lens: the old-fashioned kind. For the last few weeks, they'd been doing a unit on photography, and this camera was like the ones each student was allowed to sign out, but this one was brand-new.

"Have you ever had your own camera before?" she asked.

He shook his head.

He thought of the slide show she'd shown them last week. *Ansel Adams,* that was the landscape guy. Some old lady who took pictures of flowers. But Trevor had liked the picture of people, the *portraits,* best. Faces. Mrs. D. had explained that photographers could be artists, that a good photographer uses the light to make ordinary or even ugly things beautiful. He thought about the kind of pictures he might take, about the faces he knew.

"The school will probably do away with the darkroom eventually. Move everything to digital. But for now, I can still teach you how to develop the film. How to make prints." Her head shook back and forth like a bobblehead doll, her voice made of tissue paper. "I want to see the world the way you see it, Trevor."

He wasn't sure why Mrs. D. took such an interest in him. He wasn't a good artist. Not like Angie McDonald in his class, whose paintings always looked like what they were supposed to. The things he drew never matched what was inside his head. He couldn't get what was up there on the page, and he wasn't sure anybody would want to see that anyway. But since sixth grade, Mrs. D. had looked at him like she saw someone special inside there. Nobody had ever looked at him like that before.

He'd been thinking a lot lately about the way people looked at him. He'd grown so much since last year, he barely recognized himself in the mirror. He'd outgrown every pair of pants, every pair of shoes he owned. He felt like the Incredible Hulk, busting out of his own clothes. Kids had always been mean to him, teased him, but now the same kids moved away when he walked down the halls at school, pretending like he wasn't there but still making sure to get out of his way. His teachers, except for Mrs. D., now looked at him like he was one of the bad kids. Like *he* was the troublemaker. His mother looked at him with sad eyes mostly, though he knew she was trying not to. If pity were a picture, it would be a picture of his mother. His dad's face was full of worry too, though he tried not to show it. His little sister, Gracy, was the only one who didn't look at him with some shade of disgust or disappointment. But she was only five; what did she know?

"Thanks," he said and took the camera from Mrs. D. and turned it over in his hands, excited to give it a try. He peered through the viewfinder and twisted the lens only to focus in on Jolyn Forchette, who was jealous and smelled like green beans, scowling at him from across the room. He crammed the camera into the backpack with the math homework he hadn't turned in and a banana that had been sitting in there so long it had turned brown and soft.

"It's already loaded," Mrs. D. said. "Just shoot."

He forgot about the camera as he made his way to the cafeteria for lunch. As the sea of students parted for him, liquid and flowing, whispering and sneering, he kept his head down, his gaze at the floor. He tried to make himself invisible, though that's nearly impossible when you're six feet tall in the seventh grade and you wear a size ten shoe. Still, he tried his best to disappear. But then as he made his way past a group of snickering and pointing seventh-grade girls, he started to feel that bad metal feeling. *Corroded.* That was the only way to describe it. Like his insides were rusted out, like one of his dad's cars at the yard. He could even taste it sometimes way back in his throat. He tried to swallow it down hard, but the metallic taste lingered on his tongue, made the insides of his cheeks itch.

He tried to ignore them and went to a table near the hot lunch line. He only had $1.50, which didn't go far in the à la carte line. The few times he'd tried to get a decent meal there, he'd wound up starving by the end of the day, his stomach roiling and furious. Only losers got hot lunch, but at least the hot lunches filled him up. He threw his backpack down into a chair and grabbed a tray. That was the other good thing about hot lunch; there wasn't a wait, so there would actually be enough time to eat after he got back to his table.

Spaghetti. That meant there would be bread too and those electric orange cubes of cheese. Gray-green broccoli and chocolate pudding with skin on top. He was hungry. His mom had made eggs and bacon and hash for breakfast, but he felt hollow now. His body burned through fuel faster than his dad's pickup.

He pushed the brown plastic tray along the metal rollers and he watched as a group of seventh-grade guys went right to the table where his backpack was. He grabbed a carton of chocolate milk from the bin filled with ice and glanced over at the table, hoping they'd notice his pack and go somewhere else.

"Here you go," the lunch lady said, handing him a sloppy plate of spaghetti. He took a pair of tongs and grabbed a clump of cheese cubes and three spongy slices of garlic bread.

The guys didn't seem to notice Trevor's backpack holding his place. They were all sitting at the table, laughing and eating their à la carte burgers and French fries. Trevor shoved the money at the hot lunch cashier and made his way over to the table.

"*Fee Fi Fo Fum,*" said one of the kids.

"That's my backpack," Trevor said softly.

"*That's my backpack,*" mimicked the kid in a girly voice. He had red hair that covered one eye like a comma. Ethan Sweeney. Of course.

Trevor reached for his backpack but Mike Wheelock, with his greasy black hair and a Patriots jersey, grabbed it first.

"Hey, freakshow, what do you keep in here? Body parts? I bet he's got some dead chick's head stuffed in here," he said, laughing.

"Just give it," Trevor said.

Mike started to unzip the backpack and stuck his head in to inspect.

"Ew, what's that smell?" he said, jerking his head back. *The banana.*

The other guys leaned over to see inside. And suddenly Trevor felt the metal turning into quicksilver, mercury rushing through his veins.

"What's this?" the Sweeney kid asked, reaching in and grabbing the camera from Mrs. D.

"I said, *give it,*" Trevor said. He thought about Mrs. D., picking out the camera and paying for it out of her own pocket. He thought about what the kid might do to it.

"*Give it, give it,*" Ethan mocked, his voice high and sharp.

Normally, Trevor just tried to ignore these guys, but lately, he couldn't seem to control himself. It was like this new body of his, these new hands, had a mind of their own. So the next thing Trevor knew, the tray of spaghetti was flying onto the floor and his fists were swinging, though they connected with nothing but air. The whole cafeteria erupted, the chanting starting small and growing bigger, like a heartbeat. *Fight, fight, fight.*

His eyes stung and his mouth flooded with the taste of metal. But before he had the satisfaction of his fist making contact with Ethan's face, someone was yanking his collar hard, choking him. He shook his head like a dog on a chain, and the hands let go, making him stumble backward.

"All right, that's enough. Break it up," Mr. Douglas, the janitor, said.

Trevor blinked hard and when his eyes focused again, he noticed the way the sunlight was shining through the cafeteria window, casting his own shadow, enormous and dark on the filthy cafeteria floor. And he thought about the gift from Mrs. D. About the camera. About how he might capture this picture: his own terrifying silhouette and all of the other kids' faces staring at him with something between fascination and horror.

Elsbeth looked at the catalogues that came in the mail with the models in their bathing suits and flip-flops and dreamed herself somewhere warm. It was April, *spring* everywhere else but here in Vermont, where yards were still laced with patches of dirty snow and you could still see your breath, like ghosts, when you went outside. Her girlfriend, Twig, went on a cruise for Christmas last year. She and her boyfriend flew down to Miami and then got on a ship to the Bahamas. She came back the color of a ripe peach with streaks of sunshine shimmering in her hair, like she'd captured the sun itself and brought it home with her. This was one of those things Elsbeth ached for, another one of those things she knew that she and Kurt probably wouldn't ever be able to afford to do. Still, she marked the bright green two-piece in the Victoria's Secret catalogue with a coupon for mayonnaise she clipped earlier, and set it on the kitchen table next to the stack of neglected bills.

Elsbeth had worked at the salon all morning and then picked Gracy up from her half day at kindergarten after lunch. Gracy had fallen asleep in the car on the way home and, thankfully, stayed asleep as Elsbeth carried her inside and put her in her bed. Trevor would be at school for another couple of hours, and Kurt would be at the yard until suppertime. There was a roast in the Crock-Pot, so supper was taken care of, and so she had exactly two more hours of peace. Two more hours when she didn't have to tend to anybody else's needs except for her own. This was her guilty pleasure. This solitude. Sometimes she just lay down on the couch and closed her eyes for the whole two hours, waiting for Gracy to call for her and break the spell. She knew she could be, *should* be, catching up on the laundry. She knew she had dishes to do, grout to scrub, floors to mop, but this was the only time of day when she could hear her own thoughts. The only time of day when she was completely and absolutely alone.

She lay on the couch and glanced at the magazine. The model was bustier than she was, with more up top and in the rear than Elsbeth had. The model had flowing auburn hair, while Elsbeth's was the color of coal tar pitch. She wore it in a ponytail most days like she used to when she was a little girl; it made her feel younger than her thirty years. The model was smiling, and her teeth were even and white like Tic Tacs or a row of shiny Chiclets. Elsbeth hadn't seen a dentist in a decade. And when her wisdom teeth came in, they undid all the work the braces she'd worn in junior high had done. Still, she knew she was sort of pretty to look at. She had her dimples and big wide eyes. She was no Victoria's Secret model, but her stomach was flat and her legs were long and strong. She tried to picture herself in the bathing suit, but the only real beach here was way up at Lake Gormlaith, and only teenagers wore two-pieces there. She thought of the summers when *she* was still a teenager: those humid nights spent drinking wine coolers and skinny-dipping. She wished she'd known then that she should hold on to that feeling—of strawberry-flavored Bartles & Jaymes on her tongue and cold water on her naked skin—because now it was so far away it felt like a whisper too quiet to hear.

She closed the magazine and then closed her eyes, calculating how many minutes of freedom were left. She tried to remember sunshine, the smell of suntan lotion. The sound of loons and the splash of bodies in water. But just as she was drifting off, floating on her back looking up at a dream sky full of stars, the phone rang, rattling her nerves. She sat up and quickly grabbed it off its cradle so it wouldn't wake Gracy.

"Hello?" she said softly.

"Mrs. Kennedy? This is Principal Cross."

Elsbeth closed her eyes, took a deep breath. Waiting.

"I just wanted to let you know that Trevor will be staying after school with us again today."

"What happened?" she asked. She could hear Mrs. Cross sigh on the other end of the line.

"There was an altercation."

"A fight?"

"More of a *confrontation* really."

"What does that mean? Is he hurt?"

"No one is hurt. Mr. Douglas, our custodian, was, thankfully, able to stop the boys before it got physical."

"So it was an *argument?*" Elsbeth asked. Mrs. Cross drove her crazy.

"Mrs. Kennedy, Trevor's behavior is becoming disruptive. This is the third time this month that he's served detention. If this had escalated into a fight, if anyone had gotten hurt, he'd be facing suspension."

"But no one was hurt?" she repeated.

"No. Thankfully, not this time."

Elsbeth, exasperated, stood up. She could hear Gracy stirring in the other room.

"You may pick him up from the office at four o'clock," Mrs. Cross said.

She nodded and hung up the phone, looked at the glossy red-headed model smiling at her. Mocking her.

She didn't know what was going on with Trevor lately. He'd always had a hard time at school, with other kids. But he'd never been violent before: always more apt to flee than fight. And Principal Cross was new this year; she didn't know Trevor, hadn't seen what he'd been through since kindergarten. All she saw was this big kid always on the verge of a brawl.

Quietly she went to the room that Gracy and Trevor shared, and Gracy smiled up at her from her soft nest of blankets and pillows. Elsbeth sat down on the edge of the bed and stroked her hair. There was a sleepy seed in the corner of her eye that Elsbeth delicately extracted with one pale pink fingernail.

"Hi, Mumma," Gracy said sleepily.

"Hi, baby. Did you have sweet dreams?"

Gracy nodded. "I'm still sleepy."

"Okay, baby. Go back to sleep."

She never said it out loud, but she worried that she loved Gracy more than she loved Trevor. It was one of those truths that made her feel ashamed. What kind of mother admits that? What kind of mother even thinks something like that? But even when Trevor was just a baby, she remembered feeling like he didn't belong to her. Like she didn't belong to him. With his white-blond hair and skin, his ice-colored eyes, he certainly didn't look like her. It was like Kurt had made him all by himself, as though she'd had nothing at all to do with it. Even after nine and a half months of carrying him around in her belly, there were times when she would watch him playing or sleeping and she had to remind herself that he was her son. Her *child*.

Of course, she was only seventeen when he was born. Nobody should be having babies at seventeen. She hadn't even put away her baby *dolls* yet when she was seventeen; when Kurt used to sneak into her room at night, she'd turn them all face-down on her dresser so they wouldn't see what they were doing. She was still just a girl when she got pregnant. So for a long time, she thought maybe it was just because she was such a young mother. Maybe she resented Trevor for the loss of her freedom, blamed him for all the things she had to give up: for the prom she didn't go to, the pep rallies, the bonfires, her position as first chair flute in the band. For all the other summers she might have spent drinking wine coolers and swimming naked at the lake.

But as he got older, she realized it wasn't as simple as that. Trevor wasn't like the other children. At the playground the other mothers sometimes shook their heads at Trevor, whispered when they thought she wasn't looking. He didn't look like the other little boys, and he didn't behave like they did either. For one thing, he was so sensitive. He'd cry about just about anything. If something was too loud, if he didn't want to leave, when someone refused to play with him. He threw tantrums, *big* tantrums. Those times, she'd scoop him up in her arms and walk away from the huddled mothers, wincing as he kicked her thighs, scratched her arms, and sobbed into her hair. But despite feeling protective, angry at these women with their well-behaved toddlers, she couldn't help feeling a little bitter too. Angry at him for being such a crybaby. And she realized what she was feeling was *shame*. She was ashamed of her own son. It made her feel awful.

And then seven years and two miscarriages later, Gracy was born, and she knew for sure that while there might be something wrong with Trevor, there was something far worse wrong with *her*. Because the minute Gracy was born, she remembered feeling a whole new kind of love. Not love like she felt for her mother, for her grandpa. Not even the kind of crazy love she used to feel for Kurt. But a love so big it felt like something liquid. Something that soaked her; she felt heavy with it. A *mother's* love.

Gracy was a beautiful baby: eyes as big and dark as Junior Mints. Her hair, like Elsbeth's, was the color and thickness of molasses. She almost never cried, and when she did it wasn't because she was angry or frustrated. She never threw her body across the room and into closed doors, never tore her own hair out like Trevor did at that age. She cooed and smiled and didn't shrink away from Elsbeth's touch. (That's what killed her more than anything, the way Trevor retracted from her. It made her feel found out, accused.) Grace was just that, just the smallest bit of grace. Elsbeth's sweet reward for the agony that was Trevor. Her mercy.

Now that Trevor was older and things seemed to be getting worse rather than better, she didn't know what to do. She tried so hard to be a good mother. To make Trevor feel loved and special. But it felt false, like she was pretending, and she worried that he could sense this. That maybe she was even to *blame* for his problems, that she had failed him in some terrible way.

Of course, she would never admit that she felt this way. It was her secret. Kurt didn't know how hard she worked just to get through some days with Trevor, how exhausting it was. Thank God for Kurt. Kurt who was patient and kind. Kurt whose love was always equal. Elsbeth knew that Kurt never had such terrible thoughts. At least Trevor had his daddy. Always. She knew she needed to call Kurt, let him know what had happened. What had *almost* happened. Jesus, that woman infuriated her. She'd send Kurt to get him. Kurt would know what to do.

When Elsbeth called, Kurt was out in the yard looking for a '92 Camry hubcap. He was pretty sure they had one, but it wasn't showing up in the system. He searched through the shiny stack, like a haphazard pile of fallen spaceships, but couldn't find the one he was looking for. The customer was a lady, and he could tell she was watching the time. She was one of those coffee-break shoppers. Thinks she can show up at three in the afternoon, find what she needs, and make it back to work without anybody noticing she's gone. She was teetering on a pair of scuffed black high heels, scrunching up her nose at the smell, as Kurt sorted through the heap.

Beal came out to the cap pile, carrying the chirping cell phone like it was on fire. "It's Elsbeth," Beal said, breathless, holding the phone, which had ceased its song.

There were a billion reasons Elsbeth might be calling (something she needed him to pick up at the store on his way home, a question about where to find the hammer or Phillips head or WD-40), but today Kurt's first thought was of Trevor. Of *what did he do now?* As Beal handed him the phone and wiped the sweat off his forehead with the back of his shirt, Kurt felt a knot grow in his gut.

"Thanks," he said, looking at the screen that announced the presence of a new message.

The lady put her hands on her hips and tapped her foot, glanced at her watch. At this rate, she'd be lucky to make it back to her office without somebody figuring out she'd been gone.

"I'm real sorry, ma'am. Why don't you leave your number with Beal here and we'll give you a call as soon as we find the cap you need," Kurt offered.

"Maybe you didn't understand when I said I needed it *today*," she said, like she was talking to a four-year-old. "I'm showing a client a house in an hour, and I can't be driving around town without a hubcap. It's not professional."

He wanted to listen to Elsbeth's message, but this lady with her high heels and impatience was their first customer of the day, possibly their *only* customer of the day the way things had been going lately. They couldn't afford to lose her business, even if it was just a forty-dollar hubcap.

"Beal, see if you can find this young lady's cap for me?" Kurt asked.

"No problem," Beal said.

"Beal here will help you find exactly what you're looking for," Kurt offered, and the woman scowled.

He listened to the message as he made his way back to the shop through the maze of car carcasses, waiting until he was out of their earshot to call Elsbeth back. He leaned against the yellow husk of a 1979 Mercedes and hit the speed dial.

"Hey, baby," Elsbeth's voice said. The thick, gravelly sweetness of her voice could still make his knees go soft. "Did you get my message? Trevor's in detention again and Gracy's still napping. Would you mind picking him up at school at four?"

"What did he do?" he asked.

"I don't know. Another fight, I guess. She said the janitor stopped it before anybody got hurt. Can you get him?"

"Yeah. I'll go." He glanced at the scratched face of his watch. He had about twenty minutes. Beal could close up the shop. Hopefully he'd find that damned hubcap before the lady gave up.

As he made his way to the shop to grab his truck keys, he surveyed the sea of glass and chrome. He'd been working at the salvage yard since high school. Back when he still had plans to go to college, he'd helped Pop out every summer, socking away any money he made for his tuition. But then, after Billy took off, and later when Pop keeled over at the A&P, the stroke leaving his whole right side paralyzed, Kurt knew he wasn't going anywhere. He'd taken over the yard and been here ever since. He'd married Elsbeth, Trevor was born, and then Gracy. He had a family, and he really didn't have a choice but to keep the business going, unless he sold the yard. Not that he hadn't thought about it. Not that he hadn't been tempted. But the sad fact was that he had grown up among this wreckage. These hollowed-out skeletons of Caddies and station wagons and Volkswagen buses had been his playground as a kid. Getting rid of the salvage yard would have been like selling off his own childhood.

And the yard had actually been a lucrative business until last year. But now people were driving their cars into the ground rather than scrapping them when things started to break. It also seemed like everybody was finding what they needed to keep them running on eBay. And the folks who used to drop stuff off were trying to make a profit off it themselves, selling parts on craigslist or out of their own garages. He'd stopped looking at the books; he knew that as soon as he did, he'd have to cut back Beal's hours, maybe even let him go, and Beal's wife was just about to have twins. Despite everything, Kurt loved the yard, and it pained him that the business was going to shit. He used to think he'd pass it on to Trevor someday when he was grown.

Trevor. Ever since the episode last month, the new principal seemed to have it out for Trevor. He was always coming home with pink slips, warnings about his behavior, signed in that curlicue handwriting that looked more like it belonged to a teenage girl than a school principal. The times they'd been called into the office, Mrs. Cross hardly said anything, just shook her blond head, like he and Elsbeth should know better. Like they were at fault for his bad behavior.

Not that Kurt *didn't* blame himself. Of course he did. Trevor was his son. He was the one who had raised him. But ever since Trevor was just a little boy, he'd had a hard time with other kids.

He'd been pushed around and made fun of for one thing or another, off and on for twelve years. Up until this year it was the *other* kids whose parents were getting the pink slips and fancy handwriting and calls from the school. They'd been to the school counselor a hundred times, but she insisted that there was nothing wrong with Trevor. He was a good student, sensitive but well-behaved; it was the other boys who were the problem. The school did what they could, but Kurt knew how devious kids could be, how much they could do when the teachers weren't looking. And lately, Trevor refused to talk about it. But Kurt could still see it in his eyes. He'd seen it in his brother Billy's eyes when he was a kid. Trevor didn't have a single friend, and Kurt knew exactly how to read the pain of his loneliness. He didn't know what to do for him, didn't know how to make that sorrow go away.

But this fighting business was new. It was like something shifted inside Trevor since he turned twelve. First off, he grew seven inches. Went from being the shortest kid in the class to the tallest in just one summer. He also put on about thirty pounds. A thin line of hair started to grow above his lip. He went from *boy* to *man* in about thirty seconds flat, except for his voice, which remained that of a little boy. Kurt knew this was part of the problem: something else that set him apart from the other boys.

It wasn't two weeks into the school year that Kurt and Elsbeth got the first call from Mrs. Cross. Apparently during the seventh-grade recess some kids had been giving Trevor a hard time, pushing him around, and he'd, finally, pushed back. There had been two other "incidents" since then, the same kids picking on him, and both times instead of just taking it like usual, he'd fought back, once shoving one kid into a snowbank. Part of Kurt was proud of Trevor. These stupid asshole kids were finally getting what they deserved. But the school didn't see it that way. The same counselor who had insisted that Trevor was fine now said she "didn't know what to do with him." She thought he should see an outside professional, someone who could help him manage his anger. But even if Kurt hadn't thought that therapy was a load of shit, his insurance wouldn't have covered it anyway. He knew Trevor shouldn't be fighting, that he'd have to punish him, again, for this, but he also knew that there weren't a lot of other options.

Kurt grabbed his keys from the shop and went to his truck. The windshield was filthy. He lifted the wiper-fluid lever, and the motor buzzed. Empty. He turned the wipers on anyway, and they pushed the sludgy grime across the glass. He waited until the windshield was clear enough to see, until the road came into focus in front of him, and then sighed, backing out of the driveway and heading to the school.

Trevor sat perched on one of the wheel wells in the back of his dad's truck as they drove away from the school. He watched as the school became a dollhouse and then just a red-brick pinprick in the distance. Trevor loved riding in the back of the truck. With the wind coming at him from all sides, he held his arms out and could feel every inch of his skin. Sometimes, in the summer, his dad would take him and Gracy swimming up at Lake Gormlaith, and they'd get in the back still soaking wet, their towels flapping around like capes. By the time they got home they'd be dry, their eyes red and stinging from the wind. He loved the taste of the air, held his mouth wide open and stuck his tongue out, tasting the seasons on his tongue. Spring tasted like fresh-cut grass. Summer tasted like hay and heat. Fall like overripe fruit. It was too cold to ride in the back in the winter, but he imagined winter air might taste like peppermint. In the back of the truck, he felt free. His skin stopped prickling. His muscles relaxed. He let the breeze wash over him. It made him feel clean. In the truck, he could almost forget about school.

School. He almost wished Mr. Douglas hadn't gotten to him so quickly. If there had been an actual fight, he would have gotten suspended. And if he got suspended, at least then he wouldn't have to go back to school tomorrow.

Mr. Douglas, who restrained and then detained him, considered himself the school cop as well as the janitor. (After somebody started calling in bomb threats a few months ago, Mrs. Cross gave him a neon orange bib that said SECURITY across the front, which he wore when he patrolled the parking lot at the school.) He was fat and sweaty. When he'd pressed Trevor's head down onto the sticky cafeteria table and yanked his arm behind his back (which Trevor thought was pretty ridiculous considering he hadn't even gotten a chance to hit anybody), he'd hissed into Trevor's face, "You're in a lot of trouble, mister," and his breath smelled like hot dogs and cigarettes.

Trevor turned toward the cab and looked at the back of his dad's head. When his mom rode in the truck, his dad would stretch one arm across the backseat behind her and rub her neck. But today he had both hands on the wheel, his knuckles tight and white. Trevor wasn't sure what would happen to him when he got home. His mom would probably try to get him to talk about it, but he knew that even though she asked the questions (*What did they say to you? What did they do, baby?*), she didn't really want to hear the answers. What she wanted was for him to be like Gracy. Sweet and loveable and easy. But he wasn't any of those things, never had been.

All the other times, his dad had taken him out to the shed, made him yank down his pants, and hit him twice on his bare backside with his belt. It hadn't hurt much, but it made his eyes sting with shame. As further punishment, his dad had made him go to the yard and stack tires all day on the weekends. He couldn't get the smell of rubber off his hands, even with soap. His dad didn't try to talk to him; he was probably smart enough to know there wasn't any way for Trevor to explain. No way to describe how he felt right before he snapped. When the things they said to him pricked his skin like needles. *Freakshow, Frankenstein, Faggot.* How could he tell him about that rusted-out taste in his mouth that meant all hell was about to break loose?

When they pulled into the driveway, he stood up and hopped out of the back of the truck. He could see Gracy peering out the front window at him. She pressed her nose against the glass like a pig and blew her cheeks out. He smiled at her, and she waved, leaving greasy prints on the glass.

"Come on," his father said, exasperated, leading the way to the backyard, loosening his belt as he walked.

It was only five o'clock, but the sky was already darkening. The whole world looked bruised. They'd made this same trek a dozen times or more since last year. There was practically a path worn into the ground. When they got to the shed, Trevor closed his eyes and braced himself, leaning his hands against the cold siding.

"Damn it, Trevor." His father's voice was deep and soft, a lullaby voice. Trevor squeezed his eyes shut tighter and tried to pretend that he was only waiting for sleep. But then he heard the slide of leather through denim, the belt catching on the loops, and his whole body tensed, readied itself.

"What am I supposed to do with you?" his father said softly. "What the hell am I supposed to do?" But he wasn't talking to him, to Trevor, not really, but rather seemed to be asking the question to the dusk. To that damaged sky.

And then it was over, as if it had only been a couple of distant cracks of thunder. As if it had only been a faraway storm.

Outside the hospital window, the sky was like a fairy-tale sky. A violet sky, a *violent* sky, with a terrible moon. If this sky were flattened into the pages of a book, the moon might have a face, a sneering face. And the story would be about what happens to bad little girls when they don't listen to their mothers.

Crystal's mother sat at the side of the bed, busying herself with the remote control as if the most savage thing in the world hadn't just happened to her daughter.

"You can go home, Mom," she said. "I'm okay."

Distracted, she turned to Crystal and said, "Don't be silly." But she couldn't hide the look of relief on her face, the gratefulness for Crystal's permission to leave. For all of the arguing over the last several months, now neither one of them seemed to have any words left for the other, and they had spent the last two hours sitting in silence. "Seriously. I'm fine. They said I can check out in the morning. Just come back at nine."

The truth was, she didn't want her mother to stay. She wanted to be alone with this strange sorrow, the one curled like a cat in the corner of her mind. If her mother left, then it might leap to her lap, let her stroke its soft fur. But not as long as her mother insisted on lingering. As long as her mother was here, she had to pretend. To make believe that it was as simple as this.

"Well, only if you promise me you'll be okay," her mother said, cocking her head slightly and reaching for Crystal's hand. She ran her thumb gently, absently, over the IV needle stuck into the vein in the back of her hand. This tenderness felt like a blow. Her mother hadn't given her so much as a good-night kiss in months; she couldn't remember the last time she hugged her. But now that it was all over, now that her mother had gotten what she'd wanted, the warmth she'd withheld was suddenly released. Her lips pressed against Crystal's forehead; she squeezed Crystal's hand. "We love you," she said, speaking not only for herself but for Crystal's father, who had known enough to leave three hours ago, as well. "We're proud of you. This was the right decision."

Crystal could feel her throat thickening, the sorrow filling her body in all the new, empty places. She nodded because if she spoke she would cry. And she would not cry.

"Okay, then," her mother said, straightening. "You call if you need me to come back. Even if it's the middle of the night. I can come back."

Crystal kept nodding, willing her mother out the door. Watching, relieved, as she disappeared, as the heavy wooden door closed, leaving her, finally, alone. Her whole body felt like a limb that had fallen asleep and was just now prickling back to life. The pain was there but not there. Like some shimmering thing underwater. And the memory of what happened tonight was also soft at the edges.

She'd been out walking Willa after dinner. She hadn't been able to eat more than a few bites before she felt bile rising like mercury up the thermometer of her esophagus. Like fire in her throat. She thought that maybe if she walked, gravity would prevail, and there would be some relief.

She'd only gotten to her sister Angie's school before she needed to sit down. Her heart was skipping beats again, stuttering and stumbling and then stalling. It took her breath away each time, like a dozen small deaths. She'd looped Willa's leash to the swing set and sat down on one of the swings. The canvas cradle was not designed for a girl in her condition, but she needed to rest. She didn't feel right.

Willa hadn't found a place to relieve herself yet. She'd sniffed nearly every bush, every tree, along the way. But now she was squatting at the foot of the slide.

"Willa, no!" Crystal said.

Willa looked up at her as her body convulsed with the effort of relieving herself.

"*Jesus*, Will," Crystal said, grabbing onto the cold chains of the swing to help her stand up. She shoved her hands in her pockets, hoping she'd remembered to put a plastic baggie inside or else some poor kid would get a terrible surprise at the end of his ride.

Willa sniffed at the pile, and Crystal located a bag in her pocket. She enclosed her hand in plastic and bent over awkwardly to scoop up the stinking mess. Suddenly, she felt a shock go through her entire body, and then a deep ache across her abdomen. She stood up, hand full of shit, and swooned from the stink and the pain.

"Come on, Willa," she said, and Willa obeyed.

The two blocks home felt like two miles. She had to stop every other house it seemed, her entire body quaking with each contraction. When she walked past Ty's house, she wondered if he was inside. What would he do if she just stopped here? If she just had the baby right here on his doorstep? Would Lucia invite her in, make her some chamomile tea? She almost laughed at the thought of it.

By the time Crystal got back to her house, she realized that this was it. It was finally, really, happening. She needed to go to the hospital; the baby was coming tonight.

And now, just eight hours later, it was over. All of it. The baby had come. And gone.

She thought about her mother driving home. Her back straight, her hands at ten and two. She imagined Willa waiting at the door for her. Her father inside now, maybe catching up on some listings, trying to forget what had happened in the hospital. She thought of her sister, Angie, doing homework or drawing. Or maybe already asleep, as if this had all been a dream. As if Crystal weren't lying in the hospital feeling like her body had been split open like a ripe peach. That dark pit in the center of her, that pocked dark place now exposed.

She reached for her phone on the nightstand. Nothing. Ty hadn't answered any of her texts. Hadn't had the decency to even answer the goddamned phone. She stung. She leaked. She could feel her body emptying. Everything that remained trying to escape.

Through the wall behind her she could hear a woman moaning, like an animal. On the other side of the curtain that divided her own room in two, a baby cried, its cries like tinkling bells. Only Crystal keened silently. Her body weeping, seeping, but her eyes were absolutely dry.

Later as she closed her eyes, she allowed her mind to wander to that place she'd promised she wouldn't ever go again. To that impossible place. To imagine what would have happened if she had simply refused. If instead of handing the baby over to Mrs. Stone with her pale hair and pale yellow sweater set, she'd just held on.

As Elsbeth stood, rolling Mrs. Van Buren's whispery hair into hot rollers, she dreamed her life backwards. She couldn't help it. It was magnetic, this need to circle back again and again. To unwind the life that had been woven from that moment on, to imagine how things would be different if she hadn't met Kurt. Mrs. Van Buren's soft voice was hypnotic, and as she talked, Elsbeth drifted.

When she'd met Kurt, she was sixteen years old. Elsbeth at sixteen was doe-eyed but scrappy. She was on the girls' basketball team at school, all legs and speed. She met Kurt when she and a couple of girls from the team had gone out for pizza at Luigi's after the game. They'd won, she'd scored twenty points, and she was feeling invincible. Kurt was sitting at the booth behind them, and she'd noticed him right away when she walked back to the table, carrying the giant pizza on the hot silver tray. He had slow eyes, the kind her mother would have called "bedroom eyes." Light blue with heavy lids, thick blond lashes. Totally sexy. He looked at her, and she felt everything inside her go soft and melty.

For almost an hour, she sat giggling with her girlfriends, stealing glances at him across the back of the booth's seat, trying to make that pizza and her fountain drink last forever. He was sitting with two other guys, and every now and then he'd catch her looking at him and grin. By the time the girls' pizza was finally gone and the soda was diluted with melted ice, she felt like she was going crazy. And so when the guys started to empty the plastic pitchers of beer and stack up their cups, gathering their coats and making to go, she thought about her coach's mantra, *You can't score if you don't take the shot.* So she edged out of the seat, and then she was standing at the guys' table, every nerve ending a live wire. "Hi," she said. "My name's El." She looked straight at Kurt as she said this, trying to say a thousand other things without saying a word.

"Cool," one of the other guys said. "You girls like to party?"

And then they were all piling into Kurt's car, four in the back and two up front. Led Zeppelin blasting on the stereo, winter air coming in through the open windows. They drove out to the river, tumbling out of the car and into the woods, and somebody had a bottle of tequila and somebody had weed. And Elsbeth had a mission.

It didn't take long. Soon, the others had clumsily paired off and wandered away, finding soft places to lie down and make out. She and Kurt held hands and walked along the river's edge. She remembered that she was cold and he'd offered her his sweatshirt. Later, her tongue and lips swollen from all the kissing, she crawled into her bed, still wearing it. His phone number was scrawled on her forearm in ballpoint. His sweatshirt smelled like sawdust and pine. She was drunk and slept curled up inside the sweatshirt, dreaming the night, the kisses over and over again.

But she was *sixteen*. And she knew now that back then she would have fallen in love with *anyone* with sexy eyes who gave her a second glance at a pizza joint. With anyone who touched her like Kurt had. With anyone who kissed her like that. It was all just a matter of circumstance that it happened to be Kurt.

As she slipped the curlers out of Mrs. Van Buren's hair, the silvery curls like tiny clouds, she wandered back through that night, at all the opportunities to change her future. If she'd missed the game-winning shot and gone home to sulk over a cardboard quart of ice cream. If she hadn't been so sure of herself, so certain that she could have anything she wanted. If she'd fallen asleep on her stomach instead of her back, the ink of his number smudging into her sheets like the mascara she didn't bother to wash off.

She imagined the other lives she might have lived. The other men she might have loved. The other houses in other towns, the other jobs, even the other children. But the barb that snagged and ripped on all of this was Gracy. Without Kurt, without Trevor even, there would never have been Gracy. And the thought of that, of Gracy's absence from her life, was like imagining the world without the sun.

She used to love Kurt so much it stung. But that love had dulled like one of the knives in the set they got from her mother for their wedding. She still cared about him, of course, but she couldn't help but feel let down.

She and Kurt used to dream about leaving Vermont, about going somewhere, anywhere but here. Kurt said he'd always wanted to go to Alaska. That he'd love to work on a fishing boat. That they could get a little log cabin in the snow. Elsbeth dreamed of sunshine. California, Arizona, Florida, Hawaii. Kurt told her he heard that at certain times of the year in Alaska, the sun never set. But he also said he'd go anywhere Elsbeth wanted. These were the things they shared in the calm blue midnights of their first year together. She could still remember that tingling feeling of a possibility sometimes. That soft happiness of a shared dream. But as soon as Elsbeth found out she was pregnant, they'd put off their plans. She'd enrolled in cosmetology school so that she'd have some practical skills. A way to make a living, *wherever* she and Kurt wound up. She figured girls in Alaska needed their hair done just as much as girls in Two Rivers. Trevor would just be a minor delay.

She was haunted by the promises whispered under covers, by the trill her skin used to feel at his touch when she was still just a girl in tube socks and a basketball uniform. This wasn't the life she'd dreamed of then. Maybe this was someone else's dream, but it certainly wasn't hers.

But then again, here she was. She wasn't a dreamy sixteen-year-old girl anymore. She was a wife. A mother. She knew she just needed to do something, sharpen those dulled edges. Feel alive again.

"You have lovely hands," Mrs. Van Buren said.

"Excuse me?" Elsbeth said, untying the plastic cape with its snowfall of silver curls.

"Your hands are lovely," she said. "Do you play piano?"

She studied her hands, her long, thin fingers. It was as though she were seeing them for the first time. "No." She laughed. "I used to play basketball, though."

And despite herself, again she rewound, in slow motion, her long legs running backward down the court, away from the basket, dribbling and dodging in reverse. The pass from the sideline, returning to the hands of the other girl. A girl whose name she could no longer recollect.

By noon, her feet were tired, but it had been a busy day with two new clients she hoped might become regulars.

"See you later," she said to the receptionist, Carly, on her way out.

"Say hi to Gracy for me," Carly said, the electronic bells of the doorway chiming.

She drove to the elementary school to pick Gracy up from kindergarten, and when they opened the metal gate, Gracy ran across the blacktop into Elsbeth's arms, nearly knocking her over. "Mumma!" she said, and Elsbeth smiled. Gracy's unabashed affection nearly killed her sometimes. She couldn't remember the last time Trevor had hugged her.

Gracy's teacher came over and rubbed the top of Gracy's head. "You have quite a little artist here," she said to Elsbeth. "Gracy, why don't you show your mama what you made today?"

"What did you make?' Elsbeth asked, squatting down to help Gracy open her Hello Kitty backpack.

"I drew you a picture," Gracy said, reaching into her school folder and carefully pulling out a sheet of paper. She handed it to Elsbeth.

The picture was of a face, with big round eyes and exaggerated eyelashes. Black hair and pink lips. The neck was long and thin with a heart-shaped locket at the throat.

"Is this me?" Elsbeth asked, reaching for the locket she wore every day. The one Kurt had given her when Gracy was born, the one with a picture of Gracy on one side and herself on the other. The one she didn't take off even in the shower.

Gracy nodded.

"She was so proud of it," Mrs. Nelson said. Then she whispered conspiratorially, "It really was the best one in the class."

Mrs. Nelson had told Elsbeth more than once how special Gracy was. She had a couple of really difficult children in the class this year, including one kid who repeatedly spat on her, and Elsbeth knew that she was grateful for Gracy. Sometimes Elsbeth felt like two different people, like two different mothers. She was Trevor's mother, always sitting on the opposite side of the principal's desk, head hung in shame, and she was Gracy's mother, beaming with pride. It made her feel like shit.

"It's not as pretty as you are, Mumma. I couldn't do the nose right."

"It's perfect, sweet pea," she said, hugging Gracy tightly, feeling the little bones of her shoulders like wings at her back. But she also felt a crush of guilt, as though that other mother, *Trevor's mother,* were standing there next to her, watching this display in disgust.

"Listen, how about we go get a treat? Just you and me," and then, "We can pick something out for Trevor too."

Gracy nodded and pressed her forehead against Elsbeth's.

Elsbeth pulled into the parking space in front of the Walgreens and glanced in the rearview mirror. Gracy had already fallen asleep, and she thought for a moment about just driving home, letting her sleep. But she'd promised her a treat, and if she woke up at home, that would be the first thing she'd remember. As she lifted her out of her booster seat, she noticed a whole bunch of crumbs stuck to something hot pink on the seat's upholstery. She plucked a withered French fry from the floor and shoved it in her pocket. She thought of Twig's Mustang with its soft leather seats and freshly vacuumed floor mats and sighed.

Gracy grumbled a little as Elsbeth hoisted her up onto her shoulder, still dreaming. She was five now, almost *six,* and almost too big to be carried, but Elsbeth didn't mind. She'd carried her on her hip for the entire first year of her life; she could cut and even color hair with Gracy still clinging to her. She lugged Gracy inside and then lowered her into the front basket of one of the shopping carts. "Mumma, can I get a Butterfinger?" she asked groggily.

"Sure, baby," Elsbeth said. "Anything you want."

"Trevor likes those peanut butter cups."

Elsbeth could spend a whole day at Walgreens. She loved to wander the makeup aisle, trying the samplers of blush and eye shadow on the backs of her hands, while the glossy models on the displays smiled coyly at her, like they shared some sort of special secret. She loved walking down every aisle, letting her fingers graze the sticks of deodorant, the flip-flops, and the tacky wind chimes. She paused at the Tupperware, the hand soap, the bags of gumdrops and little jars of Vaseline. There was a comfort in all this stuff. It quieted her nerves in a way nothing else could. She let Gracy out of the cart in the toy aisle, let her pull the puzzles and dolls and squirt guns from their shelves and metal hooks. They flipped through coloring books and crossword books together. She read entire magazines at Walgreens.

Everyone steals.

This was what Elsbeth told herself every time she couldn't resist the impulse to pocket an item. Of course, she never took anything expensive: not the cameras or GPSs, not the cordless phones or expensive earbuds. But little things: a box of diet pills, a bag of M&M's, a tiny garden gnome whose little red hat poked into the palm of her hand as she pocketed it. She took something almost every single time she shopped there, though the total probably didn't add up to even a hundred dollars' worth of merchandise. The box on the top shelf of her closet was overflowing with the stolen trinkets: Matchbox cars, magazines, batteries, and gum. Once she even managed to pilfer a box of twenty lubricated condoms, despite the fact that she'd been on the Pill since Gracy was born. At home, she'd opened the box and slipped the condoms into her hand like colorful party favors. They lay scattered now next to some stolen dryer sheets and a ball of rubber bands in the box.

The box made her feel awful. She knew stealing was wrong, but the urge was so strong. It felt like the time she and Kurt had driven to Maine and she'd stood at the shore as the waves sucked at the sand beneath her feet. She was powerless to its pull. And, of course, she would never steal from a local business, but Walgreens was just one of a million chains making somebody somewhere richer and richer. *Everyone steals.* This is what she told herself.

Today, as Gracy snagged a giant stuffed Easter bunny from the clearance bin, Elsbeth felt that tidal pull toward a rotating display of sunglasses. She knew where the security cameras were. She also knew that there was only one employee on the floor right now and she was busy texting behind the counter.

"Come on, Gracy Bear," she said and Gracy ran to her, dragging the bunny across the scuffed and speckled linoleum. She scooped her back up into the cart and, without hesitation, slipped a pair of tortoiseshell sunglasses into the front pocket of her jeans. Her heart was beating hard but steadily in her chest as she pushed Gracy and the rabbit straight to the counter where she smiled at the pregnant girl behind the counter. This girl had been working there for a while, mostly on weekends, though. She'd seen her a few times before, watched as the suspicious belly bump grew into an obvious one. She couldn't be more than sixteen, and Elsbeth felt a sudden snag in her heart. She had wished she could tell her something, warn her or something, but it would be like yelling "Fire!" after a house has already burned to the ground.

"Did you find everything okay?" the girl asked, quickly shoving her phone back behind the counter.

"Yes, thanks," Elsbeth said, trying not to think about the sunglasses. She knew it was dangerous, stupid. She could so easily get caught, though she never stole unless Gracy was with her. Nobody ever suspects a *mother* of shoplifting, especially not a mother buying her cute little girl a giant stuffed rabbit and a Butterfinger. "Gracy, honey, put your bunny and the candy up there so the nice lady can ring us up."

The girl smiled at Gracy, and Elsbeth's chest ached with pride.

Elsbeth glanced at the girl's round belly again, making sure before she spoke. "Are you having a girl or a boy?"

The color drained from the girl's face, and she looked down.

"I'm sorry, that's none of my business," Elsbeth said, and suddenly she was aware of the sharp arms of the glasses poking into her hip.

"That'll be five dollars and forty cents, please," the girl said. Her eyes were watery, blinking hard.

Elsbeth handed her six dollars and Gracy grabbed the bunny from the counter, squeezing it.

"It was a girl," she said. "I already had her."

"Oh," Elsbeth said, feeling her face grow hot. She figured she'd be smart to just shut up before she made things any worse.

As she got Gracy back into her booster seat, she thought about the days right after Trevor was born, when her body looked and felt so different. She remembered staring in the full-length mirror on the back of her bedroom door, stunned to see a woman's body instead of a girl's. She remembered how cheated she felt. How devastated. She also remembered wondering if she'd made the wrong decision. Thinking, as Trevor wailed and flailed in his crib and she could do nothing but sit helplessly on her bed and cry, that maybe she should have given Trevor up to someone who would make a better mother. It was in those days, so long ago now they were hazy, dreamlike, in her mind, that she began second-guessing her entire life.

In the car, she pulled the sunglasses out of her pocket, peeling the UV sticker off the lens. She peered into the rearview mirror

at Gracy, who was cooing softly to the rabbit, a swipe of chocolate and peanut butter across one cheek. Elsbeth looked at her
own reflection and put the sunglasses on, and as she tilted her
head to the left and then the right, she thought about the bathing
suit in the catalogue, about sunshine and the ocean, and she realized exactly what she needed to do.

They needed a vacation.

And so instead of driving home, she pulled out of the lot and
drove to the grocery store. Even though she'd already blown their
grocery budget for the week, she got two thick pork chops from
the butcher and a frozen Sara Lee cheesecake. The kids could
have fish sticks, but she would need to make something special
for Kurt. On the way to the register, she grabbed a seven-dollar
bottle of Chardonnay.

Elsbeth knew that if she was going to convince Kurt to take
a vacation, she would need to start planting the seeds early on.
Like the tulip bulbs she planted last winter. She couldn't just
come out and ask him; that would never work with Kurt. He'd
come up with a zillion reasons not to before she even finished
asking. She would need to be patient. She needed to be smart
about it, subtle. She had to do in a way that made it seem like it
was *his* idea.

On Fridays after work, Kurt usually went to the store to pick up his dad's groceries for him: a carton of eggs and a jar of instant coffee, two loaves of white bread, and three cans of deviled ham. Then he'd go to the liquor store for a carton of Kools and a handle of Seagram's Seven. If Kurt bought anything else (fruit or vegetables or milk), they would only go bad in his fridge. He stopped by to check in on Pop every Friday night on his way home from work, and once every month he took him into town to the barber and then out to Rosco's for lunch. The home health nurse came by twice a week to make sure he was taking his meds. Maury Vorhies, one of Pop's neighbors, came on Monday nights to play cribbage. Kurt had asked him to keep an eye out on Pop as well.

Sometimes Kurt could hardly believe this was the house he had grown up in. It was like the cancer that had slowly rotted out his mother's belly. At first, you couldn't tell from the outside what was happening on the inside, but in the last year or so, the rot and decay and stink had started to spill out onto the front porch, the yard, the driveway, and beyond. And now that the snow had melted, he realized just how much crap there was outside. As he walked up the cracked walkway to the porch, he knew he was going to have to say something to Pop about the mess before the neighbors did.

Kurt had tried numerous times to help his dad clean up, but Pop had only gotten upset. Taken it personally. He was a *collector*, he said. Why couldn't Kurt just respect that and leave his shit alone? Kurt, of all people, should understand the value in other people's junk. Hadn't the salvage yard put food on his table his whole life? Hadn't it put this very roof over his head? The problem was Jude Kennedy *was* a collector, but he didn't collect antiques or snow globes or even those little spoons from all over the world. He collected *everything*. The bloody Styrofoam trays that cradled his ground beef, the plastic rings that embraced his beer, the junk mail that filled his mailbox. Advertisements for oil changes and grocery store fliers were as valuable to him as his dead wife's china and his own Purple Heart. The house had always been full, but when Kurt's mother was alive at least it was clean. Now it was filthy. There was one path that you could walk through, which led from the front door to the La-Z-Boy where his father spent most of his days and all of his nights and then on into the crowded kitchen and, finally, into the bathroom. Every time Kurt visited it seemed to get just a little bit worse; the pathway just a little bit narrower. He wanted to help him, to just empty the place out, give him a fresh start, but at this point he wasn't even sure where to begin.

Most Fridays, he'd sit with his father in a spot cleared off on the old couch and watch a basketball game or baseball game or just old episodes of *Law & Order*. Pop would draw hard and long on one Kool after another. The air was minty and thick; there was a layer of ash on everything. Kurt would catch him up with what was happening down at work as well as stuff happening in town. He brought drawings that Gracy had made, with *GRANDPA* scrawled across them in waxy crayon. He was usually there at least a couple of hours. But tonight, he'd promised Elsbeth he'd be home by suppertime, so he'd have to make it quick.

"Hey, Dad!" Kurt said by way of warning as he slowly cracked the unlocked door. He knew his father sometimes left the door to the bathroom open, and he didn't want to embarrass him by walking in while he was struggling to use the contraption they'd gotten at the medical supply store after the stroke.

"C'min." His father's voice crackled, scratchy and deep like the crush of fallen leaves, and Kurt pushed the door open as far as he could. Something was blocking its full arc. The light was dim inside, but it looked like a ratty footstool.

Jude wasn't in the bathroom but in the recliner, already wearing his pajamas. He didn't usually lounge around in his nightclothes; despite the state of his home, he still showered every day, used a straight razor to shave, and wore clean, pressed Dickies and collared shirts. This attention to hygiene and grooming was a relief to Kurt.

"You okay, Dad?" Kurt asked, making his way through the messy living room to the kitchen with the bag of groceries.

"What's that?" he asked. Growing up, Kurt used to be able to tell when his father had been drinking from the soft slur that signaled three or four or more cocktails. But ever since the stroke, Pop *always* sounded drunk. The only way Kurt could monitor his drinking now was by measuring how much was left in the bottle when he got there on Friday nights.

Kurt returned to the living room after shoving the perishables in the fridge and tried not to look at the mess on the counter and in the sink. Last week's bottle had about a finger left in it. "I said, *Are you okay?*"

"Why don't you ask that bitch from across the road?" he said.

"Theresa?" Kurt asked, sitting down on the couch next to a stack of newspapers and his father's breakfast plate slick with congealed eggs and bacon grease. Theresa Bouchard had been in Kurt's class in high school. They'd even gone out once or twice, but after graduation, he'd never called her again. Now she was a single mom, raising five boys, or maybe it was six. The rumor was every single one of them had a different father, though they all looked the same to Kurt. Dirty little buggers with hair in their eyes and runny noses.

Pop's eyes were glassy, and there was a sweating tumbler between his legs.

"What'd she say?" Kurt asked.

"Said she's gonna call the county, get the house condemned."

"What?" Kurt asked. He felt sucker punched. "For what?" Though he knew exactly for what.

Pop shrugged. "Complainin' about rats and raccoons. One of her snot-nosed kids come over and says he got bit." He reached for a new cigarette and lit it with the tip of the one still burning between his lips. "When I was a kid, that was called trespassin'. Those little shits are always comin' around, stealin' stuff. They're lucky I don't shoot 'em."

Kurt lifted his chin and rubbed his hand across his head. "Well, let's get it cleaned up, then. If it's just the trash out front, I can make a couple trips to the dump this weekend. Let me put some of those boxes on the porch into the garage. What else?"

"Be a good kid and get me a fresh drink?" his father said then, holding out his cup to him like a beggar, shaking it so the remaining ice cubes tinkled inside. His eyes looked as watery and viscous as the whiskey.

Kurt went to the kitchen and made a weak cocktail, loading it up with ice. He turned on the faucet to water it down, but the pipes only clanged and hissed. Jesus. "Pop, did your water get shut off?" Kurt was seething. His father always seemed to wait until the last possible moment to let him know there was a problem.

Pop stared at the television.

Kurt rubbed his temples. "Jesus, Dad. Why didn't you tell me? We can pay your water bill. How much do you owe?" Kurt had no idea how he was even going to pay his own water bill this month.

"Bah," Jude said.

"Dad, this is serious. If Theresa calls the county and they find out you don't have running water, you'll lose your house. What will you do then?" Kurt asked, though he knew exactly what he would do then. He'd have to move in with him and Elsbeth. Christ. He knew he was going to have to call Billy and ask him to send a check.

"Listen, Dad," he said. "I'm gonna bring Trevor over this weekend and we'll work on the yard. And I'll figure out what to do about the water. But you've got to let me help. You can't get all sentimental about stuff. It's time to hoe out. I'll call Bill."

"Don't you even think about calling that little prick," his father grumbled, slamming the cocktail down on the end table.

"He's your son," Kurt said.

"He's no son of mine."

On his way home, Kurt called Billy on his cell, knowing he wouldn't pick up. It was Friday night. Billy might be out after work. Kurt tried to imagine him sitting down in some dark bar, loosening his tie, ordering a drink. He tried to picture the contents of his briefcase as he rested it against the bar stool, but Kurt had no idea what he carried inside, what a lawyer's trappings were. Billy was five hundred miles away, but it felt farther than that. It felt like a whole lifetime between here and there. Between them.

"I need to borrow some money," he said into the silence. "Not a lot. Call me back."

By the time he pulled into the driveway at home, the nerves in his legs were raw and thrumming.

Trevor sat down on the couch next to Gracy. She was watching *SpongeBob,* hugging a stuffed bunny he hadn't seen before. She put her little feet up on his lap without taking her eyes off the TV. There were holes in the toes of her tights, and her big toes were both sticking out. He didn't know how she could stand it. He tickled her toes, and she wriggled and giggled.

"Stop it!" she squealed.

"Color with me?" she asked. There was a TV tray in front of her, paper and crayons all over it.

Trevor's mother was busy making dinner in the kitchen: The smells hit him like a punch in the gut. Ever since the fight the other day, he'd been skipping lunch, avoiding the cafeteria completely, eating vending-machine peanut butter crackers in the art room during lunch period. Now his head felt swimmy with hunger, his stomach knotted tight.

"Dinner!" she called.

The table looked fancy, with candles and the good place mats she usually only put out for Thanksgiving and Christmas. She dished fish sticks and green beans onto his and Gracy's plates and big juicy pork chops onto hers and his dad's. The smell of it all made his mouth fill up with saliva. It was all he could do to keep from shoveling it in with his fists.

His dad sat down and scowled. "What's all this for?" he asked.

His mother shrugged, smiling and pouring some wine into two tumblers. "You've been working so hard lately, we *both* have,

I just thought it would be nice for us to have a nice family dinner."

She smelled like flowers, and her hair was still wet. When Trevor got home from school, she'd asked him to watch Gracy while she took a bath. She was in there a long time, and when she came out she smelled sweet, the steam coming off her like hot roses.

"How was your day?" she asked, and her voice sounded funny. Too high, like a cartoon version of herself.

His dad just nodded, and his mother looked at him hard, like she wanted something. Like he was supposed to be able to read her mind. She did that to Trevor too. But his dad didn't say anything, he just started to saw at his pork chop.

His mother took a deep breath, like she was filling herself with air, and he wondered, for a moment, if she might just float away. He imagined her lifting off the ground, like a ghost, slipping out like shower steam through a crack in the front door.

Gracy was trying to explain some sort of project with lima beans they were doing in her kindergarten class. Trevor remembered doing that in kindergarten too, the beans wrapped in wet paper towels, their sprouts curling like tapeworms inside their plastic bags. It was supposed to teach them something about life cycles.

"And mine was the first one to sprout. The first one!" Gracy said, grinning as she speared a fish stick with her fork. "Mrs. Nelson says I have the best handwriting in the whole class. Do you know how to spell difficulty? It's hard. D-I-F-F-I-C-U-L-T-Y. That's funny! It's *difficult* to spell *difficult*."

Trevor's father hadn't spoken a dozen words to him since the fight at school. And Trevor was afraid to look him in the eye, so he concentrated on cleaning his plate. When he was finished, he quietly asked for more.

"Help yourself, honey," his mom said.

He scooped another pile of green beans, like slimy pick-up

sticks, onto his plate, and took the last fish stick from the greasy cookie sheet.

"I need you to come to Pop's house with me this weekend," his dad said, without looking up from his own plate.

Trevor felt sick to his stomach, but it wouldn't do him any good to argue. He hated going to Pop's house. He'd have stacked a thousand tires at the yard if it meant not having to go to Pop's. If they were looking to punish him, this was how to do it.

"What for?" his mother asked. Her voice was back to normal now, and her face looked like a fist. "I thought we could go to the outlets in North Conway this weekend. Gracy's grown out of all her summer clothes. Plus, I wanted to pick up some annuals at the nursery on the way back."

His dad looked up at her, but kept chewing. It was a good long time before he finally swallowed, like he was chewing on the words he might say. "Maybe we should hold off until the good weather sticks. Last year we got a frost in the middle of May. Ruined all those flowers you planted."

Sometimes, when they did this, Trevor could hear the warble and hiss of all the words that *weren't* being said. Of all the ones stuck inside. They were like angry whispers, squashed down. Suffocated. It made his throat feel tight. Made him feel like he couldn't breathe.

"What does Jude need that can't wait until next weekend?" she said, and set her fork and knife down. Trevor knew this meant she wouldn't eat any more until she got her way. And as much as he would love to ask for the half a pork chop, as likely as it was to wind up in the trash, he knew he shouldn't even think about it.

"Theresa Bouchard's been making some noise. He needs me to take some junk to the dump."

"Somebody oughtta take that whole *shit box* to the dump," she said softly, the word like a snake slithering out of its hiding place in the grass, and then there it was. Out in the wide open.

"Mumma, you cussed," Gracy said, her mouth open wide, half-chewed green beans inside.

"El," his dad said sternly.

His mother shook her head like she was just waking up from a dream. She reached for Gracy's hand. "I'm sorry, honey. Mommy shouldn't use bad words." She smiled and looked down at her own plate, nodding. "Okay. It's fine. We'll go another weekend."

And just like that, there was silence again. Only Trevor knew that the unspoken words were being choked, asphyxiated, that all those unsaid things were slowly dying.

Crystal lay in the bathtub in the bathroom she shared with her little sister, Angie, and watched as milk began to leak from her nipples, floating across the water like liquid clouds. Her breasts were hot, buzzing, and so large they hardly seemed to belong to her anymore. Her stomach looked different now too, like a partially deflated balloon.

At the hospital, after they took the baby away, the doctor had offered to give her medicine to help dry her milk up, but she'd declined. She told him she couldn't swallow pills and then almost laughed because that's how this happened in the *first* place. But now as she rose out of the water into the misty air, her boobs felt like bowling balls, heavy and aching, pulling on every muscle in her shoulders and back. She hesitated and then tentatively pinched one of her nipples, watching as three distinct, almost violent streams of milk squirted out, like a mini showerhead. She gasped and pulled her hand away, but it kept on spraying. The doctor had warned her not to do this, not to "stimulate" her nipples; if she just left them alone, the milk would dry up on its own and everything would go back to normal.

Normal. God, she couldn't remember what normal was anymore. Was normal back when the biggest worries she had were writing her college essay, what to wear to school in the morning, who would take her to the prom? Was normal back when she had only daydreamed about Ty, her best friend Ty—all that awful wishing, wanting, waiting? Or maybe normal was later, when Ty finally loved her back and they walked down the halls at school, his arm slung over her shoulder—the taste of Big Red gum in his mouth when he kissed her. When her whole world felt anything *but* normal. What she did know was this: There was no going back to *that* normal. Not now.

Her work shirt was still on the bathroom floor where she'd left it. The wet circles on the chest were dry now, crusty and dark. She'd need to toss it in the laundry before her next shift. She didn't want her mother to see it either; she didn't want to see the red shame on her mother's flushed face.

She'd gotten the job at Walgreens to save money for college. Her parents said they would cover her tuition, but she'd need to pay for her room and board. She kept the job after she got pregnant, because for a while she thought she might keep the baby. She'd gotten the job so she could support herself. Support both of them. But later, after everything fell apart, she kept the job because it was the only thing she had anymore that she could count on. She couldn't count on Ty; that was for sure. She couldn't count on her best girlfriend, Lena. And she couldn't count on her parents, even though they insisted she always could. That was only true now that she'd given the baby up; if she'd kept her, she wasn't sure she'd even have been able to count on a roof over her head.

The people at work didn't judge her the way the kids at school did, the way her parents did. They didn't care that she was pregnant. They didn't care that *normally* she'd be training for the state track meet, or that she'd been third in her class until all this happened. They didn't even know that she was supposed to go off to UVM in the fall, nor would they care that she was starting to think she might not even *go* to college anymore. They didn't care about her old dreams or who she was before all this; as long as she showed up on time and her register balanced out at the end of her shift, she was golden.

Crystal liked the way Walgreens smelled: like lemons floating in bleach. She liked how organized it was and that you could pretty much get everything in the world you'd need to live on here, except maybe fresh fruits and vegetables. She liked the electronic doors, the air-conditioning, and the white linoleum floors. She liked that you could go from brunette to blond with stuff from one aisle and then find everything you'd need to kill yourself in another. There was power here. There was possibility.

She had known today was probably going to be a little weird. Last week she'd been pregnant, and now she wasn't anymore. Just like that. They all knew she wasn't going to keep the baby. That wouldn't be a surprise, but still. She knew it was bound to be awkward. She hadn't even been back to school yet. That would take her a while longer, she figured.

Thank God, Howard wasn't there. Howard was the day manager on the weekends when she usually worked. Howard had a crush on her, and once, in Feminine Hygiene, he muttered something about helping her raise the baby. She'd acted like she didn't hear him and rushed back to the counter, pretending she had a customer. Today when she'd walked through the doors, it was Deena who was up on a stepladder replacing one of the fluorescent bulbs. "Hi," Deena had said, like everything was normal. Deena was no-nonsense. She wouldn't have cared if Crystal had had a litter of puppies right before her shift; there was work that needed to be done. "Someone just dropped a twelve-pack of MGD in Beverages," she said. "Mop's already out there." And then, stepping down off the ladder, she scowled. "You okay to mop?" And Crystal nodded.

Six hours later, Crystal's breasts had hurt so badly she thought she might die. Even the cheap polyester of her work shirt pressing against them was almost unendurable. And then as she was ringing up some creep buying Fiddle Faddle, socks, and duct tape, she felt her entire chest go hot and wet. The guy's bug eyes got buggier and he gawked at her, staring at her chest. When she looked down, she could see perfect circles spreading across each boob, like blood from a pair of bullet wounds.

"Shit," she said and threw the guy's change at him, ducking out behind the counter and running to the Baby Care aisle. She grabbed a box of nursing pads and made a dash for the restroom. She found Deena restocking an endcap of batteries. "I gotta put these on my tab," Crystal said, holding up the box. Ashamed.

Deena looked confused at first and then, noticing the two wet blossoms at Crystal's chest, nodded. "You can take one of my shirts from my locker," she said.

Somehow she'd managed to make it through the rest of her shift, even when the lady, the one who was always stealing shit, asked her if she was having a boy or a girl. That just about did her in. But she'd just kept working, and soon it was time to go home.

On her way to clock out, she walked down the baby aisle again, and when she saw the package of two Winnie the Pooh pacifiers, she felt a tug in her chest, a quickening of her heart. She thought about the lady slipping barrettes, Scotch tape, bubble gum into her pocket. How bold she was. How ballsy. She glanced around to make sure Deena wasn't coming and plucked the pacifier package off the rack and, hands trembling, shoved it into her pocket. But then as she waved good-bye and headed toward the door, she felt guilty and slipped a couple of bucks into the register.

Now she wrapped her wet hair in a towel, put on her sweats, and pulled the pacifiers out of the pocket of her dirty work shirt before chucking it in the laundry pile.

Downstairs, her parents and sister were watching a movie on TV, but she locked her door anyway and sat down on the edge of her bed.

Eeyore. He was her favorite character when she was a kid. She even had a stuffed one from one of their trips to Disney World. She put her finger through the plastic loop, held the pacifier to her nose, and sniffed the strange chalky latex smell. Then, after she climbed under the covers and turned out the light, she closed her eyes and put the pacifier in her mouth.

Kurt walked.
In the middle of the night, when his legs started warming up for their symphony of pain, he had no choice but to move them. He'd found that the only way to quiet his limbs was to listen to them, to stand up and let them sing. In the winter, he just walked up and down the hallway that ran through their small house, the wooden floors creaking loudly even beneath his careful feet. On warmer nights, he walked in the woods behind the house, through the neighbor's fields. Tonight, he walked down the driveway and out onto the dirt road that would lead him, if he walked long enough, into town.

It was dark and cold out, the ground still patchy with snow from the last big storm. He walked down the long, steep driveway, wondering if he should have worn gloves, a hat, and he turned to look back up at the small house, at its paper cut-out silhouette against the bright sky behind it.

He and Elsbeth had rented this house for six years before they were able to make an offer to Buzz Nolan, their landlord. The house was small, just a two-bedroom ranch with one bath, but it belonged to them. That had to be worth something. Even when they were still just tenants, Kurt had kept it up well, making most of the repairs himself. He'd replaced the loose floorboards on the front porch, installed new windows when the sills in the original ones rotted out. He'd patched the roof and re-tiled the bathroom; he'd even upgraded the kitchen countertops a few years back. He'd caulked and snaked and plumbed. He'd painted every inch of every wall.

They'd refinanced a few years ago when the house appraised at almost twice what they'd paid for it, cashing in on a chunk of equity. He'd paid off their debts, upgraded the computer system at the salvage yard, and splurged on a real wedding ring for Elsbeth, who'd been wearing a cheap 14K gold band since their wedding day. He'd never seen her as happy as the night he took her into town for dinner at Hunan East and gave it to her in its velvet case, like he was proposing for the first time. But not even a week later, it was as though it had always been on her finger, and the gratitude and joy it had brought seemed to evaporate. It shamed him now how much he spent. It shamed him that he'd mortgaged their future for that flimsy moment of happiness. Because now they were upside down on the house, and despite the state-of-the-art computer system, the website, the salvage yard was barely surviving. And on top of all that, they had to figure out what to do about Trevor and how to keep Pop from losing his house. Christ. Even if his legs weren't like live wires, he doubted he'd be sleeping.

He walked along the road kicking at rocks, studying the ditch that ran parallel to the road. When he got to the bend where two white crosses loomed ominous and sad, he stopped. The crosses had weathered three winters. You think he'd be accustomed to them by now, grown numb to the makeshift memorial. But each spring when they emerged from the melting snow a little more weathered for the wear, they never failed to startle him. A drunk-driving accident; two teenagers had been killed on the way home from a party out at the place where the rivers meet. Two boys, brothers. When summer turned to fall, he'd been the one who finally removed the rotting teddy bears, the deflated balloons with their sad ribbons, and the notes with their illegible Magic Marker scribblings. He hadn't known the boys or their family, but he still considered himself the unofficial caretaker of this roadside shrine.

He climbed down the muddy embankment to the crosses and used his jacket's cuff to wipe the dirty snow off the wood. Wind whipped across his face, stinging his eyes. He straightened the cross on the right, which was leaning awkwardly into the shoulder of the other one, and felt a pang in his gut.

Billy had called back right after he and Elsbeth got into bed. She'd been acting weird all night. First the fancy dinner. Cheesecake and *wine,* for Christ's sake. She was trying too hard. Being too sweet. When the phone rang, she'd been kissing his neck and rubbing his leg over and over with her hand. It didn't feel sincere, though; it felt like she was trying to get something from him. Something she wouldn't name. He felt like that a lot lately: like there was some secret he was supposed to figure out, but she wasn't giving him any clues. And so instead of arousing him, her gentle strokes had just made his jumpy nerves feel even more agitated.

"I've got to get this," he'd said, looking at Billy's name on the screen. He waited for him to leave a message, and then took the phone out into the living room, leaving Elsbeth in their bed.

Billy's voice hadn't changed since he was a teenager, since he left town and never came back. There was a lot of background noise. It sounded like a subway station: hollow, a loudspeaker voice reverberating. Billy waited a moment and then cleared his throat. "If the money's for you," he said. "I'll send it. If it's for Dad, he can go to hell."

And while it killed him to lie to his brother, it almost killed him more to let Billy think he couldn't provide for his own family. He'd texted a quick note back. *500 should take care of it. Pay u back next month.*

Now Kurt climbed back up the embankment and looked down at the crosses. He'd bring out some flowers soon maybe, after El's lilacs started to bloom. Get some of those cemetery vases that you can spear into the ground. That would be nice.

By the time he got back to the house, his legs seemed pacified. Ready to let him rest. He quietly opened the bedroom door and peeled off his clothes. He pulled the sheets back gently and climbed in next to Elsbeth, wrapping his arm around her, breathing the smell of her clean skin. She was sleeping deeply now. He envied her this. The way sleep could consume her. Even on nights when they'd fought, when Trevor had them both on edge, she'd been able to lose herself in sleep. To slip easily into her own private peace. Gracy was the same way. Even as a baby, she'd always been a good sleeper. A *good sleeper,* as if sleep were a skill instead of something necessary to survive.

On nights that his restless legs propelled him out of bed and into the darkness, he knew that sleep would elude him. Because even if his legs relented, his mind kept reeling. And so he held her, her body responding to his even in sleep, and concentrated on her breathing, on the steady thump, thump of her heart, as he waited for morning to come.

On Saturday morning, Trevor refused to eat breakfast. He did this sometimes, as if to punish Elsbeth. He didn't want to go to Pop's, and while she could hardly blame him, if he didn't eat, he'd be starving later, which would only make things worse.

"I don't like this wasting food," she said, scraping the food off his plate into the trash can and then thinking, too late, that she should have saved it, sent it with him for lunch.

"I'm not hungry," he said.

She looked at him, but he wouldn't return her gaze. She wished she could brush the white shock of hair out of his eyes, touch his chin, *make* him look at her. But she worried he'd only swat her hand away.

"Listen, I know you don't want to go, but your dad needs your help," she said, turning back to the counter. She knew that Trevor respected Kurt. That Kurt and he shared some sort of bond that eluded her.

At that Trevor silently stood up, grabbed the camera his teacher gave him, and walked out the front door. She watched him through the window as he climbed over the tailgate into the back of the truck, looking through the camera at the sky.

Kurt came in and sat down at the table. "Thanks," he said when she handed him his plate.

She sat down across from him and picked up her coffee, which had grown cold. "You need me to come with you today?"

"I've got Trev. You don't need to worry about it."

And truthfully, she was relieved that he hadn't accepted her offer. Like Trevor, she'd rather go just about anywhere than Pop's house on a Saturday morning. But she also knew that everything with Pop was wearing Kurt down. She'd suggested a few times that he talk to Jude about moving into an assisted-living place. If anyone could convince Jude to move out of that dump, it would be Kurt. But Pop was stubborn and proud. Like father, like son.

"You mind if I take Gracy to the salon, then? Get our tootsies painted?" she asked, stroking his leg with her bare foot under the kitchen table.

He grabbed her calf and pulled her foot onto his lap.

"I love you, El," he said.

She wriggled her foot until it was pushing into the soft lump at his crotch. She felt him stiffen, and she smiled. "Love you too, baby."

After Kurt and Trevor took off for Jude's house, Elsbeth took Gracy to Babette's to get them both pedicures. It was a freebie that came with working at Babette's Beauty Boutique, one of the few (if tiny) perks. And Gracy loved it. She'd spend all day choosing from the rows and rows of colors.

Elsbeth had been working at Babette's since she graduated from cosmetology school, almost thirteen years now. She worked five mornings a week and every other weekend. Twig shared the chair, working the afternoons and the weekends Elsbeth was off. They left notes for each other sometimes, silly scribbles on sticky notes they stuck to the mirror. Elsbeth learned about most things going on in Twig's life through these scratched missives. It would be nice if they could work at the same time, she thought. But so many things with Twig were like this: Elsbeth always feeling left out, a part of her life but still, somehow, on the edge of it.

She and Twig met at beauty school, and without Twig, she probably would never have finished and gotten her license. The first three months were the worst; the smell of shampoo alone was enough to send her running to the bathroom; perm solutions and hairspray were almost more than she could stand. (She wondered sometimes if maybe all those chemicals were partly to blame for Trevor's problems. When she was pregnant with Gracy, she didn't do anything but cut hair. No coloring, no bleaching, no nails.) Twig was her savior back then, holding her hair back as she threw up into the sink. Bringing her ice cubes to suck on. Thankfully, by her second trimester, all those noxious smells became tolerable. And by the time she got her certificate, Trevor was already born.

In school, she and Twig had studied together and practiced on each other, but it was clear from early on that Twig was a better stylist than Elsbeth, though she'd never admit it. She was an *artist,* truly, while Elsbeth was merely competent. Twig got the wealthier clients, the younger clients. All of the teenagers. She was famous for her upsweeps: May and June with their proms and weddings made Twig enough money to spend most of her time off in July and August traveling. She was always running off to Old Orchard Beach or down to Atlantic City to visit her sister. Elsbeth, however, relied on the faithful ladies from Plum's Retirement Community who got bused into Two Rivers every week. And, to be honest, she really didn't mind. They always wanted the same thing: cut and curl, the occasional color. It was easy work, and there wasn't nearly as much at stake. Elsbeth was also a good listener, and mostly the ladies just wanted to talk.

Back in the day, Babette's used to be a barber shop, and it still had the swirly barber pole out front, though it didn't work anymore. Elsbeth thought Babette might do well to renovate a little, but she wasn't really in any position to speak up. The place was caught in a serious time warp, but Babette and most of the customers (especially the retirees) didn't seem to mind.

Behind reception, there were black and white photos from the '50s and '60s hanging crooked on the walls. Elsbeth's favorite was the one of the original owner, standing with his little girl by the barber pole. Betsy Parker, that was her name. In the picture, she's sucking on an Orange Crush, and both her knees are skinned. Elsbeth always thought the girl looked a little bit like herself: long legs, black hair, restless eyes. Babette said that she'd gone off to college but then had to come home when her father got sick and couldn't run the shop anymore. Like Elsbeth, she also got pregnant when she was still just a girl. Then one night there was a terrible thunderstorm, and she got in a car crash up at The Heights. She died just as her baby was born. It was the saddest story Elsbeth had ever heard. She looked at Betsy Parker's picture at least once a day and felt her throat grow thick.

The salon was small, only five chairs and a couple of nail tables, though they had a tanning bed in the back as well. It was on the same street as the bank and the post office. Across the street was a used bookstore with a bowling alley in the basement. Elsbeth liked to browse through the used copies of *Vogue* and *Condé Nast* during her lunch breaks.

"Hey, girlies!" Twig said as Elsbeth ushered Gracy through the heavy front door, the bells jingling like Christmas. Twig was like a ray of sunshine in bright yellow capri pants and a tight orange tank top. Her shiny blond hair was spun up into a high ponytail. "I thought you were going shopping today," she said as she combed out her customer's curls.

Elsbeth sighed. "Trevor got in trouble again. Kurt's making him do time at Jude's."

"Jesus, El. What did he do now?"

Elsbeth shook her head. She shouldn't gossip about her own son. Sometimes she felt like she wasn't even talking about her own family when she told Twig about Jude, about Trevor. When she complained about Kurt. Then it would hit her, this was her *family*, the people she was supposed to love more than anybody else in the whole world, and she'd feel bad. "Same old stuff. Getting in fights. I think the new principal has it out for him."

"I'm sorry, honey," Twig said. As she spun her client around to look in the mirror, Twig whispered to Elsbeth, "You look like you could use some time in the tanning bed."

"What about Gracy?"

"I'll take care of Gracy. You go on," Twig said. "Treat yourself. Nobody's in there."

"You sure?" Elsbeth asked, feeling swollen with gratitude.

"Princess Grace will get the full spa treatment." Twig winked. "Mani, pedi, and how about a shampoo and blow-dry, Gracy?"

Gracy smiled, a big gap-toothed smile, and squeezed Elsbeth's hand. "My favorite color is sparkly purple. Can I get sparkly purple? But pink on my toes. I only like pink on my toes."

"Absolutely," Twig said and lifted her up into her chair. "Now, I'm going to need to know which Disney princess you like the best."

"I like Sleepy Beauty."

"Me too! Why is she *your* favorite?"

Gracy's brow furrowed thoughtfully. "Because her hair's the swirliest."

Elsbeth hugged Twig. "I *love* you," she said, practically running to grab the key to the tanning room.

Elsbeth stripped down to her bra and underwear and studied herself in the full-length mirror before affixing the goggles and climbing into the tanning bed. She tried to imagine herself in that Victoria's Secret bathing suit. She turned from side to side; she could use a tan. God, she was the color of milk. Glancing to make sure the door was locked, she slipped out of her panties and bra and climbed naked into the bed. And as she closed herself into that coffin of sun, she shut her eyes and dreamed of the beach. Of flamingos and oranges and Disney.

As they pulled up the long gravel driveway, Trevor peered through the camera's viewfinder at his grandfather's house. It was the same kind of house as theirs, just a shoe box with windows. But while theirs was freshly painted, with window boxes and bright blue shutters, his grandfather's house looked like a cardboard box that had been dragged through the mud and stepped on. The front porch was full of garbage bags and old furniture. The shutters hung like droopy eyelids, and the yard was littered with trash and broken-down cars. Trevor rolled down the window and clicked three photos of the house.

"Where'd you get that?" his father asked.

"School," he said. "From my art teacher."

"Well, you best return it," he said.

"She gave it to me."

His father looked at him suspiciously.

They both got out of the truck and made their way up the cracked walkway to the front steps. There were a million dandelions gone to seed springing up from the dead grass. Trevor used to make wishes on those. Used to blow them into the wind, hoping. Something about that sea of weeds, all those unwished-for wishes made him feel bad for Pop.

The last time he was here was the day after Christmas. His mom had baked a ham, studded with cloves and sticky with marmalade glaze, Pop's favorite, which she asked Trevor to carry. It was wrapped up in tin foil, hot in his hands. They had presents too, in green and red paper, and Gracy had made Pop a sparkly

Christmas ornament at school. But inside Pop didn't even have a
tree, and there hadn't been any room to sit down. After about fifteen minutes, when Trevor felt like he couldn't breathe, his
mother, thank God, said she wasn't feeling well, and they'd left.
The glitter from Gracy's ornament made a sparkly path from the
door all the way back to the car. He could see some of it still
there, like tiny shards of glass. Like fallen stars.

He didn't want to go inside. Being in there, surrounded on all
sides by boxes and trash and clothes and broken things, made him
feel like he'd crawled out of his skin and put it on again, but inside out. It made his heart beat fast. It made him dizzy.

"I'll wait out here," he said.

"You can get started with those trash bags, then. Put 'em in
the back of the truck. You better wear these gloves," his dad said,
pulling his own gloves off and handing them to him. Then his
dad went to the front door and banged on it, blowing into his
bare hands. It was still as cold as winter, even though it was already the end of April.

When his dad disappeared into the house, Trevor took pictures of the heaps of garbage, the bags half-buried in old snow. He
focused on a cardinal, crimson and still, perched on the open
drawer of a broken-down dresser. He snapped shot after shot of
something rotten on the ground that was crawling with maggots
until he thought he might gag. When he heard the door opening,
he quickly set his camera down and started lifting up the bags of
trash.

They worked for hours, taking everything that wasn't con-
tained and shoving it into giant green yard bags. Pop sat on the
porch, overseeing, occasionally making them stop so that he
could inspect the contents of the bags. More than a few times,
he'd pulled something out and held on to it. A broken stapler, a
cap gun, a nasty John Deere cap that he perched on top of his
head. Something about seeing him like that, his drooping face
and that cap sitting high up on his head, made Trevor feel sad. He
hated that he hated being here. He tried to remember what it

used to be like when his grandma was alive, but those memories were fuzzy, like what you see when you open your eyes underwater.

At lunchtime, his father ran into town to drop off the first load at the dump and to pick up some sandwiches and sodas, asking Trevor to stay behind with Pop. "Make sure he doesn't start emptying those bags out," he'd whispered to Trevor when Pop went inside to use the bathroom.

Pop was working on one of his model fighter jets at the messy kitchen table, carefully painting the wings with his good hand. The other one sat curled and useless as a cat on the table. Pop was always working on a new model. He had a whole collection of fighter planes from the Vietnam War that he'd assembled and painted. They hung from the ceiling in the living room on invisible strings, thick with dust, hovering over the piles and piles of junk like buzzards over a landfill.

Pop was lost in concentration, his cigarette burned down to nothing but ash in the plaid beanbag ashtray next to him. Trevor sat quietly across from him. A beam of sunlight found its way through the kitchen window. In it, he could see the smoke from Pop's cigarettes floating like ghosts. *Now,* he thought, and aimed his camera.

Pop looked up as the shutter released. "Your dad says you been fighting again."

Trevor nodded.

"You keep it up, they're gonna kick you out of school, you know."

That wouldn't be such a bad thing as far as Trevor was concerned.

"Now, school ain't everything," Pop said, his mouth sounding like it was full of marbles. "But it's somethin'. Even I got my diploma."

"I hate school," Trevor said.

"Maybe if you spent less time scrappin' and more time studyin', you'd like it more. Can't let shit stick in your craw."

Trevor thought about that, about holding grudges.

"You know, your dad graduated number ten in his high school class. He shoulda been the one to go to college. To get the hotshot job in the city."

"Why didn't he go, then?" Trevor asked.

Pop's eyes were milky with cataracts, and his hands shook as he reached into the pocket of his faded khakis and pulled out his wallet. Sometimes, when he was little, he used to give Trevor quarters. Linty and warm. They always smelled like the menthol eucalyptus cough drops he sucked on. But today, instead of pulling out a wilted dollar bill, his yellowed nails pinched at the edges of a picture of two little boys in matching outfits. Plaid shirts with pearly snaps on their pockets.

The photo was scratched and worn. It looked like one of the pictures his mother took him and Gracy to get taken at the JCPenney every year. Against a fake forest backdrop, both boys had startlingly white hair and pale eyes, but the older boy was solemn, scowling, while the younger one was smiling brightly, missing his top two teeth in the front.

"Your daddy's always been so serious. But a good boy. Responsible."

"Is that Uncle Billy?" Trevor asked, peering into the scuffed boyhood face of his uncle.

"Some people give and some people take," Pop said. "*Loyalty. Fidelity.* That's something you don't learn at college. That's something you either are or you aren't."

Trevor didn't know what to say, but it didn't matter because Pop returned quietly to his work. When he was finished, he held the fighter jet up for Trevor to see. "This here's a Cessna A–37 Dragonfly, son, a Super Tweet."

"It's cool, Pop."

Later, his father and Pop ate their lunches on the porch and Trevor took more photos. Of his grandfather in his pressed khakis and clean white tank top. Bright blue suspenders. He focused on Pop's long, sad face and deep widow's peak, his shock of white hair so much like Trevor's own and his father's. He clicked when his dad wiped at the mustard on the sagging side of Pop's mouth, when they laughed at something Pop said, and when his dad put his arm across the back of Pop's shoulder and patted him twice. Like he was Pop's father instead of his son.

By the time they got in the truck to take the last load of trash to the dump, Trevor had used up a whole roll of film. As much as Trevor hated school, he was looking forward to learning how to develop his pictures. He could hardly wait to get into the dark-room, to see what he'd caught.

Crystal was still bleeding on Monday when she went back to school. She was starting to wonder if she'd ever stop, if she'd ever heal. She made sure she had extra pads in her backpack, wore dark jeans and a big sweatshirt over them.

Her mother dropped her off, like she always did, pulling up in the drop-off lane and kissing her on the cheek. "Have a good day," she said, her voice as bright as fluorescent lights. "Work hard," she added, in place of her usual "Be good."

Crystal nodded and got out of the car. "I picked up a shift at work after school. I'll call at nine when I'm done."

Before her mother could protest, she slammed the door shut harder than she intended to. She couldn't bring herself to turn around and look back at her mother, who she knew was leaning over the passenger's seat and waving at her.

She tried to pretend like this was any other day, like every other day. She'd been going to this school for four years now, walking this same path from car to door without so much as a second thought. Now it felt like she was making the journey to-tally naked, with bells on her ankles and a bullhorn announcing her arrival. But worse than how exposed she felt was that she knew she'd have to see Ty. Ty who hadn't even called back after she left the message saying she was in labor, or later when she was headed to the hospital. Ty who didn't even bother to come say good-bye to the baby girl that was half his. Ty who hadn't an-swered a single one of the text messages she'd sent him since she got home from the hospital.

Their lockers were right next to each other, just like their desks all through elementary school had been: the unfortunate consequence of alphabetical proximity—his *McPhee* to her *McDonald*. They'd be stuck next to each other until graduation next month, and even then they'd have to share the stage for a moment as the diplomas were dispersed.

"What do you want from me?" he had asked, after everything had turned to shit.

She used to know exactly what she wanted from him. At first, optimistic, she'd wanted him to step up and be a man. To be a father to the baby, and, maybe one day, be a husband to her. After that, when those ideas began to seem silly, she just wanted him to be her friend again. They'd known each other almost their whole lives; how hard was it to just support her through this? She wouldn't make unreasonable demands. But then at the end, she'd just wanted him to *be* there. Just to hold her hand, to be with her after the baby was gone. And he hadn't done any of it. Instead, he'd been a fucking coward. A fucking terrible friend. Now she didn't know what she wanted from him. Now that he might round the corner any minute, she thought maybe what she really wanted was for him to *stay* disappeared.

But as the warning bell rang for first period and she opened her locker, her face reflecting grimly in the magnetic mirror stuck on the door, there he was. Before she saw his face behind hers, she could smell the detergent his mom used. It was just soap, for Christ's sake, but it seriously drove her crazy. It used to anyway. Now it just made her feel like crying.

"Hey," he said, and she felt everything starting to seep. God, her entire body was just one big leaky mess lately. Milk, blood, tears. She couldn't keep anything in.

When she turned to him, she half expected him not to be there. That he was just a figment of her imagination. But he was real. Standing there, looming over her with his six-foot-two frame, and she felt just as small as ever. Just as overwhelmed.

She ducked under his arm as the bell rang again, and turned to face him.

"Crys," he said, cocking his head in that way he did. Like he was innocent. Like he was still just a little boy. His dark hair flopped across one green eye; the other one peered down at her sheepishly. He stood there, looking exactly the same as always. How could he be so unchanged after all this, when she didn't feel even remotely like the same person anymore?

"Where *were* you?" she asked, feeling the words catch in her throat.

"Cryssy," he said. "I'm sorry."

She wanted him to touch her. To notice that she was melting. But he just stood there, not touching her.

"I need you to leave me alone now," she said, using every ounce of energy she had not to burst into tears. "Just pretend like I don't exist."

When Crystal was a little girl, she used to fill her baby pool with bubble bath and give her baby dolls baths in the backyard. For hours, she would float them on their backs, lather their hair with dish detergent, make sure not to get soap in their eyes. Afterward, she would swaddle them in her beach towels, comb their wet hair. She powdered their plastic bottoms and wrapped them up in washcloth diapers held together with tape. When her mother brought Angie home from the hospital, Crystal was only five, but her mother let her do all the things that real mommies did. She would let Crystal sit on the couch with Angie propped up in her arms. She taught her how to squirt a little bit of milk out of the bottle to make sure it wasn't too hot. She taught her how to get the bubbles out of both the bottle and the baby. She let her help change her diapers, and when Angie was taking a bath in the yellow plastic tub, she was allowed to wash her feet and her tiny little hands. She was the one who sang Angie lullabies. She was the only one who could make her laugh. When people asked Crystal what she wanted to be when she grew up, she always said, "A mommy," at which her parents would laugh and say, "After college. After business school."

Of course, as she got older, she knew it really was silly. Nobody wanted to be *just* a mom. There was college and graduate school. There were careers. Future moms didn't stay up until midnight studying calculus or making PowerPoint presentations for European Civ. None of her friends ever talked about wanting kids. They talked about drinking and sex and clothes. They talked about getting the hell out of Two Rivers and getting on with their lives. And slowly, she forgot that old dream. It was just another one of those silly things she'd said as a kid. Like the time she said she wanted to be a gorilla when she grew up after her parents took her to the Granby Zoo. Wanting to be a mom when you grew up was as ridiculous as wanting to be an ape. But still, when she found out that she was pregnant, the first thing she felt was not the horror and fear she would feel later, but a twinge of *excitement,* something she hadn't expected at all. Not at all during the weeks when she waited for her period to come. Not once during that awful trip to the Rite Aid all the way up in St. Johnsbury to buy the test where no one would know her. Not at all as she squatted over the toilet and felt warm pee accidentally running over her hand. But for a single moment, as she looked at the pink plus sign, she felt strangely *happy*. It was illogical, she knew this, and this sliver of happiness was quickly replaced by the awful realization that her life as she knew it was over. But this had less to do with the baby and everything to do with Ty.

She and Ty had been friends since kindergarten, but only hooking up for a couple of months when she got pregnant. His family lived one block behind her family; her mother used to send her to his house to play when she and her father first started their real estate business. She'd loved him since they used to catch toads behind his house, and after twelve years he'd *finally* loved her back. But now she was pretty sure he would go right back to not loving her again. And he probably wouldn't even be friends with her anymore. She knew that's what that plus sign really meant. It didn't mean having a baby as much as it meant giving up Ty. And she was right. Now she watched Ty move away from her, down the hallway, backpack slung over his shoulder. She couldn't believe how easy it was for him to walk away, to pretend like everything they'd been through didn't matter anymore. She made her way to first period, past the whispers, to her desk. She had to let go. Get back to *normal,* like the doctor had promised. She looked at the scratched surface of the desk, smelled the medicinal scent of the floor cleaner, listened to the humming fluorescent lights overhead. Here was her old life back. Only it wasn't her old life at all. It was worse. It was awful.

AP English used to be her favorite class. She and Ty used to write lines of poetry in ballpoint pen on each other's jeans. She still had one pair of jeans she couldn't bring herself to wash, knowing that the ink and the words would disappear. It didn't matter; they didn't fit anymore anyway. She took a deep breath, inhaling the smell of chalk dust and pencils and whatever that crap was they used to wipe down the desks. Then she opened her book and tried to concentrate on the lines that blurred in front of her leaking eyes.

The art room used to be the old auditorium, before the school built the brand-new one a few years ago. The rows of seats had been excavated, leaving only their metal stumps, but the stage was still there, and that's where Mrs. D. projected her art slides. The heavy blue and gold velvet curtains still hung on either side, and there was a giant screen like at the movies at the back of the stage, except it had a big gash down the center. Sometimes, Mrs. D. would let Trevor run the projector, and she would go up on the stage with her long wooden teacher's pointer and explain what they were seeing to them. Trevor loved slide-show days. He liked the quiet whir of the projector's fan and the click as each slide fell into place. He liked the hush as everyone stopped talking to listen. He liked the tap, tap of the stick against the screen. It was like music, he thought. Like a quiet song.

"Is that your camera?" Angie McDonald asked.

At first Trevor didn't think she was talking to him. *Nobody* talked to him. But he and Angie were the only ones sitting at the front table. He looked up at her and nodded. "Yeah."

Angie always looked like she had just rolled out of bed. Her hair was messy and her clothes wrinkled. It was amazing to him that her art was so tidy. Everything she drew was so precise, even her watercolors. She was working on a watercolor picture of a house. The bristles on the small brush she was using whispered across the page, the colors bleeding slowly, carefully, into the fibers of the paper. Watercolors frustrated him, the blur. The way they seemed to have a mind of their own. But she seemed to be able to control the paint.

"You like photography?" she asked.

"Yeah."

"That's cool," she said, smiling. "Me too, but I'd rather make up my own pictures."

The lunch bell rang, startling him.

"Hey, do you want to sit together at lunch today?" she asked, dipping her brush into the Mason jar, the colors bleeding into the water.

"That's okay," he said, shaking his head, and as she put away her work, he lingered at the art table.

She shrugged. "Okay. See you later."

Mrs. D. came over to him after all of the other students had filed out of the classroom. "You plan to spend lunch with me again?"

He nodded.

"Well, I could use some help sorting through these slides," she said. "Think you might be able to help?"

He sat at the long, scarred wooden table near the front of the room where Mrs. D.'s desk was and peered at the slides using the light box she'd gotten out of the storage closet for him. Mrs. D. needed to locate a good selection representing the early history of photography. She'd let him borrow some books, and he'd read them quickly, absorbing everything, touching the old photos with his fingers. He recognized the names, the photos, as he flipped through the slides. *Daguerre. Talbot. Rinehart.*

"Where's your lunch, Trevor?" she asked.

Trevor shrugged.

"Can I get you something from the cafeteria?" she asked, peering over his shoulder at a photograph of a Victorian wedding. The bride scowled miserably next to her husband in his top hat.

Trevor shrugged again. He'd already spent half of his lunch money on a bag of chips in the vending machine. But before he could say *No thanks,* his stomach growled loudly, betraying him, answering her question.

"Well then," she said as though she were speaking to his stomach. "I'll be right back." And then she shuffled to her desk, where she grabbed her big patchwork bag.

A few minutes later, she came back carrying a tray with a cheeseburger and fries and two chocolate milks. She waddled over to where he was working and set the tray down. Then she went to her desk and pulled out her own lunch bag from a drawer.

"Thanks," he said, feeling guilty. He'd assumed she was getting herself lunch too. "You didn't have to do that."

She brushed the air with her hand as if she were swatting a mosquito away. "Phooey."

Trevor unwrapped the burger and took a huge bite. He was starving, and it tasted so good. He'd been trying to figure out a way to pack a lunch, but his mother was always puttering around the kitchen in the morning, making his father's and Gracy's lunches, fixing breakfast. He had made such a case about wanting hot lunch at the beginning of the year that he wasn't sure how to tell her he'd changed his mind. But at the same time, he knew that if he was able to avoid the cafeteria, he was able to avoid Ethan and Mike for most of the day, except for during recess and math. He needed to figure out a way to pack himself a sandwich or something.

"You know you can't hide in here forever," Mrs. D. said, carefully unwrapping her own sandwich from its wax-paper envelope.

"I'm not *hiding*," he said, feeling defensive, thinking of Gracy playing hide-and-seek, squeezing her eyes shut and counting as high as she could while he hid from her.

"Can I tell you something?" she said, setting down her sandwich and wiping daintily at the corners of her mouth with her napkin, as if she were one of those Victorian ladies in the photo.

Trevor nodded.

"My brother had the same sort of, how shall we say, *difficulties* you have in school."

Trevor thought of Gracy. *D-I-F-F-I-C-U-L-T-Y.*

"He was a lot like you, actually," she said, and her voice sounded misty. Like fog on water. Like somebody trying to explain a dream.

Trevor looked up from the slide and cocked his head. No one had ever told him he was like anyone else. As far as he was concerned, there wasn't *anybody* out there who was like him.

"And because he was different, because he preferred to paint and draw and make music to roughhousing or playing sports, he had a terrible time fitting in. Children can be so unkind. He came home crying nearly every afternoon."

This made Trevor's ears feel hot. He didn't want her to think he was some sort of crybaby.

"But then one day," she continued, "he grew up and he moved away, and he made friends who appreciated him and all those qualities that nobody before had ever valued. He found someone who not only accepted him but *loved* him."

His ears still burning, Trevor felt squirmy inside. Embarrassed. Something about Mrs. D. saying the word *loved,* he guessed. This whole conversation was making him uncomfortable.

"What I'm trying to say, is that this world you live in . . ." she said, gesturing around the darkened room, "might feel unkind, but the world is bigger than this. It won't be like this forever. If you can just survive this, someday I promise you will be appreciated. And happy. And *loved.*"

Trevor nodded and peered down at his giant hands; they were trembling.

"It's like this," she said, gesturing to the slide he picked up. She held it up in her hand. "What do you see?"

"I can't see anything," he said.

"What about now?" she asked as she laid the slide on the light box, illuminating the photograph.

"A castle?"

"A *cathedral*. It's Notre Dame in Paris. And it is magnificent. But without the light there is nothing. It simply needs the right light behind it."

After math, which passed quickly and, thankfully, without incident, Trevor felt his spirits lifted. His whole body buzzed and hummed; his footsteps clicked across the linoleum like slides slipping into a projector. He found himself smiling despite himself. There was only one period left, science, and then he could go home. He wanted to go to the woods with his camera, take some pictures of the river, the new green tops of the trees. He thought about the church that looked like a castle. A cathedral in the light. He pulled his camera from his backpack and peered down the long hallway through his viewfinder.

"Hey, it's the Abdominal Snowman," Ethan Sweeney said, stepping in front of Trevor, his face filling the frame. He'd gotten his hair cut, and it stuck up from his scalp in sharp red spikes. His freckles looked like spaghetti sauce splatters on a white stove top.

"It's *Abominable*," Trevor said, quickly shoving his camera back in his bag. What an idiot.

"That's what I said, *asshole*." Ethan's already squinty eyes closed into slits like a snake. Then Ethan put his face close enough to his that Trevor could smell what he'd had for lunch. "Stupid faggot asshole."

And Trevor could feel it happening. Taste the metal filling his mouth, practically hear the clink clink clink of the bones in his hands as they also curled into fists. But just as he pulled his arm back, Mr. Douglas was standing between them, shoving both of their chests with his meaty hands, acting as a wall between them, looking back and forth from him to Ethan like the referee in a boxing match. "Do we have a problem here, fellas?"

He wasn't sure why Ethan and Mike were always pushing his buttons. If he tried, he could level them both. *Old habits die like a sonuvabitch,* Pop would say; they'd both been giving him a hard time since second grade. They probably figured he was still too afraid to really fight back. He used to just cry when they started in on him. Run away.

After the final bell rang, Mrs. Cross called Trevor over in the hallway. "How are we doing, Trevor?" she asked. He hated how she spoke in the plural, as if saying "we" made them on the same team. "I hear we had another run-in with Mr. Sweeney this afternoon?"

Her perfume was making him light-headed. He stared at the floor, at her toes poking out of her high-heeled shoes. At a wad of green gum stuck to the floor.

"Do you think it might be a good idea to have a little sit-down to talk about whatever it is that's going on between you two? Maybe if we can get some communication going between you boys, we can get to the root of this." Mrs. Cross looked awfully proud of herself, as though she'd just figured out a way to bring peace to the Middle East, though Trevor thought that might be more likely than getting Ethan Sweeney to stop bothering him.

Mrs. Cross put her hand across his shoulder as if to steer him down the hall, but at her touch his shoulder jumped, jerking her hand away. He caught his breath as her eyes widened; she looked at him in disbelief.

"I didn't even do anything!" Trevor said, feeling bile rising in his throat, and then he was running; he could hear his sneakers squeaking across the linoleum, feel his hair blowing away from his face, see the tiles moving beneath his feet. He knew if he were to look back now, Mrs. Cross would be standing there, shaking her head. He ran all the way down the hall to the exit, his backpack slamming against his spine.

"Tomorrow afternoon, Trevor. Three o'clock. Sharp. In my office." Her voice chased after him.

Kurt sat down at the kitchen table after supper and reached for the stack of bills on the counter. He'd just sent off the tax bill to the IRS; there would be no refund this year, and the numbers in the checkbook were far lower than he was comfortable with. He knew that one unexpected expense, one emergency visit to the pediatrician, one trip to the shop for Elsbeth's piece-of-shit car, could mean another major ding in their already beaten-up credit. He divided the bills by delinquency: thirty days past due, sixty days, ninety plus, the ones threatening collections. He paid the utilities first (those things they could not live without: electricity, water, gas). He opened something from their mortgage company next, tearing into this envelope with a vague sense of foreboding. He knew their ARM was coming up soon, and that he really needed to talk to the bank about some refinancing options. But since the market had plummeted, and the house was worth far less than they owed, he figured refinancing again was probably out of the question. He quickly realized it wasn't a bill at all but a notice. The ARM was apparently set to adjust at the end of the summer, and the mortgage premium was going to change accordingly. His eyes raced across the fine print, his vision swimmy, and his chest heaved as he looked at the figure for the first balloon payment. It was *double* their current payment. *Two times* the figure that already caused him monthly anxiety attacks. This couldn't be right. There was no way. No one at the bank had explained this when they refinanced the first time.

The whole kitchen smelled like supper still: it was rank with the smell of tuna casserole and green beans. He felt his stomach lurching, his whole world lurching as he tried to get a grip on what to do next. It was seven o'clock at night. The banks were closed. He thought about going to talk to Elsbeth, but he also knew that was the last thing he should do, could do. She would blame him. Not with her words, of course, she'd never ever come out and say that he was responsible, *irresponsible,* but that's what she'd feel. That's what her body would say when it turned away from him. That's what she would think every time she looked at his face.

He ran his hand through his hair, surprised by how thin it was becoming. He wondered if this awful habit alone was responsible for making his hair thin. If he had simply worried it away with his fingers over the last couple of years.

He had to think. He just needed to clear his head and think this through. It was another thousand dollars a month. A lot, yes. But if he picked up another job, he could probably swing it. He was home most nights by six o'clock; a couple of night shifts would be difficult but doable. Maybe he could work the weekends. And it wouldn't have to be forever either. Just until he could get the house refinanced again. Move the loan over to a different bank. Start fresh.

"Daddy?" Gracy said. She had wandered into the kitchen without him hearing her. She was wearing a threadbare Ariel nightie she'd had since she was three and the rainbow toe socks she got from Santa last Christmas. Her hair was wet from her bath, and her cheeks pink.

"Yeah, baby?" he asked.

She came to him and climbed up into his lap. It shocked him how far her legs dangled now. When did this happen? When did she stretch out like this? She'd be too big for this soon. Grown. She looped her finger through a loose piece of lace at the hem of her nightgown and wrapped it tight.

"Daddy, I love you more than pie."

"And I love you more than birthday cake."

He breathed the sweet smell of Gracy's shampoo and wrapped his arms around her tightly. He could feel the rapid flutter of her heart beneath his fingers like a ticking clock.

"It's my birthday in how many days?" she asked.

Kurt glanced up at the calendar hanging on the wall. "Just over a month, sweetie."

It would be okay. He just needed to be logical, methodical. Call the bank. Fill out the paperwork. If need be, he could get a second job. He was able-bodied. Strong. Willing to work. Elsbeth didn't even need to know.

Elsbeth came into the kitchen and smiled at them. She kissed Gracy's forehead and then leaned down to kiss Kurt.

"I was thinking," she said as she went to the fridge, peering into it. She pulled out the bottle of wine and poured a little bit into a tumbler. "Maybe we could take Gracy to S-T-O-R-Y-L-A-N-D for her birthday?"

Gracy puzzled over the letters, probably trying to assemble them in her mind.

"Yeah," he said. "Sure. That would be nice."

But after they went to bed the panic slowly set in. While Elsbeth slept, oblivious, his legs thrummed. When he couldn't take it anymore, he gave in to them. He walked and walked and walked. He walked the hallway, he walked circles around the living room, and then he walked to the kitchen and called the number on the back of his credit card, making sure there was enough room left to buy their tickets.

Crystal could count the things she loved about Ty on two hands and one finger. Eleven itemizable things. She thought of these qualities when she was checking at Walgreens. As if they were things you could ring up and bag.

She loved his hands. His fingers, long with square fingertips and thick knuckles. He chewed on his right index finger's second knuckle when he was thinking, and it was callused and thick. When he held her hand for the first time (seven years old, running through the fenceless backyards in their neighborhood), she knew she would go wherever that hand led her. She also loved his feet. In the summer, they were tan and bare, his arches strong and his tendons long. When they lay in the hammock under the big oak tree in his backyard, head to foot, she would study the soft bottoms, count his toes.

She loved the chipped tooth that only showed when he smiled, and she loved that she was there when it happened. (They'd been riding their bikes together when his tire got caught in the railroad tracks. He'd spilled over the edge of the bike, head-first onto the unforgiving ties. She'd come back the next day and, miraculously, found the other half of his bottom incisor, sitting in the gravel as though it had been waiting for her. She carried the tooth, this little boney sliver of him in a locket she wouldn't let him open.)

She loved that he was funny, but that he never needed to be the center of attention. Lena was funny too, but she was always making sure you knew how funny she was. Ty had a quiet sense of humor, and they had a million private jokes that she collected like shells or pretty stones.

She loved his family. His mother, Lucia, and her paisley scarves and silver rings, the way she looked like she was searching for the future Crystal in her face. "Let me look into my Crystal Ball," she would say when Crystal was only ten or eleven, holding Crystal's jaw in her hands and peering lovingly into her eyes. "I see happiness," she'd say. "I see love and laughter and so much happiness, and what's this? Lemonade? And brownies?" And then she would pour her a tall glass of freshly squeezed lemonade and cut her the best brownie from the center of the pan. She loved his father, who wrote children's books and played the bongos and used to put on puppet shows with puppets he'd made for them in their dusky basement. He was tall and skinny and reminded her of the Scarecrow in *The Wizard of Oz*. He'd play checkers or Monopoly or gin rummy with you without ever getting bored. And she loved his little sisters, Dizzy and Squirrel, who they pushed around in doll-sized strollers.

She loved his house: the funky Victorian with its slanty floors and drafty windows. With its kaleidoscope of wild climbing roses and rusty claw-foot tubs. It was so different from her family's prim Colonial with its perfect hedges and wall-to-wall carpeting. She loved the way Ty's house always smelled like cloves and cinnamon. Like pumpkin pie. She loved it at Halloween when Ty's father hung trash-bag ghosts from the trees and made creepy silhouettes out of black construction paper in all the windows. She loved it at Christmas, when his dad strung the entire house in twinkling lights, a frenetic sparkling peace sign in the center of the cupola. She loved it in the spring when tulips popped up in random places all over the yard.

She loved Ty's eyes, which were both blue and hazel at the same time, like God couldn't make up his mind. Like little greenish brown stones, ringed in blue. She loved the way he kissed her, first her top lip then her bottom, the feeling of his teeth on her flesh. She loved the way he smelled like the French lavender water his mother put in the laundry, even though he said he couldn't smell it at all. She loved his voice, which was deep and fluid, the way it washed over her like rain.

And she loved that he read books. Most boys didn't, or if they did, didn't admit it. Sometimes, they would hang out together in his room, the one in the attic with its porthole window and exposed beams, just reading for hours, and she imagined that this was what it would be like when they were grown-ups. This happy quiet, each of them alone and immersed in their own world, but still somehow together.

And for a couple of months last summer, it seemed like Ty's mother had been right. There was nothing but happiness and love and lemonade. After twelve years, Ty finally realized what had been sitting under his nose waiting patiently for him to come around.

She hadn't expected it, the first time he kissed her. They'd been swimming at the river all day and were hanging out on his front porch while Dizzy made a painting on a giant roll of butcher paper held down on the grass with two heavy stones, and Squirrel was bouncing up and down in her ExerSaucer. Crystal's skin was tight from the sun, and her hair smelled like the river. It was dusk, and one of his dad's jazz CDs was playing inside the house, the soft breeze of it escaping out into the night. She knew she should head back to her own house, to her mother's frozen lasagna and her dad's bad knock-knock jokes, but she didn't want to leave.

Ty came over and sat down next to her on the ratty wicker love seat with its faded red floral cushions.

"I love it here," she said suddenly, surprising herself. "I love all of this." And she was suddenly and absolutely overwhelmed by every single thing that she loved.

When he leaned over to kiss her, she was so startled she caught her breath. If she'd known it was coming she would have prepared, she would have known to hold on. And later, if she'd had any idea about how quickly and suddenly all of this could fall apart, she would have braced herself.

But it wasn't until two months later when she was sitting on the floor of her bathroom, clutching the pregnancy test in her sweaty hand, that she knew all of this was about to disappear: a decade of friendship, everything in the entire world that she loved.

She knew she could have dealt with it quietly. She could have (like Lena had sophomore year) driven to a Planned Parenthood in a town where no one knew who she was, and had this taken care of. But the very thought of it made her body rock with something between sickness and sadness. Every time she considered her options, she thought about her mother's hands, folded in her lap quietly at church. She wasn't sure why this was the image that came to mind, but it was. Her mother's straight spine in the harsh wooden pew at St. Elizabeth's. Her clean, polished nails and her carefully ironed skirts. Her Realtor blazers and the scarves she wore around her neck, the orange line of her foundation at her jaw. She didn't think of God or Jesus or Mary or the Bible or the dark confessional. She thought only of her mother.

She knew she would need to tell her mother, and that once she did, then all of the possible options would also disappear, leaving her with only one. She was going to college in one year. She had her list narrowed down to Georgetown, Amherst, and the University of Vermont. Ty wanted to go to Middlebury, which was close to UVM. Close enough that they could see each other all the time. But if there was a baby, there would be no college. Not for her anyway.

Her mother was surprisingly calm. Perhaps it was because she knew exactly what Crystal should do. When there is only one solution, then you simply do what you must. By the time they had finished their Diet Cokes at Rosco's where she'd met her during her lunch break, her mother had found an adoption agency on her BlackBerry, scheduled an appointment with her own OB/GYN, and written down the names of the prenatal vitamins she should pick up.

It wasn't until that night, lying alone in her bed, listening to Angie sleep, oblivious to everything that had transpired, that Crystal allowed herself to consider the other option, the one that she knew was ridiculous, but also the only one that seemed to make any sense.

What if she kept the baby? What if she simply went through the pregnancy, took the prenatal vitamins, went for her monthly visits to the OB/GYN, and then at the end, in the spring when the baby came, she just brought it home? Ty could still go to college, and she would just go with him. She could take night classes. Work part-time. They could rent a little house. She imagined a backyard with a hammock. She dreamed the lemonade. Why did that idea have to be crazy? As she lay in her childhood bed, it didn't seem crazy at all. It seemed real. She practiced what she would say, rehearsed the words until it was like a prayer, and she fell asleep to stained-glass dreams, whispering this strange rosary.

She waited until they were walking home after school to tell him. They'd only been back at school for a week, and it was still very much summer outside, despite the fact that vacation was over. "Carry me," she said, getting behind him and jumping on, piggyback. She buried her nose in his neck and tightened her legs around him. He took off running and when they got to his house, he spilled her onto the grass, lying down with her. They stared up at the blue sky and he reached for her hand. "I hate calculus," he said. "I totally failed that last test."

"I'm going to have a baby," she said. When she closed her eyes, she saw stars instead of the sun. She could feel every single blade of grass beneath her. His hand went loose for a moment before it tightened around hers again. She should have known what this meant, but she didn't want to.

"Okay," he said.

She opened her eyes and rolled over on her side to look at him. "Okay?" she asked, her throat swollen.

"Sure," he said, but there was a shadow that passed across those wild eyes.

"Okay," she'd said, as if it were this simple. An agreement. An understanding.

And that was that. She told her parents that night over dinner that she'd decided to keep the baby. That there was nothing they could do to change her mind. In six months she would be an adult, and she and Ty would do this together.

"He won't stay," her mother had said softly, but the words were sharp. They felt like splinters.

"Yes, he will," she had said.

"No," she said, shaking her head, looking at her like she was some stupid puppy instead of a girl. "He *won't*."

Her mother was right, her mother was always right, and sometimes it made Crystal hate her. Because only a month later she heard a rumor that Ty and Lena had hooked up at a party. That Ty had gotten drunk and told a bunch of people he was too young to be a dad and that Crystal had probably gotten pregnant on purpose, to keep him around. Apparently, he was crying on Lena's shoulder all night, Lena, her *friend,* and someone saw them disappear into a back bedroom together.

She asked Lena first, because she couldn't bear to hear it from Ty. And Lena just shook her head and kept saying, "I'm sorry, Cryssy. I didn't mean to." As if she'd accidentally slept with him. As if it had all been some unfortunate thing that couldn't have been prevented.

She went over to Ty's house later that afternoon. Lucia was in the kitchen washing vegetables from her garden. Crystal sat down in the chair by the window and Lucia made her tea. Ty didn't come home at all, and when the sun went down, Lucia said softly, "Sweetie, you should go home now."

That was the last time she went to Ty's house. And she and Ty

never talked about what happened. He just disappeared. Poof. Just
like she should have known he would. At school, she stopped
using her locker so she could avoid seeing him. She had the
counselor help her get her schedule changed so that she wouldn't
have to see him in calculus or AP chem.

At first she tried to imagine herself alone with a baby. With
Ty's baby. She thought about what her life might be like. She even
insisted for a few months that this was what she wanted, when
she really wondered if it was simply what she deserved. But then
in January when she slipped on an icy patch on the sidewalk on
her way home from school, landing hard on her tailbone, and a
truck full of assholes drove by with their windows rolled down,
laughing and gawking at her, belly-up on the ground like a beetle
on its back, she realized that her mother was right. When she
couldn't stop crying for three days straight, she knew there really
only ever had been one option.

She met the Stones two weeks later. Arrangements were
made. Her father started to take her to their house once every
two weeks so they could watch her grow, and then, in the spring,
she took Willa for a walk and just hours later, the baby came.

And now the baby was gone. There only ever had been one
choice.

The couple that adopted her was from Burlington. He was a
music professor at the university, and she was a poet. Crystal
looked up her books of poetry on Amazon. She read all the sad
poems, all the pregnancies and miscarriages captured in tidy little
stanzas. The Stones had been trying for ten years to have a baby;
that was almost as long as she had waited for Ty. She looked at Mr.
Stone's syllabus on the university's website. She studied the photos that the agency sent, read their carefully crafted pleas. She
knew they were written by the woman; they were almost like
poems themselves. The careful meter of loss. When they finally
met in person, at a coffee shop on Church Street and then later at
their house near the university, they both hugged her like she was
their own child. She'd liked them at the beginning, but by the

end, she couldn't stand to look at their hopeful, eager faces. All that aching want made her sick.

They'd offered an open adoption, but the idea seemed crazy to her. What kind of person could witness their own child growing up in someone else's house? How could that be fair to anyone? When you sold a car, you didn't show up at the new owner's house and expect to drive it. You didn't go by on the weekends to give it a wash in the driveway. Of course, she knew a baby wasn't the same thing as a car. But regardless, it was still an exchange. By giving the baby up, she got her life back. But what kind of trade was that?

She used to count the ways she loved Ty. Now she only counted the ways he'd ruined everything.

Trevor's mind was like a steel trap, like the ones Pop set out near the garden to catch raccoons and skunks. It was a violent thing, with sharp edges. It caught its victims and wouldn't let them go. It bit into their hindquarters, held them captive. At night when he tried to sleep, it was like this: all those thoughts trying to come loose, gnawing at themselves, while the steel teeth of his mind refused let go.

When Mrs. Cross called him and Ethan into her office, she'd made it clear that there were no chances left. She'd made them sit next to each other, facing her behind the rickety old desk as she explained how close to suspension, if not expulsion, they were.

"You behave like animals," she said. "And this is not a zoo. This is a *school.*"

Ethan rolled his eyes, and Mrs. Cross's face grew flushed, as though someone were squeezing her around her neck. Trevor almost wondered if he should remind her to breathe. "If there is one more incident. So much as a scuffle . . ." she started, and Ethan yawned. "Mr. Sweeney? Am I boring you?" Her voice was so tight it sounded like it might snap.

"No ma'am," he said and straightened up in his chair, stifling another yawn.

"And you, Trevor? Do you find this conversation tiresome?"

"*I* didn't yawn," Trevor said, flabbergasted. He'd been sitting there listening politely for the last ten minutes. What did she want him to do?

"Well, I certainly hope not. Because *this is it.* You have no more chances, mister. No more free passes. You will both be eighth graders soon. It is time to set aside any of the grievances you might have with each other and work on getting along. I don't need you to be friends, but I do need to trust that you aren't going to attack each other."

The idea that he still had a whole year left at this stupid school made his body buzz. He could hardly wait for high school. Two Rivers High was a union school, with about five towns feeding into it. It was big enough he figured he might be able to start fresh, or at least get lost in the crowd. But he had to get through not only this school year but the entire eighth grade before that would happen. And if what Mrs. Cross said was the truth, one misstep might get him kicked out. His biggest fear was that it might happen even if he *didn't* do anything wrong. If Ethan started something, it wouldn't matter if he stood there like a rock and took it. She was determined to punish them both.

And so at night, instead of sleeping, his mind clamped shut tight on thoughts of school, of Mrs. Cross with her soft-serve vanilla hair and her anxious eyes. She made Trevor think of the rabbits he and his dad hunted in the woods behind their house, the way she darted and flashed in and out of sight. Inside the metal jaws of his mind were images of those closed classrooms, the antiseptic stink of the bathrooms, the girls with their sneers and the boys with their fists. As Gracy slept, cooing and mumbling gibberish, Trevor ground his teeth.

The only time Trevor could forget about school was at the salvage yard. Trevor's dad had decided that they needed to start putting stuff up on eBay so they could get out-of-state customers too. Trevor had already been going to work with him on the weekends, but his dad said if he came to the yard after school and took pictures of the inventory, then he would give him a 2 percent commission on anything that sold. Trevor had always liked going to work with his dad. Beal's wife made homemade orange doughnuts, and his dad let him make hot cocoa from the packets for customers with the hot water that came out of the water machine. He brought comic books, and sometimes his dad asked him to help organize stuff or find things out in the yard. Other times, he just let him climb the piles. When he was really little, he used to sit inside the wrecked cars and pretend he was driving, messing with the stick shifts, turning the steering wheels. If he ignored the weeds growing up through the floorboards, he could almost imagine that he was traveling down a real road, the interstate. A superhighway. But now he was here to work.

"So I need photos, good ones, of everything," his father said.

"You'll need a digital camera for that, Dad," Trevor said.

"Beal's got one. It's not great, but it'll do the trick." He reached across his desk and grabbed a stack of papers. "This here's the inventory, all of it. I sorted it by category, that's the first column. See? All the *Air-Conditioning / Heat* items are together. Then comes the subcategories. Like here, see? *AC Compressor, AC Condenser, Actuator,* et cetera, et cetera. Then comes the Make, Model, and Year. The location, where you find it in the yard, is last. I made a blank column at the end where you'll write in the number of the picture file. It's real important, especially for the stuff that looks all the same."

Trevor took the stack and scanned the items. There were hundreds. *Thousands.* This could take him months. He wondered if his father expected him to be there all summer too. "What if I can't find this stuff? I don't even know what a compressor *looks* like."

His father scowled. "Then you ask somebody for help. Me and Beal are never too far away." His father handed him the camera, a flimsy and scratched little silver box. It felt like a toy in his hands after the camera Mrs. D. had given him. "Where do I even start?"

"At the top. It's alphabetical. *Accessories* is the first category. Most of that's in the trailer out back. Bed liners, floor mats, jacks. And when the camera batteries run out, come get me. I got another batch charging up."

Trevor took the camera and the first several pages from the

stack. He could do this, and he could use the money to buy film for his camera. To get it developed. They hadn't started working in the darkroom at school yet, and he was anxious to see what his photos looked like. It actually wasn't nearly as bad, as boring, as he thought it would be. It was almost like a treasure hunt; as he dug through the rubble of fenders and dashboards, the stacks of odometers and steering wheels and stereos, there was a certain satisfaction each time he was able to match something on the list. He snapped the photos, recorded the image names, and then at five o'clock his dad would come get him and they'd go home for supper.

Here he could forget about school. The job gave his brain something to do. It wasn't until later when he lay in bed futilely waiting for sleep that his mind snapped down on what another year at that piece-of-shit school really meant. At the yard, he didn't think about Mrs. Cross looking at him like he was some sort of pit stain. He didn't think the bad thoughts, about making Mrs. Cross and everybody else regret the way they'd treated him. He didn't think about Ethan Sweeney's squinty eyes and Mike's stupid face. At the junkyard, looking at the world through the viewfinder, *he* was the one in charge. It was only at night that the snare clamped down. Bit in hard and left his mind punctured and bruised, exhausted, by morning.

At work, Crystal watched the woman with the little girl and noticed for the first time how striking the child was. Almost difficult to look at. She reminded her a little bit of Ty's sister Dizzy, with her black hair and dark brown eyes.

It was Memorial Day weekend, which thankfully meant a short week at school and the chance to pick up some extra shifts at work. She'd been picking up a lot of extra shifts lately, squirreling her money away. She told her parents she was still saving for college, but that was a lie. She didn't know what she was saving the money for anymore. She had almost $4,000 in her bank account, though, and her parents had no idea. Plus, she actually looked forward to going to work lately. After dodging Ty all day at school, it was such a relief to disappear into the cold, clean aisles of Walgreens. She felt untouchable there. Safe.

She didn't notice them at first. Walgreens was packed today. Everyone in the entire town of Two Rivers seemed to need something. Charcoal and ice, condiments and paper plates flew off the shelves as though the entire world might be convening later for one giant picnic. Sunscreen and swimming goggles, blow-up water wings and water pistols. The official start of summer had come, despite the chilly edge to the air and the swarms of black flies that made most outdoor activities unbearable. So when the woman came up to her, the little girl riding on her hip, and said, "Excuse me, miss?" she expected someone looking for the citronella candles.

"Yes?" Crystal responded, looking up from the jammed pricing gun. "Can I help you?"

"I hope so," she said. "I need to get this film developed. Do you guys even do that anymore?"

The woman was clutching a Ziploc baggie with three old-fashioned rolls of film inside.

"Oh sure, of course. Is anybody over in the Photo Department?"

"No," she said. "Not that I could see anyway."

Fucking Howard. He was supposed to be manning the photo department, helping people upload their pictures, making prints.

"Here," Crystal said. "I can help you."

"Hi," the little girl said suddenly, lifting her head from her mother's shoulder.

"Hi," Crystal said back. Her eyes, that was it. They were almost black. Hard to look at.

"Most people have digital now," Crystal said as she walked the lady and her daughter to the photo counter.

"They're my son's. He's got one of those old-fashioned cameras. It's for school."

"Cool," Crystal said.

She helped the lady fill out the order envelope and then slipped the rolls of film inside. "It takes about three business days to get these back."

"Oh, you don't have one of those machines in the store?"

"Not anymore," she said. "Did you put your phone number on here so we can call when they're ready?"

"Uh-huh," the lady said.

"Is there anything else I can help you with?" she asked.

"No, thank you. I just have a few more things to pick up."

I bet you do, Crystal thought as the lady disappeared down the grocery aisle, the girl down now and trailing behind her, skipping.

They'd been taught at the Walgreens new member orientation how to handle shoplifters. Basically, they were told not to apprehend the shoplifter for smaller items. (And that's what most shoplifters took anyway: nothing of real consequence.) The theory behind this was that employee safety was Priority One, and that it simply wasn't worth it to lose your life over a candy bar. Crystal was pretty sure it wasn't really the employees that Walgreens was worried about so much as a potential lawsuit if some employee got killed over a pack of gum. Or, today, a plastic egg filled with Silly Putty.

Crystal watched the woman slip the red plastic egg out of its package and into her pocket, discarding the cardboard and plastic next on a shelf in the toy aisle. The little girl, oblivious, sat on the floor Indian style, thumbing through a *Princess and the Frog* sticker book, her unknowing little partner in crime. Crystal knew her modus operandi. She stole the little crap and then bought something else to make it seem like she wasn't doing anything wrong. As expected, the woman arrived at her counter a few minutes later with a six-pack of Pepsi and the sticker book. "Thanks again for your help with the film," she said, smiling at Crystal. There was something shifty about the woman's eyes. Nervous. It felt strange knowing that she had the power to bust her any second; she could have the cops taking her away in handcuffs if she wanted to. She could wreck this woman's life.

The little girl was twirling in front of the chips rack, her pink tutu twirling around her like a puff of cotton candy. She had dirty feet and ragged flip-flops, a T-shirt that said *Daddy's Little Monster*. Something about all of this, the stolen Silly Putty, the tutu, made Crystal's heart ache. What would happen to her if her mother got caught? She probably stole stuff from places other than the Walgreens, Crystal thought. A place with a less tolerant policy.

The lady paid for her stuff and then hoisted the little girl back up onto her hip. But rather than taking her bag and leaving, she stood staring awkwardly at Crystal. And suddenly, with her free hand, she reached out and touched Crystal's arm, tentatively, as if she were afraid Crystal might bite or lash out. Crystal's breath caught in her throat at the woman's touch.

"You look great," the lady said softly. "It took me like a year to lose the weight. No one would ever guess you just had a baby."

Crystal's eyes stung as she watched the lady walk through the security gate and out into the sunlit afternoon, the little girl clinging to her for dear life.

At home, she locked both doors to the bathroom. Angie had been using the counter for an art project again; there was paint splattered all over the sink. Soggy painted paper towels all along the edge of the sink. Her messes drove Crystal crazy. Angie was the kind of kid that grown-ups love. Creative and smart. She wanted to be an artist when she grew up; she'd known this since she was six years old. Her room was a chaotic disaster, and she didn't care at all about the way she looked; half the time she left the house wearing mismatched clothes. Other kids teased her, but she didn't seem to care. She got straight As at school. She was the star of every elementary school play. She won every coloring contest, every poster contest, every spelling bee. She was twelve years old, but she already knew exactly who she was, who she was meant to be. Crystal envied this single-minded certainty.

Crystal cleaned up Angie's mess, shaking her head, and then undressed in front of the full-length mirror. Angie was just on the other side of the door, she could hear her humming along to her iPod. She looked at this strange body, this stranger's body in the mirror. She touched the loose skin of her belly; it was odd to see the flesh there so flaccid and pale, like the belly of a fish. Before she got pregnant, she'd been proud of her strong stomach, flat and hard as a rock. This felt like an alien's body. Like she was living inside someone else's flesh.

On Gracy's birthday, Trevor pleaded with Kurt and Elsbeth to let him stay home, but Story Land was three hours away in New Hampshire, and Kurt was worried about leaving Trevor to his own devices for a whole day.

"Story Land is for babies," Trevor said. "What if I see somebody from school?"

"Then they'll be just as embarrassed as you are," Elsbeth reasoned. "Come on, it will be fun."

Kurt could see Trevor's eyes flashing in the way that they did when he was on the verge of losing it. There hadn't been any more fights at school, no more notices from Mrs. Cross, and he'd been a big help at the yard. But Trevor seemed anxious lately. Always with his guard up. Defensive, and keyed up.

"It's your sister's *birthday*," Kurt said, knowing that there was a soft quiet place in Trevor's heart for his sister. "For Christ's sake."

And so they drove to Story Land, Trevor sulking in the backseat. They didn't tell Gracy where they were headed until they got to the amusement park entrance. And luckily, even Trevor had to smile at her delight when she realized the surprise.

It was a gorgeous day for May, warm and sunny, offering a glimpse at better days ahead. After some coaxing from Elsbeth, Trevor reluctantly got on the Teacups and the Antique Cars with Gracy, who squealed with glee. Elsbeth was so happy, she held Kurt's hand, even kissed him sweetly on the cheek as they rode side by side in one of the swan boats. There was a candy color to the day, a sort of sweet overlay that bathed every moment in a cotton candy pink glow.

Elsbeth leaned against him as they stood by the carousel, watching Gracy and Trevor go around and around, up and down on the painted horses. She rested her head on his shoulder. She was wearing cut-off jeans and a tight white tank top. Kurt could feel the warmth of her skin through his T-shirt.

"You're getting sunburned," he said, gingerly touching her shoulder, which was bare and pink.

"Kurt, baby, isn't this nice? All of us together, as a family?" she asked. "Look how much fun the kids are having."

He nodded. It was nice.

"We should go to Disney World or something. To the beach!"

Kurt scowled; he couldn't help it. He thought about the credit card, just a hundred dollars or so from being maxed out. He thought about his futile calls to his mortgage company, the prick on the phone who just kept saying, "I'm very sorry, sir, there's nothing we can do." He thought about the calls he'd been making to his friends who had businesses. The excruciating interview for the cashier opening at the 76 station. He was still waiting to hear back from the acne-riddled manager in whose hands his future lay.

"It wouldn't have to cost a lot," Elsbeth said. "You can bid on hotels and airfare on the Internet. Twig got a whole weekend in Vegas for a hundred bucks on Priceline." As she spoke, and he shook his head, he could feel her body stiffening, a little pulling away from him. He hated that her affection was in direct proportion to his ability to give her things. It killed him.

"We can talk about it," he said, as sincerely as he could. They could. Talk about it. They could talk and talk in those endless circles they always seemed to spin with their words. Elsbeth's asking and his denying. Ask, deny, ask, deny.

Kurt watched as Trevor helped Gracy down off the horse, holding her hand as she climbed off the ride. He didn't understand how someone so gentle could be capable of such violence at school. He wished Mrs. Cross could see this. Evidence that he was a good boy. A good kid. Suddenly it struck him that maybe this was the solution to Trevor's problems. To all of their problems. Maybe they just needed *this*. Time together. A little adventure. Something other than the endless routine of work, work, work. There would be enough of that soon if he got the job at the 76. Maybe Trevor was just crying out for more attention at home. Kurt knew he had been so wrapped up in work, in the state of their finances, maybe it was possible this was his fault.

Gracy ran to him and reached for his hand. "This is the best birthday of my whole life, Daddy." Her eyes were bright, her hair in two pigtails, tethered with happy pink ribbons. She'd had her face painted with a bright rainbow-maned unicorn on one cheek.

And something about the sunlight, the warmth Kurt could still feel from where Elsbeth's cheek had been on his chest, the warmth of Trevor's smile and Gracy's little hand as it clung to his, overwhelmed him.

"*Let's*," he said to Elsbeth as she started to pull away. "Why not? Let's do it."

The rest of the day held the dreamy scent of possibility. It was amazing what a simple promise could do. Elsbeth opened up to him like a flower seeking the sun, her face checking his constantly for affirmation. Her body carried the heat of the sun, and she pressed into him, sharing that incredible warmth. He even allowed himself the distant but distinct hope that if he was careful, she would let him undress her tonight. She would turn toward him instead of away. Open her heart (and her long, beautiful legs) for him instead of close them.

But then the day came to a slow end, the sun descending behind them as they drove back home, and Kurt felt the realization of what he'd done slowly sinking in. Gracy was in a snow-cone coma in the backseat, her mouth rimmed in a terrifying blue. Trevor was lost in his own quiet reverie but finally smiling, and

Elsbeth was squeezing his hand expectantly. He should have been happy. He should have been content. But as he pulled into the driveway in front of their house (that goddamned house), he could feel his anxiety bubbling to the surface like a drowning man suddenly surging with a will to live. Fighting. Relentless and breathless.

"Come to bed?" Elsbeth said later after the kids had both passed out.

As he turned out the lights, she stood in the bedroom doorway wearing his old Zeppelin T-shirt, her sunburned thighs exposed. Still strong. Still sexy as hell.

Kurt went to her, closed and locked the bedroom door behind them, and dropped to his knees. He buried his face in her thighs, breathing the thick musky smell of her. He grabbed the tight flesh of her small ass with his hands and pressed his cheek into the warmth between her legs. He felt her body tremble, and he could barely stand it.

He stood up and they moved together toward the bed, amazed by the way their bodies remembered. The way she knew exactly where and when and how to touch him. The soft moans, the shudder, the quivering between her legs as familiar and reliable as rain.

"I love you," he whispered into her ear, tasting the salty flavor of her earlobe.

But as he made love to her, as he pushed into her and into her, he also had to push away the thoughts that all of this—the taste of her skin, the smell of her hair, the crippling thrill of it— was not his to keep. That it was all stolen, bought with promises he couldn't keep, making him the worst kind of thief.

Elsbeth went into the salon early, before Carly had even shown up, and sat down at the computer. They didn't have a computer at home; Kurt said they didn't need one. Trevor could use the ones at school, Kurt had the one at work, and Gracy was too young. She couldn't help but think that maybe Kurt just didn't trust her. Then again, why should he? Because here she was now, before she'd even put on the coffee in the break room, typing in www.victoriassecret.com and pulling the credit card, the one Kurt didn't know she had, out of her wallet. The model wearing her swimsuit on the screen was different than the one in the catalogue. This one had blond hair and even bigger breasts. She was standing on a beach, holding a cocktail in her hand. It was the color of a sunset and had a bright yellow umbrella in it.

After Elsbeth had selected her size, not her fantasy size but her real size, clicked the color she knew would look best on her (green), and clicked *Add to Cart,* her heart started to race. By the time she'd entered the credit card number, secret code, and expiration date, she thought she might be having a heart attack. She'd never felt like this before. Not in all the times she snuck Kurt in or out through her window, not the times she'd had a beer too many and driven home, tailed by a cop. Not even when she set off the alarm at the Walgreens, her pockets full of lip gloss, and had to wait for the counter girl to wave her through. It felt exhilarating. Amazing.

And so she went to Zappos next, found a pair of flip-flops with fake turquoise along the straps. She went to Old Navy for some new shorts, Target for four brand-new beach towels. She calculated the total in her head, but the numbers felt abstract; and really, weren't they? Numbers, just numbers. One hundred, two hundred. Three hundred. By the time she got to the Disney website and started looking at travel packages, she realized she'd been holding her breath. And when Carly came in, Elsbeth almost swooned as she stood up from her seat.

"Morning!" Carly said. Carly had just graduated from high school but was taking a year off to save money for college. Elsbeth liked to listen to her talk about her plans.

"Morning." Elsbeth smiled. "I was just doing some shopping."

Carly threw her purse underneath the reception desk and sighed. "Oh, I never buy anything online. I don't trust the Internet. Identity theft. All that."

"Really?" Elsbeth said. This wasn't anything she'd ever thought about before. "You mean like somebody stealing your credit card number?"

"No, I mean like stealing your whole life. My cousin in Rutland got her identity stolen. Screwed up her credit. She can't even get a car loan now. Somebody in Idaho got a hold of her numbers and went crazy."

"That's awful," Elsbeth said. "But that doesn't really happen very often, does it?"

"She says it happens all the time."

All day long, while she cut and colored hair, while she shampooed and blew-dry and swept up all that discarded hair, Elsbeth thought about somebody stealing her life. About somebody slipping in through the cracks in cyberspace and taking her identity. Stealing her name, her money, her credit. Then she pictured that poor sucker, thinking they were stealing something good and winding up with this. Her debt, her bad credit, her worries, her life. *Go on and take it,* she thought. *I dare you.*

Then she thought about the life she might steal, as if it were something that might just be hanging on a rack at Walgreens. She pictured herself browsing the shelves, choosing from the shiny selections in their glossy packages. She felt the tug and thrill as she slipped the new life in her pocket, as she carried its weight next to her hip. She felt it shift and wriggle inside as she made her way through the security detector, across the threshold and out into the world outside.

When she got back from her lunch break, she was surprised to see a man sitting in her chair. Most of her clients were women, and most of her clients knew enough to wait in the plastic chairs by the front door.

She raised her eyebrow at Carly. "What's he want?" she whispered.

"I'm guessing a haircut," she said, not looking up from her magazine.

Elsbeth took a deep breath and put on a smile as she made her way to her station. "Hi there," she said, and the man spun himself around. "Can I help you?"

"I hope so," he said. He had cocoa-colored skin, probably mixed, Elsbeth thought; he reminded her of a guy Twig dated once who had a white mother and a Jamaican daddy. But this man's eyes were bright, bright blue. It was startling, that combination of dark and light. He looked to be about her age or so. His legs were long, and his fingers were also long when he reached out his hand to shake hers.

"My name's Wilder," he said.

"That your first name or your last name?" Elsbeth asked, going to the sink and setting down her soda that she'd brought back from lunch.

"First. Montgomery's my last."

"You're not from Two Rivers," Elsbeth said. Of this she was certain.

"Well, technically, I am," he said, his slow mouth creeping to a smile.

Elsbeth scowled. "Two Rivers is a small town. I think I know pretty much everybody from around here."

The man spun around to face the mirror and studied his reflection. Elsbeth stood behind him doing the same. He was good-looking. *Really* good-looking. She felt herself blush and then a hot rush of guilt.

"You cut black hair before?" he asked.

"Sure," she said, though this was a lie. But really, how hard could it be? His hair was only about a quarter inch long all around. She pulled her clippers out.

"You want a shampoo too?" she asked.

"Why don't you give me the whole treatment," he said, his reflection smiling at hers.

"Sure thing," she said and was grateful to get to work.

After she was finished and she'd removed the bib from around his neck, he stood up and reached in his pocket for his wallet. "You can just pay the receptionist," Elsbeth said.

"Well, I'd like to tip you," he said, handing her a five. "And this is my card. I'm hoping I might take you out for coffee and ask you some questions."

Elsbeth opened her eyes wide. She didn't wear her wedding band to work because she was so afraid of losing it in one of the sinks, but she was also pretty sure she hadn't done anything to give this guy any ideas. She could feel her skin grow hot, the tips of her ears burning. She self-consciously pulled her hair over her hot ears. "Some questions about what?" she asked.

"About Two Rivers, actually. I was born here."

"So?" she said. "Lots of people were born here and don't ask to take me out to coffee to talk about it."

"I mean *here*," he said, gesturing across the street. "My father lived upstairs in that building. And his wife's father owned this shop. I think that might be her right there," he said, walking to the photo of the girl, Betsy Parker, on the wall.

"No kidding! But you don't look . . ." She felt herself blush again.

"I'm kind of adopted," he said. "I'm a journalist, but I'm working on a memoir. I'm here doing some research. It's a long story, but pretty great actually. I'll tell it to you if you meet me for coffee."

She glanced at the card in her hand: WILDER MONTGOMERY, REPORTER, THE TAMPA TRIBUNE. Her hands trembled.

"You're the owner, right? Babette?" He gestured to the glowing neon sign.

She felt herself nodding despite herself. "Babette," she said. Babette, the real Babette, was on her annual trip to visit her brother in Colorado.

"I'm staying over at the Econo Lodge," he said. "The one near the interstate?"

She looked at the business card again. "You live in Florida," she said, her heart beating hard in her chest.

He smiled again, his eyes blue, blue, blue. "That's right. The Sunshine State."

On Tuesday afternoon, Kurt stared at the stack of bills on his desk in the shop. When he first took over the shop for Pop, he'd been on top of everything. He paid the business's bills as they came in, actually feeling a sense of accomplishment each time he signed his name to one of the long business checks in the ledger he kept in the bottom drawer. Now his throat grew thick and his legs itched whenever he pulled the monstrous book out. The custom checks that had once seemed official and professional now just struck him as oversized and pretentious.

Kurt's phone buzzed in his pocket. The shock of it was like a Taser. He'd just hung up with Elsbeth and wasn't expecting a call.

"Pop?" he said.

"I need you to come by."

"Jesus, what for, Pop?"

"Now don't get your tit in a wringer," he said. "I just need some help making sense of these papers."

"What papers, Pop?"

"Love letters from some lady at the county."

"Oh shit, Pop."

From what he could gather, Irene Killjoy, the lady from the county, had come at the crack of dawn that morning with papers. Not a condemnation sign, yet, thank God, but a letter signed by every neighbor within a mile radius of Jude's house, except for Maury Vorhies, who had apparently refused to sign. Theresa Bouchard had spearheaded the campaign and gone to the county, letters in hand. The cleaned-up yard and porch had apparently gone unnoticed, but the raccoons under the porch and the possible rat infestation had not. Neither had the three inoperable, unregistered vehicles in the yard nor the exposed electrical panel where the siding had rotted away. And as a result of the complaints, the county had sent out inspectors, who had quickly come up with a list of thirty-five health and fire code violations.

Kurt dialed the number Pop had read to him and listened as Miss Killjoy primly answered the phone.

"It's uninhabitable," she said to Kurt. "It poses a serious danger to public safety."

"It's a private residence," Kurt said. "It's not a danger to anyone except for my father."

"Then you certainly must at least be concerned about his health and welfare."

Kurt felt like he'd been kicked in the stomach. "Of course I am *concerned*. Jesus Christ," he said.

"*Mr. Kennedy, please.* The reality is your father's home is in violation of multiple building codes, including the presence of numerous fire hazards," she said. "At this point, it's become a risk not only to your father but to the public as well."

"We'll get it cleaned up, but I need some time. I'm trying to run a business," Kurt said. He looked around at the sad shop, at that awful checkbook ledger.

"Listen, I understand your plight, Mr. Kennedy. And we only want what is best for your father. We can certainly send in some of the residents at the detention center, if you'd like. We frequently use opportunities like this for the inmates to fulfill their community service requirements."

The hair on Kurt's arms bristled. "You're going to send *prisoners* into my father's home? What kind of harebrained plan is that?"

There was silence at the other end of the line.

"Sir, we'll be sending the inspectors out again in thirty days. If these violations are not corrected, the county is going to take matters into its own hands. I would really consider this as an option."

Kurt considered the list of violations Pop had read off to him. He closed his eyes and imagined the inside of his father's house. It would take an army to get the place emptied out, cleaned up, and brought up to code in thirty days. He wondered if there were any legal loopholes they might find. Like he had money for a lawyer, and calling Billy again would just about kill him.

He tried to think about who he could ask for help. There were Nick and Marty; they'd practically been like brothers to Kurt when he was growing up. They'd both lay down their lives for him if he asked them to. But neither of them knew about Pop, about how bad things had gotten. He'd be so ashamed for them to see the kind of squalor Pop was living in. There were a couple of guys Pop went hunting with, a few men from his old bowling league, but cleaning up some old man's crap was hardly on the list of favors Kurt felt comfortable asking for. He didn't want to involve Elsbeth, so that left him and Trevor. And, hopefully, Maury, who, at least, had been a contractor before he retired. If Beal could watch the shop for a bit, they could get in there and clean. He could get a Dumpster in, though the rental alone would set him back $500 or more. And never mind the problem of what to do with Pop. They would never get that shit hole cleaned out with Pop monitoring their every move. He'd practically thrown a tantrum over a box of his mother's old *Ladies' Home Journals* that were rotting out on the porch.

They had thirty days. *Thirty days.*

He thought about the piles and piles of papers and trash, the mountains of debris teetering on all the flat surfaces of his father's house, and wondered if he was fooling himself. What he needed to do was to call Billy. There had to be a way to get an extension on the county's deadline, and Billy was the only lawyer he knew. But asking Billy to help with Pop would be like asking the pope to perform an abortion. Billy had left Two Rivers and never looked back. And the last time Billy and Pop had been in the same room, Pop had nearly killed him.

Kurt crouched down under the counter and opened the safe. After he spun the knob, listening to the tick, tick of the lock, he leaned his forehead against the cool metal. The thin envelope marked *Emergency* seemed to mock him. He'd been saving cash, just a bit here and there for years now, since Trevor was born. Five dollars here and there, every now and then a ten spot. He never counted it; vowed never to dip into it. It was his entire life savings. It was not to be touched. The currents in his legs were angry, but he stayed crouching, clutching the envelope, allowing the pain to travel up his legs, across his stomach, and into his shoulders. He held the envelope in his hands, shook his head, and shoved it back in the safe. By the time he finally stood up again, he felt like the wind had been knocked out of him.

He wrote *Family Emergency* in Magic Marker on a piece of paper, taped it to the front door of the shop with a piece of electrical tape, and then called for Trevor, who was somewhere deep inside a maze of mufflers and engines. He could see his white shock of hair above the sea of metal.

"Time to go to Pop's," he said, and Trevor slowly emerged from the labyrinth of parts.

"Do I have to?"

"Just get in," he said, exasperated, and threw open the truck's passenger door.

He knew right away as he turned down the road to Pop's house that something wasn't right. He felt it in the way the leaves hung too far over the dirt road, as if they were closing in, as if the truck might simply be swallowed by the foliage. It was as though he were driving into the mouth of an angry green beast. The electrical storm inside his body was quieted now, but the air outside was tight. He could smell rain. The forecast had said there was a storm coming that might last the next two or three days. The sky looked brooding, *angry*.

When they pulled into Pop's driveway, he could see that all

the work they'd done just weeks ago was for nothing. There were overflowing bins of trash all along the drive, a swarm of flies hovering over one open bag that spilled rotten food and papers onto the ground. The warming weather and the increased sunshine made whatever was in those piles start to stink, like something dying.

The porch steps were littered with coffee cans and empty glass jars, and the front door was almost completely obscured by furniture Kurt didn't recognize: a big oak dresser and roll-top desk. Goddamn Maury. Another swap meet trip he'd failed to mention to Kurt. Maury had become Pop's unofficial chauffeur to the weekend swap meets Kurt had pleaded with him to stay away from. Kurt could feel anger rumbling inside him, and the sky rumbled too as if in sympathy. He got out of the truck and slammed the door shut. He motioned for Trevor to stay in the cab.

He walked up the steps to the house and tried to push the enormous dresser out of the way, but it wouldn't budge. He cautiously opened a drawer. *Bricks.* A dozen bricks. He opened the next drawer and the next. Pop was building a fucking fortress of used furniture around his house.

Kurt managed to squeeze through the space between the bureau and the door and banged hard. "Pop!" he said, knocking. "Pop!" he hollered again and felt something between sickness and fear run through his body: a hollow free-falling feeling.

He tried the door. It was unlocked, but still the door wouldn't budge even with the turn of the knob. "Pop!" he said again, feeling panicky. Thunder growled this time, and a stray sliver of cold rain hit his face.

"Goddamn it, Pop! It's me. Open the door!" He looked to the window to the right of the door. On the other side of the glass was the living room, but the shades were drawn, the drapes pressed into the window by whatever junk was on the other side. He knocked again and then pushed the door hard with his shoulder, feeling something give. A little. He pushed again, harder this time, and winced with the pain in his shoulder. He pushed his hip into it and finally, he was able to get the door open enough to slip inside. He looked back at Trevor in the truck. The window was rolled down, and Trevor was aiming the camera at him.

"Put the goddamned camera away," he said. "And stay there."

He slipped through the crack he'd made but was faced with a wall of cigarette smoke and cardboard. Everywhere he looked there were cardboard boxes stacked like strange totems, like a child's fort. Irene Killjoy was right; a forgotten cigarette and this place would go up in flames in seconds. How could he have not noticed before how dangerous this all was?

"Pop," he said again and pushed blindly through the rubble of his father's life, feeling like he was sinking into quicksand.

He found Pop sitting at the kitchen table, though there wasn't an inch of space on its surface. The papers from the county were in front of him. His eyes were filmy and unfocused. He was shirt-less, the scar from an old surgery red and angry at the center of his chest. His entire body was speckled with liver spots, as though someone had flung a fistful of mud at him. Kurt felt the tension in his shoulders give a little, relieved that Pop was here, and alive. Kurt said softly, "Pop?"

Pop looked up but not at Kurt. Instead, he trained his eyes on the ceiling, where the model planes solemnly hovered over him.

"Pop," Kurt tried again, moving slowly toward him as he might a wounded animal.

His speech was slow, careful. "Your mother and I lived in this house forty years."

"I know that, Pop."

"You and Billy were both born in that back bedroom."

Kurt nodded and reached for Pop's bare shoulder. His skin was hot to the touch.

"I own this house," he said.

Kurt put his arm around Pop's stiff shoulder, feeling his heart beating hard in his own chest. Thinking about what his mother would think if she could see this now. Feeling shame like something white-hot in his chest.

"It's my goddamned *home*," Pop said.

Later that night after Elsbeth and the kids had fallen asleep, Kurt took the phone outside and walked out to the backyard. He sat down on the rusty edge of the slide and looked up at the sky. It had rained all afternoon. A persistent and furious rain. But now, at midnight, it had softened, not apologetic, but at least willing to give a small reprieve.

He dialed Billy's number, and because Kurt knew he wouldn't answer, he practiced what he would say to the machine. But then, just as his lips were forming the words that might convince Billy it was time to set aside old grievances, the words that might soften Billy's own decade-long storm, his brother answered.

His voice was soft but tinged at the edges with bitterness. "Kurt."

"Hi, Billy," he said, and the words disappeared. "Listen. Please just listen."

Trevor was alone in the art room during lunch on Friday. Mrs. D. had a staff meeting but said that he was welcome to hang out there until the next period started. He sat down at one of the worktables and opened a bag of chips he'd gotten from the vending machine. He'd also snagged an apple from the fruit bowl on his way out the door that morning. He was anxious for her to come back. He wanted her to see the photos he'd taken. The good ones anyway.

Taking pictures with the camera Mrs. D. gave him was different than taking pictures at the salvage yard. He didn't think about what he was seeing when he snapped the shots of the starters and alternators and clutches. He didn't have to, because as soon as he clicked the button, he could see the picture in the display. But when he was taking pictures with Mrs. D.'s camera, he had to really think about things. About centering, *composition,* she called it. He had to consider the light. She'd told him that in photography, the light is just as important as what you're taking a picture of. Something ordinary could be beautiful if the light is right. And the other way around. And even then, he had nothing to show for it, just a canister of film, pictures captive inside. He couldn't wait to learn how to develop them himself. He'd spent every dime he'd made working at the yard so far getting these rolls processed at the Walgreens, and it had taken a whole *week* for them to come back and his mom had forgotten to give them to him for almost a week after she picked them up.

"I have no idea why you don't just get yourself a digital camera instead," she had said, handing him the fat envelope, still sealed shut. "Even my phone's got a camera on it. Then you can just print 'em out yourself." Never mind that they didn't have a printer, or even a computer for that matter. He didn't know what she was thinking sometimes.

He'd grabbed the envelope from her hands and ran to his room. Gracy was in the backyard blowing bubbles; he could see her from their window, the greasy bubbles drifting into the pasture beyond their yard. He sat down on his bed and tore the envelope open. It felt like opening up a Christmas present.

He wasn't sure what he was expecting, but it wasn't this. For one thing, half of them were overexposed, the faces bright white moons. Eclipsed. The other half were out of focus. The ones of his dad and Pop weren't anything like what he'd seen in the viewfinder, what he'd imagined, and the ones of the trash before they hauled it away to the dump just looked like pictures of trash. There was one, of a trout skeleton with its head still attached, that was okay, but he was disappointed. His hands were shaking as he went through the rest of the stack.

He'd taken some silly pictures of Gracy out in the backyard goofing around on the rusty swing set, the one that had been in the backyard since he was her age. There were a half dozen bad ones, but finally, one decent one, one that came close to what he'd seen in his mind. In this picture, she was leaning away, her hair dipping in a mud puddle. The light skipped across the water in this one. Like something alive. You could also see the reflection of the crazy after-rain clouds in the murky water. It was disturbing and beautiful at the same time. After that were six more washed-out, ghostly-looking pictures, and then one he snapped the night after they came home from Story Land. In this one, Gracy was fast asleep, her legs and arms thrown out, her face full of peace. The light from the night-light lit up her white nightie, the white caps of her knees, and one side of her sleeping face. When he looked at the picture, his chest ached. Who would have known that looking at a photo could make your heart swell up like that? He yanked out all the bad pictures from the stack and tossed them into the trash can. Then he took the best ones and stuffed them back into the envelope.

He clutched the Walgreens envelope now, too afraid to take the photos out again. Maybe he'd only imagined they were any good. He wanted to show Mrs. D., but he didn't want her to be disappointed. Didn't want her to realize that maybe she'd been wasting her time with him. Didn't want her to ask for her camera back.

Mrs. D. came back into the art room, breathing heavily as she tossed her bag onto her desk. She coughed, and it sounded like something awful, like their neighbor's dog who barked half the night. She'd been coughing all week, but she said she hadn't missed a day of teaching in forty years and wasn't about to now. When she finally stopped, she smiled sadly and shook her head. "What have you got there?" she asked.

He handed the envelope to her, and she carefully pulled the half dozen pictures out with her papery hands and studied them. When she came to the first picture in the stack again, the one of Gracy on the swing, she looked at Trevor and smiled. "They're perfect, Trevor. They're marvelous."

"A lot of 'em didn't come out. I need to know more about the shutter stuff you talked about. F-stops. I don't know what I'm doing wrong."

"Trevor," she said and squeezed his hand. "You are an artist. The rest is just mechanics, technology. You can learn that. But the talent, the vision, is already there."

An *artist*. It felt like he'd swallowed a hot-air balloon, like something deep in his heart was about to take flight. But then he looked out the open door to the hallway where kids were all scattering to their classes, a steady blurry stream. At Mrs. Cross standing in the middle of them, her arms folded across her chest, nodding at them as they made their way to study hall or science or social studies. She caught his eye and he sank down into the seat, the heat lighting the fire beneath the balloon gone cold.

"Let me show you something, Trevor," Mrs. D. said and shuffled over to the bookcases by her desk. She pulled out a book and brought it back to his table. Her body shuddered as she attempted to stifle a cough. *The Photographs of Lewis Carroll,* it said. That was the guy who wrote *Alice in Wonderland,* Trevor thought. Gracy had the Golden Book version, the golden spine cracked and worn. She opened up the book and pressed it open gently with her palm. The first picture was of a little girl who actually looked a lot like Gracy. Black hair, a torn dress, the same look in her eye . . . something wild, like the feral cats that came looking for scraps of food at the junkyard.

"Who is that?" he asked.

"*That* is Alice Liddell." She smiled. Her voice was trembling, like dry leaves in the wind. "The *real* Alice. She was Carroll's muse."

"What's a muse?" Trevor asked.

"The one he who wrote his stories for. The one he wrote *about.*"

Trevor traced the picture of the girl who looked so much like Gracy.

"Every artist needs a muse," she said and touched his hand. "And I think you may have found yours."

He lifted up the book and flipped through the pages. Almost all of the pictures were of kids. Old-fashioned pictures. Serious faces and funny clothes.

"You can have this if you like," she said.

"Really?" he asked.

The bell rang and the room started to fill with students.

"When do we get to use the darkroom?" he asked.

"Monday," she said, moving away from him, returning to her desk. "I promise."

The other students threw their backpacks down and started taking their seats. He had math, but he didn't want to leave. He didn't want to deal with Mrs. Edam and geometry and worrying that Ethan Sweeney would do something to get him in trouble. He wanted to hear more about Lewis Carroll. About muses. But Mrs. D. said, "Trevor, you missed the last bell. You better hurry along. I'll see you tomorrow."

On Friday night, after he closed up the shop, Kurt dropped Pop's groceries off at his house and told Pop that he and Elsbeth had plans that night so that he wouldn't have to stay. He'd been by the house every night that week, but still had made no significant progress. Pop refused to throw anything away, and Kurt didn't know what to do anymore. Billy had, as expected, refused to come. "It's not your problem," Billy had said. "It's Pop's problem. He's a grown man."

"I'm not asking you to do anything except help me with some of this legal stuff. You wouldn't even have to see him."

"Jesus, Kurt," he'd said. "It's like you don't remember. Why is it so goddamn difficult for you to understand this?"

"I'm not defending Pop," Kurt said quietly.

"Really? Because it kind of feels like you are."

Kurt's temples were throbbing.

"Do you remember that hunting trip?" Billy asked.

"Which one?" Kurt asked, knowing exactly which one. His head pulsed with pain.

Pop had taken Kurt on overnight hunting trips every fall as soon as he was old enough to lift a rifle to his shoulder, but Billy had always stayed home. Maury had a hunting shack in the woods up in the Northeast Kingdom not far from Lake Gormlaith that he let Pop use whenever he wanted to. They took sleeping bags and slept on cots. They ate out of cans: pork and beans and beef stew. They ate venison jerky and drank homemade root beer that they kept cold in a makeshift refrigerator made out of a rusted barrel through which the river ran icy cold this time of year. When Billy was about ten, he had pleaded with Pop to take him along as well. Billy had never expressed any interest in these trips, always preferring to stay behind with their mother. When they came back, most years with a deer splayed and tethered in the back of the truck, he would hide between their mother's legs. But that particular year, Kurt remembered Billy suddenly wanting to be a part of this. Wanting to come along.

Most of these trips blurred together in Kurt's memory: the smell of the fire in the camp wood stove, the chill of autumn air in striking contrast to the warm fire of the trees surrounding them. He remembered the hushed sounds of their footsteps, the startling crack of the gunshots, and the quiet sound of a deer's body falling. He remembered the steam rising out of the bellies as his father field dressed the deer, the piquant stink of it. He recollected the hard cots, and the deep sleep that followed. He could remember the way his cheeks flushed with the warmth of the fire and the smell of his damp wool socks as they dried in the heat. Of course, there were particular moments that stood out: the year he got his first buck, Pop's face beaming with pride, the swig of Jim Beam he'd offered him that night to celebrate. He also recalled the years they had come home empty-handed, his father driving silently, defeated the whole way back. And the year that Billy came along, the only year that Billy came along. Of course he remembered.

They had been out in the woods for two days without even catching a glimpse of a deer. Billy was getting restless. He was only ten. It was hard to be patient when you had only experienced the boredom of tracking and none of the thrill of sighting a deer. Billy was at least a hundred feet behind Kurt and Pop as they quietly made their way through the woods. And then suddenly Pop stopped, cocked his gun, and *crack!*

"Did you get one? Did you kill one, Pop?" Kurt asked. Behind them, Billy's face was pale. His eyes were wide and terrified. Kurt suddenly knew that Billy probably shouldn't have come.

Pop whooped and started to trudge through the wet leaves

toward the fallen animal. Finally, realizing that his boys were not behind him, he hollered, "You kids gonna come help me with this or what?"

Billy shook his head, his eyes brimming with tears now. "I can't," he said quietly to Kurt.

"It's okay," he whispered. "Just come on." He'd felt irritated with Billy then. His reluctance suddenly evoked not sympathy but annoyance.

When they got to the spot where the deer had fallen, his father looked up at them, grinning. "Billy Boy, how'd you like to help your pop dress this beauty?"

The deer was a buck, a whitetail. It lay on its back, its legs stiff. It was cold out, and their breath made clouds in the air. Billy walked obediently to where the dead animal lay. Pop dropped down to his knees and pulled his knife out of his pocket, showing Billy the blade. "First things first. You got to know how to properly use your knife. If you bust the bladder, it'll contaminate the meat. This an art," he said. "You've got to remember that."

When he slit the deer's lower belly, the smell was strong. Kurt was afraid to look at Billy. Billy, who carried spiders out of the bathroom rather than killing them. Billy who wept inconsolably when he finished reading *Where the Red Fern Grows* and sobbed through *Old Yeller*.

"You've got to tie off the rectum first," Pop said, reaching into the deer and pulling out the lower intestines. Billy, who was trembling. Steam rose like ghosts out of the hot innards into the bright blue sky above them.

"Next, you need to slice into the breastbone and slit down the belly. Use your two fingers, like this, to guide the knife. Don't go in too deep. Gotta be careful not to cut into the stomach or the intestines. No point in killing an animal if you go ruin the meat."

Billy backed away from the deer and this grisly project, sitting down on a stump. His face had gone from white to green pretty quickly. He lowered his head.

"Buck up now," Pop said, his brow furrowing angrily. "No time to be squeamish."

Billy looked up dutifully.

"Now we've got to cut off the genitals," he said, slicing again. Then he yanked off the testicles and held them up like some sort of prize.

Billy covered his mouth with his hand, retching, and Pop laughed. Billy was clearly trying hard not to vomit. His eyes were red and watery, his whole body racked with the effort.

"What you need, Billy Boy," Pop said, winking, "are some of these." And then he chucked the testicles at Billy. They hit Billy in the chest, and then after a moment of stunned silence, Billy was off and running, leaving a trail of vomit (which looked a lot like the pork and beans they'd had the night before) behind him.

Kurt didn't know what to do, but he did know that *whatever* he did meant choosing sides.

"Help me with this here, Kurt?" Pop asked. "I need to crack the pelvis. Hold the tail, and I'll step on it. That usually does the trick."

Kurt could see Billy in the distance, bent over at the waist. He could hear the awful sound of his guts spilling out into the snow.

"Come on," Pop said.

Every ounce of Kurt knew he should go to Billy, tell him it was okay. That he'd been queasy the first time too. But he also worried that if he left Pop here to handle this alone, he might not be invited back the next year. And so he grabbed the deer's tail as his father stomped on the bone, the crack louder than any gunshot.

Sometimes when he couldn't sleep at night, Kurt ticked off a list of regrets. This moment nearly always topped the list.

"My whole life," Billy had said, his voice still soft on the other end of the line. Still so far away. "I tried to please Pop, to make him proud. And in return, he's thrown nothing but steaming shit back at me."

After he got off the phone with Billy, Kurt had known he wouldn't be able to sleep, and so he walked. He walked until his legs ached from the effort. He walked through the sleeping downtown, up by the high school, and out onto the road that led to the salvage yard, arriving back at home just as the sun was blooming pink in the sky.

Kurt had lied to Pop. He and Elsbeth didn't really have plans that night. He was just watching the kids so Elsbeth could go over to Twig's to get her hair colored.

"When will you be home?" Kurt asked as Elsbeth checked her reflection in the mirror by the door. She looked pretty, more makeup than usual on her eyes. Her hair was clean and hanging down instead of up in that messy ponytail she usually wore.

"What's that?" she said, turning around. Distracted.

"Will you be late?" he asked.

"Not too," she said.

After she left, Trevor disappeared into his room. He'd been a lot more talkative than usual at supper, excited about getting to use the darkroom at school the following week, talking about all the things his art teacher had planned for them. Usually he was so quiet, so sullen. As much as having that camera shoved in his face all the time bothered Kurt, this photography kick seemed to be good for him.

Kurt flipped on the TV and scooped Gracy up into his arms. He pressed his face into her hair, which smelled like the sour apple stuff Elsbeth sprayed in it to get the tangles out. It was a smell that nearly brought tears to his eyes. It seemed like it was only a little while ago that Trevor had been small enough to hold, and it made his heart ache that this time was slipping, that Gracy herself would soon be too big for this. Too old. That she would disappear behind slammed doors, want nothing to do with him or Elsbeth. The thought of that was almost too much to bear.

"Gracy-girl," he said as she nestled into his arm on the couch.

"I love you, Daddy," she said sleepily.

For now, she was still his little girl. Innocent. Happy. And he hoped that no matter what, he and his children would never, ever turn on each other the way that Billy and Pop had.

Crystal was getting ready for school on Monday when the robocall came. She picked up the house phone, thinking it was strange that they'd be getting a call so early in the morning. "Hello, Two Rivers parents, this is Mrs. Cross. School is canceled today due to a bomb threat called in early this morning. We are investigating this threat and taking all precautions to ensure that your children are safe. School will resume tomorrow."

In the kitchen, Angie wasn't dressed yet and was eating her usual disgusting breakfast of frozen chocolate chip waffles soaked in Aunt Jemima.

"You should eat healthier," Crystal said. "I can make you some oatmeal or something."

"Ick," Angie said, dipping a sausage link into the syrup.

Their mother and father were gone to work already. Most mornings they were out the door long before Crystal and Angie were even up. She'd been making Angie breakfast since Angie was in kindergarten.

"Who called?" she asked, mouth full.

"Robocall from Mrs. Cross. No school today." She didn't know whether or not she should tell her why. When her mother had explained 9/11 to her a few years ago, Angie been inconsolable for a week. She had slept with Crystal every night, terrified that terrorists were going to start bombing houses.

"Really?" Angie asked, wide-eyed. "How come?"

Crystal shrugged, opting to keep her in the dark this time.

No need to lose sleep over some stupid bomb threat. She could hardly believe they'd canceled a whole day of school over it.

"What are you gonna do today?" Crystal asked, and Angie shrugged.

"I could skip school too and we could hang out," Crystal said, worrying a little that Angie might rather just be alone.

Angie shrugged. "Okay."

Angie had always liked spending time with Crystal, but something had shifted after Crystal got pregnant. It was like she didn't know how to act around Crystal anymore. Though she'd never admit it, it broke Crystal's heart that Angie seemed not to want to spend time with her. She hoped it was just that she was growing up, exercising her independence, and not that she was somehow, like their parents, ashamed of her.

But Angie had said okay, so she'd play hooky. There was only a week until graduation. She had nothing to lose by skipping school. Why not? That way Angie wouldn't be at the house alone, and besides, she could use a day off. Jesus, she'd call in a bomb threat herself if it meant a day without having to dodge Ty and Lena. To overhear Lena gushing about their relationship. *Relationship*. That was just a stupid word for hooking up with the same person more than once in a row. She and Ty had had a relationship too, and look where that had gotten them. Of course Lena would never want to come across as the two-faced liar that she was, though, and so she was careful around Crystal. Whenever she rounded the corner only to find them pressed together against her locker (her locker!), Lena was always the one to pull away. As though she had a shred of dignity left. A shred of respect. She and Lena, who knew each other's deepest secrets. They had whispered their dreams to each other, sliced their fingers and pressed the wounds together. Almost sisters. Now Lena was like somebody she never knew. Crystal felt deflated and forgotten. And it only had a little bit to do with Ty; just a fraction of the hurt was because of him. It was mostly because when Lena was forced to choose between them, when Crystal had needed her most, she'd chosen Ty. Like this *relationship* would even last the school year. *Both* of them had ditched her when the going got tough, and because they were her two best friends in the entire world, it made her question her judgment.

She especially thought about this when it came to the Stones, the couple who took her baby. They looked the part, with their intellect and charm. But if she could be wrong about two people she'd known since she was in diapers, couldn't she be wrong about them too? She tried to put it out of her mind. For one thing, the Stones were grown-ups. They had jobs and a house and lives. Teenagers weren't the same thing, were they? You could trust adults to tell the truth, right?

"What do you want to do today?" she asked Angie.

"We could go shopping?"

Angie wanted to go to Burlington, but there was no way Crystal was going to risk running into Mrs. Stone on the street. The very thought of it made her whole body tremble. Angie had no idea who had adopted the baby. Their parents had kept her in the dark about everything they could still manage to hide about Crystal's pregnancy.

"Let's go to Montpelier," Crystal said. "We can go to the art store, to that book store, Bear Pond? I'll treat for lunch."

They took her dad's car and spent the morning wandering in and out of the shops. When Crystal was Angie's age, she and Lena used to save up their babysitting money all summer and then Lena's dad would drive them to Burlington to go school shopping. They'd try on clothes they couldn't afford, giggling and wriggling in and out of dresses meant for much older girls. They'd eventually blow all their cash at the mall and fall asleep in the car in a nest of bags. Crystal didn't even know what size she was anymore. She'd been wearing sweats and big sweaters for the last nine months, but now that summer was coming, she knew she'd be forced to deal with this new body. This stranger's body. She really needed to start running again. Soon.

They finally found an art store and went inside. Angie's face lit up as she dashed toward a display of brushes.

"You going to be a while?" she asked Angie, who was examining a twenty-dollar paintbrush, stroking the back of her hand with the soft bristles.

Angie looked up. "You can go somewhere else and meet me back here later."

Angie was only twelve. Crystal wasn't sure she should be leaving her alone. But it was an art store. What could happen to her? Besides, she was just going back down the street to the place that had caught her eye earlier.

"You promise you'll stay here?" she asked. Angie had picked up another brush and was pantomime painting. "Seriously, do not leave the store."

"I won't," Angie said, irritated. "God, I'm not a baby."

"Okay," Crystal said. "I'll be back in an hour. Meet me right here, at two," she said, looking down at her watch.

Angie rolled her eyes. "I'll be *fine*. Where are you going?"

Crystal shrugged, though she knew exactly where she was going.

She didn't know where she was going. What she was doing.

On Friday night, Elsbeth had made the mistake of telling Twig about that reporter, Wilder Montgomery. They'd been drinking wine, and it just came out. She showed her his business card, which she'd been carrying around in her pocket since he came into the shop. "He just wants to get coffee. He wants to ask me questions about Two Rivers, about the salon, for this book he's writing."

"Why does he want to talk to you?"

Elsbeth felt the tips of her ears getting hot. "He thinks I'm Babette."

Twig raised her eyebrows in disbelief. "You aren't gonna call him, are you?" Twig asked, pulling the foil from her hair. The air smelled of chemicals; between the hair dye and the booze, she felt kind of woozy.

"Why not?" she said. Twig was contrary sometimes just for the sake of being contrary, especially if she was drinking.

"Because you're *married?*" Twig said.

"I'm not going to *sleep* with him!" Elsbeth said, and though she meant it, she felt a little twinge of disappointment at saying this.

"Whatever," Twig said. "But you break Kurt's heart, I'll have to kill you. That man is a catch, Elsbeth. He's a good father, he works hard, and he loves you."

Each statement felt like an attack, like what Twig was really saying was that Elsbeth should just be grateful for what she had.

Like she was accusing her of something when she hadn't even done anything yet. *Yet.* Jesus, she'd had too much wine. She'd just get herself home and get rid of that damn business card. Twig was right.

But on Monday morning, after the bus from the retirement center came and she'd gotten all of her ladies situated under the dryers, she thought about him again. The thoughts were like slivers, little prickly things under her skin. She might forget about him for a while, until she felt the prick. That itchy reminder.

Twig had left her a little sticky note on the mirror in front of her chair. *Be smart,* it said. She'd plucked it off and tossed it in the trash. And then, just as she was headed out the door to go grab a Mountain Dew from the Cumberland Farms, shaking her head like she could just shake the thoughts loose, she bumped into him. Literally.

"Hi," he said. He had a newspaper tucked under one arm. He had a pair of glasses on; she hadn't remembered him wearing glasses before. They made him look distinguished. Kind of like a black Clark Kent.

"Hi," she said, feeling herself blush.

His eyes behind the glasses were an even brighter blue than she remembered. It was hard to look at him. He hadn't stopped smiling at her. Funny how she suddenly felt completely see-through, like he somehow knew that she'd been thinking about him all weekend. The way he was looking at her was like somebody who knew her secrets. But that wasn't possible, right? For Christ's sake, if he could really see through her, he'd have known she wasn't Babette.

"You on a break?" he asked.

She nodded, worried that if she opened her mouth she wouldn't have any control over the words that came out.

"How about that cup of coffee, then?"

Of course Twig was right. Twig was always right. But still Elsbeth walked down Depot Street with this strange man as if they were lifelong friends. As if this were completely normal. She was aware of her posture, standing taller than she normally did, throwing her shoulders back. Her mother had always tried to get her to stand up straight, but she was self-conscious about being tall. She felt different with her hair colored too. She held her head differently, was aware of the tips of her hair on her shoulders. Twig had suggested going lighter, maybe even a sandy blond, but Elsbeth had opted for auburn highlights. Something red. In the sun, she felt ablaze. When they walked past the jewelry shop and she caught her reflection in the glass, she barely recognized herself. She was Babette. A redheaded Babette (as opposed to the real Babette, whose hair was the color of lemon pudding). And when they went through the doors to the new little coffee shop near the railroad tracks, the one Kurt wouldn't be caught dead at, the one where a cup of coffee cost the same as a sandwich anywhere else, she could have been another woman. She could have been anyone but herself.

On Monday when school was canceled, Trevor was both re- lieved and disappointed. Today was the day they were sup- posed to finally go into the darkroom; he'd been looking forward to it all weekend. Mrs. D. had shown him where the chemicals were, the dusty packages of paper. He'd helped her clean the plas- tic developing trays and dust the enlarger. He had been taking pictures like crazy, spending every dime he made at the yard on film. He had four more used rolls. Now, with school canceled, he'd have to wait *another* day before he could develop them. But one less day of school was still, at least, one less day of school. And summer vacation was just two weeks away. When he thought of summer, it was like a shimmering rock under murky water.

Both his mom and his dad had to work on Mondays, so they spent the whole morning arguing about what to do with him and Gracy.

"Trevor can watch her until you get home," his father said as he finished up his breakfast, sopping up his eggs with a heel of toast. "It's just four hours. He's nearly thirteen years old, El. They'll be fine."

"I don't know. What if something happens? What if there's an emergency?"

"Then he can call 9-1-1."

"Why don't I just stay home?" she said.

"That's not necessary," his father had said in that voice that sounded like bricks. Like he was making a wall with his words.

His mother slammed the frying pan she'd been making eggs in into the sink, the brick wall cracking.

"El, it's just we really can't afford to have you missing work," his father said.

"I realize that. Don't you think I know that?" she asked, her eyes wide.

"I can do it," Trevor said, just wanting them to stop. "We'll have fun, right, Gracy?" It wasn't as though they hadn't left Gracy with him before. Sometimes when his mother needed to run to the store or the gas station, he'd watch her. Once she'd been gone for almost two hours. Seriously. How hard was it to play Chutes and Ladders and Candy Land all day? He wouldn't even have to make her lunch; she'd be home by lunchtime.

Finally, his mother threw up her hands and said, "Fine." She didn't say another word to anyone until she left, and even then she only kissed Gracy good-bye and said to him, "I'll be back at one. Do not turn on the stove. Don't even use the microwave. You know my cell number, and here's the number at Babette's." Then she looked for a moment like she might have changed her mind, like she might set down her purse and stay. But she only took a deep breath and said, "God, just be good."

"I'll be home late tonight," his father said. "I'm stopping by Pop's."

"Fine, then," she said. "I'll keep a plate warm." She took off in a huff, but her car wouldn't start, and so his dad had to pull his truck up to hers, their hoods popped open and their batteries connected by the jumper cables. Something about watching them like this made Trevor feel sad. Connected, stuck together, but still totally separate. His mother sat in the car scowling, and when the engine finally came back to life, his dad quickly disconnected them and slammed the hood down, and his mom took off, gravel flying up behind her car as she peeled out of the driveway.

Gracy was finishing a bowl of Froot Loops at the table. There were Barbies lined up all along the table's edge, like some weird Barbie picnic. "Do you want my rainbow milk?" she asked Trevor, motioning to her bowl.

"Sure," Trevor said and took the bowl of colored milk from her, tipping it up and drinking it in three small gulps.

"So what do you wanna do today, Gracy?"

By ten o'clock they had played five games of Chutes and Ladders, watched two episodes of *SpongeBob,* one *Dora the Explorer,* and about five minutes of *Barney,* which just about drove Trevor crazy. Gracy had already dug into her dress-up box and dressed up as Sleeping Beauty, Jasmine, and finally settled into last year's Candy Corn Witch costume, complete with striped tights. She'd convinced Trevor to be a wizard, tying a black cape around his neck.

"I'm bored," she said. "Let's go someplace."

"I don't think we're supposed to go anywhere, Gracy," he said.

"Than let's play outside," she said. "Mommy won't care if we play outside."

Trevor looked around the house anxiously, as if his mother had installed security cameras to ensure he didn't do anything he wasn't supposed to do. They had those at school now, and he felt like he was always being watched. He knew it was ridiculous, but he also knew she had, if reluctantly, trusted him. He didn't want to mess up.

"I guess we could go outside," he said. "Why not?"

Outside, Gracy played on the swing set. He pushed her, and she swung so high the chains kinked and made a loud snap. When she grew tired of the swing, they raced each other back and forth across the field behind the house until their legs were shaking with exhaustion.

"Let's go on a nature walk," she said. "We could go swimming."

"I don't know," Trevor said. "What if Mom comes home early?"

"We can leave her a note."

Trevor shrugged again. "I guess as long as we get back before Mom."

Inside Gracy changed into her bathing suit, and Trevor got his camera. He'd just take her down to the river to splash around. They'd be back in plenty of time. He'd been wanting to take some pictures in the woods. Find some *pretty* things to take pictures of for a change.

Trevor made Gracy hold his hand as they walked into the woods at the edge of the field. "You have to stay with me," he said. "No wandering off."

"Okay," she said. She had put her witch costume back on over her bathing suit. The hat flopped to one side and the rubber nose was still strapped to her face, the elastic pressing into her chubby cheeks. He snapped a couple of pictures, but she was giggling too hard to hold still.

"Let's go," he said.

They made their way through the woods to the river's edge and Gracy peeled off her costume, leaving it lying on a rock. It made him think of that scene in *The Wizard of Oz* after Dorothy throws the water on the Wicked Witch and she melts. He snapped a few photos of the empty costume and then followed Gracy to the river.

"You can wade, but don't go in," Trevor said. "The current looks really strong today."

"Brrr," she said as she stepped into the water. "It's cold!"

Goose bumps sprang up all over her arms and legs. He clicked a couple more pictures, thinking he maybe should have brought another roll. The sun on the water made constellations of light. A billion twinkling stars on the surface of the water.

"I don't want to go swimming anymore," she said. "I want a towel."

Shoot. He'd forgotten to grab a towel. "Here," he said, pulling off his sweatshirt and helping her put it over her shoulders. It hung nearly to the ground. He yanked the hood over her head and pulled the strings so that just her little face was showing. She stuck her tongue out and he clicked another picture of her.

"Let's keep walking," Trevor said. It was so beautiful in the woods, cool with warm spots where the trees opened up, allowing the sun to shine down through the foliage. He sat on a warm, flat stone by the water and advanced his film.

"Gracy, go stand over there by that tree."

"Why?" she asked. She had found a roly-poly bug and was examining it at the tip of her finger. Her fingernails were short, dirty.

"Please?" he asked. He thought about that photo of the real Alice in the book Mrs. D. gave him. He thought about what Mrs. D. had said about having a muse. "But take off that sweatshirt," he said. "It looks silly."

"It's too cold," she said.

"Please? Just long enough to take a picture."

"Okay, okay," she said. She pulled the sweatshirt over her head; her hair stood up with static. "Like this?" she asked and leaned against the tree. Pouty. His mom was right about her growing out of all of her summer clothes; the yellow bathing suit with the ripped-up skirt around the middle was way too small. Trevor didn't notice until he clicked the first couple of pictures that one of her nipples was showing.

"Wait," he said, feeling embarrassed for her even though she was just a little girl. He walked over to her and pulled her strap up so that she was covered again.

"Okay," he said. "Say *cheese*."

She only let him take a couple more pictures before she said she wanted to go home and have a snack. It was eleven; their mom would be back in two hours.

"Can we have popcorn?" Gracy asked, skipping ahead of him.

"We're not supposed to use the microwave," he said.

"Mommy lets me push the buttons sometimes," Gracy said hopefully.

"Not today, Squeak," he said.

They walked along the river's edge back toward their house, and when they got to the train trestle that traversed the water below, something caught his eye. There was the hint of something red through the green of the trees. He'd never noticed it before.

"Come with me," he said to Gracy. He grabbed her hand and they ran to the trestle. He thought about helping her climb up and then realized that probably wasn't safe. But he really needed to see what it was. It would only take a second. He looked back at Gracy. She'd plucked some dandelions and was braiding their sticky stems together. Her hands would be stained with the stems' brown circles later.

"Stay right here," he said. "Don't move. I'll be back in two seconds."

It was an easy climb, probably only about ten feet up or so. The metal was hot from the sun, burning the palms of his hands. He could still see Gracy from up there; he waved and motioned for her to stay put at the water's edge. He watched the river between the railroad ties as he made his way across to the other side, where he jumped down and entered a tangle of maple and birch and pine, as thick and dense as a stone. He could feel the branches scraping his arms, but he didn't care, because that red thing he'd seen was a *caboose*. A real caboose just sitting there in the woods! And it looked like he was the first person to find it. No graffiti, no beer cans. Not a single scrap of evidence that anyone but he knew that it was here. Not even the trees seemed to notice it; they were growing right up through the rusted floor. He climbed up onto the platform and went through the door.

Inside, the leaves pressed against the windows, making everything green. The floors were littered with leaves and twigs. It was cool and dark in here, a cave. Spiderwebs stuck to his face and chest as he moved through the room. There was a potbelly stove, some rotten mattresses, and a wooden chair missing a leg. There was also a platform, which he climbed. From up there, perched like a hawk, he could look out over the tops of some of the smaller trees. He could hear the river.

He quickly snapped a picture of the broken glass scattered on the floor below him, the spiderwebs that caught the sunlight in their careful designs. He tried to capture that color green, the inside of a chrysalis. It felt like he was taking photos of his own heart, which was still beating like a captured bird in his chest. *Mine,* he thought. This place is mine.

He wanted to stay longer, but he knew he couldn't leave Gracy. And it was too dangerous for her to climb up too. So he reluctantly left the caboose and made his way back to the river's edge where he had told her to wait. But when he shimmied down the trestle, she was gone.

"Gracy?" he asked, looking around. He was sure he had left her here. He remembered this toppled tree, its upturned roots like a giant's hair. Her witch costume was still lying empty on the rocks, the striped tights like quiet snakes basking in the sun.

"Gracy!" he hollered again, and then he felt the dull, hollow thud of panic setting in. He raced back and forth across the scattered pine needles, winding through the labyrinth of trees. His heart was beating like a drum in his ears and head. He was dizzy, feeling the ground tilting awkwardly underneath him, as if the world might just spill him off its edges. He walked slowly, terrified, to the water, and his heart stopped like a cork in his throat.

Gracy was standing ankle-deep in the water about ten yards away. The sun was bright behind her, making her a silhouette. A shadow. She had made a crown of dandelions that circled her head like a halo. The sun dappled the water with light, and the leaves made heart-shaped patterns across her bare legs. He caught his breath. Where only moments ago there had been terror, now there was nothing but relief. Where there had been blistering panic was now a lovely, hushed reprieve. She was here. She was okay. Disaster had been avoided, and in its place was the most perfect thing he'd ever seen.

She held her arms out and spun on tippy-toes in the rushing

water. The tattered skirt of the bathing suit swirled around her legs. He slowly, quietly raised the camera, peering through the viewfinder at her. He was afraid to release the shutter, afraid to disturb her, but he desperately needed to capture this feeling. This beautiful sensation. All of the fragility of the world was in this moment, though he didn't know how to articulate that except by pressing his finger. *Click.*

That night there was another robocall from Mrs. Cross saying that after a thorough search of the grounds by security, the administration had determined that it would be safe for the students to return to school. There was no bomb; it was just a threat. But in the morning, Mr. Douglas was standing at the entrance to the school with his DayGlo orange security vest, checking out every student before they entered the building, even the kindergartners. He let Gracy through and then looked Trevor up and down suspiciously before asking to see his backpack.

"Why?" Trevor asked.

"S.O.P.," Mr. Douglas said. Trevor had no idea what he was talking about. He reluctantly relinquished his backpack, and Mr. Douglas unzipped it, reached inside, and rifled through Trevor's stuff, pulling out a freezer bag. "What's this?" he asked gruffly.

"Film," Trevor said.

"What for?" he said, unzipping the Ziploc and shaking the film out into his hand. Trevor felt his stomach knotting up.

"It's for art class. Please be careful," he said.

Mr. Douglas looked like he might crush the rolls in his hands. But then he smirked and tossed the loose rolls back into the backpack, shoving it at Trevor. "Get on in there now," he said, as if Trevor had been dawdling instead of him holding him up.

Trevor went inside and went to his homeroom. Art class was second period on Tuesdays, and he was excited to finally get into the darkroom. He knew there were some good pictures on those rolls of film. He couldn't wait for Mrs. D. to see. He sat down at his desk and pulled out his social studies textbook. He stayed in homeroom for social studies. Angie McDonald sat next to him.

She came in, her hair a mess, two different-colored socks and a wild plaid scarf tied around her neck. She didn't seem to care what anybody thought; he liked her for that.

"Hey," she said as she sat down.

"Hey," Trevor said.

As he reached into his backpack and pulled out his folder, he suddenly realized that he'd forgotten his social studies homework at home. Along with the peanut butter sandwich he'd managed to hide from his mother that morning. They were both sitting on the kitchen counter. He felt sick. He was going to have to try to explain this to Mrs. O'Brien, and she was probably going to send him to see Mrs. Cross.

"Did you hear about Mrs. D.?" Angie whispered as Mrs. O'Brien walked into the room.

"Huh?" Trevor asked. He was starting to sweat.

"I heard she had a heart attack this weekend," she said.

"What?" Trevor asked, his throat swelling shut.

"Yeah, my mom heard it from someone in her office."

Trevor shook his head. His hands were trembling as he opened the empty folder again.

"The lady lives in the same apartment building. An ambulance came and everything."

"Is she . . ." Trevor couldn't get the word out.

"I don't know," Angie said. Her eyes were wide and filling with tears. This brought tears to Trevor's eyes too. "They'll probably make an announcement."

Mrs. O'Brien took attendance; she had to call Trevor's name twice, because he couldn't even manage to get the word "present" past the burr in his throat. Then Mrs. Cross's voice came over the loudspeaker. "Good morning, boys and girls, this is your principal, Mrs. Cross. Today is Tuesday, June eighth. You'll probably notice that we have heightened security at the school after yesterday's incident. Please know that your safety is our number one priority. On that note, remember that you are not allowed to bring weapons of any sort to school. This includes pocketknives.

They will be confiscated. Additionally, there is now a school-wide ban on Silly Bandz. If you are caught wearing them or playing with them, they will also be confiscated."

Angie rolled her eyes. Trevor took a deep breath.

"Today is Taco Tuesday in the cafeteria. And Friday night is the final dance of the school year. Now please join us all in the Pledge of Allegiance."

Trevor stood up and felt like he might pass out. He walked up to Mrs. O'Brien's desk and said, "I think I need to go to the nurse."

"What's the matter?" she asked, irritated.

Trevor shook his head. He couldn't begin to explain what he was feeling. It was the worst kind of sickness, like something had just died inside him.

"Fine, here's a pass," she said, handing him a paper slip. He rushed out the door into the hallway. He glanced toward the closed door to the nurse's office and then down toward the art room. He walked quietly down the deserted hallway and peered through the small window into the art room. Mrs. Lutz, the all-purpose substitute, was sitting at Mrs. D.'s desk. He slowly opened the door and peeked in. Mrs. Lutz looked up at him and scowled at him over the top of her reading glasses. "Can I help you?"

"Is Mrs. D. here?" he asked. His voice sounded like a creaking door.

"No, I'm sorry. She's ill. Can I help you?"

"When will she be back?" he asked.

Someone shot a paper airplane made with Mrs. D.'s expensive origami paper at him. The pointed part hit him square in the chest. The whole class erupted in laughter, the voices echoing in that cavernous room.

"I'm sorry," Mrs. Lutz said. "She's in the hospital. I don't know the details."

Trevor shook his head and backed out of the classroom, worried that somebody might throw something else at him if he turned his back.

Back out in the hall, he looked toward the exit. His whole body felt cold and hollow. The hallway was still deserted. No one was out. Not Mrs. Cross. Not even Mr. Douglas. He looked up at the security camera, its red eye peering at him, and then he ran. He ran and ran until he got to the front doors, and then he was outside. Free, running across the parking lot. He ran all the way home before he realized he'd left his backpack at school. Before he realized that as soon as they figured out he was gone, Mrs. Cross would be on the phone with his mother and father. Before he realized this might be the last straw for Mrs. Cross.

He found the spare key under the garden gnome and let himself inside, feeling like a thief. It was so quiet here with Gracy and his parents gone. Like an empty set on a stage. He sat down at the kitchen table and put his head in his hands. He could feel his heart beating in his temples. He found the phone book and looked up the hospital in the yellow pages. He called the information number, but when the receptionist answered, he hung up. He didn't even know her first name. He flipped to the white pages and traced his finger down the Ds. Finally he located her, *Carmen Dubois*. He punched the number into the phone and waited. No answering machine, just the hollow sound of the phone ringing, endlessly.

He looked at the kitchen clock. Nine thirty. He wondered how long he had before his parents figured out he was gone. Probably a good hour or more. Mrs. O'Brien might not have even figured out he wasn't at the nurse's office yet. He decided it would probably be best not to stick around the house, just in case they came looking for him here, and so he grabbed his camera, a handful of Cheez-Its, and a Coke, and locked the house back up. Once he was outside again, he decided to head for the woods.

He found Gracy's striped tights still sitting on a rock by the river where she'd left them yesterday when he found the caboose. She must have missed them when she retrieved the rest of her costume. He picked them up and slung them over his shoulder.

He thought about the photos he'd taken. He thought about the one of her standing in the river with the flowers in her hair.

But by the time he got to the trestle, he was beginning to wonder if he had only dreamed the caboose. The foliage seemed to have grown in thicker in only a day, almost completely obscuring the train car, enclosing it. He shoved the handful of crackers into his mouth and followed it with a swig of soda. Then he set the can down, slung his camera over his shoulder, and started to climb up the trestle. When he got to the caboose, he felt his shoulders start to relax. Inside, his eyes took a long time to adjust to the darkness. It smelled of something musty and damp. The light filtered through the leaves surrounding the caboose, casting shadows across the floor. He hung Gracy's tights up on a nail sticking out of the wall and then lay down on the scratchy mattress, looking through the viewfinder into the light. He put his hand on his chest and felt his heart as it slowly stilled. He thought about Mrs. D. About her heart. He wondered if it was like this, just slowing until it stopped. He tried to put the thoughts of Mrs. D. in some other part of his mind, but the metal teeth clanged down shut tight, ripping into them, tearing them into ribbons.

"We've got a problem, El," Kurt said.

Elsbeth was getting her station ready for the morning when Kurt called. She wasn't scheduled to see any clients for another hour, so she was taking her time, cleaning her brushes, organizing her tools.

"What's the matter?" she asked. He was silent on the other end of the line, and she felt like the wind had been knocked out of her. Was there some way Kurt could have found out about her going out for coffee with Wilder? Could someone have seen them together, could someone have ratted her out? For one awful minute she thought of Twig. Would she do something like that to her? She tried to gather the words that would explain. The denial that she'd done anything wrong. That he was just a writer conducting research, that it had simply been an interview. And it had been, hadn't it? He'd asked questions about Two Rivers, she'd answered them. They'd had coffee. He'd smiled, said he'd call her if he had any more questions, squeezed her hand, and picked up the check. She'd gone back to work. She tried not to think about how she'd blushed at the mere thought of him, how she couldn't concentrate for the rest of the day. She'd tried not to think of Twig's Post-it admonishment: *Be Smart* staring at her from the mirror as she cut and colored and curled.

"Baby?" she said, her body trembling.

"Trevor's disappeared. He was in homeroom this morning, said he had to go to the nurse, but he never went and he never went back to homeroom. A substitute said he came into the art room, but then he got upset and left. I've been calling the house, but if he's there, he's not answering."

"Jesus, Kurt. Where do you think he went?"

"I have no idea. But I haven't got my truck. Beal got a ride into work this morning, but then Sally started having contractions, so I lent him my truck to take her to the hospital. Would you mind running to the house real quick to see if he's there?"

"I've got a client coming in a half hour," she said.

"Shit," he said.

Elsbeth tried to think about where Trevor would go. He'd never run away before. For all the problems they'd had with him, he'd never *left*. He'd throw tantrums, throw his body down, but he'd never *vanished*. She thought about the boy who had gotten snatched on his way to school in Putney a couple of years ago. The thought of it, of somebody just *stealing* him, made her stomach turn.

"I'll cancel," she said. "I'm sure he's at the house."

She grabbed her purse from behind the reception desk, rustling around inside trying to locate her keys. "Can you tell Mrs. Brown I had a family emergency?" she said to Carly. "I'll call my other clients."

"Everything okay?"

"Yeah," she said. "It'll be okay."

It took four tries before her car started. Fucking starter. She was shaking when the engine finally roared to life and she backed out of the lot behind the salon and onto Depot Street. She wondered if she should get Gracy early from school. Kindergarten pickup was only a couple of hours away. But then again, she didn't want to scare her. Trevor was probably just at home, probably sitting on the couch watching TV, eating up half the contents of the cupboards. She'd yell at him, tell him how she lost a client because of him. Kurt would come home and deal with punishment. It would be okay.

But when she got to the house, Trevor wasn't there. And there was no evidence to suggest he had been there at all. She felt her muscles go liquid as she ran through the empty house. "Trevor!" she hollered down the hallway.

Silence. Only the ticking of the kitchen clock.

She tried to think about the places he might have gone. As far as she knew, he didn't have a single friend in the world, no one to ditch with. He never asked to have friends over. He was never invited to anyone else's house. Elsbeth's eyes stung. If he had a friend, he'd have a place to go. She felt sick at the enormity of his loneliness.

She went into their bedroom, hoping there might be some sort of clue there. Gracy's bed was unmade still, a mess of pink flowers and ratty stuffed animals. Trevor's side of the room was tidy. His camouflage comforter was tidily pulled up to meet his pillow. His drawers were closed, his clothes neatly folded inside. There was nothing on his dresser, and the clothes in his side of the closet hung empty on their hangers. She rifled through the top drawer of his desk, finding nothing but pencils, loose coins, and film.

The camera? Where was his camera?

He'd left it here this morning; she was sure of it. She'd seen it on his dresser when she turned out their light after he and Gracy got on the bus. But now it was gone, which meant that he *had* been here. He'd come home, grabbed his camera, and taken off again. Maybe he *had* run away. Shit.

She went to the kitchen and got her phone from her purse, dialing Kurt.

"I think he's run off," she said. "There's a sandwich on the counter I think he must have made and forgot. And his camera is gone too. That means he's been home. Nobody took him."

"Jesus," Kurt said. "Listen, I'll call the police station. Maybe you can check in with the school again. Someone there might know something. He's close to his art teacher. Maybe he talked to her."

Elsbeth called the school next, sitting down at the kitchen table.

"Hello, this is Trevor Kennedy's mother. You spoke to my husband earlier. I was hoping I could speak to Trevor's art teacher?"

"Mrs. Kennedy, Mrs. Dubois was hospitalized this weekend after a heart attack."

"Oh my God," Elsbeth said, her hand flying to her chest. "Does Trevor know?"

"He might, though we haven't told the children the details yet."

Elsbeth said, "Okay, thank you."

"Please let us know if we can help," the woman said. "You know, most of the time they come back. Probably just got upset and needed to clear his head."

Elsbeth clicked her phone shut and shook her head. What was she supposed to do now? She picked up her phone and looked dumbly at the keypad. She dialed Kurt's number again, and he picked up after the first ring.

Then the front door opened slowly. Trevor stood, hulking in the doorway, the camera slung around his shoulders. He looked like he was waiting for punishment, his head hanging to his chest.

Elsbeth felt a rush of something flood her body. Something powerful.

"Oh, honey, he's home," she said to Kurt. "He's here. I'll call you back."

"Where did you go?" she asked, trying not to let her relief turn into anger. "We thought somebody took you."

Trevor shrugged. His hair was filled with twigs. He looked like an animal, like something wild. He shrugged again, shoving his hands in his pockets, staring at the ground.

Elsbeth felt something snag in her throat. "Is this about your teacher?"

Trevor looked up at her, cocking his head distrustfully.

"Come here," she said, motioning for him to come to her. He continued to look at her suspiciously. It killed her that he seemed so reluctant to trust her. Feeling almost desperate, she stood up and went to him, hugging him hard, realizing she couldn't remember the last time she'd held him. He was so big now, a child in a man's body. She didn't recognize the smell of him. The feel of him in her arms.

"Listen," she said, pulling away, peering into his icy blue eyes, wanting only to make everything all right. He looked at her, confused, his bottom lip already quivering the way it had when he was still just a little boy. "She's in the hospital. And they'll take good care of her there," Elsbeth started, not knowing how to say this without breaking his heart.

Trevor's whole body stiffened and his eyes went dark. His fists clenched, and he started to shake his head hard. He pulled away from her. God, why didn't she wait for Kurt to come home to tell him?

"It's okay, sweetie," she tried, but his whole body was tight and angry now.

"No, it's not!" Trevor growled, and as his voice grew, his body seemed to grow as well. She realized then that he could harm her if he wanted to. If he lashed out the way he used to as a little boy, she could actually get hurt. She was, for the first time, *afraid* of him. She cowered despite every attempt not to. How could she be afraid of her own son?

"Listen, Daddy will be home soon . . . maybe he can take you to the hospital to see her?"

"No!" he screamed again, this time just inches from her face. His breath was hot and wet. And then he ripped the camera from around his neck and threw it across the room. It landed on the floor, the back opening and exposing the film inside like guts. They both looked at it in disbelief, as if it had flung itself across the room. Then he rushed to it, picked it up like a baby bird fallen from a tree, and cradled it in his hands, tears streaming down his cheeks. The anger was gone, exorcised, and now he was six years old again. Just a terribly sad little boy she didn't know how to reach.

"Can I help you fix it?" she asked, afraid he might lash out again, but he only shook his head.

When he was able to close the back again and seemed satis-
fied that it wasn't broken, he quietly went down the hall to his
room and closed the door. And then Elsbeth started to cry.

Later, after dinner, instead of taking Trevor to the shed and
punishing him for running off and scaring them half to death,
Kurt had only nodded across the table at Trevor, patting his
shoulder gently as he brought his dish to the sink. Elsbeth had
told Kurt about his teacher but not about his temper tantrum,
about how scared she'd been. She knew it wouldn't help anything.

"I'm sorry about your teacher," Kurt said. "I know she's been
real good to you."

Trevor's face was blank. Empty. It was as though he had left, as
if he'd slipped right out of his body and abandoned it at the
kitchen table. Like a wax figure at one of those museums. All that
rage from earlier was gone. There was nothing in his eyes anymore. Not anger. Not even sadness.

"What happened to your teacher, Trevor?" Gracy asked. She
had spaghetti sauce at each corner of her mouth. A splatter of it
on her T-shirt.

Trevor turned to her, startled. A sleepwalker awoken from
sleep.

She was putting peas in tidy rows on the tines of her fork. "I
love my teacher. Do you love your teacher too?" she asked.

"She might die," he said. His voice sounded strange. Far away.

"Trevor, don't say things like that. You'll scare her. Gracy,
honey, she's just in the hospital. She'll be okay."

Gracy's eyes widened. She got up from her chair and went to
Trevor, climbing up on his lap. She looped her skinny arms
around his neck and buried her face in his neck. Trevor's lip trembled, but he didn't cry. He just stared straight ahead at the door as
though he might make a run for it again.

"At least there are only a couple of weeks of school left," Elsbeth said. "It's almost summer. We can start planning our vacation," she said, smiling hopefully at Kurt.

Kurt turned the hot water on in the sink, his back to her.

"I've been looking online. There are some packages for Disney World. You know, they have hotels right there at the park? You can even have breakfast with all the princesses," she said to Gracy. Gracy lifted her head from Trevor's chest, wiping her eyes with the back of her hand.

"Really, Mumma?"

"Of course, that might be too expensive, but sometimes there are deals. I'm going to keep looking."

Kurt stopped running the water and turned around. "Trevor, go run a bath for Gracy. Gracy, go get your jammies on."

Trevor lifted Gracy up obediently and walked with her down the hallway.

"What's going on?" Elsbeth asked. Kurt had been acting strange since he got home. She thought it was because of Trevor, but now she was beginning to think it was something else all together. Something bad.

"I'm gonna be working a couple of night shifts at the 76 station."

"What?" she said.

"A second job."

Elsbeth felt her whole center getting hot.

"Only a few nights a week. Just through the summer."

"But we were going to take a vacation," she said, the hot center of her spreading to her limbs.

Kurt turned toward her, his face apologetic. "The kids will be out of school in a week, and we're going to need to pay to send them somewhere while you're working."

"You promised," she said, her breath like steam. She felt the words escape, hissing and then dissipating in the air before her face. Kurt didn't say anything. Her face flushed and tears pooled hot and heavy in her eyes.

But then she realized it had just been a dream all along. He'd just been humoring her stupid daydreams. *Of course* they weren't going anywhere. She'd been stupid to think otherwise.

"It's only temporary," he said, but nothing about this was temporary. This was just the way it was, the way it always had been, the way it would always be.

At the Walgreens that weekend, Elsbeth wandered the aisles aimlessly. She'd left the house before anybody else was even up. Kurt had worked his first shift at the 76 the night before, crawling into bed, smelling like gasoline, at seven thirty in the morning. She hadn't been able to get back to sleep, and so she left.

She never went shopping at Walgreens without Gracy. She knew it was stupid. She knew that she was asking to get caught. But after wandering the housewares aisle, she found herself drawn to the sunscreen display that had been up since Memorial Day. She lifted each bottle to her nose, inhaling the scent of coconuts. She snapped the cap off an aerosol can and pressed her finger hard on the trigger. The spray made her nose sting and eyes water. She squeezed her eyes shut and thought about the beach, about the ocean, about the sun. Then she opened her eyes, glanced quickly around to make sure no one was watching and pocketed a stick of Banana Boat sunscreen for baby faces. When she looked up again, the checker girl, the one who'd had the baby, was standing there, staring at her.

Elsbeth smiled at her, wondering if the girl could see her heart beating through her T-shirt.

"Are you finding everything okay?" the girl said, accusingly.

Elsbeth nodded, suddenly wanting the girl to say something. Willing her to say something. Willing her to call her out.

But the girl just kept standing there, hands on her hips, staring at Elsbeth's pocketbook.

Elsbeth felt light-headed. High. *Do it. You caught me. Say something.* She picked up a stick identical to the one she had pocketed, and studied it. SPF 50.

The girl's eyes widened, but she was silent.

They stood like this for so long Elsbeth felt like she might pass out. Elsbeth looked her right in the eyes. Unflinching.

"Well, you just let me know if I can help," the girl finally said and walked away, shaking her head.

Something about this pissed Elsbeth off. Her acting like she was any better than Elsbeth. She reached angrily into her pocketbook, took out the stolen sunscreen, and placed it back on the shelf. Her hands tingled and her head pounded. She left the store without buying anything. She had to sit in her car for ten minutes before her leg stopped shaking enough that she could press the clutch and hold it long enough to get the goddamned thing started.

On the morning of graduation, Crystal stood in the shower, letting the hot water beat against her face. When she opened her eyes, everything was blurry, like looking through her mother's eyeglasses when she was a little girl. When her vision cleared, she touched the tender spot, the secret spot at her hip.

The woman at the shop in Montpelier hadn't asked about the stretch marks, the red rivers that ran across her belly. She simply had Crystal lie down in her panties on the table that reminded her of the OB / GYN's office and asked her where exactly she wanted the tattoo. An hour later, she had walked out of the shop with a bandage at her hip and found Angie sitting on a bench out in front of the art store, sketching in a new sketchpad. She'd thought about how powerful a few simple brush strokes could be, about indelibility, about permanence.

Now the feathery script was healed: the secret name embroidered on her skin. She sat on the edge of her bed in her underwear, traced the calligraphy with her fingers, and looked out the window at an angry sky. Angie came in and sat down next to her, leaning her head against her shoulder.

"Hey," Angie said. "You okay?" She touched Crystal's arm, and it felt like a shock. When they were little they used to tear through the carpeted living room in the winter making sparks. Crystal used to think this was something only she and Angie could do. That it was like a super power.

She wondered if the Stones would adopt other children, if her baby would ever have a sister. She imagined her running through the labyrinth of that house, slippery socks on hardwood floors. She dreamed of pigtails and dress-up and the little girl watching Mrs. Stone do her makeup in the mirror. She thought about her legs swinging under the table at dinner, about birthday cakes and backyard parties. School dances and soccer games and dance recitals. *Graduations.* The skin at her hip pulsed with pain. This terrible call and response. Every thought of the baby made her body wince.

"Yeah. I'm fine. Is Dad still downstairs waiting?"

Angie nodded. "He's so excited."

She'd wanted to skip the graduation ceremonies; she had pleaded with her mother to understand, but she was still making her go. "It'll kill your father if you miss it," she said. Her father's wishes clearly trumped any sliver of compassion her mother might have. And so she put on the rented cap and gown, bobby-pinning the cap to her head.

"Come on, come on," he said, grinning stupidly, his camera in one hand and his camcorder in the other. He ushered her out to the front yard and made her stand in front of the giant maple tree where he'd taken a picture of her and Angie on the first day of school every year since kindergarten. In the photos she always held a sign with her grade on it. After about the sixth grade, she'd grimaced in every shot. *7, 8, 9, 10* . . . "Here you go, now don't look so glum," he said, and handed her a sign that said CLASS OF 2010! "Say Limburger!" he said, fiddling with the camera lens, her mother fussing with her hair.

She was ready to get in line and get it over with, ready to walk down the paved walkways, littered with cherry blossoms, to the football field where there was a makeshift stage assembled. Ready to get her diploma and get on with her life, whatever that meant. But the sky was ominous, dark and thundery, and it was already ninety degrees at only ten o'clock in the morning. It was clear the outdoor ceremony wasn't going to happen, and something about this break in tradition seemed fitting somehow. Nothing was going the way it was expected.

The principal announced over the loudspeaker in the cafeteria where they had all been herded that the ceremonies would be moved to the ice arena across the road from the school. Mrs. Noyes, the PTA president, with her cotton candy hair and cotton candy breath and her cotton candy dress, lined them up alphabetically and then they waited as the ice arena across the street filled with proud parents and grandparents and siblings. Finally, Mrs. Noyes made them follow her in a winding line, leading them like a caterpillar rope of preschoolers, making them look both ways before crossing the road as if they weren't all at an event celebrating their entrance into adulthood.

Inside the ice arena, it was even more suffocating and oppressive than it had been in the cafeteria. Crystal could see Angie and her parents sitting near the stage in the very front row. They'd taken out a huge ad (*Let the McDonalds Sell Your House!*) in the graduation program in exchange for front-row seats. "You scratch my back," her father had said, "and I'll scratch yours."

"Hey, Cryssy," Ty said softly. The hairs on the back of her neck and on her arms stood up.

He was standing behind her in line. She'd ignored him the best she could while everyone was hustling to get into the right spots and then as they inched their way from the cafeteria to the ice arena. But now he was talking to her. She couldn't pretend like she didn't hear him; they were smushed together too tight, she could practically feel his breath on her neck.

She turned around to look at him. His mortarboard sat crookedly on his head, his trademark flop of brown hair peeking out and covering one eye. He smiled that familiar coy smile, and for a minute, she just wanted to forgive him. To reach for his hand and squeeze it and say, "It's okay."

But instead she just nodded and said, "Hey."

"So I never found out where you were going to school," he said. "I heard you were going to UVM?"

"Yeah," she said. "What about you? You got into Middlebury, right?" Middlebury. Their big plan to go to school close to each other. Like a forgotten vegetable in the fridge, rotten now. She almost reeled from the stink of everything gone so slowly and perfectly bad.

"Actually, I'll be at UC Berkeley," he said.

"Berkeley?" She felt her throat thicken. In all the years she'd known him, he'd not once mentioned California. It was the same as if he'd said he was going to Alaska for college. To the moon. "You've wanted to go to Middlebury for, like, forever," she said. How in the world did she not hear about this?

He shrugged and straightened his cap. "My mom got a full-time faculty gig, *finally,* in San Diego. That means I get tuition free at any UC school."

"Oh," she said, feeling sweat rolling down her sides under her gown. Her head aching, her heart aching. "So your whole family's moving to *California?*"

"Well, yeah. I totally thought you knew. Your mom and dad are selling our house," he said. "They didn't tell you?"

They hadn't said a word. She glanced across the sea of people and located her mom and dad in the crowd. Crystal was hot now, steaming, and pissed off. They really thought that if they just pretended like none of this had happened, then they could undo it. That if they willed Ty out of her life, he would disappear. And they were right. Ty and his entire family *were* just disappearing. For good. Like nothing ever happened.

She thought about his family. About the afternoons she had spent with his mother in their kitchen, about the cracked blue Congoleum and her chipped Fiestaware bowls. She thought about Dizzy with her spy kit and the baby, Squirrel, stuffing things in her mouth. She thought about the basement puppet shows and all the bottles stuffed with notes she and Ty had set sail on the river. She thought about lying on the trampoline in his backyard, holding hands, looking up at the stars. She thought about his bed. The sheets worn so soft they felt like skin.

It was so hot in the arena, she could barely breathe. "When do you . . ."

"Lena and I broke up," he said, his words tumbling over hers. "In case you didn't know."

She didn't know about California, but she did know about this. She'd heard about the breakup only minutes after it happened, Marcy Madden delivering the news like some wretched present.

"Yeah, I heard." She nodded, trying not to cry.

"It was kind of stupid," he said.

"Yeah," she agreed, not knowing whether he was talking about dating Lena, or *everything* he'd done (and not done) in the last six months.

They sat next to each other in the uncomfortable metal folding chairs. She was sweating so badly, the polyester gown was making a sort of furnace. Everyone was using their programs as fans. You'd think in an ice arena they could make it a little bit cooler. The Zamboni looked like a metallic dinosaur parked at the edge of it all. The commencement speaker was some old guy, an alumnus from like a hundred years ago, who wrote a book about thermodynamics or something. Totally dull. And then, finally, they were being called up on the stage one by one.

"Crystal McDonald," the principal said, and she took a deep breath. There were a few cheers. She could see her mother and father grinning and nodding in the front row. Her mother was dressed in the red blazer she always wore for open houses; she had one immediately following the ceremony and wouldn't be joining them for the nice dinner out her father had promised.

When she got back to her seat, clutching the rolled-up diploma, she was suddenly absolutely overwhelmed with emotion. She hadn't planned on this, hadn't planned on feeling much of anything besides relief. She wouldn't have to go to school anymore. She wouldn't have to dash into the girls' room every time she saw Ty coming down the hall. She wouldn't have to spend her entire day avoiding confrontations. It was over now. *California.* He was leaving, and chances were, she would never see him again.

"You know, you could come out and visit me sometime," Ty

said, and Crystal felt her stomach clench. "Like during spring break or something?"

She turned to look at him in disbelief. So now that Lena was out of the picture, he was suddenly interested in salvaging whatever it was they had ever had? Her eyes filled with tears at his audacity, at his stupidity. She wanted to say something that would let him know how much he'd hurt her. Something that would hurt him. But words failed her. They tangled together like knotted shoestrings in her mind, so she said nothing.

They both stared straight ahead for the rest of the ceremony, as everyone with last names from N–Z got their diplomas. It was raining hard outside now; it pounded against the metal roof of the arena. When the principal said, "Congratulations to the Class of 2010!" and everyone threw their mortarboards into the air, she and Ty looked at each other before yanking their caps off. Just briefly, but long enough to make that empty place ache with pain.

Normally, after the ceremony, people would gather outside for pictures, but the rain was coming down so hard now, everyone just found their families and ran for their cars. She lost Ty as soon as they exited the arena. It took her almost ten minutes before she found her parents. By the time her dad pulled the car around for her, she was drenched, her mascara running down her cheeks. But at least nobody knew she was crying. It could have just been the rain.

LAST SUMMER

On June thirtieth, Kurt peered toward Pop's house, at the rav-
aged edges of the yard. It looked barren, stripped. Like a
victim of some violent act. Pillaged. It had been raining nearly
every day, and the driveway was just a rushing river of mud and
gravel and debris. For two weeks he and Maury had spent every
spare minute working on cleaning up the yard and making the
repairs outlined in the notice from the county. Maury had called
in a favor from a contractor friend and gotten an industrial-sized
Dumpster for the week. It was brimming with refuse now, completely full. It sat in Pop's desolate yard like a monster with its
mouth hanging open.

Beal had watched the shop for a few extra hours each day,
keeping things going, happy for the additional work. He talked
about wanting more hours now that the twins were here. His
wife hadn't been able to get the hang of breast-feeding, and for-
mula was costing them a fortune. It made Kurt feel awful, because as soon as this business with Pop was taken care of, he was
actually going to have to cut back Beal's hours. Kurt was dreading
that conversation, but he had no choice; taking over Beal's hours
himself could make the difference between making the new
mortgage or not. Even with the added income from the night
shifts at the 76, they were still coming up short now that the kids
were out of school. They'd had to dish out four hundred dollars
so the kids could be at swim camp every morning while Elsbeth
worked. Four hundred dollars he was going to have to come up

with by the time that first balloon payment came on August first. He tried to put it out of his mind, but it was nearly impossible.

Kurt had come back to Pop's today to be there when the inspectors returned with their clipboards and their checklists. He was pretty sure he and Maury had taken care of all of the infractions, but you never knew. While the outside had mostly been cleared, the dead cars and old trailers towed to the yard, the trash and debris thrown away, the inside of the house was still packed solid. Pop hadn't let them throw away anything but obvious garbage. He'd refused to get rid of pots and pans and radios and ratty paperback books. He'd gone into a rage about a collection of coffeemakers and toasters Kurt found underneath the kitchen sink when they were repairing a leak.

"This is gonna kill him," Maury had said, shaking his head.

Kurt had thrown up his hands. "No, living in a rat-infested *house* is going to kill him. Whatever that stuff growing up through the bathroom floors is, is going to kill him. The fucking exposed wires and the rotten drywall are going to kill him."

Now Pop sat on the front porch on a metal folding chair, a drink in his lap. It was ten A.M. He stood up and started to walk into the house, listing, righting himself by grabbing onto the doorway. Kurt didn't know whether it was his leg or the drink at fault.

"Pop, I think we should at least get the kitchen table cleared off before they come. So they've got some place to sit if they need to."

"No more!" Pop hollered, swaying like he was on a ship.

"We don't have a choice, Pop. They will take your house away. They'll take all this *stuff* away."

"I am a goddamn decorated veteran. I served my country." Pop looked skinnier than usual: his belt pulled tighter, the waistband gapped. He was unshaven, the few hairs left on his head sticking up. His eyes were glassy and unfocused. His face was furious, red. "Last I knew, this was a free country." He went into the house, the screen door slamming behind him.

The inspectors pulled up then, one white county car and then another. Kurt was loading up the truck with some stuff he thought he could sell at the salvage yard: some old starters and car stereos, a half dozen steering wheels. He'd assured Pop he wouldn't throw any of it away and that he'd write him a check for anything that sold.

Irene Killjoy pulled up behind the inspectors and got out of her car, straightening her skirt. "Well, let's see what sort of progress we've made, now shall we?"

Two hours later, the inspectors wordlessly got into their cars and took off.

"Well?" Kurt asked Irene. Pop, who had come and observed the inspection angrily but, thankfully, silently had now gone back into the house, slamming the door shut and locking it behind him.

"It looks like the major infractions have been taken care of," she said. "Legally, the house is now up to code. However, Mr. Kennedy, from my experience, this is just a temporary fix." She shook her head sadly, and Kurt felt his shoulders tense. "With all due respect, your father has an *illness*. Trust me, I've seen this before. The stuff will come back. He'll just fill up all that empty space. He doesn't need a housekeeper; he needs a mental-health professional. I can suggest a wonderful social worker who can work with him on his hoarding issues . . ."

"Hold on," Kurt said, trying to breathe deeply so he would not lose his temper. "The house passed the inspection, correct?"

"Well, yes. For now. But I'm fairly certain there is a deeper problem here," she said.

"Everything is up to code now. I think it is time for you to get off my father's property." Kurt raised his chin, gesturing toward her car.

She sighed, looking at him in the same way that Trevor's principal did. As if he were someone to pity. Some sad sorry fucker. He knew it was like putting a Band-Aid on a ruptured artery, but Jesus, what else could he do?

"Let me see you to your car," he said, grinding his back molars together and putting his palm against her back, pushing gently.

"Of course," she said and awkwardly navigated a string of mud puddles to her car.

"We'd like to follow up with your father at the end of the summer. Unless I receive any complaints sooner."

"There won't be any need for a follow-up," Kurt said.

Irene Killjoy got in her car and started her engine. But when she tried to back out, her car spun out in the mud.

"Oh Jesus Christ," Kurt said and went to the car.

She rolled down the window and smiled. "Would you mind giving me a little nudge?" Kurt got behind the car and pushed as she revved the engine, but as her tires finally gained enough traction to move forward, the mud was already flying, splattering his jeans. Pop wouldn't answer the door. He was probably passed out by now. He'd gone through half the bottle of Seagram's while the inspectors negotiated the piles of stuff in his house. Kurt scratched a note on an old receipt in his pocket and stuck it with the county's inspection pass notice to his window. *I'll come by Friday night—K.*

Trevor liked to swim. In the water, his body never betrayed him like it did when he was doing something as simple as walking down the halls at school. In the water, he felt coordinated and weightless, fluid. *Free.* He liked the mix of cold water and hot sun, the way the water filled up his ears, numbing his senses. He preferred to swim in natural bodies of water—ponds and rivers and lakes—but the swimming pool was the next best thing. So when his father told him that he and Gracy would be in swim camp all summer, he'd been happy.

It was finally summer. He didn't have to think about Mrs. Cross or Ethan and Mike or homework or *anything* until September. He couldn't help but think of Mrs. D. though, and every time he did, it made him feel like he couldn't breathe. He asked Angie if she'd heard anything, but she hadn't; all he knew was that she hadn't come back to school.

He kept taking pictures, but knowing he had no one to show them to made him feel untied somehow, unraveled. He collected all the rolls of undeveloped film in his underwear drawer; the spent rolls of film were like little capsules, little treasure chests for which he had no key. His last commission check from the yard wasn't enough to pay to process all of them, and he chose to spend what was left on more film.

He'd finished the inventory sheets at the yard last week. He'd also helped his dad upload the remaining pictures to eBay. The increase in business wasn't what his dad probably hoped for, but they had sold a few things so far: a starter, a catalytic converter, a

steering wheel for a '69 Chevelle. Trevor knew things weren't
going well at the shop. He could read the worry in his father's
face. He'd cut Beal's shifts back to just a couple of days a week
now, and Beal had suddenly gone from friendly and funny to
sullen and irritable. Trevor figured his dad would need his help
even more now with Beal only there half-time, but instead he
said that Trevor could have his summer off as long as he stayed
out of trouble. That wouldn't be hard with both Ethan and Mike
on the all-star team for baseball; their summers would be occupied with games and travel. If he was lucky, he might make it a
whole summer without having to deal with them.

The first week of swim camp was great. He and Gracy rode
into town with his mom on her way to work, and she dropped
them off at the pool, giving them each a dollar to get a soda or an
ice cream after they were done. Gracy went to the shallow end
where all the other little kids were, and Trevor went to the deep
end. There were only four kids in his class, and two of them were
eighth-grade girls, Savannah and Kylie, he sort of knew from
school. They didn't talk to him, but they weren't mean either. The
other boy was Rudy Hauser, a sixth grader who had just moved
to town. Their teacher was a college girl named Lisa who had
shaggy red hair and freckles everywhere. She wore a whistle
around her neck and had a tattoo of a four-leaf clover on her
ankle.

Every morning, they swam laps to warm up, and then she had
them work on a particular stroke for the next hour. Trevor liked
the backstroke the best, because then he didn't need to think
about breathing. The hour always went fast, and then they got to
take their break at eleven. Afterward they worked on their turns
or diving until it was time to go. Sometimes they had races, and
Trevor always won. When the session was over at noon, he picked
Gracy up from the kiddie end of the pool and they went to the
snack shack for Popsicles or French fries. Their mom picked
them up at twelve thirty, and then they went back to the house,
where he usually just changed out of his wet clothes and took off

for the woods. Trevor spent every afternoon that first week walking in the woods taking pictures, hanging out in the caboose. He'd cleaned it up, brought some stuff from home (some photo books and comic books and an old beanbag chair). He took a pair of scissors and cut out his favorite photos from the Lewis Carroll book Mrs. D. gave him and hung the pictures on the wall: *Alice as Beggar Girl, Agnes Grace Weld as Little Red Riding Hood, Beatrice in fancy dress.* The few pictures he had of his own looked amateurish in comparison, but he hung them up anyway. The caboose was his own Fortress of Solitude. He would have been happy if summer never ended.

But the second week of swim camp, everything changed.

Trevor knew as soon as they showed the kid at the gate their laminated camp passes that something was different. He could feel it. He walked Gracy over to her class and pulled her Sleeping Beauty towel out of his backpack. The towel was threadbare and Sleeping Beauty's eyes had worn off, making her look sort of creepy. He pulled his own towel out and went to the locker room and hung his backpack on a hook in an empty locker, stuffing his T-shirt and sneakers inside. Somebody else was in the locker room; he could see their feet underneath the bathroom stall door. He hurried into the shower to rinse off and then walked back outside to the pool.

"Check it out," a voice behind him said. "Is Bigfoot learning to swim?"

Trevor didn't turn around. He didn't have to. It was Mike Wheelock. Right behind him, breathing down his neck. He ignored Mike and walked out of the locker room to the end of the pool where, waiting for him at the deep end, was Ethan Sweeney and another kid from the baseball team. Ethan was in the water, flicking water at Savannah and Kylie, who were sitting on the edge of the pool. They were giggling, "Stop!" Just his luck, it looked like their baseball team was cut from playoffs early, and now here they were here. Of course.

Trevor's whole body was covered in goose bumps from the

cold shower. He rubbed his arms up and down and sat down next to Rudy, who watched as Mike swaggered to the pool's edge.

"What are *you* looking at?" Mike said to Rudy.

Rudy was smaller than Trevor, with a perpetually runny nose and acne. He knew it was awful, but he couldn't help entertaining the hope that Rudy might just become a new target for Ethan and Mike, take the burden off him, even just for a while.

Mike cannonballed into the pool, getting everyone at the edge wet, the two girls squealing but not really upset. When he came up for air he high-fived Ethan in the water. Trevor's eyes stung with chlorine. The air suddenly smelled dank and musty. Rotten. He was grateful when Lisa finally showed up and had them all get into the water to do laps. Today was the breaststroke, and he glided through the water.

"Thought you might be here for *synchronized* swimming lessons," Ethan said as he climbed up the ladder after he was finished with his laps. *"Water ballet?"*

"Just leave me alone," Trevor said and moved to the far side of the pool.

"Just leave me alone," Ethan mocked.

"Okay, that's enough, boys," Lisa said, gently knocking Ethan in the back of the head.

When it was time to practice turns, Lisa had them all line up next to each other. Trevor swam the length of the pool as fast as he could, and when he got to the end, he executed his turn, feeling that strange and wonderful feeling of not knowing which way is up or down. Then something brushed against him. Legs. He was tangled up with someone else. He burst, disoriented, to the surface of the water, struggling for air.

"Hey, pervert!" Ethan Sweeney screamed in his face. "Homo perv."

Mike swam up to them then, pushing his chest out. "What'd he do?"

Trevor wiped the chlorine out of his eyes. He searched frantically for Lisa, who was at the opposite end of the pool, in the water, helping the other new kid with his turn.

"He tried to *molest* me," Ethan said, smirking. His face was sunburned, his hair and eyes both red. "He had a total boner."

"Shut up! You ran into me," Trevor said, tasting metal in his throat, acrid. Bitter.

"Yeah, right," Ethan said, sneering.

Trevor's legs were suddenly weak; he was having a hard time treading water.

"Guess since your old-lady girlfriend got sick, you're lonely," Mike said, laughing. "Sorry to hear about Mrs. D. Guess now you're a full-on faggot."

Trevor felt like he was drowning.

"What's the problem over here, boys?" Lisa asked. She had swum over to them. She bobbed up and down in the water like a toy.

"No problem." Mike smiled.

"Okay then, make your way back to the other side. We're almost out of time. You too, Ethan." She dipped under the water then and disappeared like a minnow at the bottom of a lake.

Mike flicked his tongue in and out of his mouth, like some thick slug, mock making out with her.

"That's my fucking sister, asshole!" Ethan said and pushed Mike's head under the water.

His sister. Trevor let himself slip under the water, sinking slowly to the bottom of the pool, and then kicked off against the wall, swimming as fast as he could to the other side.

At home that afternoon, he told his mother he was going to go walk in the woods. She was at the kitchen table painting Gracy's fingernails. The whole room smelled like chemicals, clean but poisonous. Gracy looked up at him and smiled. "Can I come with you?" she asked, and he saw his mother stiffen. Not so much that anybody would notice, but Trevor did. He knew the way her shoulders looked when she didn't like an idea. He knew the way her mouth twitched, her eyes scrunched into slits. She didn't trust him at all anymore, not since he took off and scared her half to death. Since he threw his camera.

"Not today, Gracy," he said, so his mother wouldn't have to.

"Be back by supper," his mom said without looking up from the delicate work of painting Gracy's miniature nails.

The first thing Trevor needed to do was to replace the caboose's windows, though not with glass. What he needed was plywood, four or five sheets that he could use to keep out the light. So no one could see in. Or out.

He went to the shed and started to rummage through the piles of stuff they'd transported over from Pop's house. He dug through the rubble, looking for something that might work. Finally, he found a stack of sheet metal that looked about the right size. He was pretty sure his dad wouldn't mind, but then thought maybe he should call him anyway just to check. He was doing his best to stay on his dad's good side. He went back into the kitchen and grabbed the phone from the counter.

"Look at my fingernails, Trevor!" Gracy said, hopping down from her chair and wriggling her fingers in his face. "Do you want me to paint yours?"

"No thanks, Gracy," he said.

"Thought you were headed to the woods," his mom said.

"I forgot something." He brought the phone outside and dialed the shop. He could picture his dad at the counter, tapping away at the adding machine, the tape like a snake's tongue, flicking out of the machine.

"Dad?" he said. "I found some sheet metal. Can I have it?"

"What for?" he asked.

Trevor had anticipated the question but wasn't sure if his story would be enough to convince his father. "I'm going to build something," he said. "A tree house or something."

His father had promised him a few years ago that he'd build him a tree house in the backyard. There used to be a big oak tree that would have been perfect, but during a big summer storm it fell over and crushed the garage roof. They hadn't talked about the tree house after that.

"Aren't you a little old for that now?" Kurt asked.

Trevor shrugged but didn't answer.

"I don't care," his father said. "Go ahead, but don't cut yourself."

"Thanks," Trevor said and returned the phone to its cradle in the kitchen. He loaded the pieces into his dad's wheelbarrow. He'd need some metal screws too. The Makita. Some electrical tape or weather stripping. He returned to the shed and dug through the coffee cans of hardware that littered the wooden worktable, taking what he needed and started loading it into the wheel barrow.

He pushed it through the pasture behind the house, into the woods, and all the way to the river, navigating bushes and trees and upturned roots along the way. Then he parked it at the river's edge and made three trips up the trestle with all of his supplies to the caboose.

Inside, the light coming through the cracked windows was green, as though he were submerged underwater. As if the caboose were at the bottom of a swimming pool. He lingered in that aquatic light, trying not to think about what had happened at the pool. Trying not to think about the way his whole body had ached.

Homo perv. He had a total boner. He tried to remember what his body had felt when Ethan touched him. He couldn't recollect anything now but the disorientation of being upside down in the water. Sometimes, he felt his body stiffen despite himself; it didn't take much. It wasn't his fault, though; there wasn't anything he could do to control it. He didn't think so, but was it possible he'd actually had a hard-on? And what if he did have one? Did that make him what they said? Was he really queer?

He shook his head, tears streaming down his cheeks. He wiped them away with his shirt sleeve, rubbing the snot from under his nose afterward. Then he reached for the first piece of sheet metal and got to work.

When Twig asked Elsbeth what she and Kurt were doing for the Fourth of July, Elsbeth had shrugged. Most of the time they grilled burgers in the backyard, had some friends over, and then Kurt and his buddies would set off firecrackers in the field behind the house. But now that Kurt was working so much, they hadn't bothered to make any plans. The yard was closed for the holiday, though, so at least he had one day off. She thought she might convince him to go to Twig's party, to have some fun for a change.

"Twig's having a party up at Gormlaith this afternoon. Then fireworks tonight. You wanna come?"

"Jesus, El. I'm exhausted. I haven't had a good night's sleep in weeks. I just need to catch up a little."

Elsbeth sighed. The bed was empty three nights a week now, and Kurt was a walking zombie. When she spoke to him, she was pretty sure he was only pretending to hear her most of the time. Nodding, his eyes glazed over. She knew he was tired, but for Christ's sake.

"You go," Kurt said, rubbing the back of his neck. "Take the kids. Have fun."

"Trevor's not going to want to come without you," she said.

Trevor wasn't any better than Kurt. Both of them moping around. Eyes glassy and sad. It was depressing. So they weren't going to Disney World—it was still *summer*. Couldn't they at least enjoy that while it lasted?

"I just really need to get some sleep, El."

"Fine," she said. "You and Trevor stay here. Take a *nap*. I'll take Gracy."

Elsbeth spent the rest of the morning making food for the picnic. She boiled potatoes for salad, made deviled eggs freckled with paprika. She played the radio loudly and sang along. Gracy helped her make brownies, and they sat together on the back steps licking the bowl, watching the hummingbirds buzz against the red plastic feeder. Trevor took off for the woods again, and Kurt went back to bed.

It was a beautiful sunny day. Not too hot. She tried to focus on the sunshine.

She packed everything up into a picnic basket and tiptoed into the bedroom to grab her new suit, careful not to wake Kurt, and then ducked into the bathroom to try it on. It had arrived, along with all the other things she ordered a couple of weeks ago. She hadn't tried it on yet, though, because all those packages just made her sad. She knew she should send them all back, get the charges taken off the credit card. She'd hidden the FedEx boxes and UPS envelopes in the back of her closet.

She slipped the suit out of the plastic it was wrapped in and held the pieces up. She wriggled out of her jeans and T-shirt, unhooking her bra and letting it fall to the floor as well. She pulled the top on and studied her reflection in the mirror. Definitely no Victoria's Secret model, but she looked pretty good for thirty. She slipped the suit off again and pulled the paper panty liner out. She wouldn't be returning this one.

"I'll be back after the fireworks," she said to Kurt as she buckled Gracy into her booster. Kurt stood in the driveway, his eyes red and shadowed, his hair a mess. "Go back to bed. You look like hell," she said and immediately regretted it.

"Jeez, thanks," he said.

"Sorry. But seriously, get some sleep. I left some potato salad, and there are some burgers in the freezer for supper." She put the picnic basket on the floor and shut the car door. As they backed out of the driveway, her spirits were lifted with every inch they drove away from the house.

Gormlaith was about a forty-five-minute drive from Two Rivers. Twig's family had a camp up there. They had a dock and a motorboat and water skis. She'd only been there a couple of times, and never for the Fourth of July. She was excited. It was the first time she'd looked forward to something since Kurt squashed their plans for a vacation. Elsbeth also missed Twig; she hadn't really seen her since the night she colored Elsbeth's hair. They'd communicated exclusively through sticky notes on the mirror.

Hey, girlfriend! What's new?

Date tonight. Nothing to WEAR!

I remember dates. LOL.

HUNGOVER.

Try Vitamin B.

She hadn't heard back from Wilder, which was just as well, even though it left her feeling a hollow pang of something unfinished. He'd most likely gone back to Florida by now. If he was looking to write a whole book about Two Rivers, he'd probably been pretty disappointed with what the town to offer. *She'd* only been able to offer him a little bit about the town's history: just a couple of anecdotes and the stuff she'd learned in grade school. He'd wanted to know more about the beauty parlor, but she didn't really know much of anything. Babette would have been able to help him: the real Babette. It was good he was gone; because she could hardly pretend she was Babette now the *real* Babette was back from Colorado. Elsbeth had been stupid. Impulsive and stupid. She thought about him flying back to Florida, looking over the notes he'd scratched in his notebook while they talked. He'd come for answers and instead just got some silly woman pretending to be somebody she wasn't.

She pulled into the driveway at Twig's camp, and there were already about a half dozen cars parked in the driveway and all along the edge of the road. She hadn't expected so many people.

She recognized Mireya's car right away. Mireya was Twig's baby sister. Twig always had wild stories about her. She'd hitchhiked by herself to California during Easter break when she just fifteen. She got all the way to LA before their parents figured out where she'd gone. Mireya drove an electric blue Camaro; she waited tables at Luigi's and was the 2009 New England regional karaoke champion runner-up. Elsbeth was also pretty sure she'd gotten a boob job last year.

"Hi, Mookie!" Elsbeth said, bending down to pet Twig's rescued mutt, who sniffed her legs and begged for attention. Ollie, Twig's Italian greyhound, was barking behind the screen door.

"Ollie, shut *up! Sorry!*" Twig hollered, coming to the door. "Hey, girls!" She rushed down the steps in her bikini, giving Elsbeth a big hug. Elsbeth could feel her ribs in her back. She'd been on this cabbage soup diet for two weeks already, and it seemed to be working. Twig took the picnic stuff and the beer Elsbeth had picked up at Hudson's on the way. "Oh my God, I am so excited for your potato salad. If I ever see another bowl of cabbage soup, I'll kill myself," she said.

Gracy giggled as Mookie smothered her with kisses, almost knocking her over with her giant paws.

"Mookie, down!" Gracy reprimanded, still laughing even as she fell backward.

"Come on in! I've got appletinis." Twig winked and grabbed Elsbeth's arm.

There were only a couple of people inside the camp: a few women Elsbeth didn't know gathered around the kitchen counter, a couple of guys playing pool at a pool table in the middle of the main room. Twig grabbed two keg cups, poured them drinks from a plastic pitcher, and handed one to Elsbeth. Then she led the way through the camp, wriggling her way past the guy who was lining up his shot, "Excuse me!" and through the living room to the sun porch.

The whole cabin was so nice, exposed beams and hardwood floors, but the sun porch was the best. It was all windows, a whole wall of glass, through which you could see out over the spacious lawn to the lake. Elsbeth looked out the window, shielding her eyes against the glare of the sun. There were about twenty people outside, playing badminton on the lawn, lounging on beach chairs on the dock, and surrounding the gas grill. The smoke and smell of barbeque wafted up through the open windows.

"Gracy, you wanna go swimming?" Twig asked. "I've got some floaties, some noodles?"

"I already know how to swim," Gracy said. "I moved up to Dolphins already. I can hold my breath for a really long time."

"Wow!" Twig said. "Will you show me?"

"First let's get some sunscreen on, sweetie," Elsbeth said, reaching into her bag for the aerosol can of SPF 50, wishing she hadn't put back the stolen stick of sunscreen at Walgreens. It would have been good for her nose and cheeks. But remembering the way the check-out girl had looked at her made her skin prickle.

Outside, Gracy stripped out of her clothes; she was wearing her old yellow swimsuit underneath, and she stood with her arms and legs spread as Elsbeth coated her with a layer of sunscreen. The aerosol burned Elsbeth's nose. The suit was too small, and something about this reignited her frustration with Kurt. Gracy should have clothes that fit. It didn't matter so much now, but when she got older the other kids would notice. Make fun. They'd watched that happen with Trevor already, and the idea of Gracy being teased for something they could prevent made her hot.

"Are there any other kids here?" Gracy asked.

"Not yet, but there will be later for the fireworks," Twig said. "Where's your brother and daddy today?"

Elsbeth felt her shoulders stiffen. "At home."

"How's Kurt?" Twig asked.

"How should I know?" Elsbeth snapped. "I never see him anymore."

Sometimes with Twig, Elsbeth felt like all she did was bitch. She hated that she was always complaining. Twig never had much of anything to complain about. And even though Twig was a great listener, Elsbeth always seemed to feel worse after talking to her.

"I saw him at the 76 the other night. He looked dog-tired," Twig said, squeezing her arm sympathetically. "It must be real hard having him gone so much."

Elsbeth didn't like to be pitied. "Yeah, but it's totally temporary. We're just saving up for a real vacation."

As soon as Elsbeth finished rubbing the sunscreen into Gracy's shoulders, Gracy grabbed Elsbeth's hand. "Come watch me swim!"

"Okay, okay." She laughed. She and Twig carried their drinks down to the water's edge and found a couple of free lawn chairs at the grassy shore. Gracy waded into the water, shivering.

Elsbeth sat down, sipping on the sweet green cocktail. Twig sat down next to her and clinked her cup. "Cheers." The vodka was like liquid sunshine in her throat.

When the drinks were gone and Elsbeth was feeling warm and pleasant both inside and out, Twig said. "Let's go in!"

Elsbeth unzipped her jeans and wriggled out of them, pulled her tank top off over her head. She felt suddenly shy in her new suit. Exposed.

"Cute suit! Victoria's Secret, right? I think I have that one in red," Twig said and then, as an afterthought, "But it looks *so* much better on you."

In the water, Elsbeth floated on her back, let the water fill her ears and stared up into the bright blue sky. The muffled sounds of the party felt far, far away. Everything: Kurt, Trevor. All of her problems seemed to drift away here. She helped Gracy swim out into the deeper water, holding on to her hands as Gracy kicked her feet behind her. They were light out here. Free. She wondered if swimming in the ocean was different. If the water was warmer;

if it was harder to stay afloat. When Gracy started to shiver, her lips trembling and blue, Elsbeth said, "Let's go get our towels. Take a break."

Back at the lawn chair, she wrapped Gracy up in her Sleeping Beauty towel like a burrito. She pulled her onto her lap and nuzzled her wet hair. "I love you, Gracy Bear," she said.

"I love you too, Mommy Bear," Gracy replied.

The sun quickly dried their skin.

"Hey there," a voice said.

Elsbeth looked up, but without her sunglasses, she had to shield her eyes to see who was speaking.

Wilder.

"Hey," she said, confused. What was he doing here? "What are you doing here?"

"I came into the shop looking for you the other day, and I spoke with *Babette.*" He was smirking, his hands shoved into his pockets.

Elsbeth felt her ears getting hot, her cheeks flushing with heat. She opened her mouth to explain, but nothing came out.

"She looked at me like I was a lunatic."

"I'm sorry," Elsbeth said, feeling mortified.

Wilder smirked and shrugged. "So I said to her, 'No, no, *Babette.* You know, beautiful girl with black hair? Dark eyes. About this tall.' " He motioned in the air with his hand; if she'd been standing, his palm would have been resting on the top of her head.

"Oh God," she said, shaking her head, realizing how insane he must have thought she was. *Beautiful girl.* "I am *so* embarrassed."

"You mind?" he asked, motioning to Twig's empty seat.

She shook her head, and he sat down.

"When I was a little kid, I used to pretend I was Batman. I got a costume for Halloween and I wouldn't wear anything else until after Christmas," he said.

She studied his face.

"Sometimes, it's more fun to be somebody else."

"I just . . . I didn't . . . ugh."

"Anyway, luckily, Tamara was there and she helped me figure it all out."

"Twig," Elsbeth said.

Wilder cocked his head.

"Her nickname's Twig. Nobody calls her Tamara." She didn't know why she said that. It was true, but it still felt mean-spirited. She looked out at the lake. Twig was executing a perfect dive from the floating dock about a hundred yards out.

"Well, anyway, *Twig* invited me today. She didn't tell me you'd be here," he grinned at her. "Just got lucky, I guess."

"I thought you'd be back in Florida already," Elsbeth said, looking toward the water, concentrating on anything other than his eyes.

"I leave next week."

"Oh," Elsbeth said but she didn't know whether to be happy or disappointed.

"I'm going to interview some mermaids at Weeki Wachee next. For my book. My stepmother used to work there."

"Mermaids?"

"It's a roadside attraction. With mermaids. You know, with tails instead of legs?"

She was aware suddenly of her legs. Of every hair she'd missed when she shaved that morning. Of the one purple bruise where she ran into the bumper of Jude's goddamned Lincoln, which Kurt had towed to their house the other day.

"And who's this little mermaid?" Wilder asked, extending his hand to Gracy.

Gracy scowled at him.

"It's a pleasure to meet you," he said. "Whoever you are."

Gracy shook her head, refusing his outstretched hand.

"Gracy, be polite," Elsbeth said.

"My daddy says for me never to talk to strangers," Gracy said, shaking her head.

"Wilder is not a *stranger,*" Elsbeth said, looking at Wilder apologetically.

"He's a stranger to *me,*" Gracy said, stubborn.

Elsbeth felt her whole body flush with vodka and heat. "I'm sorry," she said.

"No, she's right. She doesn't know me. Smart girl." Wilder lowered his hand.

Gracy crossed her arms against her chest. Elsbeth rolled her eyes and then immediately felt bad. Gracy was just doing what she'd been told to do. She was *six;* it wasn't her fault.

Twig came over then, wrapped up in a fluffy pink towel, and put her hand on Wilder's shoulder. "So you decided to come after all."

Elsbeth stiffened. She wondered what else Twig had said to Wilder, wondered why she hadn't bothered to tell Elsbeth that she'd been busted pretending to be Babette.

"I see you've met Princess Grace?" Twig said, smiling.

"I did," he said.

Gracy suddenly opened up, the scowl melting from her face as Twig tickled her.

"You need to meet my sister," she said to Wilder then. "I told her all about you. I think she ran to Hudson's for more beers, but she'll be back soon."

Elsbeth felt her heart sink and then her cheeks tingle with shame as Twig said, "Hey, can I steal him for a second? I need help getting the Jet Skis out of the boathouse."

"Sure," Elsbeth said and watched as Twig and Wilder walked down toward the water, Twig laughing and punching his shoulder playfully. So she'd invited him here to meet Mireya. Then why was she being such a goddamned flirt? She watched Twig's cabbage soup butt, her tanning bed tan, her perfect haircut. God, how could she feel such loathing for her best friend?

Elsbeth had a second appletini with her lunch and was feeling drowsy and content. Gracy had started to fall asleep on the lawn chair right after lunch, and Twig had shown Elsbeth to a quiet room inside the camp where she could put her down to nap. In the clean, peaceful room, Elsbeth considered lying down herself.

"I'll be outside when you wake up, honey," she whispered. "Or find Twig."

"Okay, Mumma," she'd said sleepily and pulled the blanket up to her chin.

Elsbeth went back outside where Mireya was organizing a game of horseshoes. Mireya, like Twig, was one of those women that men flocked to. *Like flies on horseshit,* Jude would say. Right now there were three men all vying for her attention, though Wilder wasn't anywhere to be seen; Elsbeth felt a guilty twinge of relief.

"Wanna play?" Mireya asked her.

"No, that's okay." Instead, Elsbeth walked down to the dock, which was empty of people now. She sat at the far end and dangled her feet in the cool water. She felt footsteps behind her, the dock shifting and rocking beneath her with each step.

"Hey, El! You wanna come with us? I'm going to take Wilder out to the island." Twig was tipsy. She could tell by her crooked smile. She had a six-pack of beer tucked under one arm and a couple of life preservers under the other. She tossed them into the boat that was moored to the dock and started to climb in. Elsbeth thought about Twig taking Wilder out to the island and felt a little awful pang, like a rusty fishhook, somewhere inside her chest. Twig had been drinking; who knew what she might do. Maybe Mireya hadn't been interested. Now he was fair game, at least in Twig's book. None of this should matter, but it did.

"Come on!" she said, reaching for Elsbeth's hand. She glanced at her watch. Gracy had been down for a half hour. She probably had another hour or so until she woke up. She probably shouldn't leave, but she felt herself nodding. "Sure, why not?"

The ride out to the island only took a couple of minutes in the motorboat. And Elsbeth was grateful for the noise of the motor. She didn't want to have to talk. She held on to her seat and closed her eyes against the wind, which stung her skin. She'd

probably gotten sunburned. Twig cut the engine as they got close
to the island. The sudden quiet was almost deafening. Elsbeth had
figured they'd circle the island and then return, but Twig was
steering the boat into a small cove, easing it in and throwing
down the anchor.

"You think it's really still here?" Twig asked, grabbing Wilder's
arm.

He shrugged. "I hope so."

"How long ago did he say he put it here?" she asked.

"God, back in the sixties. Decades ago."

"What are you guys talking about?" Elsbeth asked, her cu-
riosity piqued.

"A letter my father wrote. To Betsy, the girl from the photo at
the beauty parlor. You know, you kind of look like her," Wilder
said, studying Elsbeth's face.

She couldn't believe he'd noticed the resemblance too. As he
examined her, she felt herself becoming Betsy Parker in his gaze.

"He buried it inside some tree on this island."

"Why did he bury it?" Elsbeth asked.

Wilder climbed out of the boat. She studied his strong forearms, the sleeves of his white cotton button-down shirt rolled up
to the elbows.

"They were best friends," he said. "She didn't know how he
felt about her when they were kids. It was a *secret*." He smiled at
Elsbeth, and she felt her knees go soft. She tried to remember if
Kurt had ever written anything to her besides grocery lists. She
didn't think so.

"That's so romantic," Twig said, swooning.

"I'm sure it's probably disintegrated by now," he said. "If it's
still there at all. But it can't hurt to look."

They all got out of the boat and started walking through the
tangled brush of the small island. There were some rusted beer
cans, cigarette butts. Elsbeth suddenly thought about Jude, about
all of that debris, and that made her think of Kurt. Of what he'd

think if he saw her right now. She shook her head as if she could shake those thoughts loose.

She had no idea how Wilder expected to find anything in these thick woods, but all of a sudden he pointed and then rushed over to a large willow tree. It was split down the middle, like it had been struck by lightning. He searched all around the trunk of the tree and then, incredibly, pulled a piece of paper out of a deep crevice in the wood.

"Holy shit!" Twig said. "Is that it?"

"I don't know," he said, gingerly unfolding it.

"What does it say?" Elsbeth asked.

He studied it, and she watched as the paper crumbled in his fingers. Elsbeth felt suddenly heartbroken. Of course, it was a miracle that he'd found it at all, but now that he had, she wanted more than anything to know what it said. As it crumbled, she felt herself crumbling. Something inside her turning to ash.

"I can just make out her name," he said, peering at the faded letter. "That's it. Just *Dear Betsy.*"

As Wilder recounted the story of the accident for Twig, Elsbeth thought about Betsy Parker, about the baby she had inside her when she died. That poor baby growing up without a mother.

"Oh my God," Twig said. "That's the saddest story I ever heard."

Wilder nodded. "I thought I might be able to find this to give to my dad."

Elsbeth's throat swelled. She tried to imagine Trevor and Gracy without her. What would happen to them if *she* just disappeared?

"I need to get back," she said. "Gracy will be up from her nap any time now."

When they pulled up to the dock, she could see Mireya holding Gracy on her hip. Gracy's face was bright red and her cheeks were streaked with tears. Elsbeth scrambled out of the boat, feel-

ing the effects of that second cocktail and the sun. Trying to right
herself, she ran up the dock until she got to the shore. Her legs
felt wobbly, and she was nauseous. She wasn't sure whether it was
from the vodka or from the boat ride.

"Oh, honey," she said, reaching out for her. Gracy shook her
head and clung to Mireya, burying her face in her shoulder. So
much for stranger danger.

"Gracy," Elsbeth said sternly, feeling like somebody had
sucker punched her in the stomach. She pried her out of Mireya's
arms and squeezed her tight. She felt Gracy's body resist and
then, slowly, soften.

"She was crying. I hope it's okay I got her," Mireya said.

"It's fine. Thank you," she said, wishing Mireya would just
leave now.

"I had a bad dream, and I couldn't find you. Where were you,
Mumma?"

"I'm sorry, sweetie. I shouldn't have left," she said and started
to walk back up to the camp with Gracy snug on her hip, leaving
Mireya behind.

"Promise you won't leave me anymore," she said.

"Never ever," Elsbeth said, feeling like she might cry.

Down by the water she could see Twig lying down on a lawn
chair, Wilder sitting next to her. Mireya flitted down toward them
like a butterfly, then took his hand and pulled him up from the
chair. Elsbeth's stomach twisted and tightened as she watched
them walk to the water, holding hands. Acid rose in her throat as
Mireya glanced back up at her, smiling like she'd just won something. What a fool she'd been. What an idiot.

"Listen, sweetie. How about we go home?"

"No firecrackers?"

"I think Daddy has some sparklers," Elsbeth said, trying to
smile.

"Aren't those dangerous for kids?"

"I'll make sure you're safe," Elsbeth said.

★   ★   ★

Back at the house, Elsbeth found Kurt in the kitchen. She wanted to let him know, needed to let him know, how sorry she was. How confused she felt. How much she needed him. She went to him, hugged him, pulled back, and gave him a kiss.

"Have you been drinking?" he asked, pulling away from her, his eyes widening.

She caught her breath, raised her eyebrows, looking at him in disbelief. She'd expected him to hug her back, to hold her. "We had such a *great* time," she said, ignoring him. "It was gorgeous. We took the boat out, and Gracy had a root beer float. We went swimming."

"How much did you have?" he asked.

She couldn't believe he was interrogating her like this. "Just a couple. Jesus, it was hours ago."

"And you *drove?* What the hell were you thinking?" Kurt's voice was loud; he was *yelling* at her.

Elsbeth's eyes widened. "I am not drunk."

"I can smell it, El," he said, and she wondered if it was possible that he was right. They were pretty strong drinks, but she would never have gotten in the car if she didn't think she was okay.

"What if you'd gotten pulled over? Jesus. You had Gracy with you." He looked disgusted with her. This wasn't what she'd wanted at all. Maybe she should have just stayed at the lake. No one there was judging her. No one there was accusing her.

"Oh, so now I'm some sort of horrible mother?" she said, and then she remembered the terrified look on Gracy's face when she found her with Mireya. She thought about Trevor, about how he'd raged at her that afternoon.

Gracy was in the living room watching videos; she could hear Dora the Explorer singing, "Backpack, backpack." Elsbeth knew she should end this now, not let it escalate into something bigger than it needed to be.

"How was *your* day?" she asked, rubbing her temples, though she honestly didn't care anymore. She didn't even want to know.

Her forehead was tender to the touch. Burned. She felt like she might explode.

"Pretty damn awful," he said. "I spent the whole afternoon looking through Pop's boxes for some legal papers Pop thinks are in there. Nothing but trash."

Elsbeth looked past him, out the kitchen window.

"I think we should go away," she said to no one.

"El, please don't start with me on this again."

"Let's just *go*. We don't have to fly. We can just pack up the car and drive. We can stay at campgrounds. We can pack a cooler so we don't have to eat at restaurants. We don't have to go to Disney World even, we can just go to the beach."

Kurt was shaking his head.

"There's a place in Florida with a live mermaid show, these ladies swim in mermaid costumes under the water," she said, her heart beating hard in her chest. "Gracy would love it. Please, Kurt, let's just go." She felt desperate, drowning.

"Stop," Kurt said.

Elsbeth realized that her words were coming hard and fast, tumbling. But she *couldn't* stop. "We never go *anywhere*," she said, feeling her voice getting louder. "We never do things like normal families do. It's no wonder Trevor is so messed up. He hasn't gotten to do anything that other kids do. Spending all his time at the goddamned junkyard . . ."

"I said stop it, El," Kurt said.

". . . lurking around, taking pictures like some sort of Peeping Tom. It's not *normal*. None of this," she said, gesturing wildly, toward the box of Pop's papers on the kitchen table, "is *normal*."

Kurt slammed his fist against the table then, startling her. She felt like she was going to be sick. "Goddamn it, El. Shut *up*."

She thought about Twig yelling at Ollie barking and barking and barking. Was that what Kurt thought of her? That she was just some annoying, yappy dog? Elsbeth felt tears coming to her eyes and wiped them away. She was suddenly at a complete loss for words. She wanted to storm out, to take off in her car, but as pissed off as she was about his accusations, what if he was right? She shouldn't be driving. She wanted to walk out the back door and just sit out on the back steps to cool off, but the steps were covered in Pop's shit. She was trapped. Trapped inside this house, inside this life, and she felt like screaming.

Kurt stared at her without speaking, but she could see the muscles in his jaw tightening. His fists clenching.

She got up and stormed through the living room, not looking at Gracy because she knew if she did she'd lose it. She went to the bathroom instead and slammed the door. She pulled off her clothes, tore off the bathing suit, and shoved it in the blue plastic trash can with the spent tube of toothpaste and the empty toilet paper rolls. She turned the shower on as hot as it would go and stepped into the steam. The hot water pounded at her sunburned skin, made her entire body feel as though it were on fire. She closed her eyes and put her face under the stream. She felt ignited, ablaze. She would burn anything she touched.

After Elsbeth fell asleep, anger pulsed in time with Kurt's heartbeat in his limbs, and he couldn't lie still enough for sleep to come. And so he got dressed and quietly left her alone in the bed. He was still furious with her, and he hoped that she'd be hungover in the morning. He couldn't understand this, any of this. Elsbeth had always been a good mother to Gracy. This was something he'd been able to count on. She and Trevor had their problems, but the way she was with Gracy more than made up for any failings she had. But now, as he watched her sleep, he wondered if he could trust her anymore. And worse, he worried that there were *other* things he should worry about.

Someone down the road had been setting off firecrackers all night, and the air stank of their burnt remains. He could also smell the hints of a coming storm, feel the tight electric promise of thunder and rain. Still, despite the warnings from the sky, his legs insisted on moving, and so he walked.

Kurt wondered what would happen if he just kept walking one of these nights. If instead of making these ever-widening circles through town, looping back home, he just kept going. What would happen if, instead of traipsing endlessly through the woods and along the river, he just walked out onto the entrance ramp to the interstate and headed north? He wondered how long it would take him to get to the border, any border, how long to walk out of this life and into a new one.

Elsbeth thought he didn't understand, but he did. He knew

what it felt like to want to flee. To escape. To leave everything behind. She thought she was the only one who wanted more than
this small life. But he also knew that a man has responsibilities,
obligations. A father to his children. A son to his father. A man to
his wife. You can't just run away. He wasn't Billy.

Thunder rumbled in the distance, but the air was dry. Electric. He shoved his hands in his pockets and kept moving. After
about fifteen minutes, he came to the place in the road where the
two crosses were. He climbed down the steep embankment to
them. They looked ominous in the dark, pale reminders of how
very precarious things are.

He wondered about these kids sometimes. The boys who
died here. He imagined them saying good-bye to their parents
that night before they headed out. How their parents might not
have even looked up from what they were doing (their mother
with her casserole, their father with the nightly news), how they
might have been distracted, their minds on other things. He tried
to imagine what they must have felt, then, later when they were
awakened by the phone call telling them that everything they
thought they had was gone now. That all those things (the football games and school dances, the grass-stained clothes and messy
rooms) they'd taken for granted had now been taken, irrevocably,
from them. That life as they knew it was over.

He brushed both dusty crosses off with his sleeve, straightened the one that was always listing to the right, and looked up at
the ominous sky. Heavy storm clouds were moving across the
moon; it looked like a painting, like something both real and un-
real at once. When thunder rumbled again, he knew he should
head back to the house, that if he stayed much longer, he'd be
walking through a storm the whole way back. But he couldn't
move. His legs were, for some reason, suddenly remarkably still.
Even as the rain came down and the sky was severed by a streak
of lightning, he was paralyzed. And with the next shock of light,
he realized:

Elsbeth was going to leave him. The revelation was like the dull ache of the flu coming on. Maybe not tonight. Maybe not even this year. But her unhappiness, her discontentment, was beginning to swell. It was like a cancer, some poisonous thing that was growing, and he worried there might be nothing he could do about it. She was teetering at some terrible precipice, but instead of grabbing hold, pulling her back, he'd been standing there dumbly watching her, waiting for her to fall. He knew he needed to do something.

The sky had warned him, but he hadn't heeded its admonishment. And so now, as he walked the two miles back to the house, the wind and rain were merciless. Punishing. By the time he walked into the midnight kitchen, his flannel shirt and jeans were heavy with rain. His hair was drenched, and his shoes were soggy. He peeled off his wet clothes and dried off as best he could, but as he crawled into bed with Elsbeth, the thunder scent of him (of the sky he carried in, in the anger that still thrummed in his chest) woke her.

"Kurt?" she muttered. "Were you walking again? In the rain?"

But instead of answering her, he just pressed his body against hers, enclosed her. Held on tight.

He dreamed about a train. About the bright headlights of a train racing toward him, about his legs once again failing him as he stood paralyzed straddling the tracks. The ground rumbling under his motionless feet. The whistle screaming in his ears. He dreamed the blinding light and deafening sounds.

"Kurt, it's your phone," Elsbeth said, pulling him from the tracks and back into the soft nest of their bed.

His heart was pounding in his chest as the world came sharply into focus. He grabbed the cell phone from his nightstand, and struggling to focus on the screen. It was Maury. It was five A.M.

"Yeah," he said.

"Kurt, you better come over real quick. It's Jude."

He listened to Maury explain what had happened and then Kurt hung up and got out of bed, yanking on his pants, which were still wet from his walk in the rain.

"What's going on?" Elsbeth asked, sitting up.

"Pop's in the hospital," he said. "He's had another stroke. Maury found him this morning. He was lying on the bathroom floor since yesterday."

Trevor planned to tell his mother he wasn't feeling well, that he might even throw up. It was true. Every morning for weeks he'd woken up feeling like his guts were tied in knots. But today especially, his stomach was cramped and angry. There was no way he could go to swimming lessons today. No way he could deal with one more morning of Ethan and Mike taunting, teasing, the girls in his class giggling, the small new kid, Rudy, laughing at him. The chlorinated sky even seemed to be mocking him with its brightness, its smug placidity.

He knew that whatever was going on with his stomach probably had to do with Ethan and Mike. It was like all the anger in him was turning his intestines into a knotted fist. And the longer he let them harass him, the tighter the fist inside him became. He knew that eventually something would have to give. He was a head taller than both of them; he was stronger. He could hurt them if he wanted to. He could hurt them really badly. And without Mrs. Cross around to put her foot down, without someone to stop him, he was afraid of what he might do.

It was early, just past seven, and his father was backing an old trailer into the backyard. As the sun rose, Trevor watched his dad carefully maneuvering the trailer into the spot where the oak tree used to be. Pop had been in the hospital for two weeks but he was getting out today, and he would be staying at their house. Well, not exactly at their house, there wasn't room for that, but in this trailer on their property. Until a spot at the nursing home opened up anyway. He knew from his parents' hushed discussions at night that until somebody at the home moved or died, Pop would be living in their backyard. *Like white trash,* his mother had said when she thought he wasn't listening. And Trevor thought about all the work they'd done on Pop's house, all the trash they'd cleared away only to have this happen.

He'd heard his parents arguing every night for the last two weeks. He'd covered his ears with his pillow, but still, somehow their words found their way in. Ever since Pop's stroke, and his father announced that Pop would be staying with them, she'd been acting crazy. She was always, always angry now. Not just at him. She was mad at Kurt. She was mad, even, at Gracy.

Earlier that morning, Gracy had reached across the kitchen table for the sugar bowl, and she'd knocked over her glass of orange juice. It spilled all over the newspaper, and all over his mom's pocketbook, which she'd left there. It dripped down onto the floor, under the table, where it made a puddle around the legs of the chair.

"Jesus Christ!" she'd screamed, startling them both. "Why do you have to be so clumsy? You have to pay attention, Gracy. Watch what you're doing."

Gracy, who Trevor was pretty sure had never been scolded before in her life, crumbled. Her face fell, her lip quivered, and her shoulders shook. He didn't know what to do. He wanted to hug her, to let her know that the world was just upside down lately, that his mother hadn't meant it. But this expression was so new, so horrifying and strange, he quietly grabbed his camera (which had escaped the flow of orange juice) instead. But when his mother realized what he was doing, she'd yanked the camera out of his hands and slammed it down next to the sink.

"Just stop it!" she screamed. "Goddamn it. This isn't *normal*. You shouldn't want to take pictures of this. If I catch you doing that again, I'm getting rid of the camera. I will take it away. Do you understand?" Her voice sounded like it belonged to someone else. "If you do anything, anything at all, it is gone."

Trevor nodded and tried not to think about how much her

words hurt. *Normal.* What was wrong with his pictures? Mrs. D. had said he was an *artist*.

"Do you have your suits on?" she asked them. They both nodded. Gracy's eyes were red, and snot was running from her nose. "Your towels are in the dryer. Gracy, come here so I can wipe your face."

"I don't feel well," Trevor tried, as his mother dabbed at Gracy's nose with a paper towel. "I don't think I can go to swimming lessons today."

His mother turned on her heel and glared at him. "Christ, what's the matter with you now?"

He felt his whole body aching. His stomach was lurching inside his body. What *was* the matter with him? If he could figure that out, then maybe he could change it. Make it better. He shook his head.

She came over to him and pressed her wrist hard against his forehead, then yanked it away. "You're fine. And besides, we don't have any choice. Your dad's working this morning and then dealing with Pop this afternoon. I have to work. If you feel bad, tell your teacher and she'll probably let you sit out. It's just a few hours. Can you do this for me? *Please?*" She looked a mess. Her hair was stringy, and she had dark circles under both eyes.

Trevor nodded, his stomach throbbing now. Bile rising sharp and acrid in his throat, turning into hot tears in the corners of his eyes.

At the pool, Mike was sitting at one of the picnic tables eating chocolate Pop-Tarts, looking at some sort of comic book or something. Ethan was nowhere in sight. Trevor prayed he was sick today. Without Ethan, Mike usually left Trevor alone. Trevor dropped Gracy off at her class and then slipped quietly into the boys' locker room. He pulled off his T-shirt and shoved it into his backpack, hung the pack inside a locker, and put his towel around his shoulders. He took a deep breath and turned to leave.

"Hey, faggot," Ethan said, shoving into him with his shoulder. Trevor's stomach pitched. He tried to keep walking, but

Ethan was pushing against him, hard, pushing him back toward the wall of lockers. He resisted, but Ethan had momentum. His breath smelled like bubblegum as he got in his face. "I should kill you," he said, sneering.

Trevor clenched and unclenched his fists. He thought about his mother, insisting that he come today. Her threats to take away his camera. What would she do to him if he fought back? If he just punched Ethan Sweeney in his face? What would his father do?

"And if I kill you, then you'll go to hell with all the other faggots." The word, *faggot,* made Trevor think of bloody Styrofoam trays, of tiny white worms crawling in and out of gray meat. It made him think of garbage and decay. It made his stomach turn.

As Ethan pushed him harder against the wall, he could feel the metal locker handle pressing into his back. He felt nauseous with the pain, sickened by the thoughts of rotten meat, disgusted by the scent of Ethan's hot Bazooka breath in his face.

Mike came to the doorway then, as if Ethan had sent him some telepathic signal, and Trevor was overwhelmed with terror. Outside the lifeguard's whistle blew shrilly, and then there was nothing but the watery sounds of summer: kids screaming and splashing, their joy deafening. He was alone. No one would hear him if he cried out.

Mike started walking toward them, and Trevor felt his stomach clench. Mike laughed, throwing his head back, and Ethan pushed harder. The metal hook dug into Trevor's kidney. His whole body throbbed with the pain.

"What's the matter?" Ethan said, feigning sympathy. "Am I hurting you?"

Trevor shook his head even as tears sprang to his eyes. His stomach hurt so badly he could barely breathe. He clenched his muscles together, suddenly aware that his bowels were intent on releasing. It was unstoppable. Unbelievable. He was *shitting* himself, the heat of his feces traveling down the back of his leg.

They didn't notice at first, and then Ethan recoiled at the smell.

"Holy crap!" he said, letting go of Trevor and jumping backward.

"Did he just *shit* himself?" Mike asked, mouth gaping, his own wad of gum like flesh on his tongue. "What a freak!"

"That's what happens when you let somebody fuck you up the ass," Ethan said. And then they were gagging and covering their mouths, racing to the doorway. "God, that is so disgusting!" Then they were gone, the laughter echoing off the cinder-block walls.

Trevor ran into one of the bathroom shower stalls and pulled off his soiled trunks, rinsing them out in the cold water of the shower and then putting them on again, watching as his excrement finally disappeared down the drain. Sobbing, he let the shower soak him, chill him, numb him. And then he stayed inside the locker room, knees curled to his chest on the cold concrete floor, until he heard the final whistle announcing that it was, finally, time to go home.

Kurt kept telling Elsbeth it was just temporary, that as soon as a spot at the nursing home opened up, he'd be moving Pop out of their backyard. But it had been three weeks already with no end to this in sight, and in the meantime, they were living like some sort of hillbillies, the trailer Kurt towed home from the salvage yard taking up half their backyard. And despite the second stroke, Pop was still, *somehow,* managing to fill the trailer up with crap, and it was starting to spill out onto the backyard. She'd had enough.

That morning, she was doing the dishes when she looked out and saw Jude tossing a grocery bag full of something out his door. It landed next to Gracy's swing set, and something metallic tumbled out. Lids. A hundred sharp tin lids. Livid, she'd dried her hands and stormed out the back door. Jude had already disappeared back inside the trailer, and so she banged on the flimsy door. Hard.

She could hear him moving around inside. For a guy who had two strokes, he sure was pretty mobile. The door creaked open on rusted hinges.

"Morning," he slurred.

Since the second stroke, his speech had gotten worse. It was difficult to understand much of what he was saying. But she didn't need him to talk; she needed for him to listen.

"Jude, I know you're in some tight quarters out here. But I need you to keep the backyard clear. This is where Gracy plays.

When you throw your trash out here, it's dangerous. She could get cut on these," she said, bending down to pick up a lid.

Jude swayed in the doorway, his head bobbing. He hadn't gotten dressed yet, and his ratty bathrobe revealed the scar on his chest. Kurt said it happened in Vietnam, his badge of honor, but looking at it, at his pale sunken chest and that raised river of flesh that ran through it, made her turn her head in shame.

"Recycling," Jude said.

"What's that?"

"It's for the recycling. Kurt said to put it by the door."

Elsbeth took a deep breath, thought about the way he'd chucked the bag out the door and into the yard.

"Well then, you won't mind if I take it to the *recycling bin*," she said and picked the bag of lids up. Most of them were still filthy, sticky with baked beans or tuna or whatever the hell else it was he ate. The recycling place would never take these.

Elsbeth turned on her heel and stomped around the side of the house where the trash cans were and dumped the bag in.

She hadn't always felt this way about Jude. Back when she and Kurt were first dating and then later married, she and Jude actually managed to mostly get along. They used to spend Sunday afternoons at Jude and Loretta's house. Jude called her "E-beth," rustled her hair, and when she was so pregnant she couldn't see her feet, he'd bring her glasses of lemonade mixed with iced tea. That was back when Kurt's mom was still alive, before she got sick. She had brought out the best in Jude. She wasn't sure if there was a best in Jude anymore. When she died, everything went to hell: Jude, the house.

She had no idea what would happen to the house now. She thought they should sell it. It was the closest thing to an inheritance that Kurt had. And even if they had to tear the place down, the property had to be worth something. It was on two or three acres that backed up to the river. She dreamed about what they could do with the money. Though she knew that as long as Pop was alive, he'd never let it go.

Inside, she went to check on Gracy. On the weekends, she let Gracy sleep late in the mornings. Kurt was working at the 76 on weekends now, so she had given Twig her weekend spots at Babbette's so she could be home with the kids.

Gracy would sleep until ten o'clock if you let her. Trevor, on the other hand, was up at the crack of dawn, even on the weekends, taking off into the woods to do God knows what. Before Jude moved into the backyard, she clung to the quiet time after Kurt's truck took off down the road and before Gracy woke up. She'd drink her coffee sitting out on the back steps, watching the sun come up, and the birds that came to the feeder Kurt put up. But now, her view was of Jude's god-awful trailer. She was never alone now. And the only birds that came by now were the filthy scavengers coming after all this garbage.

When she poked her head into Gracy and Trevor's room, Trevor was gone and Gracy was still fast asleep on top of her sheets. Kurt was in the shower; she could hear the water running. Steam seeped out from under the bathroom door.

Normally, she would have snuck into the bathroom, locked the door behind her. She would have quietly stripped off her clothes and pulled back the shower curtain. She would have soaped her hands up and washed every inch of Kurt's body. But not today. Not anymore. Jude could wander in any minute. Any bit of privacy they had was gone now. And so instead of slipping into that steamy place, Elsbeth knocked, hard, on the bathroom door.

"Kurt," she said. And she could feel all that anger she'd felt toward Jude coming back, getting mixed up inside her. "Kurt!"

He opened the door, and for one quick second it was Jude she saw instead of her husband. He was staring at his face in the foggy mirror; she spoke to his reflection. "Your father is throwing his trash in the yard. Metal lids. Sharp goddamned lids. And I swear if Gracy gets hurt . . ."

Kurt's reflection peered back at her, but it was like he was looking at her without really looking at her. His gaze fixed somewhere beyond her, his body there but his mind elsewhere. It made her feel both pissed off and completely alone.

"Kurt?" she said.

"Yeah?"

"I can't take this much longer."

"I know," he said.

"I mean it. This is our house. *Our* home."

Kurt stepped out of the shower and grabbed a towel, still looking at her, past her, in the mirror.

"I hate this," she said. "I want my life back."

As the steam escaped through the open door, the mirror cleared, and she could make out his face. And, for a moment, their eyes made contact.

"Soon," he said. "I promise."

Promise. Every now and then Elsbeth could remember what it felt like for there to be the promise of something better ahead. She could remember the excitement of all the things that might come, the hope that resided somewhere inside her ribs. *Promise,* that little bird inside the cage of her own bones that fluttered in anticipation, its wings quivering with longing. She had always been an optimist, somebody who truly believed, *trusted,* that the world had more to offer her and that one day she would find happiness. But now, at thirty years old, the realization suddenly struck her that maybe this was it. Perhaps this was as good as it was going to get.

At night, when Kurt disappeared into the darkness, going wherever it was that he went when his legs would not let him sleep, or when he worked at the station all night and she languished alone in their bed, she allowed herself the girlish, the childish, fantasies that seemed harder and harder to conjure lately: adventure, travel, fun. Her dreams were small, really. She didn't need a fairy-tale life. What she really wanted was to just be happy. But *this* wasn't happiness: her father-in-law living in the backyard, her son always in trouble, her husband so far away she felt like she barely knew him anymore. Nothing but work, work,

work, and they still didn't have two nickels to rub together. If something didn't give, she was going to lose it. Alone, in bed, she fantasized about just getting in the car and taking off, starting fresh. She would just take Gracy and disappear. She dreamed them on the road to a new life. She imagined a second chance. But then Kurt would come home and climb into the bed, enclosing her with his arms, trapping her with his biceps. The familiar smell of him would envelop her, the heady smell of hard work and something she couldn't quite put her finger on, and suddenly all those stupid fantasies became just that. Stupid dreams, and she realized the cage was locked. That bird inside her chest was getting old, listless, as it waited for her to release it. She imagined what the key to the cage might look like. A tiny golden thing no bigger than her pinkie finger.

She thought about Trevor out there in the woods doing whatever it was he was doing, thought about all of the trouble that was likely to come once school started again. She thought about Kurt stuck at the yard, stuck inside the 76 station while the rest of the world was sleeping. And she even thought of Pop in his own prison in their backyard. And she wondered if the lock on this cage, like all the others, might be too rusty to open anymore. She had been silly; it was too late. The bird in the cage was too old. If she were going to set it free, she should have done so when its wings were stronger. When it still had the ability to fly. Before it shat all over the cage and forgot how to sing.

Crystal was working forty hours a week now, happy to take the extra shifts, happy even to deal with Howard and his clumsy advances, which just kept coming. She had to admire his tenacity at least; he was not giving up. Working, even dealing with Howard, kept her occupied, kept her mind off everything else.

Crystal would work at the Walgreens for the rest of the summer and then she'd go off to college in the fall. And none of this would matter anymore. She would forget everything. She would start over again. She would forget Ty. The baby.

She had to just keep reminding herself that next month she was going to UVM. Like any other student. She was moving into a dorm room with some girl named Fiona who was from upstate New York. They'd e-mailed each other a couple of times, friended each other on Facebook. Crystal scoured the pictures Fiona had posted, and it looked like she was pretty normal. Lots of pictures of her with her girlfriends, hiking and swimming and camping. She was pretty but not too pretty. Thin but not too thin. There were a few pictures of her with her arms around a big golden retriever, and lots of posts quoting famous authors. When Crystal was stocking shelves or pricing stuff or dealing with customers, she imagined what her life would be like at college. There were entire days when she could forget this year, amnesiacal days in which she could forget almost entirely that just a few months ago, she'd given birth to a baby girl. A girl who lived in the same city where she would be going to college.

Her body showed almost no evidence anymore that she'd been pregnant just a few months ago. Her very flesh seemed to exhibit the same amnesia, that same ability to deny or forget. She assumed this remarkable elasticity was because she was only seventeen, an athlete. Her stomach had returned to its normal size, her breasts had shrunken back down to their modest A cups. Even that dark line, the *linea negra,* her doctor had called it—that line that divided her in half, that divided her life in half (*before* and *now*)—had all but faded away. She had started running again, and by July, she was completely back in top form. Her body had put all of this behind her. And if her body could forget, couldn't her mind as well?

Howard noticed, of course.

"You look *fine,*" he said. Crystal was pretty sure Howard had learned all of his social skills from TV.

"Thanks," she said.

Today Howard was working the photo counter, and she was stocking the back-to-school items on the seasonal shelves near the front and manning the front counter as well. She'd just sliced open a box of ring-bound notebooks when the door jingled.

Crystal looked up and saw her: the shoplifter lady with her little girl trailing behind. The woman looked harried, her hair disheveled. She was wearing a hot pink sundress, the kind with a stretchy strapless tube top, and flip-flops. The little girl was filthy too, her mouth smeared with chocolate, which also spotted her T-shirt. Crystal felt her heart pang. She left the open box on the dolly and moved behind the counter where she had a better view of the store. She watched as the woman moved through the aisles. There was no pattern that Crystal could discern. No method as far as she could tell. She was like an ant, determined and forward moving, but without any sort of logic to her direction. As Crystal sprayed the counter down with 409 and wiped away the sticky spots, she watched the woman walk down the makeup aisle, the hair goods, and then make a sharp turn toward the grocery aisle.

Crystal's hands were shaking, her heart racing as the woman's fingers skipped across the dusty cans of beef stew, chili, soup. Really? Soup? Behind her, the little girl was tugging at her mother's skirt, but the woman was so fixated on the canned goods, she seemed completely oblivious. It wasn't until the little girl screamed, "Mommy!" that she snapped out of it. Her hands still clutching a small can of Dinty Moore, she turned to the little girl, her face angry, twisted.

There was a thin red line running down the little girl's face. And then, as she started to cry, the blood rushed faster and faster, coming out like some horrific faucet inside her nostril had been turned on. Crystal grabbed a wad of paper towels from the roll and came out from behind the counter. She walked quickly past the chip display to them and knelt down next to the girl. "Here you go, sweetie." She handed her the clump of paper towels and helped her press it to her nose.

The woman looked bewildered, a sleepwalker startled awake.

"Do you want me to take her to the bathroom?" Crystal asked the woman, and she nodded. "It's right back there." She pointed to the sign that said RESTROOM.

The woman was still clinging to the beef stew, her eyes vacant.

"And you can just take that up to the photo counter. Howard will ring you up." Crystal gestured toward the can and studied the woman's face for any sort of sign of guilt, any acknowledgment that she'd been caught red-handed almost stealing a can of Dinty freaking Moore. "You can meet us in the restroom."

"Here, come with me," she said to the little girl, taking her little hand and steering her down the aisle toward the back, pressing the paper towels to her gushing nose. "I'll be right back," she said to Howard and walked the little girl into the handicapped stall in the bathroom.

The little girl was crying now, and the blood was not stopping.

"I used to get bloody noses when I was little," she said as she sat the girl down on the closed toilet lid. "You just need to pinch your nose and lean your head back. Here, like this."

She did as she was told.

"Now you might taste something yucky in the back of your throat, but you need to keep holding your head back. Okay?"

The little girl nodded.

As they waited for the bleeding to stop, Crystal tried to take a quick inventory of the child's body. She wasn't even sure what she was looking for, but she had a feeling that something was really, really wrong in this family. The girl didn't have any visible bruises, but she was covered with bug bites, which she had clearly scratched until they scabbed over. Her hair was in two braids that looked like they'd been slept on. She had a Band-Aid on one of her knees.

"What happened to your knee?"

"I fell down," the girl said, her nose plugged. "In the back-yard. Where Pop lives."

"Your daddy lives in your backyard?" Crystal asked, horrified.

"No, silly. Pop. My *grandpop*."

"He lives in your *backyard?*"

"He used to live in a house, but it got too dirty. There was a raccoon, I saw it. They were afraid the raccoon might bite the lit-tle kids."

Crystal nodded and stroked the little girl's hair, trying not to look shocked. Trying not to whisk her straight away. But to whom? The police? Child Protective Services? What do you do when some kid tells you their grandfather is living in the back-yard? When you've been watching her mother shoplift for months and months? *Stay calm,* she thought. *Think this through.*

"Here, let's see if it's fixed." Crystal gently took the soggy wad of paper towels from the little girl's nose and had her lean her head forward. For the moment, the bleeding seemed to have stopped. Crystal went to the sink and wet down another paper towel, which she used to wash the dried blood from her face. She also wiped away the chocolate ring around her mouth and dabbed at the tears in the corners of her eyes.

There was a knock at the door then, and as she tossed the bloodstained tissues into the trash can, the little girl's mother came in.

"Is she okay?" she asked. "You okay, honey?"

The little girl nodded.

Crystal rolled another wad of toilet paper, hands trembling, and handed it to the girl. "Take this with you, in case it starts up again, okay?"

"Thank you so much. God, the sight of blood makes me so queasy. Thank you for taking care of her," the woman said. She was smiling now. That crazy distant look in her eye was gone. Crystal wondered if the can of beef stew was in her pocketbook. She'd have to ask Howard if he rang her up.

"You ready, Gracy Bear?" the mother said sweetly.

Crystal's eyes widened, and her heart started to pound hard in her chest. "What's her name?" Crystal asked, her throat thick, suddenly feeling like she might faint.

"Grace," the woman said, still smiling. "We call her Gracy, though."

Crystal held onto the handicapped bar so that she wouldn't pass out.

Grace. G-R-A-C-E. The letters that spun their magic stitches across that wounded place. *Grace.* What were the chances? And what could it mean?

The little girl leaned into her mother and hugged her tightly around her knees. Crystal felt dizzy and had to concentrate just to breathe. When they were gone, she lifted the lid of the toilet and vomited. Then she pressed her cheek against the cold porcelain and cried.

Trevor walked Gracy to the pool entrance, careful not to let the kid checking passes see him. He handed her the Sleeping Beauty towel from his backpack and then slung the pack back on his shoulder. "Just show them your pass and go to your group. I'll be back before Mom gets here."

"Where you going, Trevor?" she asked. "What about swimming lessons?"

"Don't worry, Gracy. I just have an errand to run."

"What kind of errand?"

"Just go straight to your group," he said.

She shrugged and kissed his cheek. "Okeydokey, artichokey."

He watched to make sure she'd gone through the gate and then walked away as quickly as he could without breaking into a full-blown sprint.

The address he scrawled onto a scrap of paper was downtown, about a mile from the pool. It would have been faster if he'd walked down Depot Street, but he couldn't risk getting caught by his mom, so he took the long way, walking through the neighborhood surrounding the downtown.

When he got to the house, Trevor glanced at the address, comparing it to the brass numbers nailed to the wall, making sure he was at the right place. The house was run-down, the porch he stood on sinking. Box fans whirred in several of the windows. There was a row of mailboxes by the front door. He scanned them, looking at the peeling labels until he saw Carmen Dubois. *Mrs. D.* Apt. 4.

He slowly opened the front door, startling as, somewhere, a dog barked loudly. Heart racing, he walked cautiously into the dimly lit entrance. It smelled musty, like old cigarette smoke, and the air was thick and hot. It filled his lungs, making him feel as though he were drowning. As his eyes adjusted to the dark, he could make out the grim hallway, the tilted staircase. A dusty beam of light coming from an upstairs window. He wished he'd brought his camera.

He glanced at the doors on the main floor, and then started to walk slowly up the stairs. The paint on the railing was chipping, and the carpet on the stairs was threadbare. There was something terribly sad and lonely about all of this. For as much as he wanted to see Mrs. D., *needed* to see Mrs. D., he was starting to hope that somehow, despite the matching addresses, despite her name on the mailbox, he had been mistaken.

At the top of the stairs, he could see Apt. 4, and the dank smell of mold and must gave way to the smell of something delicious. Like Thanksgiving dinner. Herbs and meat. Something warm and simmering. He approached the door and thought again about just turning around and going home. Normal students didn't track down their teachers and go see them at their houses. Normal kids weren't friends with their elderly art teachers. But normal kids didn't shit their pants at swimming lessons either.

He hesitated for another moment and then took his hand out of his pocket and knocked cautiously on the door, his heart echoing the thump, thump, thump of his fist. There was nothing but the distant sound of the dog barking, and so he knocked again.

"Just a minute." The voice was hers, but smaller, on the other side of the door.

He took a deep breath. He could hear feet shuffling behind the door, and then the sound of locks being unlatched. He felt a wave of relief wash over him. This meant she wasn't in the hospital; she was home.

Mrs. D. looked confused at first, as though she didn't know who Trevor was, and he wondered if she had somehow already forgotten him. She looked smaller than she did at school, more stooped. She had a cane in her hand, and instead of her black wig, she had a scarf around her head. If anyone was unrecognizable, it was her.

"Trevor?" she asked. "What's the matter? You look like you've seen a ghost."

He nodded, and as he did, everything he'd been holding inside started to rise to the surface. He realized, again, that he no longer seemed to have control over any of his bodily functions. The tears were streaming down his face, hot and salty in the corners of his mouth.

"Come in, come in," she said, reaching for his hand and pulling him into her apartment.

Inside, she motioned for him to sit down on the couch. The coffee table was littered with art books and pill bottles and dirty dishes. "Please excuse the mess," she said, sitting opposite from him in a wing chair. "I wasn't expecting company."

He shook his head.

"Oh dear, let me get you something to drink. Would you like tea?" She pushed herself out of the chair, wheezing a little with the effort.

"Can I just have some water?" he asked. He'd felt like he'd been drowning before, but now he felt parched, like every drop of moisture had been drained from his body.

"Of course, of course," she said and shuffled back to the kitchen.

Trevor glanced quickly around the room. Every inch of every wall was covered with framed paintings. Many of them looked like they had been painted by students, but others were ones he recognized from the slide shows at school. Picasso, Monet, Miró. There was a fireplace, with a basket of folded laundry where the fire should be, a mantel crowded with photos, laced with cobwebs. That smell, the Thanksgiving smell, had not been coming from her apartment; her apartment smelled like turpentine, like paint. There was no television, but there were a billion books, piled up in teetering towers, all over the room. Shoe boxes of paint, brushes like petal-less flowers in glass jars.

She came back into the room and handed him a glass. The water looked milky, but he was so thirsty he took a big gulp and then set the glass down.

Mrs. D. lowered herself into the chair across from him again and smiled. "It's so nice to see you, Trevor. I'm so sorry I missed the last week of school."

Trevor's throat felt thick. Swollen shut. "I was worried that you . . ."

"Oh dear, no. Not this time. This old ticker's just not as reliable as it used to be. But I'm still here. Tell me, how are you? You must be happy to be on vacation from school for the summer. What have you been doing with your free time?"

Trevor closed his eyes tightly, willing away the smell of the locker room, the stink of his own body's waste. "We never got to use the darkroom," he said.

"Oh, Trevor, I am so sorry. The first thing I thought of, at the hospital, was that I had let you down. That you'd be disappointed."

"You promised you'd teach me." His voice was louder than he intended it to be. He wiped angrily at the tears that were spilling from his eyes.

"Oh, Trevor," she said. Her voice sounded like something fragile, swimmy and soft. Like someone trying to talk underwater. "What have they done to you?"

He shook his head. He shouldn't be here. Coming here had been a stupid, stupid idea. He had no idea what he thought she could do for him. What sort of comfort or protection she might provide.

"When school starts again, will you teach me how to use the darkroom?"

Mrs. D. reached across the messy coffee table and touched his arm. Her hands, speckled like a brown egg, grasped his. "Trevor, I won't be back at school this fall."

Trevor felt the way he did in those dreams where the earth disappears from underneath your feet. "But you're better. They sent you home. You're not sick!" Again, his voice thundered despite his every attempt to stay calm.

Mrs. D. shook her head softly. "I'm retiring, dear. I had planned to retire soon anyway, and I think this was a sign that it's time for me to stop working. To take care of myself so something like this doesn't happen again."

Trevor's eyes widened in disbelief. He shook his head again. He felt like he was three years old. The rage and frustration and panic rushing through his body, escaping through the tears in his eyes, the snot dripping down his nose, the sounds in his throat.

"Oh, Trevor, please. It's okay, it's okay . . ." Mrs. D.'s voice was so far away, it was as though the earth had indeed swallowed him whole, and she was far, far away now.

The next thing he knew he was weaving through the crowded rooms of her apartment and out into that dark hallway again. He could hear her voice calling after him all the way down the stairs, and even as he ran down her street and past his mother's work and then past the entrance to the pool where he was supposed to be with Gracy.

Crystal's mother suggested they take a girls' trip to Burlington to go shopping, to get the things she would need for her dorm room, some new clothes for college. In exactly one month they would be dropping her off at UVM for first-year orientation. And then, starting one week later, she'd be an officially matriculated college student.

When Crystal was in middle school, she used to love these back-to-school shopping trips with her mother. They were pretty much the only time that she and her mom spent alone together. They'd spend the whole day walking up and down Church Street, navigating the underground depths of the Church Street Mall. They'd eat lunch at one of the outdoor cafes, Leunig's or Sweetwaters, their bags piled in colorful heaps at their feet. But her mother hadn't taken her shopping in over a year. She'd ordered all of her maternity clothes online and put the packages on Crystal's bed in inculpatory piles while she was at school.

"I'm supposed to work on Saturday," Crystal said.

"Take it off," she said. "You work too hard."

"It's not that easy, Mom. You have to put in requests for days off like a month in advance." This was a lie. She could easily just ask one of the other girls to cover for her. All she had to do was talk to Howard, who would pick up the shift himself if he had to.

"Talk to your manager. We're going shopping on Saturday, and that is final."

Crystal didn't sleep at all on Friday night. She tossed and turned, sleeping in fits and starts, awakening in a sweat each time she did manage to drift off. Angie was passed out cold in her bed, her arms flung over her head in that careless, carefree way she had. Angie never had problems sleeping. She was out within seconds of her head hitting the pillow and she barely moved all night. If it weren't for her snoring, you might think she was dead. Crystal used to be the same way. Up until this past year. Now she was lucky to get a couple of consecutive hours. Some nights she was lucky to get any sleep at all. When she first came home from the hospital, she was waking every hour, dreaming the sounds of the baby crying, her breasts hot and angry. Even now, she slept the sleep of a new mother: the fragile sleep of someone knowing she will soon be woken.

She had been so sure about leaving Two Rivers, but now that her departure was less than a month away, instead of thrilling her, instead of filling her with a rush of excitement, the impending exodus only made her feel anxious. Worried she'd made the wrong decision. Every decision lately seemed somehow incorrect and fraught with potential disaster. When she borrowed her dad's car and drove to work, she'd go the long way, worried that if she went her normal route there would be a car waiting to swerve off the road into her. But then she would second-guess *that* notion and wonder if she'd just sealed another, perhaps worse, fate. Maybe taking this route would bring her into a head-on collision with a *different* wayward driver.

And this decision, the decision to go to UVM suddenly struck her as fundamentally ridiculous. She had picked UVM because that's where her dad had gone, because it was one of the best state universities in the country; the caliber of the school had definitely weighed in. So too had the sprawling green campus. But she'd mostly picked it because it was part of the grander scheme, the now-obsolete scheme. Ty was supposed to go to Middlebury. She was supposed to go to UVM. They were supposed to be together. They had planned weekend visits, talked about how they could take the bus to Two Rivers together for the holidays. But now Ty was *not* going to Middlebury. Ty was going to California, three thousand miles away. And her baby, *their* baby, belonged to someone who taught at that university. How could she ever go to school where the adopted father of her child worked? It was inane.

UVM seemed like some sort of paper-cutout place, like a picture in a child's pop-up book. Not a real place anymore. Not a real school where she would study and stay up giggling with her roommate, Fiona. Someplace where she would become both Crystal and somebody new all at the same time. It seemed like a dream upon waking, one of those delicate dreams shattered into unrecognizable slivers as soon as she opened her eyes.

On Saturday morning, she pretended she was not feeling well, but her mother called her bluff.

"I rescheduled four meetings with clients for this," her mother said, towering over her bed in some terribly bright yellow blouse, like the sun herself had come in to personally wake her. "I don't care if you've got typhus," she said, laughing. "Up and at 'em."

Her mother was not a cheerleader in high school, but she should have been. She had the energy of one, the ability to rouse anyone, even Crystal, out of a slump. Her mother simply didn't tolerate crabbiness. *Funk* was not a word in her vocabulary. She even affectionately referred to the McDonald family as "The Team." "Come on, Team!" she'd say whenever she needed to rally them into action.

Crystal tried again. "I really don't feel well."

"You can sleep it off in the car," her mother said, smiling and reaching for Crystal's hand. Crystal knew she had no choice and allowed her mother to pull her, like a fallen runner, up.

She tried to pretend like this was just another shopping trip with her mom, something she used to look forward to. Crystal tried to recapture that sense of propriety, of having her mom all to herself for a whole day. Her mom even made a big show of turning off her BlackBerry as they got in her car, stuffing it into the depths of her purse.

"You don't have to do that, Mom," Crystal said.

"Your father can handle anything that comes up," she said.

But her mother's attempts at normalcy were transparent. And something about all this effort seemed more sad than generous. Like watching some wounded runner limp his way across the finish line. Still, she was willing to give it one last shot. Take one for the team.

Crystal's mother hadn't driven her to Burlington in ages. The times she'd gone to visit the Stones when she was pregnant, her father had driven. He'd waited in the car while she toured their home (seen the nursery painted those candy colors), drank their herbal tea, listened to their lullaby voices speaking softly to the baby inside her. But now, as they pulled off the interstate, her mother was the one clutching the wheel. Not her father with his sad eyes staring straight ahead so he wouldn't have to look at her. Not her father and his disappointment like another passenger squeezed in between them.

"You must be getting so excited!" her mother chirped as she got off the interstate at the Burlington exit.

Crystal shrugged. "I guess," she said, trying hard to be cheery.

But as they drove past the street that would have taken her to the Stones' house, she felt like someone had tripped her. The Stones lived near the university's campus in a crooked old house that reminded her of Ty's house. At the front was a wide porch, and a widow's walk was perched on the top. Mrs. Stone had explained that the legend was that widow's walks were built for the women whose husbands were away at sea. For the women whose husbands *died* at sea. From above they could look out into the immense emptiness, to grieve. She wondered if there was an architectural feature designed for girls forced to give up their babies. She was not a widow, but she grieved like one; she felt the same vast sorrow. But she was not a widow. There were no names for girls like her.

For the first time since she had the baby, she allowed herself to think about what had happened to Grace *after*. She imagined the Stones driving back to Burlington with her strapped into the expensive car seat she'd seen on the kitchen table one time when she visited. It was green with a plaid canopy. Mrs. Stone had pointed out its safety features to her, the five-point harness, the way it virtually bolted into the backseat. Mrs. Stone had wanted Crystal to know this was proof that they would keep her safe. But it only made her feel carsick.

"You okay?" her mother asked. Her mother didn't know anything about her visits with the Stones. She never asked on those days when she came home after crying silently the whole way, her stomach muscles aching from the effort. And Crystal never offered. She hadn't talked to anyone about them. No one even asked who they were beyond the portraits they painted in the agency's application. No one wanted to think past that moment in the hospital when she let her go. But now she gripped her seat tightly and imagined their trip home from the hospital, the way Mrs. Stone would have sat in the backseat with the baby, her heart racing, her happiness and fear mixing together in some terrific emotional cocktail. Intoxicating. And she thought about the way the tires would crush the gravel in the driveway, the way the porch light might have made shadows across their faces. She considered the trellis thick with leaves and blooming morning glories; she dreamed the heady scent of spring.

"I'm okay," she said, nodding and nodding, but missing the burning flash that had now stopped coming to her breasts each time she thought about the baby. She traced the calligraphy with her fingers.

And for a little while, her mother's enthusiasm was infectious. As her mother helped her pick out fluffy towels and soft sheets and a matching brand-new comforter freckled with daisies, she almost felt like any one of the other girls she saw walking with their mothers up and down the street, arms loaded down with bags. Her mother was trying so hard, it nearly broke Crystal's heart. "You're going to need a new alarm clock," she said, looking at a display of kitschy oversized alarm clocks at Homeport.

"I've got an alarm on my phone," she said.

"As a backup, then," her mother said.

And she tried to imagine herself sleeping on those daisy sheets, her head resting on the ergonomic pillow, waking to the sound of that turquoise clock, but just couldn't. It was like trying to imagine waking up in someone else's life. And while that had seemed like exactly what she needed even a few weeks ago, she knew what she really wanted was something else entirely.

She wanted something impossible. She wanted the life she had failed to choose. She wanted to go back to that moment at the hospital when she lifted the baby and passed her like she was not a baby at all but a baton in some horrific race, trusting that the Stones would get her to the finish line.

They were sitting outside at Leunig's, in a sea of other mothers and other daughters, waiting for their food when she caught sight of a woman in the distance. She was nearly a block up the street, but she was blond, her hair in a high ponytail, and she was pushing a stroller. Crystal felt a tug in her chest as the woman came closer, as if they were connected somehow, sewn together at the chest, as if she were somehow reeling her in, pulling her closer with this invisible thread. She was filled with both a terrific sense of dread and excitement. Waiting for the moment to come, the moment when she would be able to make out the woman's face, to confirm that it was Mrs. Stone, and that inside that stroller was her baby. That it was Grace. Crystal felt like she might faint. She clutched the table, but couldn't take her eyes away. And then the woman's face came into focus. It wasn't her. And the baby in the stroller wasn't a baby but a toddler. A little boy with a crusty nose and overalls. Crystal felt like she might vomit.

"I'm not going, Mom."

"Not going where, sweetheart?" she asked, distracted. She was checking her phone for messages; Crystal had told her to go ahead. That she didn't mind.

"To school."

Her mother looked up, her bright face suddenly drained of color, making her peach-colored lipstick look alone on her face.

"Of course you are," she said. "Don't be silly."

"I can't," Crystal said. "I'm not ready."

"No one is ever *ready,* sweetie," she said. "You were like this before you went off to camp for the first time too, remember? I had to practically carry you onto the bus."

"This is not camp!" Crystal said, her voice quivery and high.

Her mother glanced around, smiling apologetically to all the other mothers, all the other daughters. "Of course not, sweetie. I'm just saying that it's natural to be nervous. To be anxious."

"I'm sorry," she said. "I can't do it. And if you make me go, I won't go to classes. I'll fail out. And I'll come home again anyway. Why not skip right to that part? Just fast-forward four months. Because that is exactly what is going to happen." Crystal felt manic, trapped at the table, trapped by the bags that were hanging off her seat, surrounding her feet. "I am so tired of pretending that none of this happened. I am sick and tired of pretending like I'm just some normal girl. I'm not. I made a mistake."

"I know," her mother said, still acting as though she were talking to a defiant child. "And you *took care* of that mistake." Her mother was smiling maniacally, as if she smiled hard enough she could make what was happening not happen.

"You don't get it, do you?" Crystal said, her chest about to explode. "The mistake wasn't getting pregnant. The mistake was letting you talk me into giving my baby up."

Her mother had gone from looking apologetic to looking mortified. "You need to stop, young lady," she said, as if Crystal were eight instead of eighteen. "You're making a spectacle of yourself." Her voice was hushed and furious.

The waitress came to their table, setting down their plates. "I can't," Crystal said, shaking her head, feeling the tears coming hot and hard. She practically knocked over her water glass as she stood up. She rushed toward the restaurant door and went inside, grateful that she was able to locate the restroom quickly. Inside the tiny room, which was decorated to look like some sort of Parisian *toilette,* she sat down on the toilet seat and waited for the heat in her head to dissipate, to somehow disperse through the rest of her body. She wondered if it was possible to bring on a fever by simple, sheer will. Finally, someone knocked on the door, and she gathered herself.

She found her mother outside, paying the waitress, both plates of food untouched. Her mother had gathered their bags together.

"I think it's time to go home," she said, without looking at Crystal.

Crystal nodded, suddenly compliant. And she did feel like a child. Like a child who had just had the biggest tantrum ever and somehow gotten her way. She followed behind her mother, scolded, all the way to the parking garage.

LAST FALL

The call came just as Kurt was getting ready to clock out at the 76 station. It was Labor Day, and he'd been there since dawn. It had been busier than usual, lots and lots of folks gassing up after a weekend on the road. Grumpy families who'd been stuck inside SUVs and RVs and station wagons for several days staggered in for energy drinks and Cheetos, road weary and miserable. He kept thinking about Elsbeth's suggestion that they drive to Florida. From the looks of these people, he was not convinced that loading his family, *any* family, into a car for three days was such a good idea. He was exhausted and just wanted to go home, have some supper, and go to bed, though he knew between Pop and Elsbeth and the kids this would be nearly impossible. School was starting tomorrow. There would be lunches to pack, school supplies to organize, Trevor to contend with. He knew that the end of summer meant the beginning of trouble.

His phone rang, and Jessica, the second-shift cashier, scootched in behind the counter, shooing him away as a customer came up with a six-pack of beer. "I got it."

He flipped open his phone and headed to the stockroom.

"Hello, Mr. Kennedy? This is Gladys Rivers over at Plum's Retirement Community. I'm just calling to let you know that a room will be opening up here soon, and your father is at the top of our list."

"That's great!" he said, his whole mood lifting. He had begun to think that Pop might live in the backyard forever. "That's terrific. When can he move in?"

"Well, the resident is actually moving to another facility, so it won't be until December first, but if you get the paperwork in now, we'll have everything ready."

Kurt punched his card in the stockroom and grabbed a Pay-Day from the rack by the register, fishing into his pocket for some change. Jessica scooped the change into her hand and smacked her gum. "Have a good one," she said.

Kurt felt light, happy. Even his legs felt free. He couldn't wait to tell Elsbeth that Pop would be leaving. That he could get the trailer and all of Pop's stuff cleared out in a matter of hours. That she could have her house back. Her life back. December first. Just another couple of months. They could do this.

Once Pop was finally out, they'd have their home back. They'd be a family again. Pop's Medicare would cover the expenses of the home, and if they could convince Pop to rent out his house, or maybe even sell it, that would mean some income. He could quit the station. Focus on the yard. Get Beal to come back full-time. Get it all together again. Maybe even take El on that vacation she wanted. He knew all of this had been temporary. It was just a matter of sucking it up and weathering the storm, which now finally seemed to be receding.

As he was walked toward the 76's doors, the bright fluorescent lights yielding to the darkening sky outside, he stopped at the rack of flowers wrapped in bright green cellophane. They were $6.95 a bunch. Way overpriced, like just about everything in the store, but he grabbed the best-looking bouquet and went back to the register.

At home, there were dirty plates on the kitchen table; they'd eaten without him. There was a frying pan white with congealed grease on the stove top, and the air smelled like burgers. All he'd eaten all day was a frozen burrito and the PayDay he had devoured in the car. The smells of dinner made his stomach rumble. He could hear the TV in the living room and the sound of a bath running. He set the flowers down and went to the bathroom door, leaning quietly against the jamb.

Elsbeth was kneeling next to the tub, her hands massaging shampoo into Gracy's hair. Gracy was giggling and splashing, her body brown from an entire summer at the pool. A Little Mermaid doll floated on her back next to her, and their hair tangled together, floating like seaweed in the water. From the doorway, Kurt studied Elsbeth as she leaned over Gracy. God, her body still just about did him in. He ached, his whole body ached, with desire for her. It was almost painful, this wanting. Excruciating.

And suddenly, he understood her longing. Her pleas to get away, to take a trip, came from the same place as this almost mournful desire he was feeling as he watched her. As he longed for her, he suddenly appreciated her own simple yearning. She'd been telling him what she needed, and he'd been denying her. How could he expect anything other than rejection from her in return? Why were her wants any less real than his? No wonder she was slipping away. It wasn't her fault; it was *his*.

"El," he said.

"Daddy!" Gracy squealed. "Look, I have rabbit ears!" She pulled her own hair up into two pointed soapy bunny ears at the top of her head.

Without looking up at him, El reached for a little purple plastic bowl that was teetering at the edge of the tub and dipped it into the water. "Time to rinse," she said. "Close your eyes tight."

"I got a call from Plum's today. There's a spot at the home."

Elsbeth turned around, her eyes wide and hopeful. "Really?"

Kurt nodded. "And if we can get his house rented out, I'm going to quit the 76."

"Are you sure?"

Kurt nodded. "Well, it doesn't open up until December first, but right after Thanksgiving everything should be back to normal."

Elsbeth stood up and came to him, her hands wet and soapy. She wrapped her arms around him and pressed her cheek against his chest. He could feel the bath water seeping into the fabric of his shirt. "Promise, things will get better," she whispered into his ear.

Kurt nodded.

She pulled back. "I'm serious, Kurt. Cross your heart."

Kurt felt his fingers making the motion across his chest, but even as his fingertips grazed the place where Elsbeth's cheek had just been, he felt the familiar buzzing in his legs. The reminding thrum of so many broken promises.

The first day of school, Trevor woke up in a cold sweat, his entire body protesting as he pulled back the covers and sat up in bed. Gracy was awake already, getting dressed in her new first-day-of-school outfit.

"Can you help me?" she asked, struggling to pull the plaid dress over her head.

"Come here," he said and undid the button at the neck so that her head could slip through. Her hair was electrified with static, sticking out all over. He patted her hair down and smiled at her. He wondered what it must be like to be Gracy, to be so happy.

"Are you excited for school?" she asked.

"Not really," he said.

"How come? You don't like your new teacher?"

Trevor shrugged. He'd gotten the envelope with the information about his classes, about his teachers, about his homeroom, but none of it mattered. What mattered was if Mike and Ethan were in any of those classes with him. What mattered was whether or not their paths would cross during the day, whether or not they'd be breathing down his neck during math, English, social studies. What mattered was, with Mrs. D. gone, where he would go during recess and lunch.

"I love my new teacher. She has curly hair. I know 'cause I've seen her before. And we can eat lunch together now that I'm not in kindergarten."

Trevor took a deep breath. The kindergartners were in a separate building, but first graders were in the same building with the older kids. Their classrooms were on the opposite side of the building, but they shared the same cafeteria, the same playground. He was worried about what this might mean. For one thing, he didn't want Mike and Ethan to have one more thing to bother him about, and having a little sister tagging along would give them plenty of ammunition. He was also afraid that being his sister might somehow make her fair game to their abuse. But his worst fear was that Gracy would see how they treated him, that she would hear the names they called him, see the hatred in their eyes. That she would grow to be ashamed of him.

"I usually go to the art room for lunch," he said. "And you'll probably have friends you want to eat with too," he said.

"No way." She smiled. "I want to be with you."

Their mother drove them to school, and Trevor leaned his head against the window, trying to cool the heat that seemed to be burning like a furnace in his stomach. It was September, but the air was hot and humid still. *Indian* summer, everyone said. And he tried to imagine himself a warrior, dignified and brave. But as they got out of the car and his mom insisted on walking them into the building, he could feel his resolve dissolving. The building with its windows like glowering eyes, the big front doors like a puckered mouth, made him feel like the school itself was scowling at him.

Mrs. Cross was standing in the doorway in a bright blue dress, smiling and saying *hello* to each of the children as they entered the building. The security camera's red eye winked at each of them as they passed.

"Well, good morning, Gracy!" she said, bending down to Gracy and touching the top of her head. "I think you've grown about six inches since I saw you last. And did you lose a tooth?"

Gracy smiled, shoving her tongue through the new space.

"Oh, *two* teeth!"

Mrs. Cross stood back upright and reached out for Trevor's hand. "Welcome back, Trevor. I trust we're going to have a good year this year?" Her face pinched together as though she had a mouthful of staples.

Trevor ignored her hand, looked to the ground and nodded. Thankfully, his mother let him head off to find his locker while she took Gracy to her classroom. "No fighting," she said softly. "Please."

Trevor pretended he was surrounded by a bubble, a thick bubble made of something impenetrable. Something that rendered him invisible. If he concentrated hard enough, he knew he could make himself simply disappear. He would mind his own business. He would speak to no one. He would not react to anything. He would become blind, deaf, and dumb. He would cease to exist.

"Hey, Ethan, it's your *girlfriend!*" Mike said, punching Ethan in the shoulder. They were standing next to his locker. Blocking it. He blinked long and hard, invisible, *invincible,* and then reached between them to open the latch. He had a padlock in his backpack, but for now, it was unlocked.

"We missed you at the pool. What happened, did your mama have to spend the rest of the summer potty training you?"

The latch came loose in his fingers, and he opened it. Ethan pressed his fist against the locker door. "What do you think you're doing?" he asked.

Trevor focused on his own hand, studied his knuckles, the architecture of bone and tendons. He willed it to stay relaxed, palm splayed rather than knotting into the fist it wanted to become.

"Aw, go ahead and let him open it," Mike said. And then Ethan lifted his hand, the metal door swinging open and crashing against the neighboring locker.

Trevor peered into the darkness and recoiled. A pile of dog shit sat inside. Wet and loose, smeared across the bottom of the locker. Trevor started to gag.

"Welcome back, fudge packer!" Ethan hissed, and then they were gone, running down the hallway.

Trevor looked down the hallway and Mrs. Cross looked back

at him, her eyes like slits. He closed the locker, shifting his back-pack onto his left shoulder, and as the bell rang, he rushed down the hallway to his homeroom.

When the last bell rang at the end of the day, he waited for the halls to empty out and he quickly cleaned out the locker, dumping mountains of soiled paper towels into the trash cans. He scrubbed the locker with the powdery soap from the restroom until it was clean. He watched carefully to make sure no one saw what he was doing. No one needed to know about this. He wouldn't tattle. He wouldn't start school off this way.

After school, he went to the woods, trudging through the heat and thick foliage, aware of the heft of his breath, the heavi-ness of his body, the way the earth yielded to him. Inside the ca-boose, he lay on his back in the darkness. With the sheet metal now secured in the windows, there was absolute darkness. Not a single ray of sunlight could find him in here. He could not see out, and no one could see in. Blind. Deaf. Dumb. Alone. This was his dominion, his kingdom. His own private tomb. He knew what he needed to do, but he wasn't sure where to begin. He would need things, things he didn't have access to at home. He would need chemicals. Equipment. He would need privacy. He would need to be left alone.

Elsbeth would try. She would give it one last shot. Kurt had promised he would make things right again. Pop would move out, Kurt would quit his night job, they'd rent Pop's house out and everything would be back to normal. They'd get Trevor some help at school. Maybe they'd even finally be able to get away. Maybe this winter.

Winter would be here soon; despite the heat of an Indian summer, the leaves were starting to turn. Just a sugar maple here and there. A bright bloom of red amidst all that green. Within a few weeks, the color would have bled through, the color spreading through the trees like something contagious. The air would chill. The sky would first brighten and then grow dark. Snow would come. The dark, cold chill of winter would be here.

She tried to remember back to those autumn days years ago, when she and Kurt were young. She tried to recollect the good feeling of his scratchy sweater against her cheek at football games. The cold bleacher seats beneath them, the hot cocoa warming her hands. The feeling that her life was just about to begin. She tried to recollect the anxious feeling she got in her stomach when she waited for him to call. The nausea that came when she knew it might be hours, a day, before she could see him again. She tried to recall the way she held her breath then. The way she thought she might explode with the need for him to touch her.

She tried to remember what it felt like when she was falling in love. The way the rest of the world blurred as the two of them remained sharply in focus. As though nothing else in the entire world mattered except for his hands, his lips, his hair, his throat, the thick, hot feeling of him inside her.

After she dropped the kids off at school, she called the salon and told Carly that she would be a little late. She didn't have any clients scheduled until eleven o'clock, so she'd only be letting down the walk-ins. She had time.

She drove downtown and parked in the far end of the big lot in front of the JCPenney. She could feel her whole body trembling. She checked her reflection in the mirror, startled by the dark circles under her eyes, and then got out of the car, suddenly more determined than she had been before.

Inside, the smell of the perfume counter was thick, sweet, almost sickening. Her nose tickled; she thought she might sneeze. A lady with a pair of glasses on a gold chain around her neck smiled at her, lifting a glass bottle of perfume up, offering to spray her. She started to shake her head and then stopped—*Why not?*—offering her the inside of her wrist. The spray was cold. She lifted her wrist to her nose and she was overwhelmed by the smell of gardenias.

She made her way past Men's Wear and Juniors and Children, touching the soft hems of dresses and blouses and coats. She wandered past the Baby section and into Lingerie. She touched the lace bras, the sexy boy shorts and thongs, filled her hands with little plastic hangers.

"How many?" the saleslady asked, barely looking up from the jeans she was folding.

"Three," Elsbeth lied and disappeared behind the dressing room door.

She tried on bras and teddies and robes. Examined herself, tried to imagine how she might look through Kurt's eyes. She touched herself cautiously, imagining Kurt's fingers on the inside of her thighs.

She knew that if she looked at the price tags on the items she'd picked, she'd lose her resolve. And so she carefully pulled the tags off, shoving them into the pocket of a robe she left hanging

GRACE

229

in the dressing room. Then she pulled her clothes back on over a black lace bra and pair of matching panties, and returned the three bras to the saleslady.

"Find everything okay?" the woman asked. "Can I get you a different size?"

Elsbeth smiled. "No thank you . . . I'm on my way to work. I'll come back another time."

On her way to the front of the store, she stopped at a rack of little girl dresses. She picked one that she knew Gracy would like, took it to the register and set it down. "Just this," she said and pulled out her credit card, feeling the lace of the stolen lingerie cool against her fevered skin.

Beyond not going to school this fall, Crystal didn't have a plan, not really. But she did know that regardless of what she decided to do now, she couldn't depend on her parents for much longer. Her mother wouldn't speak to her after their trip to Burlington except when she absolutely had to, and her father had only taken her aside and said sadly, "You have until January first. And then you either go to college or you move out." Every moment in her parents' house was wrought with a sense of exasperation and finality. They were slowly giving up on her. She recognized this acceptance of failure from a year ago when she'd told them she was going to keep the baby.

She'd deferred her acceptance to appease them. What they didn't know, or didn't want to acknowledge, was that she had no intention of ever enrolling. She pictured that girl, the one she might have been, sprawled beneath a shady tree, books spread out before her. She mourned the loss of this girl like the loss of a friend. She tried to imagine an alternative future, but every time she tried to conjure tomorrow, there was nothing but shadows. She waited for the shadows to take shape, to emerge, for their edges to sharpen. She trusted, because she had to, that they would eventually speak to her.

In the meantime, she knew that whatever she did, she needed to be smart. She had a job, and she had $6,000 in the bank. It seemed like a small fortune, though she knew that once her parents kicked her out it wouldn't go far. She knew she'd need to be careful about how she used her cash. She needed to think like a grown-up, like an adult.

The first thing she would need would be mobility. If she didn't have a car, there was no way she could even get to work. No way, once winter came, that she'd be able to get anywhere. She looked online, rode her bike past the used car dealership in town, checked the ads in the local paper. She considered asking her father for his advice, but quickly reconsidered. She knew that if she asked for his help, he'd only scoff at the pieces of shit she could afford. He'd balk at the stupidity of buying a vehicle with a hundred thousand miles on it. He'd make her take anything she had her eye on to his personal mechanic, who would likely deem it a deathtrap. He'd shake his head, throw his hands up. And so she found herself alone in the old man's driveway, sitting in the driver's seat of a 1985 Volvo wagon, talking to him through the rolled-down window.

"I'll knock the price down to a thousand if you've got cash," he said.

The man's name was Roger Lund, and she'd seen his ad on the bulletin board at the Walgreens, the blurry photo. The handwritten specs.

"It's got a leak, the power steering fluid, you should know that. I'm an honest guy. I just keep a jug in the car. It's a slow leak, nothing that you should worry about."

She sat in the car, gripping the steering wheel, nodding. The tan upholstery was torn but soft. A pine tree freshener hung from the rearview mirror. She peered into the cavernous backseat. The car was huge. She could fit everything she owned in the back. She could load up everything she had if she needed to. She could practically live in here.

"It handles real good in the snow too. Weighs about a ton," he said, patting the enormous hood. "A real good, safe car for kids. You got any kids?"

She looked at him, shocked. "I'm only *eighteen,*" she said and then realized how ludicrous it was that she was alarmed by his question. She pushed the thoughts of the baby, a car seat, out of her mind. "No, I don't," she said.

"Well then, here's the name of my mechanic. He's worked on this car since I bought it new for my wife. She passed away last year."

"Thanks," she said, taking the slip of paper and stuffing it in the visor, noticing that there was a silver St. Christopher medallion tucked in there too.

"Is this yours?" she asked, holding the medallion out to him.

"You keep it. He'll keep you safe on the road."

Something about this simple gesture made her eyes fill with tears.

"Won't get far without the key, though," he said, chuckling and reaching into his coat pocket. He handed her the key through the window. In exchange she counted out ten one-hundred-dollar bills from the envelope they'd given her at the bank. *A thousand dollars*. She'd never spent so much money on one thing in her whole life. The very thought of it nearly made her heart stop. But the most important thing was taken care of now, and as she maneuvered the giant boat of a car out of the old man's tiny driveway, she felt a rush of something she hadn't felt in a long, long time. As she drove through town, past Ty's house with her own parents' faces smiling from the For Sale sign, past the Walgreens, past the on-ramp to the interstate, she felt the wonderful trill of *possibility*.

She parked the car on Ty's old block so she wouldn't have to tell her parents right away, and she walked past his house slowly, peering at the curtainless windows and empty driveway. The Tibetan prayer flags his father had strung from the porch roof were gone now, the faded rainbow-colored mailbox replaced by a plain brass one. She stopped the car and looked in her rearview mirror to make sure no one was coming. Then she got out of the car and ran across the street to the empty house.

She was a little girl again as she made her way up the footpath, skipping over the cracks, counting the stones. When she got to the front porch, she ran her hand along the railing, careful to skip the spot right before the top of the steps. She'd gotten a splinter there once before. Lucia had taken it out with tweezers, distracting her with a homemade pomegranate popsicle. The lockbox was on the door, but she knew almost right away what the combination would be. 1993, the year Ty and she were born. 1993 was Lucia's PIN number, the password to everything. Her fingers trembled as she tried the combination, but it was with steady hands and a thumping heart that she slipped the key into her palm and then used it to open the front door.

Inside, the house was empty and light. Without curtains, the sun had full access. Scuffed wood floors; she knew the origins of most of the scars: from the ancient upright piano Lucia could never decide where to keep. From Ty's skateboard. Dizzy's roller skates.

She went upstairs slowly, anticipating every groan and sigh of the stairs. When she got to the landing, she felt ill. But she pressed on, down the long hallway, past the girls' rooms to the place where the attic stairs pulled down. She climbed the ladder to Ty's room and felt her entire body aching, like something hollow, as empty as an abandoned home.

She just needed to see if it was still there. The secret they'd sworn to keep. If it was gone, then she knew she'd be able to let go. Because it would mean that he had as well. She went to the window seat that looked out over their back lawn, studying the tops of the trees. The branches were bare now, just frail gray bones. When she and Ty had sat here that afternoon, they had been vibrant and green, obscuring the view of the graveyard beyond. Today she could see the stones in their tidy rows. All those sad memorials.

"What should we name her?" Ty had asked, touching her stomach with his fingertips, as though reading Braille. He'd pushed his fingers down beneath the waistband of her jeans, and she'd felt like she might pass out as his fingers dipped and probed.

"I don't know," she said. "We don't even know for sure that it's a girl."

"What about *Grace*?" he asked.

"Huh?" she asked. Her eyes were closed now as she felt his fingers moving against her.

"Grace."

"Why?" she asked, her breath getting caught in her throat, her hips moving toward him, magnetic.

"Remember the time Mom took us to the graveyard and we made those rubbings?"

She remembered; it was summertime, and the grass was freshly cut. The smell of it was so strong she wondered if smells were alive. They had big sheets of butcher paper, a box of sixty-four crayons.

"You got hot and my mom told you to lie down on one of the stones because they were cool," he said. "And I remembered thinking you looked like a sleeping princess. I almost kissed you to wake you up."

"You did not," she said, smacking his arm.

"I did."

"We were only five!"

"I was an early bloomer." He smirked.

She rolled her eyes.

"I used to go back to that gravestone all the time. Remember? It didn't say anything except *GRACE* in big letters. I remember thinking that was the most beautiful word in the whole world. It's a word that means a lot of things. But the definition I like best is *divine favor.* A favor from the gods. Like she's a gift."

Crystal studied his face, looking for something she couldn't name. *Grace.* "You'll stay," she said, a question. A plea. "We'll do this together?"

He looked at her, his face as serious as a granite stone, and nodded. Then he pulled his pocketknife out of his pocket and scratched the word into the windowsill.

G-R-A-C-E.

Now she ran her finger over the wood, over the word. The only word that ever mattered. He didn't sand it down or even scratch it out. He didn't destroy it; he only left it behind.

Trevor must have been crazy to think he could do this on his own. He'd managed to get the sheet metal up to block the light from the windows of the caboose, but so what? He didn't have any of the other stuff he needed. What he had was a cave. A dark, cool cave where no one on earth could find him. After school every day, he went to the caboose and tried to figure out a way to make it work, making lists of what he needed, sketching out diagrams and plans. Maybe it was a stupid idea. Maybe he should just be content with having this quiet place where no one would bother him.

The last time they were at Pop's, Trevor had found a battery-operated fan and a small generator. He'd asked his father if he could have them, and when he asked what for, Trevor said, "The fan's to put next to my bed." It was still hot. Summer still hanging on, resisting the inevitable chill of autumn. "And I just wanted to mess around with the generator. See if I can make it work." What he figured he could really do with the fan was create some ventilation in the caboose. And the generator actually *did* work; he'd need it to power the equipment. He'd also found an old utility sink in Pop's backyard. He thought he might be able to rig it up somehow. But all of this was useless without the necessary equipment. The chemicals. And the only place he was going to find that stuff was at the school.

Being at school was like walking through a minefield or getting lost in some awful fun house. He never knew when Mike or Ethan might just pop up, never knew when the next ambush might be. He tried a different route from class to class each day, hoping to throw them off course. But while he could elude them one day, on other days they seemed to anticipate his every move. Their taunts followed him; their words like snakes, hissing and curling around him, when he least expected it. He still sought solace in the art room, though without Mrs. D. there, it wasn't at all the same safe haven it had been.

The new art teacher, Mr. Franklin, had told them they would be doing a short unit on photography and then promptly showed them a bin of cheap digital cameras and two ancient computers, only one of which had Photoshop on it. Trevor's heart had sunk.

"What about the darkroom?" he'd asked quietly. He almost never spoke in class, in any class, and his voice seemed to startle everyone, including himself.

"Those chemicals are terrible," he said. "Completely toxic. The district's concerned with liability issues. Besides, it's an antiquated art form." Mr. Franklin probably would have thought that Mrs. D. was an antiquated art form herself. He couldn't have been older than Trevor's mom.

Trevor thought about all the rolls of film in his drawer. He could barely remember the images he'd captured anymore. Gracy, his *muse,* had grown so much since he started taking pictures. He bet that she'd look like a different girl in the pictures he'd taken over the summer. He loved that the camera helped him to freeze time, to hold onto something that won't last no matter how hard you try to make it. But until he developed the photos, they were just dreams captured in their canisters. Worthless.

During the first week of school, he'd somehow mustered up the courage to ask Mr. Franklin if he could spend his lunch periods in the art room. Mr. Franklin had looked at him suspiciously but said, "Ah, why not? But I'm on lunch duty, so I'll be in the cafeteria. You can hang out here as long as you don't mess with anything." He'd raised his eyebrow at Trevor, as if gauging whether or not Trevor was trustworthy.

Mr. Franklin was unimpressed by Trevor's art. He fawned over

Angie's sketches and paintings (which were beautiful but strange—mostly wide-eyed girls with giant bellies). But he pretty much ignored everyone else. Mr. Franklin was young and handsome; all the girls in the class giggled and whispered whenever he turned his back. Trevor studied him. He was tall and athletic-looking. He wore soft, worn jeans and sweater vests over crisp white cotton shirts. He always had the shadow of a beard, and his hair curled over the top of his shirt collar. His voice was deep. His hands large. Trevor wondered what he was like as a kid. If kids had ever picked on him. He doubted it. Trevor missed Mrs. D. and her ratty sweaters and musty breath. She was like a cozy chair, a favorite blanket. He felt disconnected without her there, a balloon that's been cut loose in a building, hovering above everything. Untethered and precarious but still captured. One move in the wrong direction and he might just pop.

During lunch, he waited for Mr. Franklin to leave the classroom, pretending to work on a charcoal drawing he'd started of a bowl of grapes and figs. But as soon as the doors closed behind him, Trevor quickly disappeared into the darkroom. His fingers grazed the trays. He lowered and raised the enlarger, flicked the red safe light on and off. He ran his fingers across the packs of paper, the coiled film spools, the piles of clips. He went to the locker where the chemicals and paper were kept. Mrs. D. had shown him where she kept the key, hanging from a cup hook on the opposite wall. Inside the locker there were three shelves of chemicals: *Developer, Stop Bath, Fixer,* all labeled in Sharpie, in Mrs. D.'s careful handwriting. Seeing this trace of her made him miss her more. He knew he should go see her again, but her apartment had made him feel sad, and without pictures, he wasn't sure what they could talk about.

Suddenly filled with a sense of purpose, Trevor studied the contents of one jug, *acetic acid,* then lifted it from the shelf and carried it back to the art room. His heart beating hard in his chest, he unzipped his backpack and put the jug inside. He returned to his desk, carefully setting his pack down, and continued drawing, shading, and erasing until the sides of his hands were black. When the bell rang, he heaved the backpack onto his shoulder and quickly left the art room, passing Mr. Franklin on his way back in.

"You get some work done?" he asked.

"Yeah," Trevor said, afraid Mr. Franklin might hear the sloshing of the stop bath in his pack. Mr. Franklin smiled. "You know, Trevor, I really like a student who puts in the extra effort. Any time you'd like to stay after class, you're more than welcome. And I'll take a peek at your work, see if I can come up with some pointers." Trevor thought of those lopsided grapes with the shading all wrong. The figs that looked like shriveled-up ears instead of fruit. And he thought about all those photos, the ones just waiting to be developed. All those moments just waiting to be exposed. Trevor rushed past him into the hallway, which was thick with students now, moving in swarms like buzzing insects. He kept his head down and made his way through the throngs to his class.

Later, after sixth period, he walked quickly down the main hall, past Mr. Douglas, who was engaged in a battle with a mop bucket, and it struck him that while Mr. Douglas acted like he was some sort of armed guard in the morning, by the afternoon he was more concerned with emptying wastebaskets and mopping the floors. He didn't care what *left* the school, he only cared what came in. If Trevor was careful, he could get everything he needed. Well, almost everything. When it came to the bigger stuff, he'd need to come up with a plan. But for now, he could at least get started.

Kurt knew that it wouldn't be as simple as telling his father he was moving into the retirement home. He would have to have been stupid to think that it would be that easy. He knew Pop. He thought long and hard about how he might present the news, how he might temper it, slant it so that it sounded appealing to him. He'd have to paint a picture that was based in truth but highlighted in the right places. Like a lawyer. He almost wished Billy were here to give him some advice on how to make his case.

He stood at the kitchen sink, bleary-eyed from another day and night of back-to-back shifts, his eyes barely registering the motions his hands conducted. The pouring of coffee, of milk. The wipe-down of a spill. The closing of cabinet doors. His body was operating solely out of habit, taking over while his brain got the rest it so desperately needed. He knew that he was just a few more sleepless nights away from lunacy. He'd heard that you could actually lose your mind with insomnia. Start seeing things that weren't there.

Through the window, he studied the disaster that Pop had made of the backyard in just the couple of months that he'd been living there. He tried to imagine how others might see it. What the neighbors, if they had any, might have thought. Pop was like an animal, like a rat. Collecting, gathering, protecting, and keeping. His possessions were meaningless, ridiculous, to everyone but him. Kurt had tried again and again to find the empathy a good son should have, but that well had dried up a long time ago. Now Pop's stuff just made him angry. He knew that sending him off to

the home was ultimately for his own safety, what any good son
would do, but he also knew there would be a certain satisfaction
in throwing everything away. In clearing Pop's mess out of his
life. Of confining him to the small room at the home where it
was someone else demanding order, cleanliness. He was tired of
being the bad guy, the one always making demands.

He knew Pop would resist. That he would argue and fight.
He would accuse and try to make Kurt feel as though he hadn't
done enough. He might lock himself in the trailer and never
come out. Like an angry kid throwing a tantrum.

But then Kurt thought about Elsbeth. About the reward. Two
nights before, she came to him. Took him by surprise. She offered
herself to him in a way that he'd forgotten she could. She'd undressed him and then herself, revealing some lingerie he'd never
seen before. He was too turned on to even worry how much it
had cost her. They were like teenagers again, awkward and shy
and stumbling and hungry. She'd clung to him after, her whole
body still quaking. She'd slept curled around him, the pulse points
of her body aligning with his. Music of blood. The smell of their
bodies hovering in the air.

But he also knew Elsbeth. He knew that she had shown him
this, given him this night, as a tentative promise. It was conditional. He knew that if he screwed up, she could take things away
as readily as she had given them to him. She was testing him, teasing him. She'd whispered in his ear again, "Promise."

He had promised. Promised so many things. But this time, he
knew that if he was unable to deliver, she might just finally disappear. That she might slip out from the covers, slip through his fingers, slip out the door.

He threw back the cup of coffee, which burned his throat,
and set it down in the sink. He buttoned his flannel and readied
himself for a fight. Pop needed to start packing. This was it.

The heat had finally broken, like a resistant eggshell, spilling a
cold chill. The air felt numb, liquid. Kurt went to the trailer and
knocked on the door. It struck him, as his knuckles rapped

against the flimsy metal, that there was no way Pop could survive in the trailer when the weather truly turned. It was no more than a metal can on wheels. It would have been like living inside a tuna can. He had no choice. He would be safe at Plum's. Taken care of. Warm.

He could hear Pop shuffling about inside, and for a moment, he panicked that maybe Pop was trapped under a pile of something. Buried under the rubble he'd created. But then the door flew open and Pop stood there, hair slicked back. Clothes tidy and clean. Face shaven and fists clenched.

"I know whatcha come for," he said.

"Oh good," Kurt said, startled. He hadn't been prepared for this. "I meant to tell you sooner, but I was worried you might not want to go."

Pop stared out at the empty field beyond the yard, his eyes glassy.

"Listen, they've got a room. It's a good-sized room. The food is supposed to be excellent. There's a shuttle that will take you into town whenever you'd like to go shopping, to the barbershop. And of course I'll be by all the time. You can bring your own bed if you want to, but they have a linen service. Someone will do your laundry. It'll be like living at a hotel."

Pop shook his head.

"They've got bingo and poker tournaments. Movies on the weekends. They've got cable in every room."

"I ain't going," he said.

Kurt smiled, ready for this. "I know it's a big change, but, Pop, you need to be somewhere where there are nurses. Where you're safe. You can't live here through the winter. You'd freeze to death. Plum's is a good place. It's clean and your Medicare will pay for it."

"I said I ain't going anywhere," he said. "Unless it's back to my own goddamned house."

Fall came quickly and without warning. The heat broke and suddenly it was frigid. Winter's fingers were prying; Crystal could feel them as she lay in her bed, touching her. Warning her. She thought of Ty in California. Daydreamed the palm trees and sunshine and the beach. As she shivered under the covers, she conjured dream seagulls, crashing waves, and bellowing foghorns.

She'd never been to California. Never been anywhere farther south than Boston, never farther west than Burlington. She thought about leaving. About running away. About packing up all those towels and sheets and bulletin boards her mother had insisted upon and leaving. She wondered if the Volvo would be able to take her long distances or if it would fail her, leave her stranded.

But whenever she considered fleeing, she also thought about Grace. The thought of being far from her was excruciating. It was ridiculous, she knew. She wasn't a part of her life. She was no one to her. But still, she felt bound to her as though they were tethered together.

It had been six months. A half of a year. The baby she'd given to the Stones wouldn't be the same baby anymore. She went to the parenting websites and studied the milestone charts. She looked at the photos of babies at one month, three months, a year. She tried to picture Grace, her tiny hands now grasping. Her small body maybe even starting to crawl. She tried to hear her cooing, imitating sounds. She tried to smell her, the scent of powder and milk. The sites said that by now a baby would recognize faces. Know who her mother was. Might be anxious about being separated from her. She wouldn't recognize Crystal at all. She wouldn't know her. Wouldn't love her.

Crystal wondered if she'd made a mistake not accepting Mrs. Stone's offer for an open adoption. She tried to imagine what her life would be like if she had agreed to this arrangement. If she'd just gone off to UVM like she was expected to, living so close to her. Would there be weekend visits? Would she sit in their beautiful living room full of books and thrift-store furniture and poetry, watching as Grace crawled across the floor? Would she be allowed to hold her, to smell the heady scent coming from the top of her head? To feel the tiny flutter of her heart against her chest? Who would she be to Grace? Who was she without her?

She worked. She worked and worked and worked. Forty, fifty hours a week. She spent nothing, saved every penny. She stood in line at the ATM with her paychecks, watched as the balance grew. It was all she knew how to do.

The woman, the one with the child named Grace, kept coming into the Walgreens and Crystal said nothing, even as her rage grew. Crystal watched her as she pocketed Life Savers, tea lights, greeting cards. She studied her as she pilfered packs of gum and aspirin, magazines and ballpoint pens. It both angered her and fascinated her. She watched this other Grace, oblivious, dancing in the aisles.

One morning the woman came in and went straight to the film counter, where Crystal was going through prints that had not been picked up, making calls to remind people to come in and get them.

"Brr." The woman shivered. "It's like January out there and not even Halloween yet."

Crystal nodded. The little girl was bundled up in a ratty pink jacket with a furry hood framing her face. Her cheeks were flushed red, her nose runny.

"Do you guys offer a discount when you have a lot of rolls? Like a coupon or something?" the woman asked.

"We have specials sometimes. Let me check this week's flier." Crystal reached for a flier from a stack behind the counter and thumbed through it quickly to see if there were any specials. "How many rolls do you have?"

"*A lot.* They're my son's. He's got like thirty rolls, though, so I only brought about half of them. See?" She opened up her purse and Crystal peered in, wondering how many stolen things lay beneath the mountains of film, stunned by her willingness to reveal the contents of her purse.

"I could maybe talk to my manager and see if we can get you a discount. If you leave the film here, I can just call you and let you know."

"That would be awesome. He's really into this photography thing, but it costs so much to get the film developed. His birthday's coming up, and I thought it would be nice to do this for him."

"That's cool," Crystal said. Grace, the little girl, was twirling down the aisle where the walk-in coolers were, leaving tiny muddy footprints on the linoleum.

"Hey, would it be okay if I gave her a lollipop?" Crystal asked.

"Sure," the woman said.

Crystal came from behind the counter and grabbed a couple of Tootsie Pops from the display. "Grace?" she said, the word too sweet on her tongue, and the little girl turned around. She smiled at Crystal, and she felt her heart bottom out. She bent down to her and said, "Your mom says it's okay for you to have a treat. Do you like cherry or chocolate?"

"Chocolate," she said and reached for the lollipop. Her tiny fingers closed around the stick and Crystal felt light-headed.

"You okay?" the woman asked.

Crystal stood back up, steadying herself. "Yeah. I'm fine. I think I just forgot to eat breakfast."

After they were gone, she followed the pattern of those tiny footprints with her own feet until the place where they ended at the door where her mother had scooped her up.

Trevor's days were spent dodging and scheming; his life was like an elaborate game of hide-and-seek where he was always It. He pictured Ethan and Mike, counting, giving him just enough time to hide before seeking. Stalking. After two months back at school, they were still just as relentless and intent.

On the Friday morning before Halloween, he woke up panicked. He'd dreamed about being in the locker room again, the stink of his own excrement waking him. But as he opened his eyes, afraid that he'd soiled the sheets, that his bowels had once again betrayed him, he realized it was only the smell coming from the backyard. From Pop's garbage, which he stacked in disgusting piles against the side of the house.

"Do you like my costume?" Gracy asked. She was up already, twirling in an elaborate pink dress. She was wearing a sparkly tiara and plastic high heels.

"Who are you?" Trevor asked.

"I'm *Aurora,* dummy," she said. "Sleeping Beauty. What are you gonna be for Halloween?"

"I'm too old for that," he said, but then he thought maybe it wouldn't be such a bad idea. If he wore a mask, something to disguise himself, he wouldn't have to hide. He could walk through the halls like any other kid. He could be invisible.

"Hey, where's that Jason mask?" he asked. "Is it in your dress-up box?"

"I don't like that one. It's scary!" she said.

But then Trevor was up and digging through the cardboard

dress-up box in the closet. He found the hockey mask under a pile of Hawaiian leis and a fluffy black feather boa.

"Don't put it on, Trevor. I hate that!" Gracy was starting to tear up, but fighting it.

"I won't. It's just for school."

"Are you going to be in the parade?" she asked.

Trevor shook his head. "Nah."

She shrugged and jumped off her bed, snagging the edge of her skirt on the bedpost; he could hear the fabric ripping, knew that this would send her over the edge. "It's okay, we can fix it," he said. His mother had given him a sewing kit a long time ago, in case he ever needed to sew a button on. He'd shoved it in his sock drawer and forgotten about it. It was one of those things his mother did sometimes, offering him weird little trinkets he didn't really need. He went to his sock drawer and pulled it open. He barely had room for his socks anymore since the rolls of film had been piling up.

The film. Where was his film? There must have been thirty rolls of film, and now there were only a dozen or so.

"Gracy? Did you take my film?" he bellowed. She was sitting on the edge of his bed, her tattered skirt splayed before her like a patient.

"What's film?"

And then it hit him. His mother. She hated his camera. She had been threatening to take it away from him. But he hadn't even done anything. Why would she do this? He thought about all those lost pictures. He felt that awful metallic taste in his throat. Acerbic and stinging.

"Mom?" he hollered, stomping down the hallway to the kitchen.

"She's not here," his father said. "She went into work early so she can come to your parade at school."

"Did she take my film?" he asked, feeling his hands clenching and unclenching.

"What are you talking about?" his father asked. He looked tired, purple half moons under each heavy eye.

"Nothing," Trevor said, eyes stinging.

His father drove them to school. Despite the frigid air, Trevor asked to ride in the back of the truck. The leaves had already turned to fire and then ash. The branches were bare now, gray arms reaching toward the sky. It looked like they were asking for something, pleading with the heavens. He could taste snow in the back of his throat, the cold, sharp taste of winter.

He hopped out of the back of the truck as soon as his father pulled up in the drop-off lane, and reached into his backpack for the Jason mask. Scanning the crowd of costumed students funneling into the building, he put the mask on.

"Take it off, Trevor!" Gracy cried. "I don't like it."

Ignoring her, he grabbed her hand. "It's just a mask, Gracy. It's just me."

As they made their way to the school, he felt, for the first time in a long time, as though he belonged. Monsters, vampires, princesses. No one looked like themselves. Everyone was someone else, and he thought how cool it would be if Halloween were every day. If every day he could put on a costume and transform himself into somebody different. If he could hide in other people's clothes, inside other people's skin.

"Bye, Gracy!" he said, but she was still pouting. Still mad.

Everybody was distracted. Nobody was listening to the teachers. Even Mrs. Cross's voice from the speakers in the corner of the room barely registered over the excited din of the kids. But by the time third period came around and Trevor had art, everyone seemed to have calmed down a little bit. The novelty of the costumes had worn off. And once he was safe inside the art room, he took off his mask.

Angie sat down next to him. "What are you supposed to be?" she asked.

Trevor shrugged. "Nobody."

Her hair was in two braids secured at the top of her head with flowers and ribbons, and she had penciled between her eyebrows. "I'm Frida Kahlo," she said. "Obvi. Is that your mask?" she asked, pointing at his mask, which was sticking out of his backpack. "I guess it's kind of cool, kind of retro anyway."

Mr. Franklin made them spend the entire period sketching a stupid pumpkin he'd brought in. He projected a Winslow Homer painting on the screen, *The Pumpkin Patch,* but with the lights on, it was hard to even see what they were supposed to be looking at. Mrs. D. would never have done it this way. And about two minutes into class, the projector cut out.

"I can fix it," Trevor said. "There's an extra power supply in the darkroom. That's all it is usually. There's a short in that one."

"Great," Mr. Franklin said and sent Trevor to the darkroom to retrieve it.

Trevor couldn't stop thinking about the rolls of film. His mother wouldn't have destroyed them. At least he didn't think so. But not knowing where they were made him anxious. It was like she had stolen his journal. Inside those plastic canisters was his entire life.

In the darkroom, he searched for the power cord in a box of other cables. He'd managed to sneak out a whole bunch of stuff since school started, and luckily Mr. Franklin hadn't noticed that any of it was missing. He had gallons of chemicals now. They were safe in the caboose, but now the weather was starting to turn, he worried about them freezing. He knew he'd have to act quickly, before winter came. He found the cable, tangled like a snake in the other cords and wires, and his eyes fell on the timer. He didn't have his backpack, though. He'd have to wait until lunch when he was alone.

Mrs. Cross came over the loudspeaker just as everyone but Trevor was getting ready to go to fourth period. "Good afternoon, boys and girls. Just a reminder that the Halloween parade and costume contest will be starting in five minutes. Participation is mandatory, unless you have a note from home excusing you.

When the bell rings, you should line up, and your teachers will take you out to the blacktop. After the parade, you should all go to the cafeteria for lunch. We will announce the winners of the costume contest during lunch period."

In the past, the parade had been optional, though almost everybody except Logan Monroe, who was a Jehovah's Witness, participated. Last year Trevor had spent the hour with Mrs. D.

Trevor went to Mr. Franklin's desk. "Can I hang out here during the parade?"

"Do you have a note from home?"

Trevor shook his head.

"Sorry, buddy. There's nothing I can do for you. You heard Mrs. Cross."

Outside it was freezing. Trevor had forgotten his gloves, and so he shoved his hands in the pockets of his coat. He put the Jason mask on, scanning the crowd through the plastic slits. So many masks. Ethan and Mike could be anywhere.

They marched around the blacktop, parents of the younger kids drinking coffee, taking pictures, and waving like idiots. He could see his mother standing alone near the basketball hoop. With the mask on, he wondered if even she would recognize him. He thought about his film again, and his whole body shivered with anger.

As the first graders marched past the judges' table, Trevor looked up and noticed that it was starting to snow. Just a few flakes here and there, but it was definitely snowing. He wished he had his camera. Mrs. D. had shown him a book once about a man from Jericho, Vermont, who was the first person to photograph snowflakes. She even had a print of one of them. It was like seeing the skeleton of a snowflake, its bones.

The entire crowd seemed to notice the snow all at once, and the little kids squealed, sticking their tongues out to catch the falling snowflakes. By the time it was the eighth graders' turn to march, the snow was coming down lightly but steadily, and the sky was completely white.

He recognized Mike right away, in a zombie mask, because of his Patriots jersey, which he hadn't taken off since football season started. But he couldn't locate Ethan among the crowd of were-wolves and mummies and monsters. He felt like an idiot as they circled the blacktop, and he hated Mrs. Cross for making them do this. He hated the whole school for putting him on parade like this. The parents were laughing, pointing, as they marched and marched and marched, like prisoners sent out to march in the cold.

By the time they got back into the building, Trevor was numb. The cold had seeped into his marrow, and he could barely feel his body. He felt like he was trapped inside someone else's skin. He went to the art room when the lunch bell rang and went straight back to the darkroom without even bothering to make sure he was alone. He unplugged the timer and shoved it into his backpack. He was zipping up the pack when he felt someone behind him. He froze and then turned, expecting Mr. Franklin but finding, instead, a kid in a werewolf mask staring back at him.

"Hey, faggot!"

And then the zombie in the Patriots jersey was behind him. "So is this where you and your new boyfriend come to do it?" Mike laughed.

"What are you talking about?" Trevor said, feeling the words scraping his throat. Trevor could feel himself transforming. Changing. He was not Trevor anymore, but Jason. He was Jason Voorhees, in his hockey mask and ragged coat.

"*Mr. Franklin,*" Ethan sang. "Everybody knows he sucks cock."

Trevor could feel his whole body splintering. Splitting. Part of him fled, just rose up like smoke from his body, while the other part of him grew, expanded. He could feel his chest ballooning, his shoulders broadening. He could feel his legs and arms and fists thickening.

"Whatcha got in your bag this time, Trevor?" Ethan said, grabbing his backpack.

But just as he was about to reach in, Trevor's entire body

flooded with that quicksilver flush, his blood a river of mercury. He felt their hands on him, pushing and pressing and hitting. And suddenly, every bit of restraint he'd had rushed away in the silver current. He pushed Mike off him, sending him backward into a metal locker, the noise like a gunshot. And then he wrestled Ethan, who was thrashing around underneath him, almost as strong as he was. But he was stronger, and soon Ethan went still beneath him.

"What are you gonna do, Baby Huey?" Ethan said.

Trevor felt the gears in his jaw cranking, the quick, sharp silver of his teeth. Click, click. And then his mouth filled with metal as well. Liquid and hot. Salty.

"Jesus fucking Christ," Ethan screamed, clutching his ear.

E lsbeth was already at the school when Kurt got there, pacing up and down the hallway outside the principal's office. Now, sitting on the other side of Principal Cross's desk, it felt as though they were the ones in trouble. Mrs. Cross looked smug, as usual, her lips pursed together tightly, the muscles in her neck taut.

"Mr. Kennedy," she said, shaking her head.

Kurt pressed his palms against his thighs and tried to quiet them, and then reached for Elsbeth's hand, which was clenched into a fist on her lap. His own hands were trembling.

Kurt didn't know where Trevor was, where they put kids who did things like this. He just wanted to get him and go home, but he was pretty sure it wasn't going to be that easy.

"I'm sure you understand my dilemma," Mrs. Cross started, continuing to shake her blond head, scolding. Kurt had noticed the last few times she'd spoken to them that it was as though she were talking to one of her kindergarten students instead of two grown adults.

"Trevor's behavior is simply unacceptable. My instinct is to expel him. For the safety of the other children in this school."

"But what are we supposed to do?" Elsbeth spoke up, surprising Kurt. Usually she left all of the talking to him in these situations. "I have to work. We have to *work.*"

Kurt thought about work. About the scent of gasoline. About the acres of debris at the yard. And the endless hours they each spent working, working, working.

"Mrs. Kennedy," Mrs. Cross said condescendingly. "This is not

a day-care facility. It is a school. It is a place where children come to learn."

Elsbeth's face flushed red, and Kurt felt his heart ache for her. "We know that," he said.

"I know that. I'm just . . . upset," Elsbeth said, her eyes filling with tears. "Do you have to expel him, though? The school year just started. He's been trying so hard."

It was taking everything Kurt had not to stand up and move. His legs felt like he'd been stung by a thousand wasps.

"You do understand," Mrs. Cross continued. "The *police* were called. This was an assault. You should consider yourselves lucky the Sweeneys aren't pressing charges." Principal Cross leaned toward them, as if she were going to tell them a secret. "Trevor's anger is not normal. He is a child, filled with . . . rage."

Kurt flinched. "He must have been provoked. He would never do anything like this without being provoked. You have to know how he's treated here, by the other kids. It's got to be somewhere in his file. He's constantly *bullied*. Constantly *teased*." Kurt's voice thundered, and he could feel the blood rushing to his face, hot and liquid. He pressed his fists against his angry legs.

"Mr. Kennedy, if you could please calm down. I do understand that circumstances may have aggravated the situation."

"*That Sweeney kid* aggravated the situation. He's just as much to blame for this. I guarantee it. I bet even his own parents know it. Otherwise they'd be pressing charges." Kurt threw his hands up in disbelief and then rubbed his face, his callused fingers pushing hard against his temples.

"Unfortunately, the reasons behind his behavior are secondary. This is considered *major misconduct* by the school, an extreme infraction of the school's policies. And there really are only two options at this point. The first, as I said before, is expulsion. You should be aware, though, that if we expel him, unless he attends another school, he'll need to be held back to repeat the eighth grade next year. This is where my hands are tied. As you know, there are no other public middle schools in Two Rivers.

He would need to commute, or you would need to find a private school for him."

"Do we look like the kind of people who can afford private school?" Elsbeth said, her voice high and tight. Her cheeks were red.

"El," Kurt said, reaching for her hand, but she yanked it away from him, and he felt his chest tighten.

"Seriously," she said, looking from Mrs. Cross to Kurt. "Even if we could afford it, which we *can't,* I'm sure he'd just find a way to get kicked out of there too."

"Your son is troubled," Mrs. Cross said, frowning. "He needs help. Have you looked into any of the public assistance programs available?"

"We don't need welfare," Kurt said, his legs aching now.

"There are some state programs that offer free mental-health counseling for adolescents. I can put you in touch with the Department for Children and Families."

"My son does not have a mental illness," Kurt said, the words bitter in his throat. "He's a *victim.* If I had to put up with half the shit he's put up with at this school, I'd have fought back a long time ago. It's not insanity. It's fucking self-defense."

"If you can *please* watch your language, Mr. Kennedy," Mrs. Cross said, reaching up to the top button of her clean white blouse, fiddling with it nervously.

Suddenly Kurt knew something had shifted. She looked afraid of him. And he imagined this was what Trevor felt like when he finally fought back against those asshole bullies.

"As I said before, expulsion is our *first* option. The second is for him to be enrolled, on a trial basis, in the pull-out program we have."

"What is that?" Elsbeth asked.

"It's our special-education program," she started.

"Special ed?" Kurt's throat constricted with the thought of the special-ed kids at school when he was Trevor's age. The drooling, head-banging, thrashing retarded kids who met in the room near the cafeteria.

"We would assign a team to work with Trevor. If he's classified as special needs, he'll have access to professionals, educators who work exclusively with children with behavioral issues."

Kurt's legs felt like he'd walked into an electric fence. The current would not leave his body.

"I am willing to try this on a trial basis," she said, smiling, as though she were doing them some sort of favor. "But if there is one more incident, one more act of violence, expulsion would be our only option. And I also feel that a temporary suspension is appropriate before he is moved into the pull-out program. Perhaps he can use that time to consider the consequences of his actions. It will also give us time to prepare an IEP. He could return to school after the Thanksgiving holiday."

"That's a whole month from now!" Elsbeth said, squeezing Kurt's arm.

"Where is he?" Kurt demanded.

"He's been detained in the guidance office. The police are completing their report."

"And the other child?" Elsbeth asked, the crimson flush having drained from her face. "Is he okay?"

"Ma'am. Trevor *attacked* him; he nearly bit his ear off. Luckily, another boy pulled him off before he was able to sever the earlobe. He's been taken to the hospital for stitches."

Elsbeth's eyes spilled the tears they'd been holding, which she wiped away hard with her thumb. She looked at Kurt, like this was his fault. Like he could somehow have prevented this. Like he had the power to fix it.

Kurt stood up. "I'd like to see my son now."

His mother went back to work, and his father drove him home. When they pulled into the driveway, Trevor got out of the truck and almost headed to the shed, figuring it would be best to just get it over with, but his dad stayed in the cab, rolled down the window, and said, "I've got to go back to work. You okay till your mom gets home?" He wasn't looking at Trevor but past him, through him. Like Trevor was nothing but air. And for a second, Trevor almost wished for the sting of leather against his bare skin.

"Sure," he said and slung his backpack over his shoulder. His dad rolled the window back up and backed out onto the road, gravel crushing like old bones under his tires.

Luckily, Mrs. Cross hadn't opened his backpack. She was too stupid to look inside and see all of the things he'd stolen; she'd just returned it to him after they finally let him go. As he made his way to the woods, he opened the pack to confirm that the stuff was still inside. It wasn't everything he needed, but at least he had the timer. He'd have to figure out the rest later. Luckily, now it seemed there would be plenty of time.

He wasn't sure what would happen next. He knew he was suspended for a month. That meant a whole month he wouldn't have to be at school. And after that would be Christmas break. It seemed like biting off Ethan's ear was one of the smartest things he'd done lately.

In the caboose he went through all of the supplies. Almost giddy. A whole month, but still, he needed to get to work.

After dinner, while his mom gave Gracy a bath, Trevor's father motioned for him to follow him outside. Trevor had known it was only a matter of time before he had to go to the shed. His dad had probably just been waiting until Gracy was occupied so she wouldn't ask where they were going.

Silently, Trevor pulled on his barn coat in the mudroom and followed behind his dad, closing the door quietly behind them. The moon was out tonight, like somebody had shot a hole through the sky. Trevor concentrated on the back of his father's head as they made their way to the shed.

His father didn't say anything; he never did. Usually, he'd ease his belt out through the loops of his pants and then lower his head while Trevor undid his own belt, as if he were ashamed to see Trevor's naked backside. Then Trevor would lean his head into his crossed arms against the weathered shingles of the shed, inhaling the rotten cedar smell. It would be over in just a couple of quick cracks, and then Trevor would scramble to pick up his pants. Usually Kurt would leave him alone, return to the house by himself, giving Trevor a few minutes to collect himself, to cry if he needed to. But tonight, instead of pulling his belt out, his dad just stood there, head hung low.

"You really screwed up this time," he said. "You can't just go attacking people. No matter what they do to you. You've gotta be civilized. You gotta play by their rules. It's a *school*. People are there to learn."

Trevor shook his head; these words belonged to Mrs. Cross, not his father.

"I need to know what those boys did to you, Trevor."

Trevor squeezed his eyes shut. Anger and shame pulsed in his temples as he thought about their jeering, sneering laughter. *Faggot, freak*. He thought about the way he felt like he was always, always on the verge of being attacked. Like a soldier at war, never knowing exactly when the enemy might strike. Tears swelled hot and impatient as he remembered the hot smell of his own excrement, their disgust. The taste of Ethan's ear in his mouth. *Cock-*

sucker. He shook his head. He couldn't tell him. He didn't have the words.

"They're putting you in special ed, son. And there's nothing your mother or I can do about it."

"What?" he said. The shock of his words felt like the crack of leather against his skin. Trevor thought about the classroom near the cafeteria. The kids in there were the ones who screamed and thrashed and threw tantrums. The ones who couldn't read. The blind children, the deaf children. The broken kids. The kids nobody cared about.

He felt his whole body starting to shake. It was like somebody was holding him by the shoulders and rattling him. Like a fault line ran down his spine, and it was shifting. The tears came hot and fast, and then he was tearing at his hair. The sting at his scalp echoing the sting of his backside.

"Stop it," his dad said.

But Trevor *couldn't* stop it. Didn't anybody understand this? It didn't have anything to do with him. He didn't have any control over it.

"I said *stop,*" his father said, this time taking a step toward him.

Trevor could feel the individual strands of hair coming loose in his hands. His ears buzzed.

"Jesus, Trevor. I said *stop it!*" And then his father's hands were on him, grabbing him, shaking him. "What the fuck is the matter with you? Maybe you do belong with those retards!" he hollered.

The next thing Trevor knew, his dad's palms were pushing against his chest. He stumbled backward, landing hard on the cold ground, a sharp pain shooting up through his spine. His father backed up, bleary-eyed and rubbing the top of his head. And then the earth stilled. The aftershocks just quiet tremors now. Trevor felt like he'd just woken up from a dream. He looked up at that torn sky, at the shrapnel stars.

"Get up," his father said, offering him his hand.

Trevor looked at him with disbelief.

His dad's eyes were wet. "I said *get up.*"

Later, as he tried to get comfortable in his bed, his raw, bruised backside making that nearly impossible, he noticed Gracy was still awake, lying on her side, watching him. Her eyes were sleepy, her hair tangled.

"Are you okay, Trevor?" she asked. "You look sad."

Sometimes Gracy just broke his heart. He felt tears coming to his eyes but squeezed his eyes shut against them.

"Don't be sad," she said and reached across the expanse between their beds.

"I'm okay," he said.

"Cross your heart."

"Hope to die," he said.

"Let him rot," Billy said.

Kurt hadn't expected sympathy; he'd only called Billy for advice. He wanted to find out what it would take to become Pop's guardian. It seemed like it was the only way he'd be able to get him into the nursing home. But Billy didn't seem willing to even offer his legal help.

"You're either a saint or an idiot, Kurt," Billy said.

"What the hell is that supposed to mean?"

Conversations with Billy almost always aggravated Kurt's legs. He was pacing, back and forth, probably wearing a path in the kitchen linoleum.

"Seriously, Kurt. He doesn't give a rat's ass about anybody but himself. I don't know why you bother."

"I bother because he's my father," Kurt said. "*Our* father."

"He hasn't been a father to me in fifteen years, Kurt. I swear you act like you've forgotten about that night. Like you weren't even there, like you didn't see."

But Billy was wrong. Kurt wasn't *really* there that night. Not until later. He had been out on a date with Theresa Bouchard at the movies. He could still remember the taste of buttered popcorn on her lips, the way it made their kisses slippery. He'd gotten home after Pop had already found Billy at the yard, dragged him into the truck, and brought him home.

Kurt could only piece together what happened before he got there by the angry words that rang out into the night as Pop threw all of Billy's things out into the front yard, and their mother stood in the kitchen doorway like a ghost in her nightgown, crying.

Billy and Kurt had both been helping Pop out at the yard that summer, just lending a hand where it was needed. Billy was an athlete (varsity in three sports by his sophomore year) and strong. Pop had him moving some of the heavier equipment around, loading and unloading parts. Kurt was in charge of doing the books, the business side of things. Billy came home at night worn ragged and smelling of grease. He spent all his money on fast food and beer. Kurt saved every dime he made for his tuition. He was supposed to go to Johnson State College in the fall. He planned to study American history, maybe eventually the law.

At the time, Pop's buddy Lloyd's son, Doug, was also working at the shop. Lloyd and Pop had been stationed together in Maine for basic training, and after their respective tours in Vietnam, they'd both returned to Two Rivers. Doug was home from college and wanted to make some extra cash, and Lloyd had asked Pop if he could help out around the yard. He was a nice guy. He and Billy hit it off.

Pop wouldn't talk about what he saw, but from what Kurt could gather, Pop had gone back to the yard that night to check the safe. He did that sometimes, checked and rechecked, unconvinced he'd secured everything. And when he got to the yard, he was alarmed to find the exterior light on. Though he wasn't sure he'd locked the safe, he did distinctly remember turning off all the lights. Worried that someone might be out in the yard stealing parts, he grabbed a crowbar from behind the counter and headed out into the darkness.

When he found Billy and Doug in the backseat of the 1978 Cadillac, he probably wasn't even sure what he was seeing. He must have figured it was a couple of teenagers. Maybe even just Kurt and Theresa. But instead of just walking away, leaving them be, he threw open the old car door and starting swinging.

Kurt got home from his date just as Pop was throwing Billy's stuff out into the yard. Billy was standing at the edge of the lawn, his face bloodied, his shirt unbuttoned.

"Jesus, Pop," Kurt had said, rushing past Billy up the steps. "What the hell happened?"

Billy left that night and hadn't set foot in the house since. His mom got sick for the first time that summer (suffering the first of four separate bouts with cancer), and Kurt was forced to write a letter to Johnson State telling the admissions office that he would not be attending that fall. Then Pop had his stroke, and he had to take over the yard. Billy became an emancipated minor and moved to DC, where he lived in a rooming house while he finished high school. He went to Georgetown on an athletic scholarship. He studied political science. He became a lawyer. The rest was history, so to speak.

Still. They'd grown up together inside the same walls, the walls that were threatening to fold in upon themselves like some awful house of cards. What Pop did was unforgivable. Of course it was. But he wasn't asking Billy to help Pop. He was asking Billy to help *him*. His brother.

"You're going to want to get conservatorship, which means you can also have control over his finances. If you're hell-bent on doing this."

Later that day, Maury showed up with his big truck, backing it into the backyard. Pop was dressed and standing with his walker, directing Maury as he maneuvered the truck's back end to the trailer. Kurt watched from the window over the sink and then, when he realized what they were about to do, threw open the back door and ran to the truck. Maury rolled the window down and nodded silently.

"What the hell do you think you're doing?" Kurt said.

"It's gettin' too cold for him to be livin' out here," Maury said.

"He's moving to Plum's December first," Kurt said. Billy had told him that he would simply need to prove that Pop posed a danger to himself, that he was incapable of making competent decisions. He figured his buddy Irene Killjoy at the county would be happy to assist. He'd left her three messages already.

"He wants to go home, Kurt," Maury said.

"Are you fucking kidding me, Pop? This is ridiculous. You can't live alone. It's not safe."

"You just want my money," Pop said, flicking his hands as though to brush Kurt away. "Get rid of me and take my house." His speech was now so distorted it sounded as though he were speaking with a mouthful of marbles.

"I don't want your money," Kurt said. Though it hit a nerve. That was exactly what he'd wanted. At least in part. If he had conservatorship of Pop, he could rent the house out. Sell it. He'd be able to stop working seventy-five hours a week. He wanted his life back. His wife back.

Maury leaned out the window. "Come on, Jude. I got the truck all warmed up for you. There's some hot coffee in the cup holder too."

Maury got out of the truck and went to Pop, taking his arm, guiding him around to the passenger's side of the car.

Kurt followed.

"You're not taking my father anywhere. You have no rights whatsoever here."

"Jude is a grown man. This is what he wants."

"He also wants to keep every goddamned piece of trash he finds. Save every goddamned scrap of paper, every frigging envelope. Just 'cause he wants it doesn't make it okay." Kurt felt like he might explode. What the hell was Maury doing this for? He knew Jude wouldn't be safe alone.

"I know this ain't what you want," he said to Kurt after Jude was in the car.

"It sure as hell isn't," Kurt said. "I'd think that you, of anybody, would be on my side. You know he can't live by himself. You've seen how he lives."

"What I *seen* is a seventy-year-old man living in an unheated trailer without proper plumbing. I seen a man who might as well be homeless. What I seen is a son too caught up in his own damned life to realize he's keeping his sick father like a dog on a run in the backyard." Maury's face was red and he was close enough to Kurt's face for him to smell the chew on his breath. "I wonder what your lady friend at the county would think of this. You're lucky nobody's come at *you* with papers."

"What are you talking about?" Kurt asked.

"Looks to me like a clear case of elder abuse. And it might just take one call to the right person to get you in a whole lot of trouble."

"Are you threatening me?" Kurt said. Maury had been like family for years. Like an uncle. He felt anger brewing in his gut, rage like an animal in his chest. He willed his fists to stay at his sides as Maury climbed back into the truck.

"Kurt, I'm just saying, might be best to let Pop go home now. Let him be."

That night Elsbeth was all over him. He had no idea what was going on with her. And while normally he'd be grateful for her affection, for her appetite, tonight he couldn't stop thinking about Maury's accusations. *Elder abuse.* God, his whole world had been revolving around Pop for years. He was seething. But Maury was right. Without the conservatorship, he had no right to keep his father against his will. He also had no legal right to have him put away in a home. Pop still had every right in the world to go back to his house.

Goddamn him, he thought.

"Not now, baby," he said, gently pushing Elsbeth away.

"Come on," she said. "The kids are fast asleep. Even Jude is gone."

She rolled over, throwing one leg over him then, straddling him, and he felt his body respond despite his mind, which was distracted. Elsewhere. With Pop in that freaking tuna can on wheels. With Pop back at his house. He could die in that house. It was like sending him to his own fucking grave. He closed his eyes and tried to let go. He tried to think only of her thighs, her hips rolling like waves over him, the tickle of her loose hair against his chest. Their sweat, the heat of their bodies despite the angry chill in the air.

The day before Thanksgiving, Crystal drove to work, parking her car near the Dumpsters at the far end of the building. The heater in the Volvo was powerful at least, especially since the temperature had dropped below freezing. They'd gotten snow, not a lot, but enough to change the way the world looked. It was pretty. A soft, clean layer covering everything. She pulled her scarf tighter around her neck before she opened the car door. It was windy outside, but she also knew that inside the Walgreens it would be warm. She locked the Volvo and walked up to the front doors, anxious to get out of the cold.

Then she heard the crying.

She looked around, thinking some child must be having a fit over something. That was pretty much a daily occurrence at the Walgreens. Each shift, she watched at least two or three moms wrestle with a child who had thrown itself on the floor in a fit of rage over a lollipop or a box of crayons or some other stupid knickknack. But there weren't any frustrated parents in the parking lot. No tantrums on the icy asphalt.

She followed the wailing sound to a beat-up Civic parked next to the handicapped spots. The window was rolled down, despite the freezing air, and she could make out a child screaming in the backseat. And there wasn't a grown-up in sight. She walked over to the car and quickly realized it was Grace, the other Grace, and anger bloomed hot inside Crystal's chest.

"Hey," Crystal said softly, looking around for the mother. Hoping she was just putting her shopping cart back or something. "Hey, it's okay," Crystal said and leaned into the car. The girl's dark hair was wet with sweat, her face furiously red.

Crystal reached in and touched her little hand. Her nails were painted hot pink with sparkles. The girl stopped crying for a minute and studied Crystal's face.

"Remember me? I helped you when you had a bloody nose," she said stupidly, as if this would make the girl feel safe. "Is your mommy inside?"

The little girl nodded. Snot ran down her nose from both nostrils.

Crystal reached into her purse and pulled out a clean tissue. She started to hand it to the little girl and then realized she should probably just wipe her nose for her. She blotted the snot off her face and then crumpled up the tissue and put it in her pocket.

"Listen," Crystal said softly. "I'm going to go inside and find your mommy, okay? I'll make sure she comes right out."

This seemed to make the little girl calm down, though she was hiccupping in the way that little kids do after they've been crying for a long time.

"She'll be right back, okay? Cross my heart," she said and made a crossing motion across her chest.

The little girl nodded, but as Crystal moved to go into the store, she could hear her starting to wail again. Maybe she should bring her in, she thought. But then again that didn't seem entirely smart either. She went back to the car and opened the girl's door. "Listen, I'll wait here with you until she comes, okay?"

When the woman finally came out about ten minutes later, clutching a bag of marshmallows, Crystal rushed to the electric doors. What the fuck? She left the kid alone to buy marshmallows? What kind of mother did that? Her hands and face were numb with the cold.

"Hey," she said, grabbing the woman's arm. "Your daughter is totally freaking out. You can't just leave kids alone in cars," she said.

The woman looked at her stupidly. God, she was unbeliev-able.

"Seriously," she said, feeling venomous as the woman walked away from her, rushing toward the car. "And you know what? I know what you're doing. You can't just steal shit. Not anymore. I swear to God the next time I see you take something, I'm calling the cops. You're pathetic."

The woman shook her head and then went to her car, where the little girl was still crying.

Elsbeth had been glad to have a few days off. Twig was working the day before Thanksgiving, and Babette closed the salon for Thursday and Friday. For a week now, she'd had back-to-back clients trying to get their hair cut before the holidays. Her feet were killing her. Even her hands were tired.

The kids both had dentist appointments in the morning. It seemed like every mother in Two Rivers had scheduled their kids to get their teeth cleaned this week; they had to wait nearly an hour past their appointment times. She read three entire old issues of *Us Weekly* while she waited. Gracy had two cavities, luckily both in baby teeth, but she'd promised the dentist she'd pick up fluoride and make sure she used it every day. She felt scolded. She hated the dentist.

Normally she would have left Trevor in the car and taken Gracy in the store with her, but Gracy had fallen asleep, clutching the new purple toothbrush the dentist had given her. She peered into the rearview mirror. Trevor was leaning his head against the window. Somber. Sulking. He'd been okay during the first few weeks after he was suspended, but now that he was going to be going back to school in a matter of days, he was miserable. And she felt for him, she really did. Getting put in the special-ed class was a stupid idea, and probably about the cruelest punishment Mrs. Cross could have come up with. But at least he wouldn't be around those boys anymore, the ones who were so hell-bent on making his life miserable.

"Trev, stay here with your sister, okay? I'll be right back."

She grabbed her purse and went inside, grateful for the warm blast of air that greeted her. She picked up a plastic basket and made her way down the first aisle. Her head was pounding as she walked past the makeup and the hair coloring. She wouldn't take anything today. She needed to stop. She felt the checker's eyes on her even across the store; she felt guilty, though she hadn't even done anything. She'd forgotten how to simply shop; she could barely breathe as she pretended to consider the hairbrushes and curling irons and combs. Her entire body was trembling.

She grabbed the fluoride the dentist recommended and then walked down the aisle of Thanksgiving stuff, letting her fingers skip across the silk flower arrangements, the aluminum roasting pans, the autumn-colored napkins. Normally, she would have pocketed one of the acorn napkin rings; she imagined it smooth and round in her pocket. Instead, she resisted and pretended to study the nutrition contents of a bag of marshmallows. She picked up the marshmallows and moved toward the counter, her entire body trilling in the same way as if she'd actually stolen something.

"You making sweet potatoes?" the kid asked.

She looked up at him.

"With the marshmallows, right? For Thanksgiving?"

She nodded. She was pretty sure that if she opened her mouth, the words wouldn't make it past the swelling in her throat.

"My mom does that too. It's my favorite. That and pumpkin pie."

She stared at his name tag: *Howard*.

"That's all for you, then?"

She nodded. The heat from the vents was suddenly too strong. Too much. She felt queasy as she handed him the money.

"You okay, ma'am?" Howard asked.

"What's that?" she asked, distracted. "Yeah, I'm good."

Outside, she was startled when the checker girl, Crystal, grabbed her arm. She started rambling on about not leaving her kids in the car. The girl had her hands on her hips, shaking her head at her like she was some sort of idiot. Why did this girl have it out for her? So she'd had a baby, lots of people have babies— that hardly made her an expert on parenting. And then she was yelling at her about her stealing stuff, about calling the cops.

"What are you talking about?" Elsbeth said, her whole body shaking now. She hadn't taken anything. She'd paid for the fluoride, the marshmallows.

"You left your kid alone in the car and she's freaking out," she said, enunciating every word as if Elsbeth was retarded.

"She's not alone," Elsbeth said, confused, shaking her head and rushing toward the car, where Gracy was red-faced and wailing, *alone,* in the backseat.

The girl disappeared into the Walgreens.

"Where's Trevor?" she asked, unbuckling Gracy and scooping her up into her arms. Gracy kept crying as Elsbeth walked around the snowy parking lot, looking for Trevor. She looked out at the road, but couldn't see him anywhere. He couldn't have gotten far. Jesus. Her shoulder soaked with Gracy's tears, she lowered Gracy back into her car seat and stroked her hair out of her eyes. "Honey, did Trevor say where he was going?"

"With those boys," she said. "Those boys with the mean faces."

"What boys, honey?"

"I was scared, Mommy!" Gracy cried again.

"Where did he go?"

Gracy pointed toward the side of the Walgreens.

"Over there?" Elsbeth asked.

Gracy nodded.

Elsbeth thought about leaving Gracy but knew that she'd just start screaming again. That girl *would* probably call the cops on her.

"Okay," she said. She got into the driver's side and pulled the car slowly toward the end of the building, where that goddamned girl wouldn't be able to see her through the window from her perch at the check-out.

"Listen, I'm just going to look for Trevor, okay?" Then she remembered the marshmallows. She tore open the bag and handed it to Gracy. "Here you go, sweetie."

Gracy nodded and took the marshmallows from her.

Elsbeth closed and locked the door and jogged down the walk alongside the store and then ducked behind the building. The Dumpsters were back there, and everything smelled of garbage. She gingerly stepped through an icy pile of slush and finally saw him. "Trevor?" He was sitting on the ground with his back against the wall, his face pressed into his knees.

"Jesus Christ, Trevor," Elsbeth said, both relieved and furious. "Your sister is alone in the car! What were you *doing?*"

He didn't look at her as she reached down and grabbed his arm. He just stood up, shoved his hands in his pockets.

"What happened?" she asked. "Why did you get out of the car?"

She lifted his chin up with her finger, inspected his face. He looked okay. No bruises. It didn't look like he'd been fighting again. He refused to look her in the eye.

"What happened? Did somebody hurt you?"

Nothing. Silence.

"I don't know what to do with you," Elsbeth said. "I can't do this anymore. I just can't do this." Elsbeth was fuming. It was freezing outside, but she could feel her armpits growing damp. She'd been trying so hard lately to be sympathetic, to understand him. But she couldn't understand him if he wouldn't talk to her.

Silently, they walked back to the car. Trevor got in the backseat and Elsbeth slammed her door shut. Her hands shook as she found her keys.

"Did those mean boys hurt you, Trevor?' Gracy asked.

Trevor was looking down at his lap. His hands were fidgeting. They looked just like Kurt's hands. He had the same square nails. The same fine blond hairs. A tremor ran through her body as she thought about Kurt. About what he would do to Trevor if he knew he'd left Gracy in the car by herself. What he'd think of *her*.

After the Fourth of July, he already thought she was a failure, a terrible mother. Maybe he was right.

She wished Trevor would say something, but he remained mute.

As Elsbeth turned out onto the slick road, Gracy reached between the seats. She handed him a handful of marshmallows in her tiny fist. "Here, Trevor. It's marshmallows."

Trevor looked up and accepted one of them from her.

"Thanks," he said softly.

She hated Gracy's innocence. Her kindness toward him. She hated that Gracy loved him more than she, his own mother, was able to.

Elsbeth turned to look at Trevor, wanting to say something that would make him tell her what happened, searching for the words that would get through, that might crack him open like an egg. But as she opened her mouth to speak, nothing came out, and she realized that tears were streaming down his cheeks.

"Oh, Trev, why won't you tell me what's going on?"

Gracy had been humming in her sleep in the backseat. She did that at night sometimes too. Her voice sounded like little bells, like a lullaby. Trevor had leaned his head against the cold window and closed his eyes.

The banging startled him. Ethan's and Mike's faces filled his window. Ethan's cheeks were red, his nose crusty with snot. They motioned for him to roll the window down. He knew he probably shouldn't, but the doors were unlocked, and he was worried that they might try to get in through Gracy's side. That they might hurt her.

He rolled the window down, and Ethan reached in and grabbed a fistful of Trevor's hair. He yanked it, and Trevor's head bumped the window frame. "Get out of the car," Mike said.

Trevor turned to look at Gracy, who had woken and looked terrified. "Gracy, I'll be right back. Don't go anywhere. Just wait for Mom."

He got out of the car and they shoved him toward the back of the building. Trevor glanced back over his shoulder as he heard Gracy cry.

"Heard you're comin' back to school next week, that they're putting you with the retards," Ethan said. Trevor could see the place where they'd sewn his earlobe back together, the scar like a thin, white worm. He shoved Trevor against the Dumpster. The air smelled rotten and thick. He worried about his mom coming out of the store and finding Gracy alone. He worried about what would happen next.

"Yeah, *Hannibal,* sure is lonely without you," Mike said, thrusting his lip out.

Trevor could feel his anger, that hot steel making his entire body stiff. His hands clenched into fists. But just as he was about to knock both of the kids out, he thought about the promise he'd made to his father. He'd told him he wouldn't fight anymore. His dad said that if he fought one more time, he'd lose the camera. That was it. And if he didn't have the camera, he couldn't take pictures. And then what would be left? And so he just squeezed his fists until his nails dug into his palms.

"What? You not gonna fight back this time? What's the matter? Not hungry?" Ethan hissed. "Don't want to bite my other ear off?" With that, he shoved Trevor against the Dumpster harder, clutching Trevor's parka with his fist. Trevor could feel the cold metal through his jacket.

"You know," Ethan said. "I know somethin' could solve all our problems," he said. He reached into his pocket then and pulled out a small knife. His face looked crazed, and he was licking his lips.

"What are you doing?" Mike asked then, sounding scared. *"Dude."*

"What's the matter?" Ethan said. He was talking to Mike, but he was inches from Trevor's face, his spit sharp and hot as it sprayed with each word.

Trevor watched Mike back up and then sprint, disappearing around the corner. Trevor suddenly knew it was worse now that he was alone with Ethan. He was holding the knife with one hand, his elbow pressed hard against Trevor's chest, but his other hand was fumbling around with Trevor's pants, his fingers looking for his zipper.

Ethan yanked it out, and Trevor could feel the cold metal of the zipper on his skin. The cold air on his skin. Ethan's hand was wrapped hard around him, and Trevor couldn't breathe. It was as though he were strangling him. Trevor felt himself getting hard.

He turned his face away from Ethan, felt hot tears coming to his eyes.

"What if I just cut it off?" Ethan said.

Trevor winced, terrified of what Ethan would do. As the cold metal grazed the skin of his penis, he squeezed his eyes shut, concentrated on the smells, the tangy awful scent of something gone bad. He tried to imagine what a picture of that smell would look like. Where the shadows would be. Where the light was. He closed his eyes tighter until he saw constellations. When he felt the sharp buzz, spreading from his groin to his shoulders, he opened his eyes.

"Fucking homo!" Ethan said, stumbling backward, wiping his hand across his pant leg, his eyes wide and scared. "Goddamn freak!" And then he was scrambling away, his feet pounding against the asphalt, and Trevor was alone.

Trevor zipped his pants, felt the dampness of his jeans and the dampness of his eyes and the awful frozen air, and he sank to the frigid ground.

Crystal went straight to the break room to clock in, shaking from her encounter with that horrid woman. Part of her felt like she should have called the cops then and there. But without any proof, what could she do? She wasn't even sure if it was illegal to leave a kid in the car. She also wasn't sure she'd even stolen anything this time. She'd ask Howard, but Howard had his head up his butt half the time; he probably didn't even notice. Now Howard was up front gnawing on his cuticles; he looked up from the bloody mess he'd made of his fingers and grinned at her. "Hey, Crys."

"You want to do register or photo today?" She sighed.

"You choose," he said, blushing in a way that made her hate him.

She couldn't see the woman's car from the window anymore. She figured she was probably gone by now anyway. Poor kid. People like that shouldn't have kids.

"I'll do photo," she said.

In the photo department, Crystal sorted the orders that had come in that morning, filing them by last name. She slipped each envelope into its slot, another mindless task. *Kincaid*. She thumbed through the Ks: *Kane, Keeney, Keller, Kennedy*. Kennedy. There were that lady's pictures, a dozen fat envelopes rubber-banded together. It had been weeks since she'd dropped off all those rolls of film. Crystal had been able to get her a discount, but then she hadn't bothered to come in to pick them up. She plucked the first envelope from the pile and quickly glanced around to make sure no one was watching. The store was empty except for some old guy filling a prescription in the pharmacy. She stuck her finger under the flap and lifted it gently, careful not to tear the paper. The adhesive was loose and it came up quickly. She ducked behind the print machine with the stack of photos in her hand and started to shuffle through them like a deck of cards.

She felt her stomach turn. She hadn't been this nauseous since she was in her first trimester. The pictures were disgusting. A ramshackle house, garbage everywhere. Close-up pictures of rotten food, a rusty sink filled with dishes. A stained mattress, piles of clothes and boxes, and a room filled with empty milk jugs. Some old man sitting at a table, ashtray overflowing, and model airplanes circling over his head. A bottle of liquor sitting next to him. Then there were a bunch of pictures of some sort of broken-down train in the woods. A few of the tops of trees, of a river, some ferns and then the girl. The crying little girl, *Gracy,* asleep. The first was a close-up of her face, her long eyelashes pressed against the tops of her cheeks. Then another one of her face, a shivery line of drool coming out of the corner of her mouth. The girl, ragged T-shirt riding up her body to her armpits, legs spread and a pair of Disney Princess panties showing. There must have been ten pictures of her, all of them clearly taken while she was fast asleep. Two or three of her skinny legs tangled up in the sheets. One of her standing by a tree, her bathing suit too small, her nipple showing. Crystal started to tremble. What was wrong with these people? What kind of mother let her son take pictures like this? Or maybe there wasn't a son. Crystal had never seen her with anyone other than the little girl. She felt the skin across her belly, that tight, tender, empty place aching, aching.

Crystal took the photos. Not every envelope, but six of them. When Howard was on his break, she shoved them into her purse. Her heart was pounding in her chest as she clocked out in the break room. She grabbed her coat and wrapped her scarf around her neck, readied herself for the cold, braced herself for the freezing air that was sure to meet her when the electric doors opened. It was dark out already. She'd been at the Walgreens all day.

The roads, which had merely been wet and slushy before, were turning to ice now. Luckily, driving the Volvo was like driving a tank. She felt invincible as she navigated her way home. The air was heavy, dark. There would be more snow soon. She pulled one of the envelopes out of her purse and looked at the address on the form. Beasley Rd. She knew that place. That was where those two boys had died. They were upperclassman when she was a freshman. They'd run track too. Everyone on the track team wore a green armband at the next meet in their memory. After the accident, they'd had a special assembly. She remembered because the boys' parents had been there, on the stage, the father stoic and the mother barely able to stand up. And she remembered thinking that somebody should give her a chair. She remembered thinking it was cruel to put their grief on display like this. Every time she drove past those markers in the road, she'd think of that poor mother, crippled with her sorrow. It still made her insides ache.

She had told her mother not to wait for her for dinner. She avoided most family dinners lately. A couple of months ago, they'd have babbled on about her *plans*. About her heading off to college in January. But now they just ate quietly. Thankfully, Angie picked up the slack. She always had some new project she was engaged in. The new art teacher had picked her and three other students to work on a mural in the cafeteria. She'd come to dinner speckled with paint, even in her hair, and fill all those miserable silences with her happy chatter. And besides, tomorrow was Thanksgiving; they'd probably just gotten a pizza anyway. Her mother would be up to her elbows in green beans and cranberries and sweet potatoes in the kitchen.

She drove through town, the snow sparkling as it fell in front of her headlights. Glittering. The car warmed up quickly, the heat blasting onto her hands and her feet. She turned the radio on, and the music soothed her. She felt almost like the car was driving itself, and she was just along for the ride. She would be content to never go home again. To just stay here, driving in the snow, forever. She slowed when she got to the place where the crosses were. There were no other cars on the road. She felt her throat thicken with thoughts of their mother, with thoughts of the holes, not one but two, that they must have left when they died. When Mrs. Stone took the small bundle from her, it felt like someone had torn out her heart. Like something had been stolen. She thought about Grace. Her Grace, and then the Grace in those pictures. The images of her inside those envelopes.

She studied the address on the envelope again. The house sat on a small hill with no neighboring homes around it. The mailbox at the roadside was battered and rusted, the metallic letters spelling out K-E-N-N-E-D-Y, the Y a bit torn. It was a little house, and much more well-kept than she expected after seeing the pictures. But that's the way it goes, right? What you see on the outside rarely reflects what's really on the inside. She, of all people, understood that appearances can be deceiving.

There was a truck parked in the steep driveway and the beat-up Civic she recognized, the one inside which she'd found Grace alone and crying. The lights were on inside the house, casting an orange glow on the snow that had blanketed the front yard. She tried to imagine what was going on inside, who these people were.

Suddenly the porch light flicked on, and heart racing, she pressed the accelerator and kept driving down the road. When she finally was able to breathe again, she turned around in someone's driveway. Turning that boat of a Volvo around was always a challenge because of the power steering fluid leak; sometimes she felt more like she was trying to steer an RV or monster truck. Adrenaline buzzed in her arms as she finally got turned around and on the road again. By the time she got back to her house, the snow was coming down sideways, a true blizzard. She couldn't even see her own house until she was at her driveway. She sat outside in the car with the heater blasting, bracing herself for the cold that she knew would await her both outside the car and in-side the house.

That night she tossed and turned in her bed, listening to the sounds of her mother's furious Thanksgiving preparations, while Angie snored softly next to her. Finally, she got up, went to her drawer where she'd stashed the stolen photos. But instead of studying them again, instead of trying to make sense of them, she pulled out the manila envelope she'd sealed more than a year ago. She locked herself in the bathroom and, her fingers trembling, she pulled out the filmy black-and-white paper.

The ink had already partially disintegrated, and her fingers left greasy smudges at the edges. She studied the shape of Grace's fetal body, the snail-like curve of her vertebrae. She touched the delicate profile, the tiny hands curled into fists.

She shoved the pictures back into the envelope and looked at her reflection in the mirror. Staring at her own image, she rolled the top of her sweatpants down and traced the careful cursive of her baby's name in reverse. *ɘɔɒɿᎮ Grace*. Her baby girl's name written across her skin, and that little girl's name reflected. It had to mean something: the coincidence of their shared name, the crossing of these two paths. There had to be a reason for this.

Trevor was sure his mother would know what had happened in the alley. He was sure everyone would know now what he had done. What he *was*. That they'd been right all along. That he was queer, a faggot. The whole way home, he had thought about what would happen when they got there, when his mother told his father that he'd left Gracy in the car. He flinched just thinking about his father's belt. He wondered if he could run away somehow before his father got back. But when they'd pulled up in the driveway, his father's truck was already there.

"Daddy's home!" Gracy squealed, climbing out of the car. She had marshmallow stuck in her hair.

Trevor followed behind Gracy and his mother, the denim of his pants frozen now, making the cloth stiff. He could still smell that awful smell, that pungent funk. It was a part of him. It had come *out* of him.

His father was inside sitting at the kitchen table, studying a bill. He looked up when they came into the kitchen, and Trevor winced. Waited.

"Hey, baby," his mother said, hanging her purse on the back of the kitchen chair.

She looked at Trevor, shaking her head a little, but her face was soft. Sorry even. She knew. She had to know what he'd done.

"What's the matter?" his father asked. "Something happen?"

"How about I make us all a nice dinner," she said. "I've got some steaks in the freezer."

Before Trevor changed into his pajamas that night, he took

off his clothes in the bathroom, the crotch of his jeans stiff. He knelt on the floor next to the bathtub and ran the water so hot that it burned his hands. He held the jeans under the stream until the fabric softened, hoping that any evidence of what had happened was getting sucked down the drain. He studied his body in the mirror, a body he didn't recognize anymore. It was a man's body. His father's body. It made him ashamed. He pulled the jeans out of the tub, wrung them out the best he could, and laid them across the radiator that was sputtering and hissing, hot to the touch. He got into the shower, scrubbed his skin, trying not to think about what Ethan had done to him and how his own body had betrayed him. He closed his eyes and pretended he was in the forest, in the caboose. Safe and warm. Protected. The water burned his skin, but he pretended it was only the sun. That it was only the heat of summer.

Gracy was already sleeping when he got into his bed. His skin was tender, rubbed raw. And his jeans had not dried but just started to stink like burnt denim when he took them off the radiator. He folded them, stuffed them into a plastic bag, and shoved them into the bottom of his wastebasket.

His whole body felt bruised. Even the sheets hurt. He thrashed around in his bed, the sheets getting tangled around his legs, making him feel like screaming. He kicked the blankets onto the floor and lay flat on his back.

"What's the matter, Trevor?" Gracy asked sleepily, squinting her eyes against the light.

"Nothing," he said.

"Did you have a bad dream?"

He felt tears spilling from his eyes.

"You can sleep in my bed," she said.

And then he remembered one time when he was about Gracy's age that he had a nightmare. He couldn't remember what it was about anymore; he just remembered waking up feeling terrified. Somehow he'd found his way through the labyrinth of the dark house to his parents' room. He'd opened the door and made his way through the darkness to their bed. He'd climbed in cautiously, wanting nothing more than for someone to hold him, for his mother to hold him. But Elsbeth had startled awake as he curled his body against hers. "Jesus Christ!" she'd said, sitting up. "You scared me to death!" Then she scooped him up and set him on the floor again. "It was just a dream. Now, go back to bed," she said. "I've got to work early."

His father hadn't woken up at all.

His knees quaking, he'd walked back to his room, waiting until he was in his own bed again to cry. He had stayed awake the entire rest of that night. And he'd never tried to get into their bed again.

"You sure?" he said to Gracy now.

"Come in," she said, patting the mattress. "I have plenty of room."

Trevor crawled into bed with Gracy, and she hugged him. "I never have bad dreams in my bed," she said. Her sheets were softer than his. She handed him Hugo, her stuffed hippo, and he held Hugo close up under his chin. Then he waited for sleep to come over him.

Outside it snowed, and inside the radiators clanged a metallic banging like someone was trapped inside trying to get out. When he closed his eyes he imagined the sounds were gunshots, that he was in Iraq or the jungles of Vietnam. Pop had told him about the war, about watching men getting shot around him, going down like marionettes whose strings have been cut. And so, half-asleep, he imagined Vietnam. He dream-trudged through a rice paddy, his feet so heavy he could barely lift them. The stink of murky water, the smell of corpses. Of death. But then he wasn't in the jungle anymore; the trees had disappeared, leaving him in the dark, cold alley behind the Walgreens. And still, his feet wouldn't move. He started to cry. He felt cold hands on him. On his shoulders, on his stomach, on his face. He could feel hands around his penis, the reluctant stiffening, the pain that was also good. His stomach turned with the smell of everything rotten and spoiled.

Loud cracks, explosions, gunshots? sounded all around him. And his feet, stuck in cold asphalt, like quicksand. Like being trapped under ice. He couldn't run. He couldn't move.

He startled awake. He felt his erection go soft, the sheets become wet, and tears fill his eyes. His heart was pounding like a hammer in his chest, so loud he could almost hear it. Disoriented, he thought he was still in the alley, sitting in a puddle of icy water after they left him there and before his mother found him. But then as his eyes began to focus, he realized he was in bed with Gracy, who was curled like a roly-poly bug, her body pressed against him. Her sweet-smelling body, touching his.

He scrambled out of the bed, his entire body rocking with guilt, shame like a migraine. He wanted to tear the soiled sheet off her, but he knew it would wake her. His whole body was shaking now, he couldn't stop it. What had he done? What had he done to his own sister? What kind of monster was he?

Kurt invited Jude to Thanksgiving dinner, and at first he'd stubbornly refused. He'd holed up himself up in that damn house again, and as far as Elsbeth was concerned, he could just rot there. Ever since Pop had moved back to his own house, Kurt had been trying to come up with a plan, but unless he somehow got conservatorship, there wasn't much he could do. She knew he was worried about Jude living by himself in the house, but the way Elsbeth figured it, if, no, *when* the house went to shit again, then it really would only strengthen Kurt's case (though there wouldn't be much of a case without a lawyer, and they certainly weren't in any position to hire anybody). She'd pleaded with him to try to just let Pop be. "It's not your problem. It's not *our* problem. You've done everything you can do. No one can say you didn't try." Kurt had done everything he could for him. Now Jude was just being an ass. She wished Kurt could just let it go. Let *him* go. But then the night before Thanksgiving, Jude changed his mind about dinner, and she watched Kurt on the phone nodding and pacing. "Okay, Pop. I'll pick you up."

In the kitchen, she ran cold water over the turkey. When she pulled out the plastic bag with the gizzards and liver and heart, she realized the insides were still a little frozen, little bloody crystals inside that cage of bone. She patted the turkey with paper towels and sprinkled salt and pepper inside. She prepared the box of Stove Top, and the smell, of sage and butter, reminded her of other Thanksgivings.

Kurt's mother, Larissa, was the one who had taught her how

to roast a turkey. back when she and Kurt were first married and Elsbeth didn't know the difference between a ladle and a spatula. Elsbeth's own mother hadn't been much of a cook when she was growing up. As a single mother, she hadn't had anyone, besides Elsbeth, to cook for. Most nights they just had sandwiches or frozen pizza; on special nights they ordered Chinese. When Elsbeth was pregnant with Trevor, Larissa took her under her wing like a protective mother hen and taught her all sorts of things. She showed her how to stud a ham with cloves, how to make a roast in a Crock Pot. Larissa had been like the mother Elsbeth always wished she'd had. Larissa was round and soft and warm. She was patient and gentle, the exact opposite of Elsbeth's mom.

When Elsbeth found out she was pregnant, she waited a whole month to tell her mother. She already knew what she'd say, knew exactly how she'd react.

"Well, there goes your life," she'd said, as expected.

Elsbeth knew this was what she'd say because that's exactly what had happened to her when *she* got pregnant at seventeen. There went her life. Or what she thought her life might be anyway. And the next seventeen years, the years she had spent with her mother in the two-bedroom apartment by the railroad depot, had been like watching somebody begrudgingly do what they've been told to do, despite every inch of their body resisting. "I'm not cut out for this motherhood business," was her favorite tagline. When Elsbeth found out she was pregnant, she also knew that a part of her mother would be relieved. Especially because, unlike her own father, Kurt loved her and wanted to marry her. Now Elsbeth was somebody else's problem, and her mother could get on with her own life. As if everything had simply been put on hold for all these years. And, true to prophecy, she met Nate, a pharmaceutical sales rep who came into the doctor's office where she worked as a receptionist, and they fell in love. Two years later he got a new job and they moved to California, where her mother went back to college and got an associate degree. Now she and Nate ran their own event planning business and lived in a big house with a pool and a two-car garage. Elsbeth had only seen her a few times since then.

Thankfully, after Elsbeth's mother was gone, Larissa had really stepped in, treating her like she was her very own. When Larissa died when Trevor was still just a baby, Elsbeth felt like her own mother had passed away. She felt robbed. Like she'd finally gotten what she needed her whole life and then had it yanked away from her.

She'd always been mystified as to how Larissa wound up with Jude. She didn't know how she could listen to the garbage that came out of Jude's mouth sometimes. Larissa was eternally shaking her head, never speaking up, just rolling her eyes and shrugging her shoulders. Defeated. Or resigned maybe. Kurt was like that with Jude too, never speaking. Never calling him on his racist, sexist, prejudiced bullshit. Kurt had told her only a little bit about why his brother took off when he was still a kid. But knowing Jude, she wasn't at all surprised. He was such a goddamned bigot, hated nearly everybody.

She didn't want her family to turn into this. To become a whole bunch of people who couldn't stand each other stuck under one roof. She didn't want Trevor to run away from home at seventeen and never come back. She didn't want Gracy to hate her. For Kurt and her to merely tolerate each other.

She stuffed the dressing into the turkey carcass and tethered the legs together with a piece of twine. She soaked some cheesecloth in melted butter and draped it over the bird like a blanket, her hands remembering all those other Thanksgivings.

Kurt came into the kitchen and stood behind her, wrapping his arms around her. She could feel his breath on her neck. She closed her eyes and tried to concentrate only on the smell of him, that familiar scent of her husband.

"I love you, El," he said. "You know that, right?"

Elsbeth nodded. She nodded and nodded.

*   *   *

The week before at work, Carly had handed her a postcard addressed to her.

"What's this?" Elsbeth asked, taking it from her.

Carly had shrugged.

On the front was the word *Florida* spelled out in big letters, each letter with a picture inside: beaches, oranges, palm trees. On the back, in smudgy letters, it said, *Thanks again. It was terrific getting to hear your stories. Someday, hopefully, you'll read mine. And if you're ever in Florida, I'd be happy to show you the sights.*

She'd laughed out loud then. First because she knew she'd never be in Florida. That had been a silly dream, a silly girl's fantasy. And secondly, because anything she'd thought about Wilder being interested in her, flirting with her, was just as inane. He was simply a man writing a book. He'd asked her some research questions. She'd pretended to be someone she wasn't. What an idiot she had been. She was so embarrassed.

She almost tossed the postcard in the trash, but instead she carried it home, put it in the box with all the other stolen things, and tears had come to her eyes. She was making the right decision in staying with Kurt. Her family was the only thing in the world that really belonged to her; how could she have even considered throwing it away?

"I love you too, baby," she said to Kurt, who was still holding her tight. "Now let me go. I've got to peel some potatoes. You'll be home by five thirty for dinner, right?"

At dinner, Pop pushed his turkey around his plate, picked at the burnt marshmallows on the sweet potatoes, and drank. Trevor watched his mother's jaw clench, watched with each of Pop's sips the way her lungs filled with air.

"Larissa used to make those green beans I like, with the crunchy onions," Pop said, the effort of speaking laborious, his words like rocks in his mouth. The entire left side of his face drooped now, his left arm hanging like dead weight at his side. "You ever make those?" he asked Trevor's mom.

"Not this year, Jude," she said.

"That woman was a fine cook. Didn't even have to use a recipe for anything."

Trevor's dad looked at his mom as if to say *sorry* with his eyes.

Pop lifted a forkful of sweet potatoes to his mouth, struggling to get it in. It was like watching a baby try to feed himself. His dad grimaced.

"Listen, Pop. I checked in with Plum's, and the room is actually still open for December first," he said. "That's just next week. Maybe we could at least go check it out this weekend? You don't have to commit to anything, but it might be nice to at least go see."

Pop set his fork down, defeated but defiant. "Don't you get started with that bullshit again."

Gracy's eyes widened.

"Jude," his mom reprimanded.

"Well, if you stay at the house, maybe we should hire some-one to help out," his dad said. "You know, just with the yard. Someone to help keep the place up."

His mother stiffened, scowling. "And how exactly do we plan to pay for that?"

Kurt set his fork down and shook his head. "It wouldn't have to cost a fortune."

"I don't . . . need help."

Trevor ate until he felt like his stomach might burst, until he felt sick. But as long as his mouth was full, he wouldn't have to speak.

"Got trouble at school again, huh?" Pop asked.

Trevor felt a jolt rush through him. He nodded, tasting the bitter combination of green beans and squash on his tongue.

"Your dad says some boys givin' you a hard time," he said.

His father must have told Pop about the fight.

"They're meanies, *super* meanies," Gracy said, pouring gravy over a small mountain of mashed potatoes.

"Careful, baby," his mother said, helping her with the heavy boat.

Trevor wanted them to talk about something else, anything else. Even if it meant going back to their stupid argument about money.

"Your dad says you got 'em, though. Got 'em real good."

"I didn't say that, Pop," Trevor's dad said, his chapped face red-dening even more. "We're not encouraging the fighting. There are other ways to handle this. The school's stepping in."

"You startin' to sound like your brother," Pop said.

"What's that supposed to mean?" his dad asked.

"I raise a *couple* of pansies? Couple of goddamned pussies?" He held up one hand, limp at the wrist, and Trevor felt his entire body flood with heat, and the edges of his vision went black, his ears filling. He couldn't hear anything but Pop's laughter. He watched as half of Pop's mouth opened, the spray of orange sweet potatoes that splattered on the clean white tablecloth. Trevor tried to make this picture flat, just a snapshot. Just a frozen image, something he could tear up and toss away.

"Jude," his mom said, standing, slamming her hands on the table. "I'm done. Get out of my fucking house."

Pop stopped laughing and closed his mouth, wiping at the wet dribble of potato with his shirt sleeve. "You," he said, slurring and pointing at her, "you don't talk to me like that."

"I'll talk to you any damn way I please. You're an ignorant ass-hole, and I want you out of my house. Kurt, I need you to take Jude home."

His dad nodded, standing. "I'm sorry," he said to his mom. "Come on, Pop."

"You've always been an ungrateful bitch," he said. "Getting knocked up and ruinin' any chances Kurt had to make something of himself. Working two jobs while you sit on your boney ass all day."

"Jude, we have children at this table. I need you to go now."

"Pop, *let's go,*" his dad said, gripping the table angrily.

Gracy was starting to cry. Normally, Trevor would have reached for her hand and said, "Come on, Gracy. Let's go play Chutes and Ladders." But he was afraid to touch her now, and so instead he stood up and went to his bedroom alone. Inside, with the door shut, he tried not to let Pop's words splinter and sting him. He tried to ignore the sounds of the chairs scraping, the muffled argument still raging in the kitchen. He pretended that the sound of the door slamming and the truck's engine roaring to life and his mother's crying were just TV sounds, special effects. That they weren't real, that they didn't belong to anyone he knew.

Not much later, he heard his dad's truck pull in and the sound of the door opening, his boots banging against the jamb, the hushed whispers between him and his mother. Just insects in the grass. Just wind whistling through the tops of trees.

★ ★ ★

That night Trevor watched his body moving through the world without feeling anything but a dull ache. He watched his own hands as they pulled on his socks, as they tied the belt around his robe, as they ran across the cowlick on the top of his head. He studied his fingers as they held the toothbrush and made it move up and down and in circles, remembering the motions, the bristles not registering against the numbness of his gums and tongue. He looked at himself in the mirror, and while he recognized his own face, he felt as though he were looking at a stranger.

The house was warm and still smelled like Thanksgiving. Like every other Thanksgiving. Outside it was cold. Trevor touched the glass of the window. It was still snowing. The crystalline white kept coming down, relentless, covering everything in a layer of pristine white. He imagined it blanketing the house, the yard, the cars and people it touched. If it never stopped, maybe they'd all be buried in snow. Maybe they wouldn't be able to open their doors, and he'd never have to leave the house again.

Four more days. Four more days before he had to go back to school. His suspension ended on Monday. On Monday, he was expected to return to that building, to the classrooms, to Ethan and Mike. To pretend as though nothing had happened. As though he were just a bad kid who'd been punished and forgiven. As if he weren't changed. Weren't found out. Weren't proven to be the freak he was always afraid he was.

As he pissed, he couldn't look at himself. He felt ashamed even holding himself to aim. He felt acid rising in his throat as he thought about what he'd done to Gracy. He was sickened by himself, his whole body quaking with shame. He knelt at the toilet, the lid still lifted, and vomited until there was nothing left inside him. Retching, his body feeling like it was trying to turn itself inside out. Until he was absolutely hollow, and then he felt his fingers wipe his cheeks with a bit of toilet paper. And watched, around and around, up and down, as they brushed his teeth again.

He tried to picture himself returning to school, dreamed the walk down the halls, the smells of the cafeteria, the sound of the bell, the *hush hush* of the other kids as they whispered behind his back. The feel of Ethan's hands pushing him into lockers, into desks, into anything that would hurt him. He tried to pretend that any of this was possible. That life could go on as it always had. Monday. *Monday.* For everyone else, it would be just another day. Just another beginning to just another week. But to him, it felt like the end of the world.

He walked out of the bathroom, aware of the sound of his feet on the floor but unable to feel anything. Nothing. It was like his entire body had fallen asleep, not the prickly sensation of raw nerves, just the dead heaviness of sleep. He went back to his room, and Gracy was just coming out.

"Do you want some punkin pie?" she asked. She was clutching her hippo. Trevor couldn't even look at her, he was so ashamed.

Everywhere across the country, families were sitting down to Thanksgiving dinner. Crystal tried to imagine them. A hundred million different families. Each of them convening over the same meal. Every father's face peering over a turkey, every mother fussing over smudges on the silver, spots on the wineglasses. Kids arguing, babies crying. All of America sitting at an enormous table. When she was a little girl, thoughts like this were both comforting and terrifying. The notion of a shared experience like this, in whatever form it might take, made her feel small. She was just one of a billion children, digging into her mashed potatoes, hiding a creamed onion in her napkin. Just one, indistinguishable from all of the others.

When she and Ty were still best friends, she used to eat dinner with her own family and then, after she had helped her mother finish washing all of the dishes, she'd walk to his house and join the McPhees for what Ty's dad called "Secondinner." Their house on Thanksgiving was like a looking-glass reflection of hers. While she and Angie were expected to sit quietly in their straight-back chairs, hands and napkins in their laps, Ty's house was loud and chaotic and wonderful. It was never just the McPhees. There were always cousins and aunts and uncles and friends. Music cranked up loud on their old-fashioned stereo. Their regular dining room table was too small for all the guests, so they cobbled together a string of tables, a mishmash of chairs. Her favorite was always the piano stool that spun up and down; no matter how old she was, how tall she was, she could always adjust it to the right height.

Crystal's mother never let anyone in the kitchen to help her. She seemed to want to make it seem like the entire meal had appeared magically on the dining room table, as though she hadn't spent the entire night before and day of preparing it. At Ty's house, Lucia invited everyone into the kitchen, handed everyone a peeler or knife or rolling pin. By the time she was nine, Crystal had helped make apple pies, acorn squash, and buttermilk biscuits. Dinner itself was a loud affair, served on the McPhees' collection of china dishes, each one hand-picked from flea markets and yard sales and secondhand shops. She loved the one with the yellow roses, and Lucia always made sure that one was in her spot. The food was different every year. Sometimes instead of turkey they had ham or beef stew or, one year, each plate had a trout with its head still on. The tradition was in the company, not in the various courses.

When Crystal was pregnant, she had imagined that first Thanksgiving with the baby. She imagined them passing her back and forth, taking turns holding her as they ate, the entire family clamoring to hold her, to pinch her cheeks and tickle her belly. She would feed her sweet potatoes from a tiny little spoon. She could hardly wait to sit by the fireplace after the meal, sprawled out on the worn Oriental rug with her as Ty's father and his friends played old Van Morrison songs on their guitars and mandolins, the sound of the stand-up bass like a heart beating through the floorboards.

But here she was, just a year later, and Ty was gone. The entire McPhee family was gone. The house that had once been filled with people and music and good smells was empty. There was no baby. She was just a name etched in skin, a name carved in a windowpane.

Crystal sat at the dinner table, hands in her empty lap, as her mother moved purposefully and silently from the kitchen to the dining room, covering the table with the same food she and a million other mothers had spent the day preparing. Light from the brand-new candles caught in the wineglasses, each rubbed with a soft cloth until they were so clear they were almost invisible.

Her father sat at the head of the table where he had sat every single Thanksgiving of her entire life. The turkey carcass lay before him like an offering.

"Just think, next year you'll be coming home from college for Thanksgiving. Maybe have a new boyfriend with you?" her mother said cheerfully.

Crystal felt her entire body tense.

"I can't believe my little girl is so grown up," she said. "Eighteen years old already."

"I'm moving out," Crystal said.

Her mother's perfectly plucked eyebrows raised, and her eyes went dark beneath them.

"Of course you are," she said, laughing. "Your dorm assignment came last week."

"I'm not going to live in a dorm," she said. "I'm moving away."

Angie sat quietly next to her. Crystal didn't mean to hurt her, and it killed her as she watched Angie's eyes fill with tears.

"That girl Fiona's roommate is transferring to another college next semester. She sent me the nicest e-mail. We both put in requests that you be placed with her."

"You've been e-mailing her?" Crystal said, stunned.

"I wanted to surprise you," her mother said, frowning.

"I don't think you heard me," Crystal said. "I said I am not going to school. I'm moving out." Her voice grew and she felt her chest expanding. "I'm eighteen years old. You can't tell me what to do anymore."

"Well, Crystal, if I hadn't told you what to do, you'd be sitting here with a screaming baby on your lap right now," she said. Her face was red and furious. "You've at least got to be grateful for that."

Crystal felt like she might explode. "I'm not just some shitty piece of property you can slap a For Sale sign on, Mom." She was screaming now, saying anything she could that would make her mother hurt as much as she did. To make a hole in her heart as big and wide as the one that the baby had left behind. "Did the Stones pay you or something? How much did you make? How much was your commission on my life?"

Her father cleared her throat then, slamming his fists down on the table. When he spoke, she knew exactly what he would say.

"Crystal, it's your turn this year. Can you please say grace?"

On Friday, Kurt went to the salvage yard and took the envelope of emergency money out of the safe. For the first time in five years, he counted it. There was three thousand dollars inside: a fortune by anybody around here's standards. Just nickels and dimes over years and years. His heart had nearly burst out of his chest as he counted the wad of cash again.

Goddamned Pop.

On the work computer, he did a quick search for local lawyers, grimacing at their smiling faces, their suits. "Fuck it," he said to no one. Then he started typing in the names of some of those sites Elsbeth had mentioned. That one Will Shatner did the commercials for. He was shaking as he plugged in the dates. April 9–16. The kids' spring break. Burlington, VT, to Orlando, FL. Airfare. Hotel. $525 per person. That would still leave about a thousand dollars. Tickets to Disney World. Meals. Rental car. He knew it was crazy, but also knew that this might just save everything.

And as he printed out the itinerary, he couldn't stop smiling. He thought about the beach, pictured Elsbeth, legs long and tan. And so much sand. He thought about himself, swimming in the ocean, taking Gracy into the water, holding her on his shoulders. He thought about Trevor, about teaching him how to ride the waves.

Kurt hadn't gone swimming in years. It seemed crazy now; when he and Billy were kids, they were always in the water. They used to swim in the river, in all the small ponds and larger lakes, in any body of water they could find.

When Kurt was about ten, his mom had talked Pop into taking them all to Maine for a weekend. She said she wanted the boys to see the ocean. To be able to swim in the Atlantic for once in their life.

Pop hadn't been happy about leaving Lloyd in charge of the shop, but Larissa had been so insistent. "These boys deserve a vacation. *I* deserve a vacation." And so Pop had reluctantly packed up the station wagon and driven them silently along Route 2, past all the weird roadside attractions: Santa's Village and Six Gun City, the sixty-foot Indian in Skowhegan and the giant Paul Bunyan statue in Bangor. Kurt knew that somewhere there was a picture of him and Billy sitting next to Paul Bunyan's big boots. He recollected the strange feeling of being at the feet of a giant. And by the time they got to Acadia National Park, even Pop seemed to have relaxed a little and was enjoying the sights.

Though it had been warm in Two Rivers when they left, it was still only June, and remarkably freezing cold and windy at the beach. They parked in an empty lot and clambered over the rocks at the beach's shore to the sand below. The wind was so cold it made Kurt's ears ache. Kurt and Billy stood looking at the crashing waves.

"Go on," Pop said. "I didn't drive all this way for you to just look at it."

"Jude," Larissa said. "It's too cold."

Kurt looked at Billy, whose teeth were chattering, wondering what to do. Billy bit his lip and glanced back at Pop.

"Come on," Kurt said softly to Billy. "Let's just get this over with."

Kurt slipped his sneakers off and rolled his pant legs up. He motioned to Billy, and Billy followed him hesitantly to the water's edge. It felt like ice water as the waves crashed around their bare ankles. Kurt glanced back at Pop. Pop was standing there, arms folded across his chest. Smug. Kurt knew he wouldn't be happy until they'd both gone in. Really, better to just get in and get it over with, he figured.

The beach was deserted. Kurt pulled his shirt over his head and pulled off his jeans. Billy followed suit and Kurt said, "Let's just go in, real quick. It'll be over before you know it."

Kurt ran into the glacial water, and his entire body went immediately, gratefully, numb. Billy next to him, they allowed the waves to pummel them, not resisting the pull of the undertow, and then, finally, when they couldn't take another second of it, they dragged their anesthetized bodies out of the water and collapsed on the sand. They yanked their clothes back on and trudged through the heavy, wet sand to where their father stood, alone now, at the shore.

"Where's Mom?" Kurt asked, his lips feeling like the time he'd gotten a shot of Novocain at the dentist.

Larissa was in the car, staring silently out the window.

"Happy now?" Pop said to her as he slammed his door shut and the boys shivered in the backseat. "Nice vacation, huh, Riss?"

"Don't be such an asshole," she'd said.

And it was like somebody had turned the light on in Pop's dim head.

"I mean *really*, Jude. They're just kids."

"I'm sorry," Pop said, putting his hand on the back of her neck, rubbing the tight tendons there as if he could simply will her to relax. "Rissy, let me go get us some dinner. You like those lobster rolls, right? With pickles?" He turned to the backseat, smiling a big, broad smile. "What do you boys want? Cheeseburgers? Some fries?" He knew he'd screwed up. Only Larissa was capable of making him see when he'd gone too far.

Pop dropped them off at the small cabin they had rented, and inside Larissa ran a warm bath. Both boys shivered as they climbed in, grateful for the steaming heat. Grateful for the water that enclosed them like a watery blanket. They stayed in the tub only until the water cooled, and then buried themselves under the blankets in one of the double beds.

Pop came back with giant milkshakes and greasy paper bags filled with food. They stayed up late watching reruns of *I Love Lucy,* Larissa and Pop sharing one bed, Billy and Kurt the other. It was the only time they all slept in the same room together.

"How about tomorrow we go fishing?" Pop said after the lights were out. "Maybe rent a little boat."

And that night Kurt dreamed of the ocean. Cold watery dreams, the deafening sound of crashing waves. But in the morning, Kurt awoke in excruciating pain. Billy too was miserable. They had caught matching ear infections, it seemed, and so instead of staying in Maine for the rest of the weekend, they had to turn around and go home. As they both sobbed, their ears throbbing, in the backseat of the car, Larissa ran inside the little mom-and-pop shop near the cabin, and came out with Dramamine, offering them each enough to knock them out for the entire long drive back to Two Rivers. Kurt remembered nothing now about the drive but incredible pain, and then the sudden sucking relief of sleep.

"El," he said on the phone. "I got a surprise."

It was easier than he thought it would be. School was out for the entire week of Thanksgiving, which meant nobody was in the building. He knew from the school calendar that the hockey team had a game that Friday, an away game. But the team would meet in the boys' locker room first, to get their equipment. The bus would pick them up out front. His mom had taken Gracy out shopping with her, and his dad was working back-to-back shifts between the 76 and the yard. He was alone.

He knew his dad had played hockey in middle school and high school; he was a goalie. He'd seen his dad's old duffel bag in the closet before: *Two Rivers Hockey* in peeling red letters. Trevor dragged it out of the closet, amazed that it still had his old uniform and pads inside. The only thing that was missing was the mask; luckily he still had the Jason mask left from Halloween.

The walk to school took twenty minutes. He got to the school and could feel every inch of his skin prickling with fear. The hockey guys were all milling around outside the entrance to the gym, waiting for the coach to come and let them in. He hung back, near the Dumpsters by the cafeteria, waiting for his window. Once most of the guys had disappeared into the building, he pulled on the hockey mask and followed, hoping that anyone watching, that those little red eyes watching from the cameras above him, would think he was just another hockey player.

He pushed the door, relieved to find it unlocked. He could hear the distant echoing voices of the guys, laughing and slamming their locker doors open and shut. But instead of heading down the stairs into the basement locker room, he kept going, through the breezeway, to the main building where he took off the mask.

The art room was dark, but he knew his way around like a blind man knows his own home. He felt his way past Mrs. D.'s old desk, past the wooden tables, to the darkroom. He unzipped his duffel bag, and within a few minutes, he was done and ready to go. He couldn't believe how simple it had been. Of course, this was the easy part. But still, he felt lighter as he made his way down the long, dark corridor back toward the gym.

He could hear the sound of the hockey players making their way toward the exit as well, and so he hung back. He was worried that if he was the last to go, he might get locked in, so he knew that timing was everything. He heaved the duffel bag onto his shoulder and, head down, moved toward the door.

"Hey, Miller!" a voice said.

He ignored the voice and kept moving toward the exit. Once he was out, he would just dash toward the woods behind the school and wait until the bus was gone.

"What's the matter, Miller? You deaf?"

Miller was the team's goalie. The only other kid in the school nearly as tall as Trevor. Trevor quickly put the hockey mask back on and turned around.

"Get a move on!" the coach said. "The bus leaves in five minutes. And take that fricking mask off," he said.

Trevor nodded and moved quickly toward the exit. Luckily, no one seemed to notice as he ducked behind the Dumpster again and then ran as quickly as he could toward the woods. When the school bus lurched away from the school, plumes of exhaust curling like dragon's breath behind it, Trevor could barely believe his luck. *He'd done it.*

On Friday night, they were eating Thanksgiving leftovers for dinner. Each of them had two pieces of white bread smothered with turkey and hot gravy. Kurt scooped some cranberries on top; he liked the cold bite of them, the sting.

"So what's the big surprise?" Elsbeth asked. She was still pissed off about Pop ruining Thanksgiving. When he'd gotten back from dropping Pop off that night, she'd said, "We are not spending one fucking cent on that bastard. I swear to God, Kurt. It is time to just let this go."

"There's a surprise?" Gracy said, excitedly. "What did you get, Daddy? Is it a treat for me?"

"It's actually a treat for all of us," Kurt said. The electronic tickets were folded into his back pocket. He could barely stand the anticipation.

Trevor looked up from his plate.

Kurt set down his fork and smiled as he slowly pulled the tickets out of his pocket. He smoothed them out and laid them on the table. "How would you all like to go to Disney World for spring break?" he asked.

Elsbeth reached across the table and grabbed the tickets, turning them over and over in her hands, peering closely at them like she was making sure they were authentic.

"Disney World!" Gracy squealed.

Elsbeth looked at Kurt, her eyes full. "Are you sure we can do this?" she asked softly, and Kurt nodded.

She stood up and came to him, sitting down in his lap and wrapping her arms around his neck. "Thank you, baby," she whispered in his ear. "Thank you."

"What do you think, Trevor?" he asked, peering at Trevor over Elsbeth's dark hair.

Trevor smiled. "It's good," he said.

Gracy disappeared into her room and came back out dressed in her Sleeping Beauty costume. "Let me dance on your shoes, Daddy?" she asked, pulling Kurt's hand. Elsbeth got off his lap and he stood up. Gracy slipped off her plastic heels and climbed onto his boots, encircling him with her arms. Elsbeth clapped her hands together, and even Trevor was smiling. He hummed "Once Upon a Dream," that sappy melody, and felt his heart swell. *This,* he thought, *is my family. This is mine.*

His phone buzzed on the table, and he hoisted Gracy up onto his hip as he went to see who was calling. Maury again. He considered sending it to voice mail, but then he had the optimistic, though unrealistic, thought that maybe Pop had finally changed his mind. Maybe he'd realized how silly it was to turn down a chance at a spot at Plum's. Stranger things had happened, right?

"Hello," he said, lowering Gracy carefully to the floor.

"Kurt?" Maury said. His voice was muffled, buzzing with static. There was a lot of background noise. Loud voices. Sirens. Pop's TV turned up too loud, probably. "It's the house," Maury said.

"I can barely hear you," Kurt said, walking with his phone into the mudroom.

"If it hadn't been for Theresa . . ." He was breathless. "He could have been trapped in there. She got him out just in time."

"Slow down, Maury," Kurt said, pulling his coat from the coat hook. "What happened?"

"There's been a fire."

The house was still standing, but the air smelled charred as Kurt pulled up the driveway. There was one fire truck and an ambulance. Pop was sitting on the fender of his Lincoln, his head in his hands. Maury was standing next to him, arms folded across his chest. Theresa Bouchard, surrounded by her brood of boys, was speaking to one of the firemen. The fire truck's beams painted the dark sky in crimson sweeps of light.

"What happened?" Kurt said.

"Not sure yet, maybe a forgotten cigarette. Seems to have started in the kitchen. Miss Bouchard saw smoke coming out the front door and called 9-1-1. Then she went into the house and got him out. We were able to get the fire out pretty quickly, but there's still quite a bit of damage."

"How bad is it?"

"The kitchen is gutted. It doesn't look bad from out here, but there's some structural damage. The fire inspector's inside. You can talk to him when he's finished." With that he turned and started to unspool a roll of yellow tape, circling the yard.

Kurt went to Theresa. "Thanks. I really appreciate your being here."

She nodded. "I been telling him something like this was gonna happen," she said. "That's why I got the county involved, you know. No hard feelin's, right?"

"None," Kurt said and squeezed her shoulder.

He went over to the Lincoln then, where Pop was still sitting, peering across the lawn at his wrecked house. "I'll let you two talk," Maury said.

"Hold on," Kurt said, pulling Maury over to the edge of the lawn out of Pop's earshot. "You got room for him at your place until the room opens up at Plum's next week?"

Maury hung his head low. "Course. Listen, I didn't think this would happen. I really didn't or else I never woulda helped him move back."

Maury's accusations had stung. The idea that he'd neglected Pop, that he'd been abusive toward Pop, had made Kurt so hot he could have screamed. But now Maury looked on the verge of tears. "S'all right," Kurt said. "I know you didn't want anything to happen to him."

Kurt made his way back to Pop. It was cold out, and someone had draped a blanket over Pop's shoulders.

"You all right?" Kurt said, sitting down next to him on the cold chrome fender. "What *happened?*"

"Set the house on fire," Pop said, looking up at him. His eyes were bleary, his face smudged with soot. He coughed into his hand. "This was whatcha wanted, right? Happy now?" he asked.

He couldn't go into the school on Monday. This was all Trevor knew when his mother dropped him and Gracy off at the front of the building, the other cars lined up like a funeral procession behind them.

"Do you want me to come in with you?" she asked. "I don't have to go into work today. I can walk you to your new class?"

"No," he said. The car was hot, the heater blasting at his face and feet. It made his skin itch. He almost wished for the cold air outside the car.

"You sure, baby?" she asked. "It's no trouble to walk you in."

He shook his head. Ever since everything that happened over the weekend (first Disney World and then the fire at Pop's), his mom had been acting different. *Nice.* It was like she had gotten everything she wanted: Disney World and Pop finally agreeing to go to the nursing home. She'd been especially nice to his dad. She even went with him over to Maury's with a turkey potpie she'd made with the rest of the Thanksgiving leftovers. There had been so much excitement at home, there had hardly been time to think about school. But now Monday morning had come, and here he was, about to go into that building. It was like somebody walking out onto the ledge of a skyscraper. Like someone point- ing a gun at their own head.

He couldn't go into the school. Not today. But he knew he needed to at least pretend he was going in if he was going to get her to leave.

"Well, have a good first day back," she said and squeezed his hand. Her touch was so foreign, so strange. "It's going to be better, Trevor. I promise."

"Bye, Mommy!" Gracy said, popping out of the backseat, her backpack thunking behind her.

"I'll be back to get you when school gets out," she said. And then she reached through her open window and reached for Trevor's hand. "It'll be okay, baby. Just keep your chin up." And for a moment, he almost believed her. Maybe it *would* be okay. But after she pulled away from the school and he stood staring up at its scowling face, as he heard the bell ring like some sort of death knell, he knew he couldn't go inside.

"Go ahead, Gracy," he said, pushing her gently toward the front doors, a lump as thick as a cork in his throat. "I forgot something. I'll be right in." He pictured her going to her classroom on the elementary school side of the building. She would be okay.

"But Mommy's already gone," she said. She was wearing last year's pink winter coat, which had a big hot cocoa stain on the front. It was too small for her, the sleeves exposing two pale forearms. The fur around the cuffs and collar was dingy, gray. Her dark hair was poking out from underneath a sparkly pink hat with a sad pom-pom on top. He pulled his camera out of his backpack and knelt down.

"Smile," he said and then he took her picture, the school looming behind her.

"Go on in," he said. "I'm right behind you."

But then as soon as she disappeared inside the school, he turned away. And ran as fast as he could, not stopping until he couldn't breathe, until the cold air seemed to have frozen his lungs. He knew he didn't have long before the school called, before everything came crashing down around him. But for now, his instinct was simply to flee.

After Elsbeth left to take the kids to school, Kurt got ready for work. He showered and dressed and pulled on his boots. It was cold out, the sky white and heavy. The air smelled like snow. He stepped outside to check the temperature. The forecast said it might drop below zero by late afternoon. It would be cold at the yard. Colder outside, where he would be adding the pile of stuff he'd been able to salvage from Pop's house to the inventory all afternoon. He had half a mind to take it all to the dump. The fire inspector had shown him where the fire had destroyed one of the main support beams. It was like a goddamn house of cards; a storm might take down what was left of the house.

Back inside, he got his heavy down jacket, his neck warmer and wool hat from the mudroom. His good gloves weren't in the bench where he usually put them. He rifled through the cedar trunk, finding nothing but Gracy's tiny mismatched mittens and Trevor's hats and scarves. He went to the bedroom, thinking maybe Elsbeth had stored their winter stuff in the closet. She sometimes did that when spring came; after a brutal winter, she sometimes couldn't stand the sight of anything to do with snow.

In the closet, he pulled the chain for the bare lightbulb that hung down over their sorry collection of clothes. He felt a pang as he touched the edges of Elsbeth's old dresses and sweaters and shirts. He wished he could take her shopping, let her buy a whole new wardrobe. She'd had some of these clothes since they started dating. He wanted to get her a new swimsuit before they went to Florida.

He reached up to the top shelf, grabbing hold of a blue plastic storage bin. Whatever was inside was heavy, and as he tried to
ease it off the shelf, he knocked over a shoe box that was sitting
next to it.

"Shit," he muttered as the box and its contents tumbled down.

He bent down to pick the stuff up and then stopped. It was
like the contents of some strange piñata. Trinkets. Junk. Just a
bunch of crap. A yo-yo, some bubblegum, batteries. Little plastic
army men and a box of dryer sheets. Unopened packs of gum,
erasers, Chapstick, and chocolate bars. Hairbrushes still tethered
to their cardboard backs, playing cards, and a two-pack of lighters.
It was as though a junk drawer had fallen from the sky, but none
of the junk had been used before.

He reached down and started putting the items back into the
box, but then his fingers skipped across something he thought at
first was only candy. But it wasn't. It was a condom. A *condom*.
And then another and another. He felt like someone had kicked
him in the chest. He sat back on his heels and took a deep breath.
They hadn't used condoms since they were kids. And even then,
clearly, not that often. Elsbeth had been on the Pill since Gracy
was born. He rifled through the crap, searching for something,
anything that would explain. A book of crossword puzzles, a key
chain, a bottle opener shaped like a flip-flop. His head was reeling, and his stomach turned. He coughed without covering his
mouth and felt bile rising in the back of his throat.

He threw everything back into the box and shoved it up onto
the shelf again. He didn't even know what he was looking for, but
he was suddenly desperate, looking for anything to justify or dis-
pel this awful feeling in his gut. He opened her drawers, rifled
through Elsbeth's underwear and bras, her socks and T-shirts and
jeans. He went through the laundry pile, pressed his face into her
dirty clothes, like a dog tracking the scent of anything unfamiliar.
He looked under her side of the bed, reached into all of her
pockets. Nothing. He went back to the closet and was about to

pull the box down again when he noticed something he hadn't before. A postcard. From Florida.

His first instinct was to confront her. If it had been anything else—finding out Trevor had gotten in another fight, catching Gracy in a lie—he would have been quick to act. He believed in holding people accountable. That people, including himself, should take responsibility for their actions, but when Elsbeth came in the front door and then into the bedroom where he sat at the edge of their unmade bed, he felt paralyzed. If he confronted her, then she might just tell him exactly what he did not want to hear.

He had put the box back in the closet, pocketed the condoms.

"What are you doing here?" she asked. "I thought you'd be at work already."

He didn't say anything.

She cocked her head and smiled at him. Teasing. Had she done this with this Wilder guy? Had she looked at him like this? *Florida.* Was this why she was so fucking obsessed with Florida?

"Can you be a little late?" she asked then, pulling off her sweater and tossing it on the floor next to his feet.

He sat on the edge of the bed, silently, as she kicked off her shoes and wriggled out of her jeans. He studied the familiar ladder of bone that was her spine, the star-shaped birthmark on the back of her thigh. His dick pulsed with the remembrance of her legs wrapped tightly around his waist, with the vivid possibility that these same legs had spread wide open for someone else.

But instead of anger, he felt heavy with a new kind of sadness. It was like a sucker punch, like an unexpected blow to the gut. He'd known things weren't going well, that everything was precarious, but he hadn't seen this coming. He hadn't expected *this.* None of his fears involved a third party. Her unhappiness, her boredom and frustration and disappointment, were the only things he feared. He had never imagined another man. That she was having sex with someone else. He felt completely deluded, deceived. He and El had had their share of problems over the last thirteen years, but betrayal had never been one of them. He'd always trusted her. He'd never once considered that she might be a liar, that their life together, that all of this, might be a lie.

His boner would not relent. Somehow, each pang of sadness, of disenchantment, made the ache of his body, the want of his body, all the stronger. And as she bent over to pull off her panties, he stood up and walked over to her, pressing his body against hers, as if mere contact might relieve this tremendous pressure. She caught her breath but did not turn to look at him. In the mirror over the dresser, he could see her squeezing her eyes shut. And something about this, her unwillingness to open her eyes, to see their reflection in the mirror, turned that sorrow into rage.

He unzipped his pants and spread her flesh open with his. She gasped, her whole body resisting his, clamping down. And every quiver of resistance, every shudder of revulsion or disgust or whatever it was she now felt for him, made him all the more determined. The ache and longing all the stronger.

He studied her hands as they clutched the top of the bureau, her manicured nails digging into the soft wooden top, and he kept going. Even as her whole body resisted, he continued, pressing his face into her clean hair, until his whole body trembled with both lust and loathing. When he was finished, he stumbled backward, feeling drunk, his legs failing him as he staggered out the bedroom door, leaving her behind, stunned and trying to catch her breath.

In her room, Crystal got out the pink and green plaid suitcase she'd had since she was a little girl and started to pack. It was cold out, so she made sure to pack long johns, turtlenecks, wool sweaters and socks. But she would need her summer clothes too. She pulled the bin from her closet and decided to just bring the whole thing. The Volvo was big enough; there would be plenty of room. She looked at her bed, at the place where she had slept every night since she was too big for her crib, and her throat swelled. She grabbed her sock monkey, the one she'd had since her very first Christmas, and put it in the suitcase. The afghan her grandmother had made. As she zipped the suitcase shut, she wondered if she should bring along any other relics of her childhood. She ran her hand across Angie's pillow, tried not to think about breaking her heart.

She opened her desk drawer and took out the envelope she'd gotten at the bank two days before, and counted the twenties again. Then she shoved it in her backpack, along with the envelope of pictures she'd stolen from the Walgreens and the ultra-sound pictures of Grace.

It took three trips to get all of her stuff downstairs. She was breathless when she finally locked the door behind her. Outside, it felt like dusk instead of late morning. The sky was dark and thick. Looming. The sun was just a small yellow hint, reluctant behind a thick gauze curtain. Even the trees seemed cautious of the threatening sky.

She put her suitcase in the back of the Volvo, opened the

door, and sat down in the driver's seat. The upholstery was hard and cold, and her hands shook as she found the car key on the ring. While she was determined, part of her almost hoped it wouldn't start. Because she knew that once the engine roared to life, there was no going back. She counted softly to three and turned the key. She pressed her foot on the gas, the seat shook beneath her, and the radio blared. Exhaust puffed out behind her, and cold air blew through the open vents. She turned her headlights on, illuminating the road in front of her. A few snowflakes peppered her windshield as she headed east. She passed the bend in the road where the two crosses reminded her to drive carefully, and she slowed in deference to the lost boys.

This was the easy part; she simply pulled the car up close to the mailbox at the edge of the road, undid her seat belt, and leaned over the passenger seat. She unrolled the window and reached out into the cold air, pulling open the door on the mailbox. It was empty, so she simply slipped the photos inside and then lifted up the red flag at its side.

Heat spread through her entire body as she glanced toward the house. Her heart pounded in her chest, her ears, her hands. She could do this. She *had* to do this.

She looked away from the house and quickly rolled up her window. Then she was pressing her foot on the gas and moving forward. In the next driveway, she turned the Volvo around and then she was on her way.

Tights made her feel itchy. But it was cold out and she had wanted to wear her purple dress. It was too cold out to wear a dress with no tights, so she'd sat at the edge of her bed as her mom helped her put them on this morning. They were a little bit small, so her mom did the trick where she lifts her up by the tights, which stretches them out and puts them on all at the same time, the waistband coming practically up to her armpits and making her giggle. But now, they were hanging down again; she could barely sit Indian-style on the rug, the middle part practically to her knees again, making it hard to cross her legs.

They were sitting on the carpet for the morning weather report. Her spot was the red square in the front row sandwiched between Connor With an *O* and Conner With an *E*. This put her right at Mrs. Kelly's feet when she sat in the teacher's chair. She liked to look at Mrs. Kelly's shoes. She had the fanciest shoes she'd ever seen. Her favorites were the shiny black ones with the little silver bows at the toes. They were made of metal, and just shaped like a bow, not really tied. She also liked the brown ones that had ribbons that wrapped around her ankles like a ballerina. Today she was wearing her plain brown ones, the ones with the tassels. Boring.

She uncrossed her legs and stretched them out into the blue square next to her where Conner With an *E* would be if he weren't absent today. He was absent a lot of days because he got ear infections, and head lice once. He came back to school after three days with a shaved head, and he had to hang his coat with a garbage bag over it so the lice didn't jump to the other coats.

"Okay, let's see," Mrs. Kelly said, leaning toward the chore chart on the wall. "Who is our Weather Reporter today?"

Her arm shot up into the air. She'd been waiting to be Weather Reporter for so long. The last time she was Weather Reporter, it was still hot outside. She didn't like the face on the sun magnet. It looked creepy. But today it looked like snow. She loved the snow magnet. It was a smiling puffy cloud with snowflakes coming out of it.

"Okay, Gracy, come on up," Mrs. Kelly said, smiling.

But just as she was going to the board to pluck the snow magnet from the pile, Mrs. Moody, the lady from the office, poked her head into the classroom. "Excuse me? Can you send Grace Kennedy to the office? Have her bring her coat and backpack."

Gracy looked at Mrs. Kelly, who shrugged. "I'm sorry, sweetheart. You can do the report tomorrow, okay?"

"Okay." Disappointed, she went to her cubby and got her backpack and her jacket. Then she took the hall pass from the hook by Mrs. Kelly's desk and opened up the heavy door to the hallway. It was kind of spooky in the hallway when the other kids weren't there. Her boots made squeaky sounds on the floor. Like a funny music. She stopped for a drink of water and wondered if there was any way she could pull up her tights.

A man wearing coveralls was standing by the girls' bathroom. He had a mop bucket, but he wasn't mopping. Usually Mr. Douglas mopped the floors. Maybe he was a substitute. "Hi, pretty girl," he said, smiling. But she didn't smile back.

In the office, Mrs. Moody nodded at her to have a seat in one of the orange plastic chairs by her desk. Maybe she had a dentist appointment, she thought. But she'd just been to the dentist last week.

She sat there for a long time, her legs dangling off the edge of the seat. Nobody paid any attention to her, and so she pretended she was invisible. It was fun. Then the door opened, and a lady came inside. She smiled at her. "Hi, Gracy," she said. She could see her!

"Hi," she said. And then she remembered where she knew her from. It was weird seeing people where they weren't supposed to be. One time she saw Mrs. Kelly at Luigi's getting a pizza with her husband. It made her feel shy.

Mrs. Moody wasn't in the office anymore, but Mrs. Bell, the nurse, was. She was at the counter looking through some papers. "You can just sign her out there," she said to the lady, pointing to the clipboard on Mrs. Moody's desk.

"I'm going with you?" Gracy said to the lady.

"Yep," she said. "Your mom asked me to pick you up."

"Bye!" she said to Mrs. Bell and hopped down off the chair. She reached for the lady's hand. Together their boots squeaked all the way down the hall to the door.

Outside, Gracy climbed into the backseat of the lady's car. "I'm supposed to be in a booster," she said.

"Shoot," she said. "I don't have a booster seat, but you should be fine as long as you buckle up." The lady buckled her seat belt and then got into the car. She looked at Gracy in the rearview mirror.

"Where are we going?" Gracy asked.

The lady pulled away from the curb and headed down the street, the school disappearing behind them. "Just for a ride," she said, glancing up at the rearview mirror and smiling at Gracy's reflection. She was pretty. And nice. She taught her what to do when you get a bloody nose. But still, it was kind of weird seeing her without her Walgreens shirt on.

Elsbeth sat at the kitchen table with her cup of coffee, unsure of what had just happened in the bedroom. Kurt hadn't said a word. Even afterward, when they were both covered in sweat and breathless, he had simply staggered into the bathroom. Shut and locked the door, run water into the sink. Elsbeth had completely undressed and pulled her robe on, looked at her startled self in the mirror.

Glancing down the hallway to make sure he wasn't coming, she slowly parted her robe and reached between her legs. The place between her thighs was tender. She might even be black-and-blue tomorrow. She stung. He'd never been so rough with her. Never anything but gentle. Gentle to the point of boredom even. She didn't know whether to be thrilled or frightened.

She could hear him in their bedroom, his heavy footsteps as he moved across the floor. She tried to read the sounds, the silences. She had no idea what was going on in his head. What had brought this on. He'd seemed almost angry.

The bedroom door slammed. He coughed. Then his familiar footsteps echoed down the hallway. On any other day, he'd come to the kitchen, gather his coat and wallet and keys, kiss her gently on the forehead, and mumble, "Have a good day. Love you." But now she felt her whole body stiffen; for the first time in ages, she couldn't predict what would happen next. She pressed her hand against her chest, felt the rapid percussion of her heart against her bones.

Kurt stood in the doorway, his hand against the door frame, and looked at her. She raised her eyebrow and cocked her head. Tried and failed to read his expression.

"Well, good morning," she said, hoping to sound playful, but her voice cracked.

He stared at her, his eyes wide. He shook his head.

"Baby?" she asked, feeling suddenly scared.

He closed his eyes and kept shaking his head.

"What's the matter?"

"Goddamn you, you . . ." he said, his voice like a blast, but then there was another sound. Also loud. Also terrible. It was far away, but loud enough to make both of them turn their heads toward the front door.

Kurt swung the door open, and Elsbeth followed behind him in her robe, careful not to slip as she navigated the icy steps. It was freezing outside, snowing now. Her entire body was trembling. There was already easily an inch on the ground, and it was sticking. She could feel the icy earth through the thin soles of her slipper socks. Wind whipped through the thin fabric of her robe. "What *was* that?" she asked, reaching for his arm.

"I don't know," Kurt said, pulling away from her and walking quickly down the driveway. He peered out into that thick white sky.

"I think it was some sort of explosion," he said. "Do you see that smoke?" He pointed to a place in the distance beyond the tops of the trees, and she could see enormous billows of gray smoke rising up into the sky. A vague orange glow.

There were several more loud cracks.

"What the hell?" Kurt said.

His cell phone rang in his pocket, and then inside the house phone started to ring.

It was third period, art, and Angie was working on a still life of three apples and a banana. Mr. Franklin had set up the display a week ago, and the bananas were brown now. Rotten. The whole room smelled vaguely of things gone bad. Remarkably, over Thanksgiving break, her own oil pastel bananas remained ripe and yellow on the page. That was the great thing about art, she thought. It preserved things.

She studied her fingers, smudged with every color in the box. She didn't mind getting messy. Not like her sister. Crystal couldn't stand getting dirty. She was always rolling her eyes at Angie's messes in their shared bathroom, muttering in disgust when she cleared the table and Angie's place setting inevitably was littered with crumbs and spilled food. They'd had a thousand arguments over their bedroom. Angie never made her bed, couldn't seem to keep her junk from spilling onto Crystal's side of the room, had a bad habit of leaving her dirty clothes on the floor rather than stuffing them into their shared hamper.

She looked toward the wooden bowl of rotten fruit and felt a pit in her stomach. Something was weird with Crystal. Well, something had been weird with Crystal for a long time now, ever since she had the baby. But that was just her being sad. Anyone who knew her could figure that out. But this morning had been different.

Angie usually slept until the last possible second before tearing herself from her bed, from the soft, warm nest of her comforter and sheets. Most days, Crystal got ready quietly, letting her sleep. She was careful not to turn on the light or make any noise as she pulled open her drawers to get dressed. It was one of those things that Angie loved about Crystal. Their mom would run the vacuum at six in the morning, bang pots and pans, have loud conversations on her phone right outside her door, but Crystal was always thoughtful. She would have made a good mom, Angie thought sometimes. She knew she shouldn't think like that; the baby was gone, not hers anymore. But Angie knew it was true.

But this morning, instead of letting Angie sleep, she had woken her up, gently nudging her shoulder. She was sitting on the edge of Angie's bed, already dressed.

"Hey, Ang," she had said. She wasn't wearing her Walgreens smock, which meant she wasn't going to work. Why was she up, then? Angie could never understand that. On days when she didn't have school, she slept until it was time for lunch.

Angie had sat up, rubbing the sleep from her eyes. "Yeah?"

"I want to give you something," she said.

"What?" Angie asked. Couldn't this have waited until she was up? Or at least awake?

But Crystal looked like she was going to cry. "Here," she said, pressing whatever it was into Angie's hand. Then she stood up, all business. "Mom wants you to come down for breakfast. She's leaving for work in five minutes."

Angie opened her fist. In her hand was the charm bracelet that Crystal had gotten for her birthday a few years ago. The one that Angie had borrowed without asking, and, within hours, lost. It was missing for almost a whole week before their dad finally found it behind the toaster. It had probably slipped off her wrist when she was making a piece of toast. She knew Crystal had to have been furious, but she hadn't said.

"I added a charm," Crystal said as she stood in the doorway. "One that's just for you."

Angie looked at the silver chain in her hand: at the shamrock charm, the heart, the soccer ball. There was a *16* with a space where her birthstone used to go and, of course, a striding runner.

But near the clasp was the new charm: a palette, a tiny silver palette and brush, with gemstones like miniature dollops of paint: red, yellow, and blue.

"Why?" Angie asked.

Crystal, still looking like she might cry, just shrugged.

Angie had put the chain on her wrist, felt the heft of it, the cold metal against her skin. Now, at the art table, as she studied the brown bananas and the bruised apples, trying to remember what the fruit looked like before it started to decay, the bracelet felt strange. Too heavy. Too cold. Something was wrong. For as generous as Crystal was, she didn't just give up her stuff for no reason.

Next to her, Heidi Lemeau's bananas looked like summer squash. Her apples were like cartoon apples: too round, too red. The two boys at the end of her table weren't even drawing; they were horsing around with a stolen banana, making obscene ges- tures behind Heidi's back. As weird as he was, she really missed that kid Trevor. At least he took art class seriously. But she'd heard he got suspended, and somebody said they'd put him in the special-ed classroom. She felt bad for him. She knew some of the other eighth-grade boys were really mean to him. He was always getting in fights, but she was pretty sure that he wouldn't be fighting if they weren't always teasing him. The special-ed kids didn't come to the art room, as far as she knew. That was just sad.

Mr. Franklin was sitting at the desk at the front of the room, looking bored. If Mrs. D. was still there, she would be walking around, looking at what they were doing, clapping her hands to- gether or putting her hand on her hip and leaning in close for a better "look-see." Angie was pretty sure that any excitement Mr. Franklin had had about his new job was gone now; most days he just gave them an assignment and then sat back, leafing through a magazine while they worked. They had pop quizzes once a week about whatever artist he told them to read about in the lame textbook he'd passed out the first day. He wouldn't let them into any of the messy stuff: clay, oils, Cray-Pas.

She watched him glance at his watch. There was still forty minutes left of class.

She raised her hand, felt the charm bracelet slip down her arm. The cold silver sent a chill down her back.

"Yes, Angie?" he asked, when he finally noticed her.

"Can I use the restroom?"

He nodded and reached for the enormous wooden pass labeled *Girls* in red Sharpie. She stood up and went to the desk and took it from him. He smiled miserably.

She walked down the empty hallway to the girls' bathroom and looked out the window next to the handicapped stall, touched her nose to the cold glass. Snow was falling outside, and for a minute the dizzying display gave her vertigo. But she stayed, watching the snow falling up, blowing sideways. Upside down.

But then there was a shudder, a tremble, and a crack. Like thunder. And in the split second before everything went black, she thought, *How strange.* She'd never heard of thunder during a blizzard.

At that crooked little house downtown, Trevor made his way up the creaky stairs and knocked on the door. He heard Mrs. D. shuffling around inside, but when she opened the door, he barely recognized her. She wasn't wearing her wig, and her skin and hair were the same silvery color. It made his ears hot, as though he'd caught her without her clothes on.

"Trevor," she said, reaching for him. "Oh dear, come in. You look half-frozen."

He followed her inside. It was dark but warm. He could smell whatever she had had for breakfast. Coffee. Toast. The snow that had dusted his shoulders and hair started to melt. Soon, his clothes would be wet.

"Can I get you something to drink? Maybe some hot tea?" Her voice sounded weak, smaller than before. "Can I take your coat?" She coughed, and her entire chest rumbled like thunder.

He shook his head and, without taking his coat off, without waiting for an invitation, he sat down on the worn couch.

"Did you have a good Thanksgiving?" she asked.

He nodded and his heart panged momentarily with the thoughts of the argument with Pop. He squeezed his eyes shut and saw only the splatter of sweet potatoes, the fury on his mother's face. He thought of Disney World. Of airplanes and beaches. The cold crash of the ocean. All of those dreams seemed to belong to someone else now. A figment of someone else's imagination.

"My brother was here for the holiday," she said, sitting next to him. "The one I told you about. He brought me these," she said, motioning to a box of a thousand watercolors, which looked like a tray of candy, on the coffee table. There was an open sketch-book, a still life of a melon and a single dimpled orange. Loose papers scratched with pencil drawings lay scattered across the table.

"How is school?" she said, her face crumpled with concern.

Trevor looked out the window at the street below. The sky was white, achingly bright. It made his head throb, his eyes unable to bear all that light. He thought about all the things she'd told him. About how the quality of light is the only thing a photographer should ever really care about. That beauty lies simply in illumination. That a good photographer can use the light to change the way we see things. He wondered if there was any light that could shine on him and change who *he* was.

"I did something," he said.

"What do you mean?"

He turned to her and studied the lines on her face. Her skin was like paper in an old book. "I hurt somebody," he said.

She reached for his hand. When she touched him, he felt his entire world starting to crumble. Like paper that's been burned. Like something turning quietly to dust. Outside the snow was falling hard now, ashen flakes covering the entire world. "Did you have another fight?" she asked.

He shook his head. His entire body ached, and he knew the end started here. He only needed to say the words. To admit the truth.

"They're right about me," he said. "They're all right."

Crystal had downloaded maps from the Internet, the route that would take them away from here. She had memorized the directions, repeated them like a mantra each night to fall asleep. Even now as she clicked her right-hand turn signal and peered through her windshield, a kaleidoscope of crystals, at the entrance ramp to the interstate, the path was like a prayer: 91, 11, 279, then west, west, west. Farther and farther, until the world itself ended.

She'd called Lucia from work the day after Thanksgiving, surprised and grateful that she hadn't changed her cell phone number yet. Grateful that she could still be found. Sobbing, Crystal had tried to get the words out to explain, and Lucia had soothed her, waited for her to catch her breath.

"It'll be okay, sweetie," Lucia said. "Everything will be okeydoke." She assured her again and again that they would figure something out.

Sitting in the back office at the Walgreens, Crystal had hugged her knees to her chest and imagined herself in Ty's old kitchen, Lucia making cocoa from scratch at the antique wood-burning stove top. She knew that Lucia was in California, in a different house, a different life, but the smooth calm of her voice brought her back to that warm kitchen. A dog at her feet and the smell of cloves and bay leaves.

When she first found out she was pregnant, Crystal told Lucia first. Before Ty. Before her own mother even. She'd gone to the house when she knew Ty would be at soccer practice and sat at the counter like she had so many times after school. Now that Angie was older, she had things to do after school; the house was too quiet without her. But Lucia was always home. Always in the kitchen ready to talk.

Crystal had broken down as she told her about the test, about the baby. About her fears of losing Ty. But instead of looking horrified, like her own mother would just days later, Lucia softened and moved toward Crystal instead of away. She enclosed her. Held her. Enveloped her. Inside her bangled arms, Crystal felt safe. She knew that, at least for now, everything would be okay.

Crystal had looked up from her knees at the boxes and boxes of meaningless crap stored in the stockroom, and Lucia offered what Crystal had prayed she would.

"You can come here. You can come be with us. Ty is living in the dorms. We have an extra room. As soon as you establish residency, you can go to school. One of the community colleges."

"I shouldn't have given her up," Crystal cried, her entire body racked with pain from the hole Grace left when she was born. "I did the wrong thing."

"It's okay. Crystal. You have a family that loves you."

She didn't know which family she was talking about, but it didn't matter anymore. She had somewhere to go.

And she started to think that maybe it was possible for a mother other than your own to love you just as much, if not more. Her whole life, Crystal's mother had given her nothing but ultimatums. *Conditional* love. Love with strings. Lucia, on the other hand, was patient and understanding. Made no demands. Crystal had wished a hundred times that Lucia could adopt her. Funny how the world works.

She didn't tell her about the other Grace. She wasn't even sure then about what she should do. What she did know was this: Here was her chance to save a little girl. To make her world right. To be a mother to Grace when her own mother had clearly failed her. She only had to look at those photos to know that something had to be done. She thought about Grace's mother, wandering the aisles pocketing trinkets. Stealing all those incidental things that no one would miss. Wasn't this the same thing?

But now, as she turned that giant beast of a car onto the interstate, accelerating through the whiteout with someone else's child in her backseat, now that she could smell that child smell of Cheerios and Play-Doh, hear the sound of tiny lungs inhaling and exhaling, she worried that maybe she was losing her mind.

The little girl was looking out the window, her face concerned.

"It's a big storm," Crystal said. "But this is a very safe car," she said, feigning cheerfulness. Her entire body rocked with nausea. She'd kidnapped a child. She'd stolen someone's little girl. And it had been so easy. How could it be so simple? She'd called this morning and pretended to be her mother. Told the woman that Grace's sitter was coming to get her. That there had been a family emergency. *And the sitter's name?* the secretary had asked. *Crys,* she had started. What a fool. *Chris Johnson.*

"What is that?" Grace asked.

"What?" Crystal said. She looked in the rearview mirror again. Grace was leaning across the seat toward the opposite window.

"That smoke?" she said, pointing.

Crystal turned back around and looked out her own window. From the interstate, she could see down into the valley where Two Rivers lay nestled. Plumes of black smoke curled up from the whiteness.

"It looks like a fire maybe," Crystal said.

"There was a fire at my grandpa's house," the little girl said. "You shouldn't smoke cigarettes."

Crystal's phone vibrated on the seat next to her. She reached for it before it could shimmy across the seat and onto the floor. Her mother's name flashed across the display. She thought for a moment about answering, but then sent the call to voice mail.

Elsbeth and Kurt stood in a crowd of parents held back by the police tape that circled the entire periphery of the school, a bright yellow ribbon enclosing a horrific package. How many "gifts" like this would he receive? First Pop's house. Now this. It struck Kurt as ridiculous how readily and unthinkingly the parents obeyed the flimsy boundary. How easy it would be to duck under, crawl over, or even just break through the tape. The only thing stopping him was what was on the other side of the tape. What was inside this particular package: from where they were standing, they could see an entire wall blown out, a classroom's contents spilled onto the snow.

Flames reached like liquid blue and orange fingers through the black smoke into the cold sky. The sound of ambulances was muffled by the snow. The white sky reflected the red and blue lights. The air was so thick with smoke, Kurt could barely breathe. And it was still snowing, still freezing. Elsbeth's skin had lost all of its color: her lips blue, her skin like snow itself. His own face stung, his bare hands were numb, and his legs felt electrified, ready to detonate. His children were possibly somewhere inside that burning mess, and there was nothing he could do.

"Where are the kids?" a woman screamed as she came running from her car, which she had pulled off the road, not bothering to slam her door shut. Kurt could hear the radio blaring inside. She was wearing a baggy pair of flannel pajama bottoms and Ski-Doo boots, a bright green parka. She looked like she'd just rolled out of bed. She ran to the woman in the orange vest, the one who had been standing there with a clipboard, taking parents' names, and said, "I've got a first grader, a third grader, and twins in the fifth grade in there. I need to go in." She clearly didn't know the rules, these stupid rules to which the rest of the mob was mindlessly in obedience.

The clipboard woman's phone rang. "Hold on a second," she said, her voice like corn syrup, too thick, too sweet. She glanced down at her cell phone and then moved away from the crowd to take the call.

"Can you believe this?" the woman in the pajamas said, turning to Kurt, as if he had some sort of explanation. Like he had any control over the situation. Her face was pocked with acne scars, her teeth bad.

Kurt went up to the woman in the clipboard and said, "Excuse me, ma'am?"

She shook her head, glaring at him, and returned to the call.

The currents in both of Kurt's legs were hot. Relentless.

"That was Principal Cross," she said, admonishing him. "All of the children are being escorted in small groups to buses to be transported to the high school. Principal Cross has said that there will be a list of the students' names posted at the municipal building's doors next door, along with the children's locations. There will also be a list of the students who have been taken to the hospital. If your child's name is not on the list, they have not yet been accounted for."

"What do you mean *not accounted for?*" Kurt hissed.

"I mean, they may still be inside the building."

"Come on," Kurt said to Elsbeth, grabbing her hand and leading her away from the crowd, which was growing now in both size and volume. Mothers with young children were weeping into each other's arms, fathers were rumbling angrily. Kurt wondered how long it would take before the angry mob stormed the burning building.

"Who did this?" Elsbeth asked as they ran through the snow to the auditorium on the back side of the building.

"What do you mean?" he asked.

"I mean who set off the bomb?"

"What makes you think it was a bomb? It could have been a gas leak. A furnace explosion."

"The school's in *lockdown,* Kurt," she said, her eyes widening in horror. "That means someone did this on purpose. And they haven't caught whoever did it yet. There could be more explosions. Whoever did this might still be in there."

Kurt felt the world go soft then; his blood, which had been running through the exposed wires of his veins, suddenly felt slow and liquid. Like liquor. The world tilted underneath his feet, and he struggled to keep from dropping to his knees with the weight of it all.

"I'm sure the kids are out. We'll just go check the list. They're probably at the high school," he said, knowing even as the words exited his mouth how phony they sounded.

The mob at the front of the municipal building was almost as big as at the school. A couple of volunteers were trying to get people into two single-file lines. It was like herding cats, though, herding a hundred hissing, scratching, wailing cats.

He and Elsbeth stood waiting, Elsbeth squinting her eyes and leaning forward as if she might be able to read the fine print from twenty feet away. They moved slowly forward, most of the parents finding their children's names on the list and then nearly collapsing in relief.

Finally, they got to the front, and Kurt stepped toward the sign with the names of the children who had been taken to the hospital. He quickly scanned the list and was relieved to see that neither Gracy nor Trevor was on it. He was elated as he made his way to the sign, where he searched for *K* names to see where they had been taken. He ran his finger down the list, searching for Trevor. Searching for Gracy. Nothing. He figured he had somehow missed them and started over again.

"Please hurry," the woman behind him whispered.

He turned on his heel and got close to her face. "You can wait another goddamned minute while I find my kids."

She looked at him, both terrified and simultaneously offended, and something about her fear made his skin prickle. *How dare she?*

But they weren't there. Neither Gracy nor Trevor was on either list. Which meant they were still inside the building. Somewhere inside that burning wreckage, where whoever was responsible for this might still be wandering around.

Just then Principal Cross came out of the building, her hair a mess, her cheeks flushed red. She teetered on her high-heeled pumps as she made her way across the icy pavement. She held up a bright blue megaphone. "Parents," she said, smiling. *Smiling.* "Thank you so much for your patience during this emergency situation. We are doing everything we can to make sure that all of your children are safe. If they have been injured, we are doing our best to get them out of the building and taken to the appropriate facilities for treatment. Thank you." Without giving any further explanation or answering any questions at all, she turned on those high heels and disappeared back inside the building, ushered by some guy who looked like he might be a janitor or something.

"Stay here," Kurt said to Elsbeth, who looked bewildered, shaking her head in disbelief at the closed door.

"Where are you going?" she asked.

"Please just stay here. I'm going to find them."

Elsbeth reached for him, clung to him, and then it hit him again as though for the first time. She'd screwed someone else. Their children might be dead, and she had *fucked* some asshole named Wilder from Florida. He pulled away from her silently and started to run back toward the school, his legs grateful for the running. The pounding of his head, of those words, of all the terrible things that might be about to unfold, echoed in the pounding of his feet on the hard-packed snow.

Instead of taking the shortcut, past the school, Trevor walked the long way home. He knew the sooner he got there, the sooner he'd have to explain. The sooner all hell would break loose. And so he took his time, despite the blistering cold and relentlessly falling snow.

Mrs. D. had told him that he needed to talk to his mom and dad. To explain all of the things that were messed up inside his head. The things about those boys, about what they had called him. About what Ethan had done to him that day behind the Walgreens. He needed to tell her about Gracy, about how afraid he was. About how confused he was, about how sad. It made him sick just thinking about how he might explain. He knew it would kill her. That she would hate him. That she would think he was a monster. But he was so tired of the secrets; exhausted from the lies. He knew that whatever came of it couldn't be any worse than the hell he was living in.

The snow was still coming down, and the entire world was covered in a thick layer of white. He could hear police cars and ambulances the whole way home. He thought about fires. About accidents. He tried to shove those bad thoughts away, but there was hardly any room anymore. Those spaces were already filled. By the time he got to the house, his entire body was numb from the cold. And surprisingly, the numbness made him feel stronger. He knew he could handle almost anything. If his dad took him out to the shed, he might not even feel the belt.

His mom's car was in the driveway, but his dad's truck was

gone. He felt his shoulders relax. But when he got inside the dark kitchen, he realized the house was empty. The only sign of life was the lingering smell of coffee and the blinking light of the answering machine. Where was she? Where would she have gone without her car? He steeled himself to find out what disaster those messages might carry.

He immediately recognized Mrs. Cross's voice, and his heart sank. "Mr. and Mrs. Kennedy, this is Mrs. Cross from Two Rivers Graded School. I'm certain you are aware of the situation at the school right now. I need you to call me immediately. The police commissioner will be in touch shortly. He has some questions regarding Trevor."

His whole body began to quake. He deleted the message.

"Mr. and Mrs. Kennedy, this is Sergeant Jenkins with the state police. I understand your son and daughter were both away from school today. We need to speak with your son as soon as possible, as he is a person of interest in our investigation. We'll be sending a patrol car by. Please be prepared at that time for your son to be taken to the station for questioning."

Trevor was out the door and running before he could listen to the last message. He ran until it felt like he had inhaled the entire blizzard, until his lungs and heart were nearly frozen in his chest. He didn't stop until he had leapt across the frozen river, climbed the bank, and was inside the caboose.

He'd never even managed to get the darkroom set up. The enlarger he'd stolen on Friday sat in the corner like a hulking, sulking skeleton. The chemicals were frozen, the safe light and timer good for nothing. He'd been such a fool to think he could have this. That he could ever make anything beautiful out of this life. There wasn't light enough in the whole world to illuminate the good parts of him.

He tore down the sheet metal he'd put up on the broken windows, slicing his left hand on the rough edge. He winced and clutched his hand to his chest. Crying, he went and picked up the enlarger, carrying it out to the embankment and hurling it into the water, his hand dripping blood on the snow. Back and forth. He made his way from the caboose with everything he'd worked so hard to collect. And one by one, he threw everything into the river. By the time he was back inside the caboose, his hand was bleeding heavily, and he was starting to feel light-headed. He knew he needed to stop the bleeding, but as he looked around the empty car, he couldn't find anything that would work. He couldn't go back to the house, though. He'd rather die than go back there. He didn't know what had happened, but he knew that he was being held responsible.

He pulled his coat tightly around him and curled up on the ratty old mattress on the floor. He tucked his hand tightly between his knees, hoping the pressure would stop the bleeding, and put his face down into his coat so that his own hot breath might keep him warm. He was safe here. No one would find him. He closed his eyes and tried to conjure the images he'd cared about so much, tried to recollect when he could see the promise of beauty, that distant shimmering hint. But no matter how hard he tried to fill his mind with light, all he could see was Grace.

"Are we here?" Grace asked as they hurled through the blizzard.

What a funny question, Crystal thought. *Of course, we're here. Wherever here was.*

"Not yet," Crystal answered.

"I need to go to the bathroom," Grace said.

"Right now?" she asked.

Crystal pulled over at the first rest stop they came to, which was only about thirty miles outside of town. There was one eighteen-wheeler in the lot and no other cars. Most people knew better than to be out on the road on a day like this. She was glad. She had hoped to get out of state before she had to pull over. She figured if she just kept driving, she could be in California in a few days. Lucia would know what to do. She could help her fix this.

She opened the car door and the wind slammed it shut after her. She wrapped her unzipped coat around her tightly and went to the other side of the car. Grace had unbuckled herself and was looking at Crystal expectantly.

"My mom always carries me when there's snow on the ground," she said, reaching her arms out.

"Oh," Crystal said and leaned over her, picking her up and easing her out of the car and into her arms. She was heavy, and as she lifted her, Grace's head hit the door frame.

"Ow!" Grace howled and then started crying loudly.

"Oh, I'm sorry," Crystal said and felt her chest tighten. "I'm so sorry, sweetie."

She examined Grace's head, and there was already a small egg forming there. She touched it gingerly with her fingertip, and Grace winced. "I want my mom," she said quietly.

The wind was howling, and Crystal ignored her.

"I want my *mom!*" she said again, this time right into Crystal's ear as she clung to her neck.

Crystal walked as quickly as she could toward the rest area. She used her one free arm to open the door and took Gracy inside. There was, thankfully, no one there. The last thing she needed was for Gracy to start crying about her mother. When she felt Grace's grasp loosen, she lowered her down to the floor.

"This way," Crystal said, pointing to the women's room.

Grace led the way and disappeared into a stall.

"I'll be right out here," she said. Grace didn't answer.

She could hear her pulling down her tights and watched her feet lift from the ground as she got on the toilet. But then there was nothing. Grace hopped back down and, without flushing the toilet, came out of the stall.

"Did you go?" Crystal asked, knowing full well she had not.

"I don't have to go anymore."

Crystal sighed. "Are you sure?"

Grace nodded.

"Maybe you should try again, because we can't stop for a long, long time."

Grace shook her head again. "I don't have to go."

"Seriously, maybe if you just try one more time."

Grace put her hands on her hips and pushed her chin out. "No!"

"Okay, okay," Crystal said, glancing quickly to the door, terrified that someone might walk in and Gracy might say just the wrong thing.

"Where are we *going?*" Grace whined as they walked back out into the storm.

"To a friend's house," Crystal said, trying to conjure an image of California, of Lucia in the kitchen. Orange trees, eucalyptus, salt in the air.

"I'm tired," Grace said.

Crystal smiled and carefully lowered her into the car this time, managing to avoid smashing her head. "You can go to sleep if you like," she said. "It's a long drive. Here, I brought a cozy blanket. Why don't you snuggle this?"

Grace took the afghan that Crystal's grandmother had made her when she was about Gracy's age. It was purple and yellow, raggedy but soft. Crystal tucked it in around her and Grace smiled sadly. "My mom probably misses me," she said.

A sharp gust of wind blew across the parking lot then, and it cut through her clothes like a blade. She closed Gracy's door and then got in the driver's seat. She was shaking with the cold, shaking with fear, and suddenly she felt like she might vomit. She shook her head, as if the simple action might clear away her doubts, but instead, it just added to the nausea. She put the key in the ignition and turned it. The engine sputtered and clunked. She tried again, a tremendous sense of panic starting to grip her. Fucking car. What if the car died here? At some fucking rest stop in southern Vermont? She'd have to wait for somebody to come by with jumper cables, and then what if it wasn't the battery? And how on earth was she going to explain Gracy?

Hands shaking almost uncontrollably, she turned the key again, pressed the gas pedal hard but not too hard, and when the engine roared to life, tears sprang to her eyes. She looked in the rearview mirror to see if any of her panic had registered with Gracy, but the little girl had already fallen asleep. Her head leaning against the cold glass, her breath making a hot, wet circle in the frost.

She pulled out of the parking lot and back onto the ramp, the car skidding a little on the ice. She steered into the skid, correcting the way her father had taught her, and then they were back on the road. Heading back into the dizzying snow. Her phone buzzed again, but this time she ignored it completely, not seeing the text from her father reading *9-1-1*.

They stopped Kurt, of course, from entering the burning school. Getting past the yellow tape proved to be easy, but getting past the police was a whole other story. While the other parents watched on, he ducked under the tape and made his way down the slippery hill to the school's back entrance. Within seconds someone was steering him back, explaining that the area was unsafe. That no civilians were being allowed inside the area, let alone the crumbling portion of the building.

"My son and daughter are in there," he said. "And I need somebody to tell me when they plan to get them out."

"Sir, we are actively engaged in an SAR. These are professionals. You need to trust us to do our job."

"SAR?"

"Search and rescue, sir."

"You mean you still haven't found all of the kids yet?"

"We're looking for all unaccounted-for students. But the building is precarious, and it's a slow process. The fire's under control, but the structural damage is significant. We don't want anyone getting hurt."

Kurt squeezed his eyes shut, thought about things catching on fire, walls crumbling. Everything falling apart. "Who did this?" he asked. "Is he still inside?"

"Sir, we don't have all the answers. I'm sure Principal Cross will be making a statement shortly to explain the situation. I'm not at liberty to say."

"Jesus Christ," Kurt said, breathing heavily, letting the cold air feel his lungs.

"I'm sorry, sir. We'll do our best to bring your children out safe and sound."

Kurt scrambled up the embankment, feeling as though he were letting down the expectant mob waiting for him.

"What did he say? Who did it?" they roared. Their voices and the wind were sharp, piercing. He shook his head and took off down to the road to go find Elsbeth.

It had been nearly an hour since the explosion. The smoke was still thick, but dissipating. The entire world smelled burned, though. Most of the ambulances were gone now, and only two fire trucks remained. There were still police cars there though. State police. The local cops too.

Elsbeth stood in front of the municipal building in a dwindling group of parents. They were the unlucky ones, the ones whose children had not yet been found. The ones who might never see their children again. It was below freezing outside, snowing, and the wind was howling. Elsbeth couldn't tell the difference anymore between fear and cold. Dread was like ice water in her bones.

There were people from the TV stations in Burlington there now, setting up their lights and cameras and sound equipment. Someone had brought a beaten-up podium outside, and the secretary had come out and said there would be a press conference at noon.

Elsbeth checked her watch again. Kurt had been gone for fifteen minutes. One parent, one who had happily been reunited with her own children, had returned with an urn of hot coffee. She and her two daughters were handing out hot Styrofoam cups to the people in the crowd.

"You're Gracy's mom, right?" the woman asked, cheerfully handing Elsbeth a steaming cup of coffee.

Elsbeth nodded grimly. She held the coffee to her lips, and it burned her tongue.

"You must be so relieved you picked her up early today," the woman said.

"What?" Elsbeth asked.

"Noelle said Gracy got pulled out of class this morning."

"What are you talking about?" Elsbeth asked.

The little girl with fat red cheeks and a turned-up nose, Noelle, nodded next to her. "She was supposed to be the Weather Reporter, but she went home, so I got to do the report. This is the first time we used the snow magnet."

"Gracy didn't come home," Elsbeth said, shaking her head, her damaged tongue like something foreign in her mouth. "Gracy and Trevor are in the school."

Noelle cocked her head and looked confused. "You can ask my teacher. I did a really good job on the weather report. She said so."

Elsbeth felt a new kind of panic growing in her chest, swelling. She looked around frantically for Kurt. Where the hell was he? Finally, she saw him walking briskly up the road, his hands shoved into his pockets. His brow furled into one low, angry scowl. She ran to him then and tried to explain the conversation, but then the front doors opened and the school secretary came out again with a new sheet of paper, a new list of names. Following behind her was a policeman.

He stood up to the podium. The cameramen positioned themselves around him, and the lights illuminated his face as though he were about to give a performance rather than explain a tragedy.

"Good afternoon, my name is Sergeant Carl from the state police. As you all know, there was an explosion at the school at approximately ten thirty-five this morning, followed by several smaller explosions. The first explosion, which started in the girls' bathroom on the main floor of the building, ignited a fire, which quickly spread to the art room and cafeteria. Due to the suspicious nature of the explosion, the school has been put on lockdown and the uninjured children have been escorted to buses and transported to the high school. The children injured in the blast have been taken to area hospitals. A search-and-rescue mission is in progress. There are currently five children unaccounted for in the building. As for the cause of the explosions, the fire marshal is still conducting his investigation, but it does appear that this was a criminal act and that these explosions were the intentional result of several homemade bombs, which were likely planted in the school during the holiday break last week. We are currently reviewing surveillance footage."

"Do you have any suspects?" a small, rat-faced reporter asked.

"We have a person of interest who will be brought in for questioning. But there are no official suspects and no arrests have been made." He gestured toward another reporter. "Yes?"

"How many children were injured? And are there any fatalities?"

"There are no confirmed fatalities at this point, though there are twelve children currently hospitalized. Several are undergoing surgery at this time. We should have more details soon."

"Is the person of interest associated with the school? Was it a student?"

"I'm sorry. I'm not able to give any answers at this time. Thank you very much."

The secretary then stuck the new list to the doorway, and the remaining parents rushed to the door. All of them broke down in tears: some in relief and the others because their children were still missing.

Kurt hit his hand against the brick wall and then headed up the steps to the building's entrance, catching the door before it could lock behind the secretary.

"Stop," Elsbeth said. "They're saying Gracy wasn't in school today. That someone picked her up."

Kurt's eyes were wild. He looked insane. For the first time in all the years she'd known Kurt, she was terrified of him. "I'll be right back," he said and pushed his way through the municipal building's doors. Elsbeth ran up the steps and followed behind him, lowering her head and praying as she did. Praying for Trevor, and praying for Grace.

Trevor listened to the wind howling outside the caboose, to its mournful lament. He wondered how long it would take before they found him out here. And what would happen when they did.

He lay on his back on the mattress, which was hard, almost frozen beneath him. His hand was throbbing now; the bleeding had stopped, but the cut was deep. The metal had been rusty, and he knew that was how you got tetanus. He couldn't remember the last time he'd had a tetanus shot. He studied his hand, the ragged cut; it made his head feel light and fuzzy. He thought about trying to start a fire in that little potbelly stove, but he knew the smoke would only call attention to his hiding place. He could always go home, of course, and he thought that maybe that would be the best thing to do. But at the same time, the longer he was here, the longer he was safe. But he wasn't stupid; he knew he couldn't stay out here forever. He'd die if he stayed here through the night. For now, it was warm enough to snow, but by the time the sun went down, the temperature would plummet as well. He would freeze to death.

He closed his eyes and listened to the music of the wind through the trees. He thought about what the bare branches, bowing with the weight of all this new snow, might look like through his viewfinder. He thought about the man who photographed the snow. He thought about all the things he wanted to take pictures of still: rain, grass, fireflies, the moon. He wanted to capture all of those things, all the beautiful things. Hold on to them tightly. *Grace*. He thought about his sister, and the way her face lit up when she saw him. He wanted to seize that love before it disappeared, because he knew it would one day fade, just as his own mother's love had once he was old enough to know he needed it. Suddenly his body was quaking, and he was sobbing. His stomach muscles tensed with the effort. His entire body ached, and the tears froze as soon as they left his eyes.

He wasn't sure when he finally fell asleep. It was less like falling asleep than letting go: allowing his body to relax, to accept the cold, to embrace it. He willed each muscle to soften, tried to think of the cold not as a feeling but as a sound. Just something to listen to. It sounded like that wind song, that frozen lullaby outside. And soon, he was in the warm rapturous sleep he hadn't had since he was a little boy. Before he was in school even. Before Gracy came along. And even as he dreamed, he listened to the forest's music, he could hear violins, the whisper of the pine trees' lyrics.

At first he thought it was only a signal, a shift in the song: the loud percussive barking. But as he willed his eyes back open, he knew it was not music at all, but animals. Dogs. And they were coming for him.

Kurt rode with the police officers in the patrol car, and Elsbeth followed behind in Kurt's truck. She never drove his truck; it felt strange to be this high up above the road. She was grateful for the four-wheel drive though, for the sheer size of the vehicle. She followed the police car, its blue and red lights spinning kaleidoscope colors on the snow, grasping the wheel tightly.

The sun was already starting its slow descent behind the western hills. It would be dark in an hour or so. The days were so short at this time of year, just slivers of days. The slipping away of the daylight filled her with dread.

The officer said they had footage of a boy who fit Trevor's description entering the school during the holiday weekend. A tall boy in Trevor's clothes. A hulking boy with snow-white hair and a Halloween hockey mask. They had numerous witnesses who recalled the Jason mask from Halloween.

The officer had assured her that as soon as they found Trevor they would find Gracy as well. That he clearly had pulled her out of school so that she wouldn't be hurt in the explosion. The name on the sign-out sheet was "Chris Johnson." No one she had ever heard of. The secretary insisted that she'd gotten a phone call from Elsbeth saying that Chris Johnson would be by to pick Gracy up. But after the police kept suggesting that maybe it was a male caller, she faltered. "Well, maybe. I don't remember. This day has been so insane. Maybe I'm not remembering things right. I'm sorry. I'm really sorry."

Elsbeth tried to comfort herself with the knowledge that

Trevor loved Gracy. That he would never put her in harm's way. If
he was, indeed, the one who had done this, then he would have
made sure she wasn't there. He would have done anything to
keep her from getting hurt. But accepting this version of events
also meant accepting that Trevor *had* done this. That something in
him had finally snapped, that he'd set out to hurt, even kill, people. Her eyes filled with tears and she wiped at them futilely. Mrs.
Cross had been telling them how dangerous he was for over a
year now, and they hadn't believed her. They couldn't stand to believe her. And if that were the case, it was as much Elsbeth's fault,
Kurt's fault, as it was Trevor's. Mrs. Cross had sat there as the police
questioned them, smug in her pale yellow suit with her pale yellow hair and her white, white teeth. *Happy* almost that something
had finally happened that proved she was right. She was a winner
now. Now that a dozen kids were in the hospital. Elsbeth felt sick.

Elsbeth searched for the windshield wipers to clear away the
snow, which was still falling hard from the sky. She wondered, if
Trevor had taken her, *where* he would have taken her. She hoped
they were both just at the house. That they were somewhere
warm. Somewhere safe. They were her babies, and the thought of
losing either one of them was suddenly almost more than she
could stand.

There was so much snow, and the visibility was so poor, she
might have missed the house completely if not for their mailbox.
The red flag was up, though she knew it hadn't been when they
left the house. And instinctively, she slowed the truck, rolled
down the window, reached across the seat, and opened the mailbox.

Inside was a bundle of envelopes from Walgreens, Trevor's
pictures.

She didn't think she had asked to have them mailed to her,
but here they were. How strange. It had been so long since she
dropped them off, maybe someone had decided to deliver them.
But she hadn't even paid for them yet.

At the top of the driveway, the police were already out of the car, opening up the back to get the dogs out. Blood rushed in her ears, rendering her almost deaf for a moment. She hesitated at the foot of the drive, quickly opening the pictures and sifting through them as though for clues.

There were some horrible shots of Pop's house. God, she was mortified that anyone had seen these, even if it was just some Walgreens photo person. She stopped rifling through them when she got to the pictures of Gracy.

Gracy standing in the river, her bathing suit half falling off, the light in her hair. Light, like fireflies, skipping across the water. A look of pure innocence on her face. Nothing but peace. Gracy. Her sweet, beautiful Grace. And suddenly she knew that this was all the evidence in the world that she needed to know that Gracy was safe. This was how Grace looked through Trevor's eyes. He *loved* her.

After today, he would be vilified. The entire town would probably hold him up as an example of what bad parenting can do. But these pictures were proof enough to her that despite what he might or might not have done at the school, he was just a sad, gentle boy. Her boy. And now, more than anything, she just wanted to find him and tell him she loved him, even if it was already too late.

Trevor startled at the sound of the dogs. He thought for a moment that he was in the middle of some terrible dream. Or, maybe, he had simply frozen to death, and this was what hell felt like. Not fire and brimstone, but the numbing ache of snow. Dogs ready to tear him limb from limb.

He could hear footsteps crunching in the snow down at the river's edge, and he scrambled to his feet, peering out the window, which overlooked the river. He could see all of the equipment he'd discarded, stuck in the slush and snow, the river ignoring the detritus, bending around it as its icy current rushed downstream. He could hear the panting of dogs, see the steam rising from their bellies and their wet noses.

"Whoa boy, hold on," someone said, and then Trevor saw the man in his black jacket: *Police* in reflective yellow across his back. Trevor moved away from the window, pressed his back against the wall. But then the voices and the snuffling sound of the dogs came closer.

"Holy shit," a male voice said. "Look at all this blood."

Trevor's hand started to throb again, reminded of its injury. His heart rapped against his chest like a knock on a door.

"I think we've got him," another voice said.

And then the voice was amplified. It reminded him for a moment of Mrs. Cross making the daily announcements on the loudspeaker at school. But this wasn't school. And this wasn't Mrs. Cross. This was a police officer with dogs and probably guns. "Trevor, we know you're in there. You need to send Grace out."

Grace?

"Trevor, send your sister out immediately, or else we're coming in."

Why did they think he had Grace? His nose was running now, snot coming down both nostrils. It was hot, steaming. He rubbed his temples with his good hand; it seemed the cold had penetrated his head now and his entire brain was cold and numb.

"I don't have her," he said, but his words were small, frozen slivers.

He could hear movement outside the caboose.

"I don't have her!" he said, listening as the words echoed inside the metal car.

"Come out with your hands above your head, Trevor," the voice said.

And Trevor did what he was told to do.

Outside the sky had grown dark. He couldn't tell what time of day it was. It could be dawn or dusk for this twilight sky. Everything was almost bluish. If he had his camera this is what he would have seen: two German shepherds, pulling at their leashes, eyes wild. Two men, necks strained and faces like square blocks. Guns aimed at his chest, the barrels like eyes.

"Where's Grace?" they asked.

Trevor shook his head. "I don't know."

And then he was down on the ground, face buried in the snow, arms yanked behind his back.

Kurt stood alone in the empty caboose as the police hand-cuffed his son and read him his rights. As Elsbeth stood shivering and crying in the doorway. As the snow continued to fall.

It was dark and cold inside the caboose. A cave. A black hole. But the light from the doorway illuminated the meager furnishings, the contents of Trevor's clandestine asylum. Kurt recognized some items from the house: a beanbag chair, an end table, a couple of milk crates fashioned into bookcases. He looked at the walls, at the photos nailed haphazardly there. He walked closer to the pictures, his head pounding as he examined them. Most of them were old black-and-white photos, like the kind you find in antique stores. Old-fashioned photographs of children, of little girls. Sullen faces, sepia faces. Creepy nineteenth-century pictures of little girls, many of them in costume. Kurt stepped back, as if changing his perspective might help him make sense of what he was seeing. There were other pictures too, snapshots. Trevor's own photos, he figured. There was one of Pop's house from a distance, one of a dead fish. One of Gracy on the swing set in the back-yard. *Gracy*. Where *was* she? What was he looking for here?

He reached for something hanging from a nail on the wall. It was striped, and slippery in his fingers. Fabric? A scarf? *Tights*. A tiny pair of Gracy's tights. He dropped them as he might a live snake.

Kurt's nerve endings were raw. His entire body felt electrified, as though he'd been struck by lightning. He stumbled backward, tripping over something on the floor.

"Shit," he said, catching himself before he fell.

He looked down and saw it was only a mattress. A filthy, bare mattress on the floor. As his heart thumped in his chest, he leaned forward to see what was on the mattress. He reached down and touched the dark spot. Blood.

His hand flew to his mouth, and he stumbled backward on his ineffectual legs, reeling as he fled the caboose. His body was so hot, the snow seemed to crack and sizzle when it hit his skin.

Through the snarl of trees, he could see the cops escorting Trevor back toward the house. He watched Elsbeth as she struggled to keep up behind them.

He sank to his knees in the snow, his legs failing him. His entire body failing him. It took every remaining bit of energy he had to stand up again and move toward his family, disappearing in the distance.

Crystal didn't know how long they had been driving. The clock in the Volvo only worked intermittently, and her cell phone battery had died. She had a car charger somewhere in her suitcase, but she didn't want to stop again; she was worried that Gracy would wake up. She was hungry, though, and she knew that Grace would likely need to eat something soon too. She had just seen a sign announcing GAS—FOOD—LODGING and could also see a pair of golden arches in the distance. Gracy might even stay asleep if she went through the drive-thru.

She pulled off at the exit and followed the signs that said FOOD and was happy to see that there wasn't a line at the McDonald's drive-thru. She glanced at Gracy in the backseat. She had shifted positions but was still fast asleep. She ordered a Happy Meal for her, trying to think whether she'd like a cheeseburger or chicken nuggets better. She got a Big Mac meal for herself, super sized; they probably wouldn't eat again until morning.

There was a gas station next to the McDonald's, and she figured it was probably a good time to gas up as well. If both the car and the people inside were fueled up, they could make it out of Vermont without having to stop again. She pulled up to the first pump, checking through the window to make sure Gracy was still sleeping. She was surprised the smell of the McDonald's food hadn't woken her up. She had to use cash to pay, which meant she was either going to have to wake Gracy up or leave her in the car. She glanced around. The place was deserted. Gracy would be safe. It would only take a couple of minutes.

She went inside the bright mini-mart, the electronic bells announcing her entrance, though the kid at the counter was watching TV, her arrival barely registered with him.

"Can I put twenty dollars in pump number two?" she said to his profile.

"You been watching this?" he asked, gesturing to the TV.

She looked up. It was a news station, and there was some sort of fire.

"That's just up in Two Rivers. I got a cousin up there."

In the blue banner beneath the footage, it said, BOMBING AT ELEMENTARY SCHOOL. SUSPECT IN CUSTODY.

"What happened?" she asked, feeling vertiginous, swirling.

"A bomb went off up at some school in Two Rivers. Some crazy kid set off a whole bunch of explosions. Boom!" he said.

Angie. Oh my God.

The aerial shot disappeared, and a newscaster came on. "While there are no fatalities reported so far in this tragic bombing, several children are currently undergoing surgery, and several others have been airlifted to Boston Children's Hospital."

She had to get home. Angie was at the school. Her entire body was shaking uncontrollably now, as though her heart were the epicenter of some horrific earthquake. She turned to go out the door, leaving the twenty-dollar bill on the counter, knowing she'd need the gas if she was going to make it all the way back to Two Rivers without stopping. But just as she was heading back out through the doors, the scene on the TV changed. The man said, "And beyond the obvious tragedy here today, there has been an alarming twist in this case. The suspect's six-year-old sister is currently missing. It is unclear at this time whether the suspect has anything to do with her disappearance, but the school has confirmed that she was removed from the school just prior to the first explosion."

Crystal stood, paralyzed, staring at the screen.

There was a photo then, a school picture of a little girl. A dark-haired girl with dark eyes. A lopsided smile and uneven bangs. *Grace.* Holy shit.

Elsbeth and Kurt sat on the orange plastic chairs they'd been offered when they got to the station. Elsbeth had accepted the watery, lukewarm coffee the woman at the front desk poured for her. She was the only person who'd looked either of them in the eyes in the last hour, and she was grateful. But she couldn't drink it.

Trevor was in the other room with the police officers who had found him out in the woods, and Kurt was on his cell phone, trying again to get through to Billy. They'd taken Trevor into custody, and Kurt had told Trevor to make sure he asked to have his lawyer present. Kurt told Elsbeth they had to honor that request. Now he just needed to get through to Billy, to get him to come home.

"Billy, turn on the news, for Christ's sake. We need your help. Please call me back," he said, then clicked his phone shut. He set his coffee down, rested his elbows on his knees, and put his head in his hands.

Elsbeth stared blankly forward at the institutional green cinder-block walls of the station.

"Where is she?" she had asked Kurt over and over again. She asked Trevor too, the cops, but no one would answer her.

They'd put out an Amber Alert, but she knew it was just a gesture. The cops truly believed that Trevor had done something with her. That he'd hurt her. They'd asked them to provide a photo of Gracy for the media, and she'd given them her first-grade picture. They'd just come back from the school that week and she hadn't even cut them apart from each other. Hands shaking, she had cut one of the wallet-sized photos from the repeating pattern of Gracy's face. She kept thinking about the other pictures of Gracy, the ones in her purse right now. The way the light had touched her hair. The soft glow of her bare shoulders. Her tiny hands. She felt the sorrow filling her, like water in a tub. It started at her feet as they came back to life after standing outside in the cold for so long, and then it traveled up her legs, spread across her hips, and finally up into her throat. She thought she might choke on it. That it might suffocate her.

Kurt's phone rang and he grabbed it quickly out of his pocket. "Billy?" He nodded and nodded, silently, listening to whatever it was that Billy was saying on the other end of the line. "Thank you," he said. "God, thank you. Call when your flight gets into Manchester." He looked at Elsbeth, his eyes filled with tears. "He's at the airport. The next flight out is in an hour. He'll be here by seven or eight."

Elsbeth reached for his hand, that familiar hand, the one she'd held since she was just a girl. The one that had cupped her face to kiss her. The one that had stroked her back as she labored with Trevor. The one that had cradled Trevor when she was bone tired, the one that had stroked Gracy's hair. His palms were rough, callused from years and years of work at the yard. Chapped by too many winters spent working outside. She let it enclose her own hand, watched as the knuckles bent and fingers curled around hers. Studied the veins and tendons. Examined the blood that coursed blue beneath that battered skin. She looked at him, but he wouldn't look at her. Wouldn't meet her glance.

"Kurt," she said, his name like a marble lodged in her throat. He looked at her then, startled, as if he didn't recognize her at all. "Baby?" she asked.

But then his hand let go, and her own hand felt exposed. Alone on her lap. She felt the liquid sorrow rising up her throat, filling her mouth and cheeks and eyes and head. She was drowning, and no one was there to save her.

Kurt didn't want to leave the station, but the rental agency at the airport was out of four-wheel drive vehicles, and the roads were bad. It was just a forty-five-minute drive to the airport. He could be back with Billy by eight thirty, even if they had to go slow.

He hadn't seen Billy since he left. Not once in all these years. He wasn't sure if he'd even be able to recognize him anymore; he was just a kid when he took off. Now Billy was a grown man. A thirty-year-old man. Kurt was trembling as he pulled up to the curb next to where Billy had said he'd be waiting.

But there he was, as though he hadn't aged a day. A thinner, more gentle version of Kurt himself. The same blond hair, wide shoulders, blue eyes. A better haircut, though, a nicer coat, not so many years in the lines of his face. He shielded his eyes from the glare of Kurt's headlights and smiled when he recognized him inside the cab.

Billy threw his suitcase into the bed of the truck and opened the passenger door. He climbed into the cab and blew into his hands. "Wow, it is fucking cold out there."

"Hey," Kurt said, feeling a thousand different things at once, some of them good, but most of them awful.

"Hey," Billy said and put one of his gloved hands on Kurt's shoulder. "I'm here, buddy. Everything's going to be okay."

They drove quietly back to Two Rivers, Kurt peering intently at the road, grateful for his need to focus on the icy pavement as an excuse for their silence.

Billy asked only basic questions, and Kurt answered them the best he could. *When did you last see Trevor? Gracy? Do you know anyone who would want to harm Gracy? Did Trevor admit to anything? Has he been acting strangely lately? Did you make sure to demand your lawyer be present?* He answered the questions, but he couldn't bring himself to tell Billy about what he'd seen in the caboose. He was afraid that if he did, then Billy would have the only answer he needed.

As they pulled into the dirt parking lot at the police station, Billy took a deep breath and asked the one question Kurt couldn't answer: "Do you think Trevor did what they say he did?"

Kurt sighed and looked into Billy's face, his own face, a stranger's face, his brother's face. "I don't know a goddamn thing anymore."

Crystal was trying not to drive too fast; she knew that if she wasn't careful, she could get them in an accident, and that was the last thing she needed. The car still smelled like greasy fries and burgers. Gracy had woken up and devoured her cheeseburger and fries and chocolate milk and was playing with the Strawberry Shortcake doll that had come inside the Happy Meal. "When are we going home?" she asked.

"Right now," Crystal had said, forcing the words past the frozen block of ice in her throat.

"Good. Because it's past my bedtime," she said, and this made Crystal smile.

She still hadn't figured out what to do about Gracy. She knew she couldn't just drop her off at her house. With everything that was happening, she was pretty sure no one would be there. She also couldn't take her to her own house. She thought about taking her to the police station, saying that she'd found her somewhere, but she was also fairly certain that Gracy would blow that story. She needed to get to Angie, but she wasn't even sure where Angie was. She looked at her dead phone. Angie might be in Burlington or Hanover. She could be in Boston for all Crystal knew. *No fatalities.* She clung to the newscaster's words. No one had died in the blast. She was still alive.

She pulled off the interstate at the Two Rivers exit, and she realized what she needed to do. The clock at the bank across from the Walgreens said 11:04 P.M. The Walgreens was the only place besides the 76 station in town that was open all night. It was

Monday. Howard would be there until midnight. She pulled into the parking lot.

"Why are we at the Walgreens?" Gracy asked sleepily in the backseat.

"Your mommy will come get you here, okay? And my friend, Howard, is going to take care of you, okay?"

Gracy shrugged. "Can I get a Butterfinger?"

"You can get anything you want."

Gracy unbuckled her seat belt, and Crystal picked her up without needing to be reminded and carried her into the store. The lights were so bright, they almost burned her eyes. Gracy blinked against the glare as well. They were like newborns just coming into the bright world.

She set Gracy down and took her hand, leading her to the photo department, where she searched through the envelopes looking for one of her mother's packets of photos. Luckily, the ones that Crystal hadn't stolen were still there, with Mrs. Kennedy's cell number right on the front. She scratched the number down on a piece of tape she pulled from the roll on the register.

"Howard?" she said.

Howard, like a dog, came wagging his tail over to her.

"I need you to keep an eye on my friend, Gracy. Her mother will be here to pick her up soon. And if anybody asks, you didn't see who dropped her off. Do you understand?"

Howard looked terrified, but he blinked hard and nodded. "Of course," he said. If she asked him to rob a goddamned bank, he probably would.

"Miss Grace," she said, kneeling down next to Gracy, who had already torn into a Butterfinger, "your mommy will be here soon, okay?"

She thought about telling her not to say anything about who had taken her, but she knew there was no way that would work. She could imagine it already, "That girl at Walgreens picked me up at school and took me for a long, long drive. We went to McDonald's too."

She had bigger things to worry about now, though. She'd returned Gracy. Hopefully her mother would just be so grateful to have her back, she wouldn't say anything. Do anything. She thought then about what it meant to be sending her home. With a brother who set a bomb off at his school. Her only hope was that she'd get removed from the house after this, placed with a foster family. Adopted even, by someone who really could take care of her.

Crystal's mind was reeling as she left Grace there and got back into her car. She dug through the suitcase in the back of the station wagon and found the phone charger. She got in the driver's side and plugged it in. Her hands were trembling as she dialed the number she'd scratched on the slip of paper.

"Mrs. Kennedy. I just wanted to let you know your daughter is here at the Walgreens. She's fine. She's waiting for you."

She clicked the phone shut, and then dialed her voice mail, listened to her mother's thousand tearful pleas for her to please come home.

Kurt and Billy had sent Elsbeth home. "In case Gracy comes back," they said. "You'll want to be there if she comes home, right?" Though Kurt knew Gracy wouldn't just walk through the front door. Though he had seen the blood himself, like bright cherry Kool-Aid on the snow.

Billy disappeared inside the interrogation room with Trevor, and Kurt paced. His legs wouldn't let him sit, not even for a moment. He walked back and forth, back and forth until the woman at the front desk who had initially seemed kind started to glare at him.

At about ten o'clock, Billy came out of the room, followed by Trevor.

"What's going on?" Kurt asked.

"He's going home. For tonight anyway. He's got an alibi that's been corroborated by his art teacher."

"What?"

"He was with his art teacher when the explosion went off. They're still trying to determine if the bombs were detonated remotely or not. But they can't hold him here until they come up with some concrete evidence that he's the one who planted the explosives. They've got some footage of a kid with a hockey mask and a duffel bag entering the school over the Thanksgiving break, so they're going to do another search of the house. But right now, they've got nothing but a whole bunch of suspicions. And suspicions aren't enough to keep a minor in custody. Not with me as his lawyer anyway."

"What about Gracy?" Kurt asked.

"God, Kurt, I don't know. But at least the lab results for the blood found in the woods matches it to him. He and Gracy are different blood types. He cut his hand. There's nothing but circumstantial evidence linking Trevor to her disappearance."

Kurt felt his entire body go limp, as if someone shut off the supply of electricity that had been coursing through his body for months now. He nearly collapsed. Maybe Trevor hadn't done this. Maybe it was all some terrible mistake. But the simple, horrific fact remained that Gracy was gone. His baby girl.

Billy reached for Kurt's arm, as if to keep him from falling. "They want him back here in the morning for more questioning. If you can just drop me at that motel we drove by, we can meet back here tomorrow."

"You can stay with us," Kurt said.

"That's okay," Billy said, shaking his head. "I plan to work through the night. And as crazy as it sounds, you need to try to go home and get some sleep. They've got people out looking for Gracy, there's an Amber Alert in place. They're going to find her, and we're going to clear up all of this stuff with Trevor. I promise."

Kurt's eyes stung, his stomach was empty, but he couldn't even think of eating. He tried to imagine Elsbeth at home, wondered what on earth she would be doing all alone in the house.

Trevor stood behind Billy, shoulders slumped, head hung to his chest.

"Come on, then," he said, and they all went outside to the truck.

When Elsbeth's cell phone rang, she didn't recognize the number and assumed it was Kurt calling from the police station. He'd been on his phone so much, it was probably dead. The girl's voice on the other end of the line was soft. Tentative. She couldn't hear her at first, and thought maybe it was just a wrong number.

"Your daughter is here at the Walgreens," she said.

"What?"

"She's fine. She's waiting for you."

"Who is this?" she asked, feeling her heart pounding in her temples and shoulders and chest.

The girl hung up without answering, and Elsbeth was out the door without even bothering to grab her coat or purse.

As she raced into town, she repeated the words again and again in her head. The Walgreens? Why on earth would she be at the Walgreens? And then the realization struck her in the chest like a bullet.

That girl. The one with the baby. Or without the baby. That teenaged girl who had confronted her, the only other person in the world who knew her secret. She thought of all the things she had stolen: the little trinkets that had accumulated, the box of stolen treasures like some terrible shrine. The evidence. The proof that she was nothing but a thief. She thought then about the photos that had appeared in the mailbox. That girl had stolen them, and then she'd stolen her daughter. In the parking lot that day, she had threatened to call the police, to have her arrested for shoplifting, but then instead she'd taken from her the only thing in the world she really cared about. Was this some kind of twisted lesson? And who was she to cast her moral judgment on Elsbeth? She was no different than her, just another girl who got pregnant at seventeen. Whose girlhood was stolen. They were the *same*. God, they were exactly the same.

She didn't bother turning off the engine when she got to the Walgreens. She simply threw the car door open and ran down the slippery walkway to the doors. They opened and she rushed into the store screaming, "Gracy? Gracy?"

Gracy was sitting on the counter at the front of the store, playing with some sort of little doll, legs dangling off the edge.

"Baby!" she said rushing to her and scooping her up in her arms.

The boy at the register said, "You her mom?"

"Of course," she said.

"She's safe. It's okay. I hope you don't mind I gave her a candy bar."

"Hi, Mumma," Grace said, and Elsbeth buried her face in her daughter's hair. Elsbeth pulled back and studied her for any evidence that she had been harmed.

"Did she hurt you?" she whispered into her hair.

"No," Gracy shook her head. She shrugged and smiled. "She was nice. She took me to McDonald's."

Elsbeth lifted her off the counter.

"Maybe you should give me some ID or something?" the kid asked. "I probably shouldn't just let her go with anybody."

Elsbeth shook her head in disbelief and then instinctively reached to her hip where her purse usually hung. "I don't have my purse," she said. "Jesus Christ. This is my kid. Look at her. Isn't that ID enough?"

"Yeah, I guess," the kid said. "I actually think I've seen you all in here together before. It's cool."

Gracy clung to Elsbeth's neck as they made their way back to the car.

"I missed you, Gracy Bear," she said, tears coming down now, hot and fast. It was snowing again, and Gracy's hair was speckled with snowflakes.

"I missed you too, Mumma."

Kurt did not speak to Trevor after they dropped Billy off at the motel. Trevor stared out the window, and he focused on the road. He was afraid to ask him the simplest question. He was afraid to know the answer. *How had this happened?* He racked his brain. He thought about Pop, that garbage heap of a house. How he'd been so consumed with saving Pop that he couldn't save his own son. His own marriage. Bile rose in his throat as he thought about the condoms he'd found, about Elsbeth cheating. His own pride had kept him from noticing that his son was clearly changing, transforming into someone capable of the unthinkable. Kurt hadn't managed to protect him from those kids, and so he'd taken matters into his own hands. Kurt hadn't even managed to protect his own daughter. He was a failure. A complete failure.

All he wanted was to go to Elsbeth, to comfort her. To be comforted by her. He knew if he couldn't do this, if she wouldn't do this, he was as good as dead. But when they got to the house, Elsbeth's car wasn't there, and a new panic set in.

"Go to your room," he said to Trevor, and he wordlessly obeyed, disappearing silently down the hallway.

The lights were on in the kitchen. There was even a hot pot of coffee still on. Elsbeth's coat was slung over the back of one of the kitchen chairs, and her purse was on the table. What the fuck? Where the hell was she? Did she run off with that asshole? Maybe *he* was the one who had Gracy. Maybe that had been the plan all along. Make it look like she'd been kidnapped, and then swoop in and steal his wife. Had this dick decided to steal not only his wife, but his entire life?

He took her purse and pulled it opened, the magnetic snap popping. He tipped it upside down and dumped its contents onto the table. A compact, a hairbrush. He rifled through her wallet, looking at the receipts, looking for anything. Coins spilled on the table and rolled onto the floor. A ratty paperback, a pack of gum, a flier for an after-school art program. A bundle of photo envelopes from Walgreens. He tore the first envelope open and spilled the pictures on the table. Trevor's pictures. The junkyard, Pop and his model airplanes. The woods. The green, green canopy that in all these years had not changed. His heart panged. He flipped through the pictures, laying them down on the table like a dealer. Hoping that the bigger picture they made might show him something.

And then there was Gracy. Gracy in bed. Gracy asleep. Gracy standing half-naked in the woods, leaning against a tree, one leg up, her lips parted. He felt his stomach turn. Gracy sleeping. Gracy in the water. Gracy's bare legs, her nipple exposed. He squeezed his eyes shut and the images of Gracy blurred with those strange sepia pictures of other little girls. Gracy's tights, strung up like a prize. And the blood, the blood on the mattress that the cops hadn't seen. They hadn't tested that blood to make sure it didn't belong to his little girl.

It was like someone had flicked the breaker on again, and the next thing he knew his entire body was electrified as he tore down the hallway to his bedroom, where he rifled through his drawer looking for the ammunition. In the living room, he unlocked the gun cabinet, and then he went to Trevor's room and threw open the door.

"Get up!" he said.

Trevor was lying face-down on his bed. He turned his head to face him. His pale cheeks were streaked with tears, red tracks, like blood in newly fallen snow.

"I said get the fuck up."

He shoved him down the hallway to the mudroom. He motioned for him to put the boots on, and Trevor obeyed, sobbing as he tied his laces.

And then Kurt said, "Outside. Now."

If Trevor had his camera, this is the way the world would look through his viewfinder: crystalline and blue. As the clouds parted, even as the snow kept falling, the hushed light of the moon was gentle. The whole world was numb and quiet and cold. Everything sparkled. It was beautiful; it was terrible.

He could hear his father's labored breath behind him as they marched from the house out past the shed to the field behind the house. The snow was getting deeper and deeper; Trevor felt himself sinking into the cold. Like quicksand, sucking him in.

He turned to look at his father. This photo of his father would be nothing but shadows and wild eyes. He was terrified. They were both terrified.

"Daddy," he said, the words like icy slivers in his mouth.

They kept moving forward until they were at the top of the hill. From up there you could see the entire valley below them. Only a few lights twinkled now. It made him think of the little Christmas village that his mother set out on the mantel every Christmas. Just a tiny little make-believe place. If he had his camera, this picture would be of a snow globe, a father and son trapped inside.

"Daddy, please don't," he said again, feeling as though his body was turning inside out. When he spoke, his words burned his throat.

His father was aiming the gun at him now, and he realized that this might be the end. Any moment now, he would be gone.

Just a memory. Maybe he deserved this, though. Maybe, without him, the world would be a better place. He knew he was a mistake. He'd known that every day of his life. He had been nothing to them but trouble and pain.

"What did you do to Gracy?" his father asked through his teeth.

Trevor squeezed his eyes shut tight and conjured the pictures, the good ones he'd made. Gracy, sweet Gracy. He squeezed his eyes so hard, trying to rid his mind of the image of himself in her bed, his penis thick and hard against her back. The thrill of his skin against her nightgown and that awful, awful release.

"Did you touch her?" he asked.

Trevor was crying hard now; it was hard to stay upright. "I'm sorry," he said. "I didn't mean to hurt her. I love her."

He watched his father's body convulse. It looked like he'd been struck by lightning. Shaken.

"Where is she?" he hissed. "Where did you take her?"

Trevor shook his head. "I didn't . . ."

"Where is she?" he screamed now, his voice echoing in that hollow air.

"Stop!" The voice came from behind his father, but it was disembodied. Just an owl's hoot, the mournful cry of a dove. "Kurt, no!"

His father lowered his gun and turned as his mother came up over the hill. She was holding Gracy in her arms, running and stumbling as she made her way to them. "Don't hurt him. God, don't hurt him. What is wrong with you? He's our son."

"Mama," Trevor said as she ran to him. And then her free arm was around him. And her tears were warm as they pressed against his cheek, and her lips were warm as they kissed his away.

Elsbeth left Kurt standing alone in the field. She clung to both children as they struggled through the falling snow back to the house. He watched as their three bodies slowly merged into one dark form that disappeared into the distance. Kurt blinked the snow out of his eyes. His vision was blurred; he struggled to focus through the icy crystals.

The gun was cold at his side now. Without gloves, his hands had grown numb. His entire body stilled, breathless, as the snow continued to fall. He closed his eyes, concentrated on the bone-numbing cold, on the blistering splinters of ice that kept falling.

He thought about the gun. Also perfectly still.

He dropped to his knees and looked up into the sky, letting the shards of ice fall into his eyes. He wondered how long it would take until the snow buried him alive. He opened his mouth and let it fill his throat. Would it asphyxiate him? Would he choke? He pictured himself frozen in supplication to this unforgiving sky. Would this be his demise? Would this be the way it all came to an end?

He peeled off his coat, tore his hat off, clutched the gun. He imagined the cold barrel in his mouth. The metallic clank of it against his teeth. He squeezed his eyes shut, the tears freezing before they fell.

And then he remembered this:

Winter. He was twelve years old. He and Billy had taken their metal flying saucers up the steep hill near their house. They had bread bags tied around their feet inside their boots to keep their socks extra dry. It was snowing. Cold. For hours they dragged their sleds up the hill and then raced down. Crashing into rocks and roots, their muscles spent, their backsides bruised. The sky was the color of faded dungarees. Starless, moonless. Still.

Kurt sent Billy down the hill one last time with a push, listening to his voice trilling in the quiet night. And he sat down, exhausted, in the soft snow, lay back and let it press all around him, filling his ears, touching his neck. He closed his eyes and listened to its crunch, its hush.

"That was wicked fun!" Billy said, his voice breaking through the silence, his boots crunching the icy snow. "Get up," Billy said. "Kurt, get up! Let's go again!"

Spring. Waking up in the soft pink glow of morning in Elsbeth's childhood bed, her skin hot and soft against his. Outside, the calling out of birds, the close click-clack sound of the train. Underneath them, the rumble and hum. He'd pressed his hand against her stomach, cupping it with his large palm, amazed. She stirred, arching her back in a stretch. He buried his face in her hair, let the darkness swallow him. Sun on his exposed shoulder, the chill of spring and the cold lilac smell of possibility. Clean white sheets. "Get up," Elsbeth whispered, turning to face him, her breath across his cheek. "You need to get up before my mom wakes up."

Summer. Trevor took his hand and led him through a labyrinth of raspberry brambles that pricked and scratched their bare legs. Kurt watched the back of his head as he led him through the summer foliage, the green so brilliant it almost hurt his eyes. Like looking into the sun. Like looking into cold white snow.

"Where are we going?" Kurt asked, but Trevor didn't answer.

Suddenly they came to the place where the brush gave way

to an open field, littered with wildflowers. It was sunset, and the sky looked as though it were melting.

Trevor turned to Kurt, smiling sadly. "Sometimes, I lie down here and I don't want to ever get up," he said.

"Yeah?"

Trevor nodded and lay down in the grass.

Kurt lay next to him, dandelions gone to seed sighing next to him, exhaling in quiet puffs. And they stayed this way, studying the sky as dusk surrendered to evening.

"Time to go," he said Trevor. "It's beautiful. But we have to get up."

And Trevor had nodded and reached for his hand.

Fall. "Get up, Daddy," Gracy said, leaping onto the couch where Kurt had fallen asleep with the TV still on. His entire body so tired from work, so exhausted he felt like an old man. Like someone at the end of his life.

He'd willed his eyes open. Her hair was messy, and her cheeks bright pink and smudged with dirt. She'd been outside playing all morning, trying to make summer last.

"I made something for you, but you have to get up!"

And so despite his body's defiance, its desire, every inch of him wanting nothing but sleep, release, he'd taken her hand and she'd pulled him through the house and out the door to the front yard. The driveway was buried under a blanket of leaves. The trees were barren without them. On the brown grass she'd lined up six silver pie tins, each filled with mud. It was cold out, and their breath was like smoke in the air.

"I made these for you. Let's pretend it's your birthday. And my birthday."

He had looked at her then in her old coat and frayed scarf and felt something he didn't have words for. Something so powerful it felt almost dangerous. And so, fighting back tears, he'd nodded and said, "Thank you. It's exactly what I wanted."

Now Kurt opened his eyes, listened to the silence. The snow had stopped falling finally, and around him the entire world glistened. He was alone, and he knew the house was empty now, but still he got up. He got up and pulled his coat and hat back on. He got up and grabbed his shotgun. He got up and started the long trek back home.

GRACE

Kurt pulls his truck up next to the curb at the airport and turns on his hazards. The sun has come out, but the snow remains. The combination is almost blinding, the whiteness making that place behind his eyes throb in time with the blinking lights.

"You got everything?" he asks Billy.

"Think so," Billy says.

Billy stayed for two weeks. He relinquished his motel room to Elsbeth and the kids, and he stayed with Kurt at the house, doing what he could to help. Thankfully, he was able to clear Trevor of all charges; there was simply no connection between him and the disaster except for a series of unfortunate coincidences. Trevor showed the police to the place in the river where he'd dumped the stolen equipment, explained that that was why he'd been carrying a duffel bag out of the school that day. He explained that he'd only been trying to set up a darkroom in the old caboose. Billy also somehow convinced Mrs. Cross not to pursue any charges of burglary or vandalism against him for stealing the equipment. And luckily, it didn't take long before the fire marshal came back with the report, which confirmed there was no way the bombs could have been set off remotely. Someone was in the building that morning. Someone else set the bombs off and ran. The surveillance cameras had caught video of a young man in coveralls fleeing the building moments before the blast. Dark hair, dark eyes, short in stature. The opposite of Trevor. The police received an anonymous tip with a name, an address, and after

searching the man's apartment, an arrest was made. He was a for-
mer employee of the school district who had grievances after
being let go. He'd been calling in bomb threats from a pay phone
for over a year. He'd written a manifesto and posted it on the Internet. He was someone troubled. Someone truly capable of
harm. He was no one they knew.

Billy suggested they press charges against the school for all
the damage they'd done with their accusations. For defamation.
For leaking Trevor's name to the press. Kurt had nodded as Billy
explained the logistics of this abstract justice. But he knew that
nothing Mrs. Cross or the school had done could compare to the
wounds he himself had inflicted on his only son.

Billy had slept in the kids' empty room those two weeks; he
and Kurt ate breakfast together each morning and then recon-
vened for dinner each night.

"They'll never forgive me," he said to Billy as he pushed his
food around his plate. "And even if they do, I'm not sure I can
forgive myself."

What he didn't say was that he worried he'd done exactly
what Pop had done all those years ago. Worse. That he wasn't sure
he even deserved forgiveness. But Billy knew; Billy had always
known what Kurt was thinking. "The difference between you
and Pop is that you're *sorry*," he said. "And that has to count for
something."

Elsbeth didn't speak to him for those two weeks after she
found him in the pasture with Trevor. She couldn't even stand to
look at him. She refused his calls. She wouldn't let him see the
kids. She said that when Billy left, she'd check out of the motel
and go stay with Twig.

"Give her time," Billy said. "That's about all you have left to
offer."

Kurt knew she was on the verge of flight, and Billy was right.
There was nothing that Kurt could do except wait. To set her free
and hope that she would come back. To prepare for what would
happen if she didn't.

As for Trevor, he wasn't sure where to begin in making those kinds of amends. How do you fix a hole that big, the one that lived between them now? A chasm with no bottom. A terrible abyss. There were no words that could undo what he had done. What he needed to do was to earn his trust, to earn his forgiveness. But how to do that was a mystery to Kurt.

During those terrible lonely weeks, he spoke with the school, got the names and numbers of the agencies Mrs. Cross had recommended that fall. He arranged his work schedule so that he would be able to drive Trevor to Burlington every week to see a therapist. He spoke to the therapist himself, and she assured him that Trevor was not damaged beyond repair, that unlike glass, children cannot shatter. They are resilient, and over time these terrible fissures could be mended. He accepted the blame he knew everyone would place on him, and he vowed to fix the broken places, to do everything he could to repair the damage he had done. It was all he could do.

And Billy helped. On the days when Kurt began to wish he *had* simply turned the gun on himself that night, that he'd simply ended everything in that field of snow, Billy was there. He also became the bridge between him and Trevor, visiting Trevor first at the motel and then later at Twig's. Billy told Kurt that he and Trevor were able to talk, that maybe Trevor just needed an ear. An ear that wasn't attached to anybody he knew, but also to someone who knew exactly what he was going through.

"He's going to be okay," Billy promised.

And Kurt just has to trust that this is true.

"I got everything in order with Pop too," Billy says, reaching into the cab of the truck to shake Kurt's hand. "Make sure you check in at the court on Monday. There shouldn't be any issue with the conservatorship now. Not after the fire. Then you can put Pop's house on the market. Get on with your life."

"Thanks, Billy," he says.

"I don't understand why you feel compelled to help him still, but I respect it." Billy has Pop's habit of nodding his head emphatically whenever he is trying to convince himself of something.

"Don't be a stranger," Kurt says, leaning in to hug his brother.

He waits until Billy has disappeared through the terminal doors before he turns off the hazards and pulls away from the curb. As he drives away, he realizes how much he will miss having Billy there at the table each morning and each night. How much he's missed having him in his life all these years. It makes him angry at Pop. All this time, he's blamed Billy for stealing the life he'd once wanted, but the truth is it was *Pop* who was the thief. The one who stole his brother from him, stole his future.

Kurt pulls onto the interstate, flipping the sun shade down to shield his eyes from that blinding light. Tucked behind the visor is the school picture of Gracy, the one they'd given to the police that awful night when she disappeared. He studies her face, her two missing teeth, the slow sparkle in her big dark eyes.

Thank God for Grace: the constant reminder of everything they almost lost. The miracle of a second chance. Grace is what had held them together; and he has to believe that Grace is what will save them now.

As winter slowly turned to spring, Elsbeth, like the bitter cold, began to feel her icy grip loosening, her rage softening. As the snow that had clung to the ground began to melt, leaving the earth soft and yielding beneath it, she felt her resolve melting. The frozen wall she'd built around her and the kids started to crack like ice on the surface of a frozen lake.

"Please come home," he said into the telephone when she finally answered his call. His voice sounded like something broken. Like shattered glass. It cut her; she could feel his words like icy splinters. And then, finally, she went to him.

"Turn out the light," she said. She couldn't look at him. Not yet. And so in the dark, they talked. He asked her questions, and she answered. She spoke, and he listened.

She explained the shoe box. She told him that she'd been stealing things for most of her life, that she was so full of wants she didn't know what to do with all that need. That taking things made her feel whole, that the trinkets helped close up the empty spaces. She told him about the man, the one who had come from Florida. She confessed her longing for him too, as if he were just something else that might be pilfered. She told him that he had been nothing but a dream, though, that he had never touched her, and she knew Kurt had to believe her because he had no other choice. They talked about her lost childhood. About everything he'd lost when Billy left. They talked about how they had failed Trevor, and how they had failed each other.

And all the while, Kurt waited. She was pretty sure he would wait forever, and so in late March, when the snow was just a memory, though the chill lingered in the air, she and the kids came home.

Now Elsbeth walks through the Walgreens, noticing that they are already putting out the sunscreen, the seasonal aisle already filling up with picnic items. The promises of summer. She puts a can of sunscreen in the cart. Their trip is only a couple of weeks away now, and it cripples her with guilt. She had suggested to Kurt that they turn in their tickets, but they were non-refundable. Kurt said it didn't matter. They should go anyway, try to enjoy themselves.

Gracy is too big for the cart now, nearly seven, so she walks by Elsbeth's side.

They wander down the toy aisle, and Gracy finds a Tinker Bell coloring book. "Can I have this, Mumma?" she asks.

"Not today. You have a thousand coloring books at home."

Grace juts her lower lip out in a shameless attempt to convince her. Elsbeth ruffles her hair. "We're here for your brother," she says. "If you stop begging, I might take you for ice cream later."

"Okay," Gracy grumbles.

They walk to the photo department, and Elsbeth braces herself.

Crystal is there; she is always there now. They have never spoken about what happened that night, but there is an understanding between them.

"Would you like the Fuji again?" she asks. Elsbeth is in at least once a week for film.

"Yes, please," she says.

She finds the film behind the counter and hands it to her.

"How is your sister?" Elsbeth asks.

Crystal nods. "Okay. She's making progress."

"That's great," she says.

Word travels fast. The story about Angie McDonald will become the stuff of local legend, she suspects. She was the girl who was in the bathroom when the bomb detonated. She had left art class to use the restroom, and the next thing she knew she woke up in the hospital with third-degree burns over 75 percent of her body.

"She's lucky to have you," Elsbeth says, and she means it.

An article about the bombing in the local paper talked about how Crystal delayed her acceptance to college to stay home and care for her sister. That she'd organized a run-a-thon to raise money for the other children injured by the fire. There had been a picture of her and Angie, before the burns destroyed her face, on the front page.

She still isn't sure what was going through Crystal's mind that day she took Gracy. She only knows that Gracy came home safe. That while she was with her, she wasn't harmed. She tried to explain to Kurt and Billy how it was that she could forgive her. They wanted her to go to the police. To press charges. But from the start Elsbeth refused. She knew they were more similar than different, she and this girl.

And then a week ago as she was sweeping up a pile of Mrs. Van Buren's gray curls from the linoleum floor at the salon, the door jingled and Crystal walked in with her sister.

Crystal looked startled to see Elsbeth, but she only nodded and asked softly, "Can you help us?"

Elsbeth spent over an hour trimming and styling Crystal's sister's hair. She was gentle as she combed through the fine tangles. Careful of her damaged skin. And with each snip of the scissors, she felt a tremendous sense of having done something right. Something good. For the first time since she started working at the salon, she felt like she had the ability to change the way someone saw themselves, to change the way they felt inside their own skin. It was overwhelming, this amazing sense of purpose.

"Come see?" she said at last to Crystal, who had been perched on a chair near her station. And they'd looked together at Angie in the mirror. She was smiling, and Crystal's eyes were filled with tears.

"Your hair is coming in so nice and thick, Ang," she said softly. "You look so pretty."

When Crystal opened her wallet to pay, Elsbeth shook her head.

"It's okay," she said. "It's on me."

Elsbeth knew then for sure that to take Crystal away from her sister was a cruelty she couldn't even begin to consider.

"Anything else today?" Crystal asks, and Elsbeth shakes her head. "Howard can ring you up," she says.

"Thank you," Elsbeth says. She goes to the register with the film and the sunscreen. She reaches into her pocketbook and pulls out her wallet. "How much do I owe you?" she asks.

Crystal dreams of Grace sometimes, her Grace. She would be a year old now, *is* a year old now, but in her dreams she is still that tiny bundle she'd held only for a moment. Crystal cries in her sleep; she knows this because she wakes up and her pillow is wet.

Every morning, she helps her mother change the dressings on Angie's burns. It's a delicate job and requires a delicate touch. She is as gentle as she can be as she unwraps her, applies the ointment, and then swaddles her again. She brushes her hair, careful not to pull at her sensitive scalp. She makes her breakfast, her favorite things, and never gives her a hard time about how gross they are.

Her mother can't stand the smell of Angie's skin, the wreckage that is Angie's body. But Crystal doesn't find it disgusting at all. She is single-minded in her care for her. She feels, for the first time, like she truly has a purpose. She thinks that maybe one day she'd like to be a nurse.

She wrote to Lucia, to let her know what happened to Angie. Lucia wrote back right away, and Ty e-mailed a few days later. They write to each other now, e-mails filed with so many careful words. The friendship they used to have is gone now, abandoned or lost, she's not sure which, but they have forged something new, a quiet forgiveness maybe. A bit of peace. Lucia sends her things in the mail. Books of poetry, homemade cookies, hand-knit hats that look silly on her head. Crystal gives them to Angie, who wears them to cover the few places where her hair still hasn't grown back in.

"You look pretty," she says today as Angie affixes one of Lucia's hats over her hair. They look at each other in the reflection of the mirror and Angie grimaces as she smiles. "No, really, look at the way the light is hitting your eyes," she says. Because despite all the damage, her eyes were, thankfully, unharmed.

She reads to Angie in the afternoons, biographies mostly. They are just finishing the one about Frida Kahlo. Angie is obsessed with Frida Kahlo. They are similar: both victims of tragic accidents, their damaged bodies like prisons. Nothing but art to save them.

After she is able to sit upright, she asks Crystal if she can get her an easel for her bed, some paintbrushes and paint. The pictures she paints bring tears to Crystal's eyes. They, like most important things in life, are both terrifying and beautiful.

"Ready?" his dad asks.

Trevor is taking pictures of what remains of Pop's house. The long shadows it makes across the burnt grass of the lawn. The cracked windows. For a moment, he imagines Pop's face peering out.

"I guess." He shrugs and climbs into the back of the truck.

As they drive away, he aims his camera at the house and watches it become smaller and smaller in his viewfinder, until it is nothing but a speck. Nothing but a memory.

Pop's house is empty now, every last piece of trash, every broken thing removed. For the second time. For the last time. They'd filled his father's truck ten times more with debris they hauled off to the dump, most of it stinking of the fire. Without Pop there to refill it, it slowly emptied out until finally, it was just the hollow shell of a place he once lived. As if Pop had never been there. Erased. Gone. It was like those photos from the first roll Trevor took. All those images that were washed away by the light, like dreams rubbed out. Just that afternoon Mrs. McDonald in her bright red skirt came and pounded a sign into the ground by the driveway. FOR SALE. His dad says that whoever buys it would do well to just knock the whole thing down and start over.

He and his dad go visit Pop every weekend, take him cigarettes and the chocolate-covered pretzels he likes. At first he wouldn't speak to them, he was so angry. But his resolve is weakening. He has to know he is safer here, that he is taken care of. He likes the food they serve. The nurses are kind, and he gets better reception on his TV here than at his old house.

Trevor talked Pop into letting him keep his model airplanes. At the house, Trevor had stood on a stool and used his fingernails to pry the thumbtacks and fishing lines from the ceiling. They were all covered with dust, and when he tried to blow them off, he realized that the dust was probably trapped in the paint. Pop had probably hung them up when they were still wet, and the dust and grime had become a part of them. He wondered about that, about filth attaching itself to you. About being stained, tainted. He told his therapist that he worries about this, that this might be what he's most afraid of. She told him that you can't be ruined by things that others do to you but only by what you do to others. He liked that idea, and he made a quiet promise to himself to remember this whenever he began to feel undone.

He also has his mom. Surprisingly, after that night in the field, she wanted nothing more than to listen as Trevor told her everything that was going on inside his head. Maybe working with the chatty ladies at the salon for all those years had made her a good listener. At first, he was reluctant. It seemed strange to spill those secrets. To let them out. But every night after Gracy fell asleep, first in the motel and then in the room they all shared at Twig's, he was able to tell her almost everything that had happened. And she listened. She really listened. She held him and stroked his hair like she used to, to calm him down when he was little, and she told him that whenever he was ready, she would make sure something was done so that Mike and Ethan never ever bothered him or anyone else again. Uncle Billy would help them. He only needed to say the word.

He hasn't talked to his father about what happened that day behind the Walgreens. He doesn't have the words yet to explain. They also haven't really spoken about what happened out in the field. But he knows that his dad is sorry; all of the anger in his face has turned to regret. Everything he does is an apology.

The night after they all moved back into the house, he heard noise outside his window and watched as his father went to the shed. The porch light shone eerily, casting a strange orange glow over the entire backyard. It was beautiful. The swing set looked skeletal, like the rusted bones of some large creature. And his father's silhouette was like a shadow, a strange choreography. In and out he moved, purposeful, and certain. By morning, there was a new roof and the windows were filled in to block out the light.

"A proper darkroom," he said, showing Trevor everything he had done, offering it to him like a gift.

They managed to save the enlarger and some other equipment from the river's edge, and what they couldn't save his father had somehow replaced. His dad had even gotten the shed wired with electricity, plumbed so that he'd have running water. His father called Mrs. D., and she promised she'd come to the house that summer, to show him how to develop the film, how to enlarge the pictures and make prints.

His mother gave him the hundreds and hundreds of photos she'd had developed for him, and he felt terrible for thinking she'd stolen them from him.

"You're a really good photographer," she'd said, looking through each of the photos with him at the kitchen table. "You know that, right?"

He'd nodded then, embarrassed but proud.

"Can I keep this one?" she'd asked, holding up the one of Gracy standing in the river.

She took the negative to Walgreens and had it enlarged, then she framed it and hung it in the living room, right where everybody could see it.

Now he lies down in the back of the truck and peers through the viewfinder of his camera up at the sky. He can feel the road under his back. It makes his heart and lungs feel like they are being pummeled. It hurts, but the view is worth the pain. Storm clouds crowd out the sun, stealing the little bit of warmth remaining. It is still spring, still cold, but summer will be here soon. Every single thing tells him this is true: the tops of the trees turning green. The crisp chill to the air, the smell of fertilizer and sunshine. Even the breeze tastes different, sweet.

The school is shut down for the rest of the year. He won't ever have to go back there. As long as he passes the tests they send in the mail, he'll be able to go to the high school in the fall. Start over.

Ethan was hurt in the explosion. Badly. Trevor heard that both of his hands were burned when he was trying to get out of the cafeteria. He heard that they were worried for a while that they might not be able to save them. He thought about Ethan without hands, how powerless he was now. How impotent. Mike wasn't hurt. He'd been at a doctor's appointment or something that morning. But after the explosion his parents decided to move away; Angie told him that her parents were selling their house.

He visits Angie sometimes. He takes her art supplies. Her sister, who stays home to take care of her, always leaves them alone, brings them snacks and stuff to drink.

He asked Angie the last time he was there if he could take a photo of her.

There is something amazing about a body that's been harmed the way hers has, something incredible about its stubborn insistence upon healing itself: all that damaged skin sloughing off, replaced by the new, fresh pink flesh. The hopefulness of it is what gets to him.

"It's beautiful," he said as he peered through his viewfinder at her. At all that shiny hope emerging.

"Shut up," she said, but she smiled too. As he clicked and clicked and clicked.

Next week they're going to Florida. He's excited to fly, both afraid and thrilled. He thinks about looking at the clouds from the inside. In the back of his dad's truck, he tries to concentrate on the clouds, to think only of flying. For now, he has nothing to worry about except sunshine. Nothing to worry about except how he might capture the light.

Acknowledgments

This book was, in many ways, a collaborative project. It was not written alone, and it is with humility and gratitude that I offer my thanks to everyone who contributed and conspired:

To my family, whose support sustains me always. To Patrick and the girls, who give purpose to my work (and all the necessary diversions from it as well). Thanks especially to Kicky for Dizzy and Squirrel; I promise the rest of their story will come soon.

To Jim Ruland and Rich Farrell, the other two-thirds of the Dub Club triumvirate, who stood by as this little bird incubated, giving me both nest to keep it safe and, later, the worms to feed it. And who watched as the ugly little thing finally grew into something worthy of both flight and song. (A special thanks to Jim for your eleventh-hour suggestions. Phew.)

To Mireya Schmidt, Tim Hussion, and Angie Vorhies for your generosity and to Georgia Bilski for the swirliest hair.

To Peter Senftleben for always seeing what I cannot. To everyone at Kensington for helping make beautiful books and finding people to read them. To Henry Dunow for looking after me, and to all my best teachers: the ones who taught me the importance of perspective, and the power of light.

Discussion Questions

1. When Crystal first goes to the Kennedys' house, she observes: "What you see on the outside rarely reflects what's really on the inside. She, of all people, understood that appearances can be deceiving." Discuss the idea of perception in this novel. Compare Crystal's assumptions of the Kennedy family through the photos and her interactions with Elsbeth and Gracy with each of the characters' own narratives. Do you think her view of them is accurate at all? Talk about Elsbeth's and Kurt's opposite reactions to Trevor's pictures of Gracy. Further, consider how your life might look to an outsider and how accurate that perception is or how it differs from the truth.

2. Discuss the various father-son relationships: Kurt and Trevor, Jude and Kurt, Jude and Billy. Are there patterns to be found? Any broken? How is Kurt like his father? How is he different? What parallels are there between the opening scene and the one in which Jude catches Billy with a man in the junkyard?

3. Trevor is a victim of Ethan and Mike's bullying, but is he also victimized by those people who fail to protect him? Who do you believe is at fault for the way he is treated? How do you think he handled the bullying? Should he have fought more, reported it, ignored it? What could have been done to protect him and other students?

4. What purpose does Elsbeth's shoplifting serve for her? What is missing in her life? Do you think she will stop now? Discuss her need for things and Jude's hoarding. Are the two more similar than different?

5. Talk about the theme of stealing in *Grace*. Elsbeth shoplifts, Trevor steals equipment and chemicals from school, and Crystal steals Gracy. What else is stolen, figuratively and literally, over the course of the novel?

6. Photography allows Trevor to see the world as an artist. Does this make his world more endurable to him? What impact does art—in the form of photography, drawing, tattoos, etc.—have on each of the characters in *Grace*?

7. Put yourself in Kurt's position as a son or daughter to an aging father with an obvious illness. How would you have handled the situation? Do you think Kurt did the right thing by setting him up in the trailer in the backyard, or should he have left Jude in his own home like he wanted? Do you think it was abuse like Maury suggested?

8. Why is Crystal so consumed by Elsbeth and Grace? How does her relationship with the Kennedys change her? Did this event actually, in the end, help her get over the loss of her own Grace or make her more regretful?

9. Do you think that Kurt and Trevor will ever be able to get past that awful night in the pasture? Is there any amount of healing or love that can mend such a rift?

10. Discuss Elsbeth's feelings regarding Trevor and Gracy. Do you believe it's possible for a mother to love one child more than another for no reason? Are she and Kurt bad parents? Why or why not?

11. Discuss the concept of grace in this novel. Think about all of the definitions and uses of the word.

Have you read all of T. Greenwood's
critically acclaimed novels?
Available in trade paperback and as e-books.

NEARER THAN THE SKY

*In this mesmerizing novel, T. Greenwood draws readers into the
fascinating and frightening world of Munchausen syndrome
by proxy—and into one woman's search for healing.*

When Indie Brown was four years old, she was struck by
lightning. In the oft-told version of the story, Indie's life was
heroically saved by her mother. But Indie's own recollection of
the event, while hazy, is very different.

Most of Indie's childhood memories are like this—tinged
with vague, unsettling images and suspicions. Her mother, Judy,
fussed over her pretty youngest daughter, Lily, as much as she ignored Indie. That neglect, coupled with the death of her beloved
older brother, is the reason Indie now lives far away in rural
Maine. It's why her relationship with Lily is filled with tension,
and why she dreads the thought of flying back to Arizona. But
she has no choice. Judy is gravely ill, and Lily, struggling with a
challenge of her own, needs her help.

In Arizona, faced with Lily's hysteria and their mother's insta-
bility, Indie slowly begins to confront the truth about her half-
remembered past and the legacy that still haunts her family. And
as she revisits her childhood, with its nightmares and lost innocence, she finds she must reevaluate the choices of her adulthood—including her most precious relationships.

THIS GLITTERING WORLD

*Acclaimed author T. Greenwood crafts a moving, lyrical
story of loss, atonement, and promises kept.*

One November morning, Ben Bailey walks out of his Flag-
staff, Arizona, home to retrieve the paper. Instead, he finds Ricky
Begay, a young Navajo man, beaten and dying in the newly fallen
snow.

Unable to forget the incident, especially once he meets
Ricky's sister, Shadi, Ben begins to question everything, from his
job as a part-time history professor to his fiancée, Sara. When Ben
first met Sara, he was mesmerized by her optimism and easy confidence. These days, their relationship only reinforces a loneliness
that stretches back to his fractured childhood.

Ben decides to discover the truth about Ricky's death, both
for Shadi's sake and in hopes of filling in the cracks in his own
life. Yet the answers leave him torn—between responsibility and
happiness, between his once-certain future and the choices that
could liberate him from a delicate web of lies he has spun.

UNDRESSING THE MOON

Dark and compassionate, graceful yet raw, Undressing
the Moon *explores the seams between childhood and
adulthood, between love and loss. . . .*

At thirty, Piper Kincaid feels too young to be dying. Cancer
has eaten away her strength; she'd be alone but for a childhood
friend who's come home by chance. Yet with all the questions of
her future before her, she's adrift in the past, remembering the
fateful summer she turned fourteen and her life changed forever.

Her nervous father's job search seemed stalled for good as he
hung around the house watching her mother's every move. What
he and Piper had both dreaded at last came to pass: Her restless,
artistic mother, who smelled of lilacs and showed Piper beauty, finally left.

With no one to rely on, Piper struggled to hold on to what
was important. She had a brother who loved her and a teacher
enthralled with her potential. But her mother's absence, her father's distance, and a volatile secret threatened her delicate balance.

Now Piper is once again left with the jagged pieces of a shattered life. If she is ever going to put herself back together, she'll
have to begin with the summer that broke them all. . . .

THE HUNGRY SEASON

It's been five years since the Mason family vacationed at the lakeside cottage in northeastern Vermont, close to where prize-winning novelist Samuel Mason grew up. The summers that Sam, his wife, Mena, and their twins, Franny and Finn, spent at Lake Gormlaith were noisy, chaotic, and nearly perfect. But since Franny's death, the Masons have been flailing, one step away from falling apart. Lake Gormlaith is Sam's last, best hope of rescuing his son from a destructive path and salvaging what's left of his family.

As Sam struggles with grief, writer's block, and a looming deadline, Mena tries to repair the marital bond she once thought was unbreakable. But even in this secluded place, the unexpected—in the form of an overzealous fan, a surprising friendship, and a second chance—can change everything.

From the acclaimed author of *Two Rivers* comes a compelling and beautifully told story of hope, family and, above all, hunger—for food, sex, love, and success—and for a way back to wholeness when a part of oneself has been lost forever.

TWO RIVERS

Two Rivers is a powerful, haunting tale of enduring love, destructive secrets, and opportunities that arrive in disguise. . . .

In Two Rivers, Vermont, Harper Montgomery is living a life overshadowed by grief and guilt. Since the death of his wife, Betsy, twelve years earlier, Harper has narrowed his world to working at the local railroad and raising his daughter, Shelly, the best way he knows how. Still racked with sorrow over the loss of his life-long love and plagued by his role in a brutal, long-ago crime, he wants only to make amends for his past mistakes.

Then one fall day, a train derails in Two Rivers, and amid the wreckage Harper finds an unexpected chance at atonement. One of the survivors, a pregnant fifteen-year-old girl with mismatched eyes and skin the color of blackberries, needs a place to stay. Though filled with misgivings, Harper offers to take Maggie in. But it isn't long before he begins to suspect that Maggie's appearance in Two Rivers is not the simple case of happenstance it first appeared to be.

**Read on for a special preview of another extraordinary
novel by T. Greenwood . . .**

BODIES OF WATER

In 1960, Billie Valentine is a young housewife living in a sleepy
Massachusetts suburb, treading water in a dull marriage and car-
ing for two adopted daughters. Summers spent with the girls at
their lakeside camp in Vermont are her one escape—from her
husband's demands, from days consumed by household
drudgery, and from the nagging suspicion that life was supposed
to hold something different.

Then a new family moves in across the street. Ted and Eva Wilson have three children and a fourth on the way, and their
arrival reignites long-buried feelings in Billie. The affair that follows offers a solace Billie has never known, until her secret is revealed and both families are wrenched apart in the tragic
aftermath.

Fifty years later, Ted and Eva's son, Johnny, contacts an elderly
but still spry Billie, entreating her to return east to meet with
him. Once there, Billie finally learns the surprising truth about
what was lost, and what still remains, of those joyful, momentous
summers.

In this deeply tender novel, T. Greenwood weaves deftly
between the past and present to create a poignant and wonder-
fully moving story of friendship, the resonance of memories, and
the love that keeps us afloat.

This is what I know: memory is the same as water. It permeates and saturates. Quenches and satiates. It can hold you up or pull you under; render you weightless or drown you. It is tangible, but elusive. My memories of Eva are like this: the watery dreams of a past I can no more easily grasp than a fistful of the ocean. Some days, they buoy me. Other days, they threaten me with their dangerous draw. Memory. Water. Our bodies are made of it; it is what we are. I can no longer separate myself from my recollections. On the best days, on the *worst* days, I believe I have dissolved into them.

It was the ocean's tidal pull that brought me here to this little beach town forty years ago, and later to this battered cottage perched at the edge of the cliffs, overlooking the sea. It is what keeps me here as well. And while I may not be able to escape my memories, I have escaped the seasons here; this is what I think as summer turns seamlessly into fall, the only sign of this shift being the disappearance of the tourists. During the summer, the other rental cottages are full of families and couples, the porches littered with surfboards and beach toys, the railings draped with wet swimsuits and brightly colored beach towels. Sometimes a child will line up shells along the balustrade, a parade of treasures. At summer's end, the kindest mothers will pack these up as they pack up the rest of their things, slipping them into a little plastic bag to be stowed inside a suitcase. The other mothers toss them back toward the sand when the child is busy, hoping they will forget the care with which they were chosen. I understand both inclinations: to hold on and to let go.

But now, in September, the flip-flops and buckets and shells are gone and the children have returned home, the inevitability of fall, the certainty of autumn just another textbook fact as they sit wearily in their September classrooms. But I imagine they must keep this magical place somewhere in their memory, pulling out the recollections and examining them, marveling at them, like the shimmery inside of a shell: a place without seasons, as far away as the moon. Their mothers have returned to their kitchens or offices, their fathers to their lonely commutes. Only I remain, in my little cottage by the shore, as summer slips away soundlessly, and, without fanfare, autumn steps in.

At night, in the fall when the tourists are gone, there are no distractions. No blue glow of a television set in a window, no muffled sound of an argument or a child's cry. There are no slamming doors or moody teenagers sneaking out to a bonfire on the sand below. There is no laughter, no scratchy radio music, no soft cadence of couples making love. There is only the sound of the lapping waves, the lullaby of water. It is quiet here without them.

I don't have a landline. When someone wants to reach me, they call the manager's office and I return the call on my cell phone, its number known only to my daughters and sister. My eldest, Francesca, calls once a week on Sundays, dutifully reporting on her life in Boston, detailing the comings and goings of my grandchildren. Mouse is less predictable, more like me, calling only when the spirit moves her. She sends beautiful letters and postcards and photographs, though, that offer me glimpses into her gypsy life. The wall behind my bed tracks her travels in a clut-tered collage. Only my sister, Gussy, calls every day. She relies on me more than she used to. We are both widows now, and growing old is lonely. We need each other.

I expect her call each night like I expect the sunset. "Hi, Gus," I say. "What's the news?" Though there is never any news, not real news anyway: a broken pipe, a sale on prime rib, a silly conversation in line at the bank. More often than not she calls to read me one of the increasingly frequent obituaries of someone we used to know.

Tonight, I slip into bed for our conversation, watching the sun melt into the horizon from my window. When summer is over, I no longer bother to close the shades, modesty disappearing with the tourists.

"I got a letter today," she says. "The strangest thing."

"Who from?"

She is quiet on the other end of the line. I picture her, nestled in her husband Frank's old recliner, cradling the phone between her chin and her shoulder as she knits something for Zu-Zu or Plum.

"Gus?"

"The letter was from John Wilson. Johnny Wilson."

I feel a hollowing out in my chest, and worry for just a frac-tion of a second that this is it. I am waiting now, for that failure of my body that will, finally, remove me from this world. But then my heart, this old reliable heart, thumps again, a gong, and my whole body reverberates. "Why?" I ask.

"He's looking for *you*."

I take a deep breath and study the sky outside my window, looking for an answer in the confusion of colors, in the spill of orange and blue.

"He just got out of rehab or some such thing. Doesn't sur-prise me at all, frankly. Probably part of his twelve steps, making amends and all that."

It does not surprise me to hear that he's had these sorts of problems, though why he would want to talk to *me* is a mystery. Johnny Wilson would have nothing to apologize to me for; if anything, it should be the other way around.

"He says he wants to talk to you about his mother. But he wants to see you in person. He wants to know if I can help him find you."

My eyes sting. Suddenly the sunset is too bright. I stand and pull the curtains across the windows and sit down on the bed again. Breathless.

"*Can* I help him?" she asks. "Find you?"

"Where is he?"

"He's still in Boston. But he said he could come up to Vermont if you might be up for a visit. He must not know you're in California."

Of course he wouldn't know this. I haven't spoken to Johnny Wilson in decades.

"You *could* come for a visit, you know," she says. "Make a trip of it. Francesca could come up too, meet us at the lake?"

Lake Gormlaith. I haven't been back to the lake since 1964. Johnny was still a little boy then. A child. My heart (that swollen, weakening thing in my chest) aches for him: both the little boy he was and whatever damaged man he has now become.

"I don't know," I say. "I haven't flown in so long. Doesn't security make you take your clothes off or some such nonsense now?"

"*Shoes.*" Gussy laughs. "You only have to take off your *shoes*. Come home, come see me. Let Johnny say what he needs to say. And you can see Effie and the girls."

Effie, my grandniece, and her family live year round now in the cabin at the lake. I haven't met the children, and the last time I saw Effie she was still a teenager. I haven't even seen Gussy for nearly two years now, and she was the last one to visit. I know it's my turn. Still, I am happy here at the edge of the world where none of the rules, even those regarding the changing of seasons, apply. Why would I leave?

"Please?" Gussy says.

"What did the letter say exactly?" I ask, wanting to hear her name, hoping she will say it.

"It just says he needs to talk to you about Eva." And there they are, the two syllables as familiar, and faint, as my own heartbeat. "He says there are some things you should know."

"What do you suppose that means?" I ask.

"I don't know, Billie. Just come home and find out."

I look around my tiny cottage, peer once again at that predictable sky. In Vermont, the leaves would be igniting in their autumnal fire, the whole landscape a pyre. There is no such thing as escaping the seasons in New England.

"Let me think about it," I say. "I'm not too wild about getting naked for just anybody who flashes a badge."

Gussy laughs again. "Think on it. I'll call you tomorrow."

"Tomorrow," I say, committing to nothing.

In the morning, I wake to the blinding reminder of daylight through the pale curtains in my bedroom. Outside, the waves quietly pat the shore as though they are only reassuring the sand. Each day begins like this; only the keening of the foghorn tells me that today it is autumn, that the sky is impenetrable.

My whole body aches, though it has for so long now that the pain no longer registers as unusual or worrisome. I rise anyway— what else can one do?—slip out of bed and into my bathing suit, which I keep hanging on a hook on the back of my door. I sleep in the nude, which makes this transition easier: no cumbersome nightgown to fuss with, no pajamas to unbutton or from which to undress. I realized long ago that I'd only ever worn nightclothes as a barrier anyway: a fortress of flannel or silk.

The bathing suit I wear these days is bright green. It complements my eyes, or it would if the cataracts hadn't rendered them this icy blue. My hair isn't the same color anymore either. Still, I wake up every single morning expecting to see the red-haired woman I used to be in the mirror, but instead I see an old lady with milky eyes and an untamed white mane. I have, on the darkest days, demanded to know who she is.

Sometimes I try to imagine what Eva would look like now, but she remains fixed in my memory the way she looked back in the summer of 1960 when I first met her. Only I have aged. Only I have watched my body slowly abandon me. I am alone in this slow decay. Nevertheless, I do imagine her here, though she appears as a ghost, and I wonder what her morning would be like. Would she also slip into her bathing suit at the break of dawn? Would she walk with me from the bungalow down the stone steps to the beach? Would she peer through the thick marine layer that hangs like a white stole on the sea's shoulders and then wink at me before tossing her hair back and running headlong into the water, disappearing into the ocean leaving me to wonder if she would resurface again? Would she leave me at the edge, fearful—an old woman with cataracts and high blood pressure— looking for her through the gauzy morning? Would she emerge from the water, riding a wave in to shore, coming home again, or would she simply vanish?

I'm never truly alone on the beach, even in autumn, even this early in the morning. The surfers come in their wet suits, carrying their boards under their arms. They paddle out to wait for the waves, bobbing and dipping like shiny black seals. The bums who sleep under the pier emerge, scavenging for food, for half-smoked cigarette butts left in the sand. Middle-aged women rise early and walk up and down the beach, purposeful in their velour tracksuits, still believing that the inevitable might be delayed, if not halted entirely. They rarely acknowledge me; I am evidence of the one thing they cannot change, the reminder of a future they aren't ready to imagine. But if they were to look, to *really* look, this is what they would see: an elderly woman in a green bathing suit walking slowly toward the water's edge. She is old and she is thin, but there are shadows of an athlete in her strong shoulders and legs underneath that ancient skin. She is a swimmer, peering out at the water as though she might be looking for someone. But after only a moment, she disappears into the cold, her arms remembering. Her whole body remembering, her whole body *memory,* as she swims toward whatever it is, whomever it is she sees in the distance. If they were to listen, to really listen, they would hear the waves crashing on the shore behind her, beating like a pulse: *Eva. Eva.*

Connect with U s

Visit us online at
KensingtonBooks.com
to read more from your favorite authors, see books
by series, view reading group guides, and more.

Join us on social media

for sneak peeks, chances to win books and prize packs,
and to share your thoughts with other readers.

facebook.com/kensingtonpublishing
twitter.com/kensingtonbooks

Tell us what you think!

To share your thoughts, submit a review,
or sign up for our eNewsletters, please visit:
KensingtonBooks.com/TellUs.